Buckhorn County, Kentucky, may not have any famous natural wonders, but it does have the breathtaking Buckhorn Brothers. Doctor, sheriff, heartthrob and vet—all different, all irresistible, all larger than life. There isn't a woman in town who isn't in awe of at least one of them. But somehow they've managed to hang on to their bachelor status. Until now.

In this first of two special volumes, you'll meet Sawyer, the doctor, and Morgan, the sheriff. Be prepared to fall in love!

Dear Reader,

My BUCKHORN BROTHERS series experienced phenomenal success—thanks to you! So for any who missed it in its first go-around, here they are again, four of the nicest, hunkiest, most popular guys I've ever written, in two special, beautifully packaged reissues. First is *Once and Again,* featuring Sawyer and Morgan.

I've had people write me and ask if guys like my fictional heroes really exist. Well, I'm pleased to tell you that *yes,* they do. I personally know four of them. I have dibs on one, because we've been married since graduating high school, and like fine wine, he gets better with every year, so I'm not about to give him up. And the other three aren't old enough yet—so hands off. (I'm speaking of my sons, of course. You'll see that this series is dedicated to them, and rightfully so.)

You remember the old song about the woman who can bring home the bacon and fry it up in a pan? Well, ladies, what about a guy who can do that? What about a guy who accepts housework as part of his responsibilities? Or a guy who refuses to believe that raising the kids is strictly the woman's job? This is a new millennium. Times have changed. The men I write about reflect the men of today, the men I admire and respect and, yes, many of the men I know. As you read about these brothers—and hopefully fall in love with them—remember to laugh, remember to keep some ice water handy and please, remember to believe.

Watch for the second book, *Forever and Always,* with Gabe and Jordan, coming soon!

All my best to all of you!

Lori

P.O. Box 854, Ross OH 45061
Lorifoster@poboxes.com
http://www.eclectics.com/lorifoster

LORI FOSTER

Once and Again

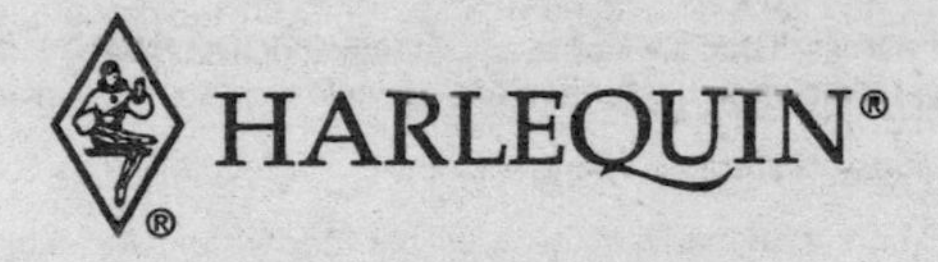

TORONTO • NEW YORK • LONDON
AMSTERDAM • PARIS • SYDNEY • HAMBURG
STOCKHOLM • ATHENS • TOKYO • MILAN • MADRID
PRAGUE • WARSAW • BUDAPEST • AUCKLAND

ISBN 0-373-83527-2

ONCE AND AGAIN

This edition published by arrangement with Harlequin Books S.A.

Visit us at www.eHarlequin.com

Printed in U.S.A.

CONTENTS

Two very special dedications
for two very special men in my life:

First, for my son Aaron.
You've always been one of the most unique,
independent people I know. And one of the finest.
I wish I could claim responsibility for that, but the
truth is, all I've done is love you—and that has always
been so easy to do. To say I'm proud would be an
unbelievable understatement. But then, what the
heck? I AM so proud, and I love you very much.

And to my son Jake. If a strong will can make the
world right, there's no doubt you'll have it fixed in
no time. I don't know anyone who possesses more
sheer determination or a keener mind. What's so fun
is the incredible sense of humor wrapped around it
all! You make me laugh so much with that quick, dry
wit, and you awe me with your unshakable logic.
I love you, Jake, very, very much.

SAWYER

CHAPTER ONE

ONE MINUTE he'd been reveling in the late afternoon sun, feeling the sweat dry on his shoulders and neck before he could wipe it away.

In the next instant, she was there.

He'd just glanced over at his son, Casey, only fifteen, but working as hard as any man, tall and strong and determined. His smile was filled with incredible pride.

The last two weekends he'd been caught up with patients, and he'd missed working outside with Casey, enjoying the fresh air, using his hands and body until the physical strain tired him.

Summer scents were heavy in the air, drifting to him as he layered another replacement board on the fence and hammered it in. A warm, humid breeze stirred his hair, bringing with it the promise of a harsh evening storm. He'd inhaled deeply, thinking how perfect his life was.

Then his son shouted, "Holy sh—ah, heck!" catching Sawyer's attention.

Not knowing what to expect, Sawyer turned in the direction Casey pointed his hammer and disbelief filled him as a rusted sedan, moving at breakneck speed, came barreling down the gravel road bordering their property. The turn at the bottom, hugging the Kentucky hills, was sharp; the car would never make it.

Sawyer got a mere glimpse of a pale, wide-eyed female face behind the wheel before, tires squealing, gravel flying, the car came right through the fence he'd just repaired, splintering wood and scattering nails, forcing him to leap for cover. Sheer momentum sent the car airborne for a few feet before it hit the grassy ground with a loud thump and was propelled forward several more feet to slide hood first into a narrow cove of the lake. The front end was submerged, hissing and bubbling, while the trunk and back wheels still rested on solid land, leaving the car at a crazy tilt.

Both Sawyer and Casey stood frozen for several seconds, stunned by what had happened, before ungluing their feet and rushing to the edge of the small cove. Without hesitation, Casey waded waist-deep into the water and peered in the driver's window. "It's a girl!"

Sawyer pushed him aside and leaned down.

His breath caught and held. "Girl" wasn't exactly an apt description of the unconscious woman inside. In a heartbeat, he took in all her features, scanning her from head to toes. As a doctor, he looked for signs of injury, but as a man, he appreciated how incredibly, utterly feminine she was. He guessed her to be in her mid-twenties. Young, a tiny woman, but definitely full grown.

The window was thankfully open, giving him easy access to her, but water rapidly washed into the car, almost covering her shins. Silently cursing himself and his masculine, knee-jerk reaction to her, he told Casey, "Go to the truck and call Gabe at the house. Tell him to meet us out front."

Casey hurried off while Sawyer considered the situation. The woman was out cold, her head slumped over the steering wheel, her body limp. The back seat of the car was filled with taped cardboard boxes and luggage, some of which had tumbled forward, landing awkwardly against her. A few open crates had dumped, and items—bric-a-brac, books and framed photos—were strewn about. It was obvious she'd been packed up for a long trip—or a permanent one.

Sawyer reached for her delicate wrist and was rewarded to feel a strong pulse. Her skin was velvety smooth, warm to the touch. He carefully placed her hand back in her lap, keeping it away from the icy cold water.

It took some doing, but he got the driver's door wedged open. If the car had surged a little deeper into the lake, he never would have managed it. More water flooded in. The woman moaned and turned her head, pushing away from the steering wheel, then dropping forward again. Her easy, unconscious movements assured Sawyer she had no spinal or neck injuries. After moving the fallen objects away from her, he carefully checked her slender arms, slipping his fingers over her warm flesh, gently flexing each elbow, wrist and shoulder. He drew his hands over her jeans-clad legs beneath the water, but again found no injuries. Her lips parted and she groaned, a rasping, almost breathless sound of pain. Frowning, Sawyer examined the swelling bump on her head. He didn't like it that she was still out, and her skin felt a little too warm, almost feverish.

Casey came to a skidding, sloshing halt beside him, sending waves to lap at Sawyer's waist. His gaze was narrowed with concern on the woman's face. "Gabe offered to bring you your bag, but I told him I'd call him back if you needed it." He spoke in a whisper, as if afraid of disturbing her. "We're taking her to the house with us, aren't we?"

"Looks like." If she didn't come to on the way to the house, he'd get her over to the hospital. But that was a good hour away, and most people in Buckhorn chose him over the hospital anyway, unless the situation was truly severe. And even then, it was generally his call.

He'd decide what to do after he determined the extent of her injuries. But first things first; he needed to get her out of the car and away from the debilitating effects of the cold water and hot sun.

Luckily, they weren't that far away from the house. He owned fifty acres, thick with trees and scrub bushes and wildflowers. The lake, long and narrow like a river, bordered the back of his property for a long stretch of shore. The ten acres surrounding the house and abutting the lake were kept mowed, and though it couldn't be called an actual road, there was a worn dirt path where they often brought the truck to the cove to fish or swim. Today they'd driven down to make repairs to a worn fence.

A crooked smile tipped up one side of his mouth. Thanks to the lady, the repairs to the fence were now more necessary than ever.

Sawyer carefully slid one arm beneath her legs, the other behind the small of her back. Her head tipped toward him, landing softly on his bare, sweaty shoulder. Her hair was a deep honey blond with lighter sun streaks framing her face. It smelled of sunshine and woman, and he instinctively breathed in the scent, letting it fill his lungs. Her hair was long enough to drag across the car seat as he lifted her out. "Grab her keys and purse, then get the shirt I left by the fence." He needed to cover her, and not only to counter the chill of the lake water.

He was almost ashamed to admit it, even to himself, but he'd noticed right off that her white T-shirt was all but transparent with the dousing she'd taken. And she wasn't wearing a bra.

He easily shook that observation from his mind.

Even with her clothes soaked, the woman weighed next to nothing, but still it was an effort to climb the small embankment out of the lake without jarring her further. She'd lost one thin sandal in the wreck, and now the other fell off with a small splash. The mud squished beneath Sawyer's boots, making for unsure footing. Casey scrambled out ahead, then caught at Sawyer's elbow, helping to steady him. Once they were all on the grassy embankment, Casey ran off to follow the rest of his instructions, but was back in a flash with the shirt, which he helped Sawyer arrange around her shoulders. Sawyer kept her pressed close to his chest, preserving her privacy and saving his son from major embarrassment.

"You want me to drive?" Walking backward, Casey managed to keep his gaze on the woman and avoid tripping.

"Yeah, but slowly. No unnecessary bumps, okay?" Casey was still learning the rudiments of changing gears, and he used any excuse to get behind the wheel.

"No problem, I'll just..." His voice trailed off as the woman stirred, lifting one limp hand to her forehead.

Sawyer stopped, holding her securely in his arms. He stared down at her face, waiting for her to regain complete awareness, strangely anticipating her reaction. "Easy now."

Her lashes were thick and dark brown tipped with gold and they fluttered for a moment before her eyes slowly opened—and locked on his. Deep, deep blue, staring into him, only inches away.

Sawyer became aware of several things at once: her soft, accelerated breath on his throat, the firmness of her slim thighs on his bare arm, her breasts pressing through the damp cotton of her shirt against his ribs. He could feel the steady drumming of her heartbeat, and the way her body now stiffened the tiniest bit. He felt a wave of tingling awareness shudder through his body, from his chest all the way to his thighs. His reaction to her was out of proportion, considering the circumstances and his usual demeanor. He was a physician, for God's sake, and didn't, in the normal course of things, even notice a woman as a woman when medical treatment was required.

Right now, he couldn't help but notice. Holding this particular woman was somehow altogether different. So often, he put aside his tendencies as a man in deference to those of a doctor; being a doctor was such an enormous part of him. But now he found it difficult to separate the two. The doctor was present, concerned for her health and determined to give her the best of his care. But the man was also there, acutely aware of her femininity and unaccountably responding to it in a very basic way. He'd never faced such a pickle before, and he felt equal parts confusion, curiosity and something entirely too close to embarrassment. For a moment while they stared at each other, it was so silent, he imagined he could hear her thoughts.

Then she slugged him.

Though she had no strength at all and her awkward blow barely grazed him, he was so taken by surprise he nearly dropped her. While Casey stood there gawking, making no effort to help, Sawyer struggled to maintain his hold and his balance with a squirming woman in his arms.

Out of sheer self-preservation, he lowered her bare feet to the ground—then had to catch her again as she swayed and almost crumpled. She would have fallen if both he and Casey hadn't grabbed hold of some part of her, but she still made the feeble effort to shrug them both away.

"No!" she said in a rough, whispering croak, as if her panicked voice could do no better.

"Hey, now," Sawyer crooned, trying the tone he'd often heard his brother Jordan use when talking to a sick or frightened animal. "You're okay."

She tried to swing at him again, he ducked back, and she whirled in a clumsy circle, stopping when her small fist made contact with Casey's shoulder. Casey jumped a good foot, unhurt but startled, then rubbed his arm.

Enough was enough.

Sawyer wrapped his arms around her from behind, both supporting and restraining her. "Shh. It's okay," he said, over and over again. She appeared somewhat disoriented, possibly from the blow to her head. "Settle down now before you hurt yourself."

His words only prompted more struggles, but her movements were ineffectual.

"Lady," he whispered very softly, "you're terrorizing my son."

With a gasp, she glanced up at Casey, who looked young and very strong, maybe bursting with curiosity, but in no way terrorized.

Sawyer smiled, then continued in calm, even tones. "Listen to me now, okay? Your car landed in our lake and we fished you out. You were unconscious. It's probable you have a concussion, on top of whatever else ails you."

"Let me go."

Her body shook from head to toe, a mixture of shock and illness, Sawyer decided, feeling that her skin was definitely too hot. "If I let you go you'll fall flat on your face. That or try to hit my boy again."

If anything, she panicked more, shaking her head wildly. "No..."

After glaring at Sawyer, Casey held both arms out to his sides. "Hey, lady, I'm not hurt. I'm fine." His neck turned red, but his voice was as calm and soothing as his father's. "Really. Dad just wants to help you."

"Who are you?"

She wasn't talking to Casey now. All her attention seemed to be on staying upright. Even with Sawyer's help, she was wobbly. He gently tightened his hold, keeping her close and hindering her futile movements. "Sawyer Hudson, ma'am. I'm the man who owns this property. Me and my brothers. As I said, you landed in my lake. But I'm also a doctor and I'm going to help you." He waited for a name, for a reciprocal introduction, but none was forthcoming.

"Just...just let me go."

Slowly, still maintaining his careful hold on her, he turned them both until they faced the lake. "You see your car? It's not going anywhere, honey. Not without a tow truck and some major repairs."

She gasped, and her entire body went rigid. "You know my name."

He didn't understand her, but he understood shock. "Not yet, but I will soon. Now..." He paused as her face washed clean of color and she pressed one hand to her mouth. Sawyer quickly lowered her to her knees, still supporting her from behind. "You going to be sick?"

"Oh, God."

"Now just take a few deep breaths. That's it." To Casey, he said, "Go get the water," and his son took off at a sprint, his long legs eating up the ground.

Sawyer turned back to the woman and continued in his soft, soothing tone. "You feel sick because of the blow to your head. It's all right.'' At least, he thought that was the cause. She also felt feverish, and that couldn't be attributed to a concussion. After a moment of watching her gulp down deep breaths, he asked, ''Any better?''

She nodded. Her long fair hair hung nearly to the ground, hiding her face like a silky, tangled curtain. He wrapped it around his hand and pulled it away so he could see her clearly. Her eyes were closed, her mouth pinched. Casey rushed up with the water bottle, and Sawyer held it to her lips. ''Take a few sips. There you go. Real slow, now.'' He watched her struggling for control and wished for some way to lessen the nausea for her. ''Let's get you out of this hot sun, okay? I can get you more comfortable in a jiffy.''

''I need my car.''

Didn't she remember crashing into the water? Sawyer frowned. ''Let me take you to my house, get you dried off and give your belly a chance to settle. I'll have one of my brothers pull your car out and see about having it towed to the garage to be cleaned…''

''No!''

Getting somewhat exasperated, Sawyer leaned around until he could meet her gaze. Her lush bottom lip trembled, something he couldn't help but make note of. He chided himself. ''No, what?''

She wouldn't look at him, still doing her best to shy away. ''No, don't have it towed.''

''Okay.'' She appeared ready to drop, her face now flushed, her lips pale. He didn't want to push her, to add to her confusion. His first priority was determining how badly she might be hurt.

He tried a different tack. ''How about coming to my house and getting dry? You can use the phone, call someone to give you a hand.''

He watched her nostrils flare as she sucked in a slow, labored breath—then started coughing. Sawyer loosened his hold to lift her arms above her head, supporting her and making it easier for her to breathe. Once she'd calmed, he wrapped her close again, giving her his warmth as she continued to shiver.

She swallowed hard and asked, "Why? Why would you want to help me? I don't believe you."

Leaning back on his heels, he realized she was truly terrified. Not just of the situation, of being with total strangers and being hurt and sick, but of him specifically. It floored him, and doubled his curiosity. He was a doctor, respected throughout the community, known for his calm and understanding demeanor. Women never feared him, they came to him for help.

Looking over her head to Casey, seeing the mirrored confusion on his son's face, Sawyer tried to decide what to do next. She helped to make up his mind.

"If...if you let me go, I'll give you money."

He hesitated only two seconds before saying, "Casey, go start the truck." Whatever else ailed her, she was terrified and alone and hurt. The mystery of her fear could be solved later.

She stiffened again and her eyes squeezed tight. He heard her whisper, *"No."*

Determined now, he lifted her to her feet and started her forward, moving at a slow, easy pace so she wouldn't stumble. "'Fraid so. You're in no condition to be on your own."

"What are you going to do?"

A better question was what did she *think* he was going to do. But he didn't ask it, choosing instead to give her an option. "My house or the hospital, take your pick. But I'm not leaving you here alone."

She took two more dragging steps, then held her head. Her body slumped against his in defeat. "Your... your house."

Surprised, but also unaccountably pleased, he again lifted her in his arms. "So you're going to trust me just a bit after all?"

Her head bumped his chin as she shook it. "Never."

He couldn't help but chuckle. "Lesser of two evils, huh?

Now you know I gotta wonder why the hospital is off-limits.'' She winced with each step he took, so he talked very softly just to distract her. ''Did you rob a bank? Are you a wanted felon?''

''No.''

''If I take you in, will someone recognize you?''

''No.''

The shirt he'd draped around her was now tangled at her waist. He tried not to look, but after all, he was human, a male human, and his gaze went to her breasts.

She noticed.

Warm color flooded her cheeks, and he rushed to reassure her. ''It's all right. Why don't we readjust the shirt I gave you just a bit?''

She didn't fight him when he loosened his hold enough to let her legs slip to the ground. She leaned against him while he pulled the shirt up around her, slipping her arms through the sleeves. It was an old faded blue chambray shirt, the sleeves cut short, the top button missing. He'd often used it for work because it was soft and ragged. She should have looked ridiculous in it, wearing it like a robe. Instead, she looked adorable, the shirt in stark contrast to her fragile femininity. The hem hung down to her knees, and it almost wrapped around her twice. Sawyer shook his head, getting his thoughts back on track once again.

''Better?''

''Yes.'' She hesitated, clutching the shirt, then whispered, ''Thank you.''

He watched her face for signs of discomfort as they took the last few steps to the truck. ''I'm sorry,'' he said softly. ''You're in pain, aren't you?''

''No, I'm just—''

He interrupted her lie. ''Well, lucky for you, I really am a doctor, and for the moment you can keep your name, and why you're so frightened, to yourself. All I want to do right now is help.''

Her gaze flicked to his, then away. Sawyer opened the

door of the idling truck and helped her inside. He slid in next to her, then laid his palm against her forehead in a gentle touch. "You're running a fever. How long have you been sick?"

Casey put the truck in gear with a rough start that made her wince. He mumbled an apology, then kept the gears smooth after that.

With one hand covering her eyes, she said, "It's... just a cold."

He snorted. Her voice was so raspy, he could barely understand her. "What are your symptoms?"

She shook her head.

"Dizzy?"

"A little."

"Headache? A tightness in your chest?"

"Yes."

Sawyer touched her throat, checking for swollen glands and finding them. "Does this hurt?"

She tried to shrug, but it didn't have the negligent effect she'd probably hoped for. "Some. My throat is sore."

"Trouble breathing?"

She gave a choked half laugh at his persistence. "A little."

"So of course you decided to go for a drive." She opened her mouth to protest, but he said, "Look at me," then gently lifted each eyelid, continuing his examination. She needed to be in bed getting some care. On top of a likely concussion, he suspected an upper respiratory infection, if not pneumonia. Almost on cue, she gave another hoarse, raw cough. "How long have you had that?"

She turned bleary, suspicious eyes his way. "You're a real doctor?"

"Wanna see my bag? All docs have one, you know."

Casey piped up with, "He really is. In fact, he's the only doctor Buckhorn has. Some of the women around here pretend to be sick just to see him." He smiled at her. "You don't need to be afraid."

"Casey, watch the road." The last thing he needed was his son filling her ears with nonsense, even if the nonsense was true. He had a feeling she wouldn't appreciate the local women's antics nearly as much as his brothers or son did. Sawyer treated it all as a lark, because he had no intention of getting involved with any of the women, and they knew it.

He had a respected position in the community and refused to take advantage of their offers. Driving out of the area was always difficult, not to mention time-consuming. He'd had a few long-distance, purely sexual relationships when the fever of lust got to him and he had to have relief. He was a healthy man in every way, and he didn't begrudge himself the occasional weakness due to his sex. But those encounters were never very satisfying, and he sometimes felt it was more trouble than it was worth.

She turned to him, her blue eyes huge again, and worried. She nervously licked at her dry lips. Sawyer felt that damn lick clear down to his gut, and it made him furious, made him wonder if another out-of-town trip wasn't in order. She was a woman, nothing more, nothing less. And at the moment, she looked pale, on the verge of throwing up, and her mood was more surly than not.

So why was he playing at being a primitive, reacting solely on male instincts he hadn't even known he had?

Her worried frown prompted one of his own. "You had a lot of stuff stowed in your back seat. Moving?"

She bit her lip, and her fingers toyed with the tattered edge of the shirt he'd given her, telling him she didn't want to answer his questions. After another bout of coughing where she pressed a fist to her chest and he waited patiently, she whispered, "How do you know my name?"

He lifted one brow. "I don't."

"But..." It was her turn to narrow her eyes, and the blue seemed even more intense in her annoyance, shaded by her thick lashes, accompanied by her flushed cheeks. Then the annoyance turned to pain and she winced, rubbing at her temples.

Compassion filled him. Finding out the truth could wait. For now, she needed his control. There was no faking a fever, or that croupy cough. "You're confused. And no wonder, given how sick you are and that knock on the head you got when your car dove into the lake."

"I'm sorry," she mumbled. "I'll pay for the damage to your fence."

Sawyer didn't reply to that. For some reason, it made him angry. Even the little talking they'd done had weakened her; she was now leaning on him, her eyes closed. But she was concerned for his damn fence? She should have been concerned about her soft hide.

Casey successfully pulled the truck into the yard beneath a huge elm. Gabe sprinted off the porch where he'd been impatiently waiting, and even before Casey killed the engine, Gabe had the truck door open. "What the hell's going on?" Then his eyes widened on the woman, and he whistled.

Sawyer leaned down to her ear. "My baby brother, Gabe," he said by way of introduction. She nodded, but kept silent.

To Gabe, he answered, "A little accident with the lady's car and the lake."

"Casey told me the lake got in her way." Gabe looked her over slowly, his expression inscrutable. "What's wrong with her? And why aren't you taking her to the hospital?"

"Because she doesn't want to go." Sawyer looked down at the woman's bent head. She was shying away from Gabe, which was a phenomenon all in itself. Gabe was the most popular bachelor in Buckhorn. He smiled, and the women went all mushy and adoring, a fact Sawyer and his brothers taunted him with daily and an accolade Gabe accepted with masculine grace.

Of course Gabe wasn't exactly smiling now, too concerned to do so. And the woman wasn't even looking his way. She'd taken one peek at him, then scooted closer to Sawyer, touching him from shoulder to hip.

In almost one movement he lifted her into his lap and stepped out of the truck. He didn't question his motives; he was a doctor and his first instinct was always to care for the injured or sick. She didn't fight him. Instead, she tucked her face close to his throat and held on. Sawyer swallowed hard, moved by some insidious emotion he couldn't name, but knew damn good and well he'd rather not be feeling. Gruffly, he ordered, "Casey, get a bed ready and fetch my bag."

Casey hurried off, but Gabe kept stride beside him. "This is damn strange, Sawyer."

"I know."

"At least tell me if she's hurt bad."

"Mostly sick, I think, but likely a concussion, too." He looked at his youngest brother. "If I can't handle it here, we'll move her to the hospital. But for now, if you're done with the interrogation, I could use your help."

One of Gabe's fair brows shot up, and he crossed his arms over his chest. "Doing what, exactly?"

"The lady had a lot of stuff in the back seat of her car. Can you go get it before it floats away in the lake or gets completely ruined? And get hold of Morgan to have her car towed out." She lifted her head and one small hand fisted on his chest. Sawyer continued before she could protest, meeting her frantic gaze and silencing her with a look. "Don't take it to the garage. Bring it here. We can put it in the shed."

Gabe considered that a moment, then shook his head. "I hope you know what the hell you're doing."

Slowly, the woman looked away, hiding her face against him again. Sawyer went up the porch steps to the house. To himself, because he didn't want to alarm anyone else, he muttered, "I hope so, too. But I have my doubts."

CHAPTER TWO

IF SHE HAD her choice, Honey Malone would have stayed buried next to the warm, musky male throat and hidden for as long as possible. For the first time in over a week, she felt marginally safe, and she was in no hurry to face reality again, not when reality meant villains and threats, along with an aching head and a weakness that seemed to have invaded every muscle in her body. In varying degrees, she felt dizzy and her head throbbed. Every other minute, her stomach roiled. She couldn't even think of food without having to suppress the urge to vomit. And she was so terribly cold, from the inside out.

At the moment, she wanted nothing more than to close her eyes and sleep for a good long time.

But of course, she couldn't.

It was beyond unfair that she'd get sick now, but she couldn't lie to herself any longer. She *was* sick, and it was sheer dumb luck that she hadn't killed herself, or someone else, in the wreck.

She still didn't know if she could trust him. At first, he'd called her honey, and she thought he knew her name, thought he might be one of them. But he denied it so convincingly, it was possible she'd misunderstood. He'd certainly made no overt threat to her so far. All she knew for sure was that he was strong and warm and he said he only wanted to help her. While he held her, she couldn't find the wit to object.

But then his strong arms flexed, and she found herself lowered to a soft bed. Her eyes flew open wide and she stared upward at him—until her head began to spin again. "Oh, God." She dropped back, trying to still the spinning of the room.

"Just rest a second."

More cautiously now, she peeked her eyes open. The man—Sawyer, he said his name was—picked up a white T-shirt thrown over the footboard and pulled it on. It fit him snugly, molding to his shoulders and chest. He wasn't muscle-bound, but rather leanly cut, like an athlete. His wide solid shoulders tapered into a narrow waist. Faded jeans hugged his thighs and molded to his...

Face flaming, she looked down at the soft mattress he'd put her on. Her drenched, muddy jeans were making a mess of things. "The quilt—"

"Is an old one. Don't worry about it. A little lake water isn't going to hurt anything." So saying, he pulled another quilt from the bottom of the bed and folded it around her chest, helping to warm her. She gratefully snuggled into it.

That taken care of, he looked over his broad shoulder to the door, and as if he'd commanded it, his son appeared, carrying a medical bag. Casey looked nonplussed to see where his father had put her. "Ah, Dad, I already got a bed ready for her, the one in the front room."

Sawyer took the medical bag from Casey, then said, "This one will do."

"But where will you sleep?"

On alert, Honey listened to the byplay between father and son. Casey was earnest, she could see that much in his young, handsome face, but Sawyer had his back to her so she could only guess at his expression.

"Casey, you can go help Gabe, now."

"But—"

"Go on."

Casey reluctantly nodded, casting a few quick glances at Honey. "All right. But if you need anything else—"

"If I do, I'll holler."

The boy went out and shut the door behind him. Nervously, Honey took in her surroundings. The room was gorgeous, like something out of a *Home Show* magazine. She'd never seen anything like it, and for the moment, she was distracted. Pine boards polished to a golden glow covered the floor, three walls and the ceiling. The furnishings were all rustic, but obviously high quality. Black-and-white checked gingham curtains were at the windows that took up one entire wall, accompanied by French doors leading out the back to a small patio. The wall of glass gave an incredible view of the lake well beyond.

There was a tall pine armoir, a dresser with a huge, curving mirror, and two padded, natural wicker chairs. In one corner rested a pair of snow skis and a tennis racket, in the other, several fishing poles. Assorted pieces of clothing—a dress shirt and tie, a suit jacket, a pair of jeans—were draped over bedposts and chair backs. The polished dresser top was laden with a few bills and change, a small bottle of aftershave, some crumpled receipts and other papers, including an open book. It was a tidy room, but not immaculate by any measure.

And it was most definitely inhabited by a man. *Sawyer.* She gulped.

Summoning up some logic in what appeared a totally illogical situation, she asked, "What will your wife—"

"I don't have a wife."

"Oh." She didn't quite know what to think about that, considering he had a teenage son, but it wasn't her place to ask, and she was too frazzled to worry about it, anyway.

"Your clothes are going to have to come off, you know."

Stunned by his unreserved statement, she thought about laughing at the absurdity of it; that, or she could try to hide.

She was unable to work up enough strength for either. Her gaze met his. He stared back, and what she saw made her too warm, and entirely too aware of him as a man, even given the fact she was likely in *his* bedroom and at his mercy. She should have been afraid; she'd gotten well used to that emotion. But strangely, she wasn't. "I—"

The door opened and a man stepped in. This one looked different than both Sawyer and the younger man, Gabe. Sawyer had dark, coal black hair, with piercing eyes almost the same color. His lashes were sinfully long and thick and, she couldn't help noticing, he had a lot of body hair. Not too much, but enough that she'd taken notice. Of course, she'd spent several minutes pressed to that wide chest, so it would have been pretty difficult *not* to notice. And he'd smelled too good for description, a unique, heady scent of clean, male sweat and sun-warmed flesh and something more, something that had pervaded her muscles as surely as the weakness had.

Gabe, the one now fetching items from her car, was blond-haired and incredibly handsome. In his cutoffs, bare feet and bare chest, he'd reminded her of a beach bum.

His eyes, a pale blue, should have looked cool, but instead had seemed heated from within, and she'd naturally drawn back from him. His overwhelming masculinity made her uneasy, whereas Sawyer's calm, controlled brand of machismo offered comfort and patience and rock steady security, which she couldn't help but respond to as a woman. Accepting his help felt right, but the very idea alarmed her, too. She couldn't involve anyone else in her problems.

Now this man, with his light brown hair and warm green eyes, exuded gentle curiosity and tempered strength. Every bit as handsome as the blond one, but in a more understated way, he seemed less of a threat. He looked at her, then to Sawyer. "Casey says we have a guest?"

"She ran her car into the lake. Gabe and Casey are off taking care of that now, getting as much of her stuff out of it as they can."

"Her stuff?"

"Seems she was packed up and moving." He flicked a glance at Honey, one brow raised. She ignored his silent question.

"Care to introduce me?"

Sawyer shrugged. He gestured toward her after he took a

stethoscope out of his bag. ''Honey, this is my brother Jordan.''

Jordan smiled at her. And he waited. Sawyer, too, watched her, and Honey was caught. He'd called her by name again, so why did he now look as if he was waiting for her to introduce herself? She firmed her mouth. After a second, Jordan frowned, then skirted a worried look at his brother. ''Is she...?''

Sawyer sighed. ''She can talk, but she's not feeling well. Let's give her a little time.''

Jordan nodded briskly, all understanding and sympathy. Then he looked down at the floor and smiled. ''Well, hello there, honey. You shouldn't be in here.''

Honey jumped, hearing her name again, but Jordan wasn't speaking to her. He lifted a small calico cat into his arms, and she saw the animal had a bandaged tail. As Jordan stroked the pet, crooning to her in a soothing tone, the cat began a loud, ecstatic purring. Jordan's voice was rough velvet, sexy and low, and Honey felt almost mesmerized by it. It was the voice of a seducer.

Good grief, she thought, still staring. Was every man in this family overflowing with raw sexuality?

''A new addition,'' Jordan explained. ''I found the poor thing on my office doorstep this morning.''

Rolling his eyes, Sawyer said to Honey, ''My brother is a vet—and a sucker for every stray or injured animal that crosses his path.''

Jordan merely slanted a very pointed look at Honey and then said to Sawyer, ''And you're any different, I suppose?''

They both smiled—while Honey bristled. She didn't exactly take to the idea of being likened to a stray cat.

''Jordan, why don't you put the cat in the other room and fetch some tea for our guest? She's still chilled, and from the sounds of her cough, her throat is sore.''

''Sure, no problem.''

But before he could go, another man entered, and Honey

could do no more than stare. This man was the biggest of the lot, a little taller than even Sawyer and definitely more muscle-bound. He had bulging shoulders and a massive chest and thick thighs. Like Sawyer, he had black hair, though his was quite a bit longer and somewhat unruly. And his eyes were blue, not the pale blue of Gabe's, but dark blue, almost like her own but more piercing, more intent. She saw no softness, no giving in his gaze, only ruthlessness.

He had a noticeable five o'clock shadow, and a stern expression that made her shiver and sink a little deeper into the bed.

Sawyer immediately stepped over to her and placed his hand on her shoulder, letting her know it was okay, offering that silent comfort again. But she still felt floored when he said, "My brother Morgan, the town sheriff."

Oh, God. A *sheriff?* How many damn brothers did this man have?

"Ignore his glare, honey. We pulled him from some unfinished business, no doubt, and he's a tad...disgruntled."

Jordan laughed. "Unfinished business? That wouldn't be female business, would it?"

"Go to hell, Jordan." Then Morgan's gaze landed heavily on Honey, though he spoke to Sawyer. "Gabe called me. You mind telling me what's going on?"

Honey was getting tired of hearing Sawyer explain. She looked up at him and asked in her rough, almost unrecognizable voice, "Just how many brothers do you have?"

Jordan smiled. "So she does have a voice."

Morgan frowned. "Why would you think she didn't?"

And Sawyer laughed. "She's been quiet, Morgan, that's all. She's sick, a little disoriented and naturally wary of all of you overgrown louts tromping in and out."

Then to Honey, he said, "There's five of us, including my son, Casey. We all live here, and as it seems you're going to stay put for a spell, too, it's fortunate you've already met them all."

His statement was received with varying reactions. She was appalled, because she had no intention at all of staying anywhere. It simply wasn't safe.

Jordan looked concerned. Morgan looked suspicious.

And in walked Gabe, toting a box. "Nearly everything was wet by the time I got there, except this box of photos she had stashed in the back window. I figured it'd be safer in the house. Casey is helping to unload everything else from the truck, but it's all a mess so we're stowing it in the barn for now. And it looks like it might rain soon. It clouded up real quick. I think we're in for a doozy."

Honey glanced toward the wall of windows. Sure enough, the sky was rapidly turning dark and thick, purplish storm clouds drifted into view. Just what she needed.

Sawyer nodded. "Thanks, Gabe. If it starts to lightning, have Casey come in."

"I already told him."

"Morgan, can you get the county towing truck in the morning and pull her car out of the lake? I want to put it in the shed."

Morgan rubbed his rough jaw with a large hand. "The shed? Why not Smitty's garage so it can be fixed? Or do I even want to know?"

"It's a long story, better explained *after* I find out what ails her. Which I can't do until you all get the hell out of here."

The brothers took the hint and reluctantly began inching out. Before they could all go, though, Sawyer asked, "Any dry clothes in her things, Gabe?"

"Nope, no clothes that I saw. Mostly it's books, hair stuff...junk like that." He dropped the box of framed photos on the floor in front of the closet.

"I don't suppose any of you have a housecoat?"

Three snorts supplied his answer.

If Honey hadn't been feeling so wretched, she would have smiled. And she definitely would have explained to Sawyer that the clothes she wore would have to do, because she wasn't about to strip out of them.

"Any type of pajamas?"

He got replies of, "You've got to be kidding," and, "Never use the things," while Morgan merely laughed.

Squeezing her eyes shut, Honey thought, *No, no, they're not all telling me they sleep in the nude!* She did her best not to form any mental images, but she was surrounded by masculine perfection in varying sizes and styles, and a picture of Sawyer resting in this very bed, naked as a Greek statue, popped into her brain. Additional heat swept over her, making her dizzy again. She could almost feel the imprint of his large body, and she trembled in reaction. She decided it was her illness making her muddled; she'd certainly never been so focused on her sexuality before. Now, she was acutely aware of it.

She opened her eyes and would have shaken her head to clear it, but she was afraid the motion would make her unsettled stomach pitch again.

Casey stuck his head into the room. "I have an old baseball jersey that'd fit her."

"No, thank you—"

Sawyer easily overrode her. "Good. Bring it here."

The brothers all looked at each other, grinning, then filed out. Sawyer leaned down close, hands on his hips, and gave her a pointed frown. "Now."

"Now what?" All her worries, all the fears, were starting to swamp back in on her. She coughed, her chest hurting, her head hurting worse. She felt weak and shaky and vulnerable, which automatically made her defensive. "I'll be fine. If...if Morgan would pull my car out, I'd be appreciative. I'll pay you for your trouble...."

Sawyer interrupted, shaking his head and sitting on the side of the bed. "You're not paying me, dammit, and you aren't going anywhere."

"But..."

"Honey, even if he gets your car out in the morning—

and there's no guarantee, figuring how it's stuck in the mud and it looks like a storm's on the way—but even if he did, the car will need repairs."

"Then I'll walk."

"Now why would you wanna do that? Especially considering you can barely stand." His tone turned gentle, cajoling. He produced a thermometer and slipped it under her tongue, making it impossible for her to reply. "We have plenty of room here, and you need someone to look after you until you're well."

She pulled out the thermometer. "It's...it's not safe."

"For you?"

Honey debated for a long moment, considering all her options. But he was trying to help, and with every second that passed, she grew more tired. The bed was so soft, the quilt warm, if she was going to move, it had to be now before she got settled and no longer wanted to. She started to sit up, but Sawyer's large, competent hands on her shoulders gently pressed her back on the bed.

Not bothering to hide his exasperation, he said, "Okay, this is how it's going to be. You're either going to tell me what's going on, or I'm going to take you to the hospital. Which'll it be?"

She searched his face, but the stubbornness was there, along with too much determination. She simply wasn't up to fighting him. Not right now.

"It's not safe because..." She licked her lips, considered her words, then whispered, "Someone is trying to hurt me."

Sawyer stared at her, for the moment too stunned to speak.

"Is this something I should know about, Sawyer?" Morgan asked.

He almost groaned. Wishing he could remove the fear from her eyes, he gave her a wink, then turned to face his most difficult brother. "Eavesdropping, Morgan?"

"Actually, I was doing tea duty." He lifted a cup and

saucer for verification. "Hearing the girl's confession was just a bonus."

"It wasn't a confession. She's confused from—"

"No." Trembling, she scooted upward on the bed, clutching the quilt to her chest. She chewed her lower lip, not looking at Morgan, but keeping her gaze trained on Sawyer. After a rough bout of coughing, she whispered, "I'm not confused, or making it up."

Sawyer narrowed his eyes, perturbed by the sincerity in her tone and the way she shivered. If anything, she sounded more hoarse, looked more depleted. He needed to get the questions over with so he could medicate her, get her completely dry and let her rest. "Okay, so who would want to hurt you?"

"I don't know."

Morgan set the tea on the bedside table. "*Why* would anyone want to hurt you?"

Tears glistened in her eyes and she blinked furiously. One shoulder lifted, and she made a helpless gesture with her hand. "I..." Her voice broke, and she cleared her throat roughly. Sawyer could tell how much she hated showing her vulnerability. "I don't know."

Agitated, Sawyer shoved Morgan away from where he loomed over her, then took up his own position sitting next to her on the bed. "Honey—"

The sky seemed to open up with a grand deluge of rain. It washed against the windows with incredible force. Within seconds the sky grew so dark it looked like midnight rather than early evening. Lightning exploded in a blinding flash, followed by a loud crack of thunder that made the house tremble and startled the woman so badly she jumped.

By reflex, Sawyer reached out to her, closing his hand over her shoulder, caressing her, soothing her. "Shh. Everything's okay."

A nervous, embarrassed laugh escaped her. "I'm sorry. I'm not normally so skittish."

"You're sick and you're hurt." Sawyer leveled a look on

his brother. "And you aren't going anywhere tonight, so put the thought from your head."

Morgan promptly agreed, but the curling of his lips showed how amused he was by Sawyer's possessive declaration. "Sure thing. We can sort everything out in the morning after you're rested." He slapped Sawyer on the shoulder. "Let the doc here fix you up. You'll feel better in no time."

Casey came in with the baseball jersey. "Sorry, it took me a little while to find it."

Sawyer accepted the shirt. "Good. Now we can get you out of these wet clothes."

Jordan lounged in the doorway, a small half-smile on his mouth. "Need any help?"

And once again, Sawyer had to shove them all out the door. You'd think they'd never seen an attractive woman before, the way they were carrying on, when in fact they all had more than their fair share of female adoration. But as Sawyer closed the door and turned back to her, seeing her lounged in *his* bed, her long hair spread out over *his* pillow, her wide, watchful gaze, he knew he was acting as out of sorts as the rest of them. Maybe more so. He'd just never been so damn *aware* of a woman, yet with this woman, he felt he could already read her gaze. And he strongly reacted to it.

That just wouldn't do, not if he was going to be her doctor.

He laid the shirt on the foot of the bed, resolute. "Come on." After pulling the damp quilt aside, he hooked his hands beneath her arms, lifted her, then proceeded to unbutton the shirt he'd loaned her as if he did such things every day. She was silent for about half a second before suddenly coming to life. With a gasp, she began batting at his hands.

"I can do it!" she rasped in her rough, crackly voice.

He cradled her face in his palms. "Are you sure?"

For long seconds they stared at each other, and just as his heartbeat began to grow heavy, she nodded.

Pulling himself together, Sawyer sighed. "All right." He suffered equal parts relief and disappointment. "Get those wet jeans off, and your panties, too. You're soaked through to the skin and you need to be dry and warm. Leave your clothes there on the floor and I'll run them through the wash." He slid open a dresser drawer and retrieved his own dry jeans and shorts, then as he was reaching for the door to leave, he added, "I'll wait right out here. Call me when you're done or if you need help with anything."

He stepped into the hallway and ran right into every single one of his brothers. Even his son was there, grinning like a magpie. He glared at them all while he unsnapped and unzipped his wet jeans. They smiled back. "Don't you guys have something to do?"

"Yeah," Gabe said with a wide grin. "We're doing it."

"At times you're entertaining as hell, Sawyer," Jordan added with a chuckle.

Sawyer shucked off his clothes, content to change in the middle of the hallway since they pretty much had him boxed in. He was annoyed as hell, but unwilling to let them all see it. As he stripped down to his skin, Gabe automatically gathered up the discarded clothes, helping without being asked. Then he handed them to Jordan who handed them to Morgan who looked around, saw no one else to give them to and tucked them under his arm.

After he was dressed again, Sawyer crossed his arms over his chest, returning their insolent looks. "And what's that supposed to mean, exactly?"

Morgan snorted. "Only that you're acting like a buck in mating season. You're looming over that poor woman like you think she might disappear at any minute. You're so obvious, you might as well put your brand on her forehead." Morgan pushed away from the wall and ran his hand through his hair. "The problem is, Sawyer, we don't know who she is or what she's hiding."

Sawyer disregarded his brothers' teasing remarks and frowned over their concerns. He didn't need Morgan to tell him there were going to be complications with the woman. His own concern was heavy. "So what do you want me to do? Take her back to her car? Do you want to lock her up for the night until you fit all the pieces together? The woman is sick and needs care before her situation becomes critical."

Casey frowned. "Is she really that bad off, Dad?"

Rubbing his neck, trying to relieve some of the mounting tension, Sawyer said, "I think she has bronchitis, possibly pneumonia. But I haven't exactly had a chance to check her over yet."

Just then every window in the house rattled with a powerful boom of thunder, and in the next second, the lights blinked out. It was dark in the hallway, and all the men started to grumble profanities—until they heard a thump and a short, startled female yelp of pain in the bedroom.

Sawyer reacted first, immediately reaching for the doorknob, then halting when he realized all his brothers intended to follow him in. One by one they plowed into him, crushing him against the door, muttering curses. Over his shoulder, Sawyer barked, "Wait here, dammit!" then hurried in, slamming the door in their curious faces.

The wall of windows in his room offered some light from the almost constant strobe of lightning, but not enough. He searched through the shadows until he located her, sitting on the floor by the bed. Her wide eyes glimmered in the darkness, appearing stunned.

But it was nothing compared to how Sawyer felt when he realized her damp jeans and silky panties were around her ankles—and her upper body was completely bare.

The breath froze in his lungs for a heartbeat, every muscle in his body clenching in masculine appreciation of the sweet, utterly vulnerable female sight she presented. Lightning flickered, illuminating her smooth, straight shoulders, her full round breasts. Her taut nipples. Her fair hair left silky trails down her body, flowing sensuously over and around her breasts. He felt the stirrings of a desire so deep it was nearly painful, and struggled to suppress his groan of instant need.

Then, with a small sound, she dropped her head forward in defeat and covered her face with her hands. That was all it took to shake him out of his sensual stupor. Determined, he started forward, dredging up full doctor mode while burying his instinctive, basic urges.

But one fact rang loud and clear in his head.

Damn, he was in deep—and he didn't even know her name.

CHAPTER THREE

SHE WANTED TO DIE. To just curl up and give up and not have to worry about another thing. She felt beyond wretched, more embarrassed than she'd ever been in her life, getting more so with every second that passed, and she was so tired of worrying, of finding herself in impossible situations, giving up seemed the best option. She was just so damn weak, she couldn't do anything.

So instead, she got obnoxious. Without raising her head, she asked, "Are you done gawking?" Her voice was a hideous thin croak, a mixture of illness, embarrassment and pain. It was all she could do to keep herself sitting upright.

"I'm sorry." He crouched down and lifted her as if she weighed no more than the damn cat Jordan had been petting. Very gently, he placed her on the edge of the bed, then matter-of-factly skimmed her jeans and underwear the rest of the way off, leaving her totally bare. In the next instant, he tugged the jersey over her head. He treated her with all the attention and familiarity he might have given a small child, even smoothing down her hair. "There. That's got to be more comfortable."

His voice sounded almost as harsh as her own; she couldn't quite return his smile.

After pulling back the covers, he raised her legs onto the mattress, pressed her back against the headboard with a pillow behind her, then said, "Wait right here while I get some light."

He was gone only a moment, but from the time he stepped out into the hallway until he returned, she heard the drone of masculine voices, some amused, some concerned, some insistent.

God, what must they think of her? She was an intruder, a pathetic charity case, and she hated it.

Sawyer returned with an old-fashioned glass and brass lantern, a flashlight and a small plastic tote of medicine bottles. He closed the door behind him, shutting out the brothers' curious gazes. For that, at least, she was thankful.

"Now, back to business." He unloaded his arms next to the bed on the nightstand, turning up the lantern so that the soft glow of light spread out, leaving heavy shadows in all the corners of the room. "The town is so small, we lose electricity with nearly every storm. It's not something we get too excited over. By morning the lights will be on."

Morning?

He shook the thermometer, and again stuck it in her mouth. "Leave it there this time."

Oh, boy. He was done with stalling, now operating in total efficiency status. Well, fine. She didn't want to talk to him away. Talking took energy, which she didn't have, and hurt her raw throat and made her stomach jumpier than it already was. She honestly didn't know how much longer she could stay awake. Lethargy pulled at her, making her numb.

He approached again, sitting beside her on the bed. He was so warm, heat seemed to pour off him. He gave her a stern look. "I'm going to listen to your lungs. Just breathe normally through your nose, okay?"

She nodded, and he opened the neckline of the jersey and slipped his hand beneath. He didn't look at her, staring at the far wall instead as if in deep concentration. But his wrist was hot, a burning touch against her sensitive skin, contrasting sharply with the icy coldness of the stethoscope.

She forgot to breathe, forgot everything but looking at his profile, at his too long, too thick lashes, his straight nose, his dark hair falling over his brow in appealing disarray. The lantern light lent a halo to that dark hair and turned his skin into burnished bronze. His jaw was firm, his mouth sexy—

"Normal breaths, honey."

Oh, yeah. She sucked in a lungful of air, accidentally filling her head with his delicious scent. She immediately suffered a coughing fit. Sawyer quickly retrieved the thermometer and looked at it with the flashlight. "Almost a hundred and two." He frowned. "Can you sit forward just a second?"

Without waiting for her reply, he leaned her forward, propping her with his body, practically holding her in an embrace against that wide, strong chest. His arms were long and muscled, his body hard and so wonderfully warm. She wanted to snuggle into him but forced herself to hold perfectly still.

Again, he seemed oblivious to thc intimacy of the situation.

She was far, far from oblivious.

He lifted the jersey to listen to her lungs through her back. Honey merely closed her eyes, too mortified to do much else. After a long moment, he made a sound of satisfaction.

He carefully leaned her back and recovered her with the quilt. "You've definitely got bronchitis, and if you'd gone on another day or two, you'd have likely ended up with pneumonia. On top of that, I'd be willing to bet you have a concussion." He gently touched a bruised spot on her forehead with one finger. "You hit the steering wheel hard when the car dove into the lake. I suppose I can only be grateful you were wearing your seat belt."

He sounded a bit censuring, but she nodded, so exhausted she no longer cared.

"Are you allergic to any medications?"

"No."

"Can you swallow a pill okay?"

Again she nodded, words too difficult.

He started to say something else, then looked at her face and hesitated. He sighed. "Honey, I know this is hard for you. Being in a strange house with all these strange men wandering about, but—''

''Your brothers are a bit overwhelming,'' she rasped in her thick voice, ''but I wouldn't exactly call them strange.''

He smiled. ''Well, I would.'' He raised his voice and shouted toward the door, ''I'd call them strange and obnoxious and overbearing and *rude!*''

Honey heard one of the brothers—she thought it was Gabe—shout back, ''I know a lot of women who'd object to the obnoxious part!'' and a hum of low masculine laughter followed.

Sawyer chuckled. ''They mean well. But like me, they're concerned.''

He patted her knee beneath the quilt, then handed her the tea. ''You can swallow your pills with this. It's barely warm now.''

Honey frowned at the palm full of pills he produced. After all, she didn't really know him, and yet she was supposed to trust him. Even knowing she had no choice, she still hesitated.

Patiently, he explained, ''Antibiotics and something for the pain. You'll also need to swallow some cough medicine.''

''Wonderful.'' She threw all the pills down in one gulp, then swallowed almost the entire cup of tea, leaving just enough to chase away the nasty taste of the cough liquid he insisted she take next. Whoever had made the tea went heavy on the sugar—which suited her just fine.

Sawyer took the cup from her and set it aside, then eyed her closely. ''The door next to the closet is a half bath. Do you need to go?''

Why didn't she simply expire of embarrassment? She was certainly due. ''No,'' she croaked, then thought to add, ''thank you.''

He didn't look as if he quite believed her, but was reluctant to force the issue. ''Well, if you do, just let me know so I can help you. I don't want you to get up and fall again.''

Yeah, right. Not in this lifetime. That was definitely a chore she would handle on her own—or die trying. ''I'm fine, really. I'm just so tired.''

Sawyer stood and began pulling the quilts off her. They were damp, so she didn't protest, but almost immediately she began to shiver. Seconds later he recovered her with fresh blankets from the closet. He laid two of them over her, tucking her in until she felt so cozy her body nearly shut down.

''Go on to sleep. I'll come back in a couple of hours to check on you—because of the concussion,'' he added, when she blinked up at him. ''I'm sorry, honey, but I'll have to wake you every hour or two just to make certain you're okay. All you'll have to do is open those big blue eyes and say hi, all right?''

''All right.'' She didn't really like the idea, because she knew she wouldn't be able to sleep a wink now, worrying about when he'd come in, if she'd be snoring, if she'd even make sense. Usually she slept like the dead, and very little could disturb her, but since this had started she'd been so worried, and she'd had to be on her guard at all times.

At least now she could rest in peace and quiet for a while, and that was more than she'd had recently.

Sawyer tucked a curl of hair behind her ear and smoothed his big thumb over her cheek. The spontaneous, casual touches disconcerted her. They weren't what she was used to and she didn't quite know what to think of them. He acted as if it were the most natural thing in the world for him to pet her, which probably meant it was merely his way and had no intimate connotations attached. He was, after all, a doctor.

Still, his touch felt very intimate to Honey. Like a lover's caress.

''Holler if you need anything,'' he said gently. ''The family room is close enough so one of us will hear you.''

He moved the lantern to the dresser top and turned it down very low, leaving just enough light so she wouldn't wake disoriented in the strange room. Outside, the storm still raged with brilliant bursts of light and loud rumbling thunder.

He picked up the flashlight and damp quilts and went out, leaving the door open a crack. Honey rolled slowly to her side and stacked her hands beneath her cheek. His bed was so comfortable, the blankets so soft and cozy. And it smelled like him, all masculine and rich and sexy. Her eyes drifted shut, and she sighed. Sleep would be wonderful, but she really didn't dare. As soon as the storm let up, she had to think about what to do.

Sawyer was a nice man. His whole family was nice; she couldn't put them at risk, couldn't take advantage of their generosity and their trusting nature. She supposed she could call a cab to take her into town and buy another used car there. The one she'd been driving didn't have much value anyway, hardly worth repairing.

But her stuff. They'd unloaded everything into the barn, Gabe said. She hadn't even noticed a barn, and if she found it, could she retrieve everything without alerting them to her intentions? She had no doubt they'd feel honor bound to detain her, thanks to her illness.

She just didn't know what to do. Since she knew she wouldn't be able to sleep, she figured she had plenty of time to come up with a plan.

TWENTY MINUTES LATER Sawyer peeked in on her—again. He couldn't quite seem to pull his gaze away for more than a few minutes, and his thoughts wouldn't budge from her at all. She was in his bed—and he knew it, on every level imaginable.

It had taken her less than two minutes to fall deeply asleep, and since then, he'd been checking her every few minutes, drawn by the sight of her cuddled so naturally, so trustingly in his bed. He leaned in the door frame, watching her sleep, enthralled by the way the gentle lantern light played over the curves and hollows of her body.

"She doin' okay?"

Sawyer quickly pulled the door shut as he turned to face Jordan. "She's asleep, and her breathing sounds just a little easier. But she's still really sick. I think she needs some rest more than anything else. She's plain wore out."

"If you want, we can all spell you a turn on waking her up through the night."

"No."

Jordan's eyes narrowed. "Sawyer, it's dumb for you to do it alone. We could—"

"I'm the doctor, Jordan, so I'll do it." He was determined to get his brother's mind off altruistic motives and away from the room. "The rest of you don't need to worry. It's under control."

Jordan studied him a long minute before finally shrugging. "Suit yourself. But I swear, you're acting damn strange."

Sawyer didn't refute that. His behavior did seem odd, considering his brother didn't know why he was so insistent. But when Jordan walked away, Sawyer again opened the door where she slept. Nope, he didn't want his brothers seeing her like this.

The little lady slept on her stomach, and she kept kicking her covers off; the jersey had ridden to her waist.

Damn, but she had a nice backside. Soft, white, perfectly rounded. The kind of backside that would fit a man's hands just right. His palms tingled at the thought, and his fingers flexed the tiniest bit.

With a small appreciative smile, Sawyer once again covered her. At least her fever must be lower, or she'd still be chilled deep inside. The fact she felt comfortable enough not to need the blankets proved the medicine was doing its job. Still, he touched her forehead, smoothed her hair away, then forced himself to leave the room.

When he walked out this time he ran into Morgan.

"We need to talk."

Sawyer eyed his brother's dark countenance. He'd have

been worried, except Morgan pretty much always looked that way. "If you're going to offer your help, don't bother. I'm more than able to—"

"Nope. I figure if you want to hover all night over the little darling, that's your business. But I want to show you something."

For the first time, Sawyer noticed Morgan was gripping a woman's purse in his fist. "Our guest's?"

"Yep. I decided I didn't like all this secretive business, and being she's staying here, I was fully justified—"

"You snooped, didn't you?"

Morgan tried to look affronted and failed. "Just took a peek at her wallet for I.D. I'm a sheriff, and I had just cause with all this talk of someone hunting her and such."

"And?" Sawyer had to admit to his own overwhelming curiosity. He wondered if the name would match the woman. "Don't keep me in suspense."

"You won't believe this, but it's *Honey Malone.*" Morgan chuckled. "Damn, she sounds just like a female mobster, doesn't she?"

It took Sawyer two seconds before he burst out laughing. *Honey.* No wonder she thought he knew her name. He was still grinning when Morgan poked him.

"It's not that funny."

"Ah, but it is! Especially when you know the joke."

"But you're not going to share it?"

Sawyer shook his head. "Nope. At least, not until I've shared it with Miss Malone."

Since he had the arrogant habit of refusing ever to let anyone rile him, Morgan merely shrugged. "Suit yourself. But you should also know I braved this hellish rain to run out to the car radio and run a check on her. Nothing, from either side of the law. No priors, no complaints, no signed statements. If someone is trying to hurt her, the police don't know a damn thing about it."

Sawyer worked that thought over in his mind, then shook his head. "That could mean several things."

"Yeah, like she's making it all up." Morgan hesitated, but as he turned to walk away, he added, "Or she's more rattled than you first thought and is delusional. But either way, Sawyer, be on your guard, okay?"

"I'm not an idiot."

"No." Morgan pointed at him and chuckled. "But you are acting like a man out to stake a claim. Don't let your gonads overrule your common sense."

Sawyer glared, but Morgan hadn't waited around to see it. Ridiculous. So he was attracted to her, so what? He was human, and he'd been attracted to plenty of women in his day. Not quite this attracted, not quite this...*consumed.* But it didn't matter. He had no intentions of getting involved any more than necessary to get her well. She was a patient, and he'd treat her as such. Period.

But even as he thought it, he opened the door again, drawn by some inexplicable need to be near her.

Damn, but she looked sweet resting there in his bed. Incredibly sweet and vulnerable.

And once again, she'd kicked the blanket away.

HONEY WOKE slowly and struggled to orient herself to the sensation of being in strange surroundings. Carefully, she queried her senses, aware of birds chirping in near rapture, the steady drone of water dripping outside and a soft snore. Yet she was awake.

Her throat felt terrible, and she swallowed with difficulty, then managed to get her heavy eyes to open a tiny bit. As soon as she did, she closed them again against a sharp pain in her head. She held her breath until the pain ebbed, easing away in small degrees.

Her body felt weighted down, warm and leaden, and a buzzing filled her head. It took a lot of effort to gather her wits and recall where she was and why.

She was on her stomach, a normal position for her, and this time she opened her eyes more carefully, only a slit, and let them adjust to the dim light filtering into the room.

As her eyes focused on the edge of a blanket, pulled to her chin, she shifted, but her legs didn't want to move. Confused, she peered cautiously around the room. The rain, only a light drizzle now, left glittering tracks along the wall of windows, blurring the image of the lake beyond and the fog rising from it. The gutters must have been overloaded because they dripped steadily, the sound offering a lulling, soporific effect. The day was gray, but it was definitely morning, and the birds seemed to be wallowing in the freshness of it, singing their little hearts out.

Frowning, she looked away from the windows, and her gaze passed over Sawyer, then snapped back. She almost gasped at the numbing pain that quick eye movement caused.

Then she did moan as the sight of him registered.

Wearing nothing more than unsnapped jeans, he lounged in a padded wicker chair pulled close at an angle to the foot of the bed. His long legs were stretched out, his bare feet propped on the edge of the mattress near her waist pinning her blankets in place. No wonder her legs didn't want to move. They couldn't, not with his big feet keeping her blankets taut.

She remembered him waking her several times throughout the night, his touch gentle, his voice low and husky as he insistently coaxed her to respond to him, to answer his questions. Her skin warmed with the memory of his large hands on her body, smoothing over her, resettling her blankets, lifting her so she could take a drink or swallow another pill.

She warmed even more as she allowed her eyes to drink in the sight of him. Oh, she was awake now. Wide awake. Sawyer had that effect on her, especially when he was more naked than not, available to her scrutiny. He was a strong man, confident, even arrogant in his abilities. But there was an innate gentleness in his touch, and an unwavering serenity in his dark eyes.

The muscles of his chest and shoulders were exaggerated

by the long shadows. She felt cool in the rainy, predawn morning, yet he looked warm and comfortable in nothing more than his jeans. His abdomen, hard and flat, had a very enticing line of downy black hair bisecting it, dipping into those low-fitting jeans. Her heart rate accelerated, her fingers instinctively curling into the sheets as she thought about touching him there, feeling how soft that hair might be and how hard the muscles beneath it were.

One of his elbows was propped on the arm of the chair, offering a fist as a headrest. His other arm dangled off the side of the chair, his hand open, his fingers slack. He was deeply asleep, and even in his relaxed state his body looked hard and lean and too virile for a sane woman to ignore. He appeared exhausted, and no wonder after caring for her all night. She studied his whisker-roughened face a moment, then gave in to temptation and visually explored his body again. A soft sigh escaped her.

She needed a drink. She needed the bathroom. But she could be happy just lying there looking at him for a long, long time.

"G'mornin'."

With a guilty start, her attention darted back to his face. His eyes were heavy-lidded, his thick black lashes at half-mast, his dark gaze glittering at her. Honey closed her own eyes for a moment, trying to get her bearings. His voice had been low, sleepy, *sexy*.

Ahem. "Good morning." The words, which she'd meant to be crisp, sounded like a faint, rusty impersonation.

Sawyer tilted his head. "Throat still sore?"

She nodded, peeking a glance at him and quickly looking away again. "You're, ah, pinning my blankets down."

She heard the amusement in his tone when he murmured, "Yeah, I know."

Then he dragged his feet off the bed and stood and stretched—right there in front of her, putting on an impressive display of flexing muscle and sinew and masculine perfection. Without even thinking about it, she rolled to her back to watch him, keeping her blankets high.

With one arm over his head, she saw the dark silky hair beneath his arm, the way his biceps bulged, and she heard his growled rumble of pleasure. As he stretched, his abdomen pulled tighter and the waistband of his jeans curled away from his body. Her vision blurred. He ran both hands through his hair and over his face, then he smiled.

She tried to smile back, she really did. But then he scratched his belly, drawing her gaze there, and she saw that his jeans rode even lower on his slim hips and that his masculine perfection had changed just a tad. Okay, more than a tad. A whole lot more.

He had an erection.

She didn't exactly mean to stare, but since he was standing only a foot away from the bed and she was lying down and he was so close, it was rather hard to ignore. Heat bloomed in her belly, making her toes curl.

He reached out and placed a warm palm on her forehead. "Your fever seems to be down. Luckily, the electricity came on in the middle of the night, otherwise, without the air-conditioning, the house would have been muggy as hell. If this rain ever stops, they're predicting a real scorcher, and with you being sick I'd hate for you to suffer through the heat, too." He smoothed her hair away from her set face, looking at her closely. "You want to use the john?"

She was so flustered by his good-natured chatter in light of her lascivious thoughts, she couldn't answer, even though her situation was beginning to get critical.

He solved the problem for her. Whisking the covers aside, he hooked one arm behind her and levered her upright. She scrambled to get the jersey shirt pulled down over her hips, covering her decently. He didn't seem to notice her predicament.

"Come on. I'll help you in, then wait out here."

She didn't want him waiting anywhere, but he hustled her out of the bed and toward the bathroom, holding her closely, not really giving her time to think about it. He walked her right up to the toilet, then cautiously let her go. "If you need anything, don't be too squeamish to call out, okay?"

Never, not in a million years. She stared at him, blinked twice, then nodded, just to get him out of the room. With a smile and a touch to her cheek, he backed out and pulled the door shut.

Even in her dazed state, Honey was able to appreciate the incredibly beautiful design of the bathroom. Done in the same polished pine but edged with black ceramic tile, it looked warm and masculine and cozy. The countertops were white with black trim, and there was a shower stall but no tub, a black sink, and a small blocked window with the same black-checked gingham curtains. Amazing that a household of men would have such a nice, clean, well-designed home.

After she'd taken care of business, Honey washed her hands, splashed her face and took a long drink of water. She looked at herself in the round etched mirror over the sink and nearly screamed. She looked horrid. Her hair was tangled, her face pale, the bruise on her forehead providing her only color, and that in shades of gray and purple and green. God, she looked as sickly as she felt, and that was saying a lot!

She glanced longingly at the shower, but then she heard Sawyer ask impatiently, "Everything okay?"

It would take more time and effort than she could muster to make herself look any better. With a sigh, she edged her way to the door, holding on to the sink for support. She barely had the door open and he was there, tall, shirtless, overwhelmingly potent. Without a word he wrapped his arm around her and practically carried her back to the bed.

He tucked her in, then asked, "Would you like some tea or coffee?"

Her mouth watered. Now that she wasn't so tired, she noticed other needs, and hot coffee sounded like just the thing to clear out the cobwebs and relieve her sore throat. "I'd kill for coffee."

"When you don't have the strength to swat a fly? Never mind. Nothing so drastic is necessary. The coffee is already on. Morgan and Gabe are both early risers, so one of them has already seen to it because I smell it. Cream and sugar?"

"Please."

He started to turn away, and she said, "Sawyer?"

He looked at her over his shoulder. "Hmm?"

"My things..."

"They're safe. Gabe and Casey got everything stored in the barn before the worst of the storm hit, but if you like, I'll check on them after I've dressed."

After he'd dressed. The fact of his partial nudity flustered her again, and she felt herself blush. She'd simply never been treated to the likes of a man like him before. Her experiences were with more...subtle men. Sawyer without his shirt was more enticing, more overpowering, than most men would have been buck naked.

She cleared her sore throat. "I'd really like my toothbrush. And...and I'd dearly love to shower and get the lake water off—"

"I dunno." He gave her a skeptical look and frowned. "Let's see how you do after eating a little, okay? I don't want you to push it. You still sound like a bullfrog, and I'm willing to bet you have a bit of a fever yet. But first things first. Let me get the coffee. It'll make your throat feel better."

His peremptory manner set her on edge. Straightening her shoulders as much as she could while lying huddled beneath a layer of blankets, she groused, "It's not up to you to decide what I can or can't do."

He halted in mid stride and slowly turned to face her. The intensity of his dark gaze almost made her squirm, but after a good night's rest, she felt emotionally stronger, if not physically, and she couldn't continue to let him baby her or dictate to her. Now was as good a time as any to assert herself.

Tilting his head, he said, "Actually—I can."

"No—"

He stalked forward, startling her with the suddenness of it. His bare feet didn't make a sound on the polished flooring, but he might have been stomping for the expression on his face. Bracing one hand on the headboard and the other on the pillow by her cheek, he leaned down until their noses almost touched. Her head pressed into the pillow, but there was no place to retreat to, no way to pull back.

His breath touched her as he studied her face. "You're seriously ill, and I didn't stay up all night checking on you just so you could turn stubborn this morning and set yourself on a decline."

She mustered her courage and frowned up at him. "I know I'm not a hundred percent well, but—"

He made a rude sound to that statement. "It's a wonder you even made it to the bathroom on your own. I can tell just looking at your flushed cheeks and lips that you still have a fever. What you need is plenty of rest and medicine and liquids."

She hated to sound vain, so the words came out in a rough, embarrassed whisper. "I smell like the lake."

At first his brows lowered and he stared at her. Then, almost against his will it seemed, he leaned closer and his nose nearly touched her throat beneath her ear. She sucked in a startled breath, frozen by his nearness, his heat, the sound of his breathing. He nuzzled gently for just a moment, then slowly leaned away again, and his gaze traveled down her throat to her chest and beyond, then came back to her face, and there was a new alertness to his expression, a sensual hardness to his features.

She swallowed roughly and croaked, "Well?" trying to hide the effect he'd had on her, trying, and failing, to be as cavalier.

His lips twitched, though his eyes still looked hot and far too intent. He touched her cheek, then let his hand fall away. "Not a single scent of lake, I promise. Quit worrying about it."

She couldn't quit worrying, not when he stayed so close. And she knew a shower would revive her spirits, which she needed so she could think clearly. She tried a different tack. "I'm not used to going all day without a shower. I'll feel better after I clean up."

He continued to loom over her, watching her face, then finally he sighed. "Somehow I doubt that, but then, what do I know? I'm just the doctor." When she started to object, he added, "If you feel such a strong need to get bathed, fine. I'll help you, and no, don't start shaking your head at me. I'm not leaving you alone to drown yourself."

"You're also not watching me bathe!"

He started to grin, but rubbed his chin quickly instead. "No, of course not. The shower is out because I doubt you could stand that long. And as wobbly as you seem when you're on your feet, I'm not taking the chance. But this afternoon, after I've seen a few patients, I'll take you to the hall bath. We have a big tub you can soak in. By then I'll have your clothes run through the washer, and you can wear your own things. We'll manage, I think."

Worse and worse. "Sawyer, I don't want you doing my laundry."

"There's no one else, Honey. Morgan has to go into the office today, and Jordan is making a few housecalls. Casey has never quite learned the knack of doing laundry, though I'm working on him, and if I know Gabe, he'll be off running around somewhere."

She stared at him, dumbfounded, then shook her head. "Let me clarify. I don't want *any* of you doing my laundry."

"The clothes you came in are wet and muddy. By now, they probably do smell like the lake. Unless you want to continue living in Casey's shirt, someone needs to do it, and you're certainly not up to it." She started to speak, and he held up a hand. "Give over, will you? I doubt doing a little laundry will kill me. If it did, I'd have been dead a long time ago."

She seemed to have no options at all. With a sigh, she said, ''Thank you.''

''You're welcome.''

His continued good humor made her feel like a nag. Trying to get back to a more neutral subject, she asked, ''Do you see patients every day?''

He straightened from the bed. ''Don't most doctors?''

''I really don't know.''

''Well, they do. You can take my word on it. Illness has no respect for weekends or vacations. And since I'm the only doctor around for miles, I've gotten used to it.''

Nervously pleating the edge of the blanket, she wondered if this might be her best chance to slip away. It was for certain if he didn't want her up to shower, he wouldn't want her up to leave on her own. ''Do you have an office close by?''

He crossed his arms over his chest. ''Very close.''

''Oh?'' She tried to sound only mildly interested.

''You're not going anywhere, Honey.''

Her tongue stuck to the roof of her mouth.

''Don't look so shocked. I could see you plotting and planning.''

''But...how?'' She'd kept her expression carefully hidden. At least, she thought she had.

''I can read you.''

''You don't even know me!''

He looked disgruntled by that fact. ''Yeah, well, for whatever reason, I know you well enough already to see how your mind works. What'd you think to do? Hitchhike into town when we were all away from the house?''

She hadn't, simply because she hadn't thought that far ahead yet. But it might not have been a bad idea. She'd be able to tell by the license plates if the driver was local or not, ridding the risk of being picked up by the people who were after her.

When she remained quiet, he shook his head and muttered, ''Women.'' He went out the door without another word, and Honey let him. She had a lot to think about. This might be her only chance to save Sawyer and his family from getting involved. She'd left in the first place to protect her sister. The last thing she wanted to do was get someone else in trouble.

Especially such an incredible man as Sawyer.

CHAPTER FOUR

SAWYER TAPPED on the door and then walked in. Honey was in the bed, her head turned to the window. She seemed very pensive, but she glanced at him as he entered. He saw her face perk up at the sight of the tray he carried.

Grinning, he asked, "So you're hungry?"

She slid higher in the bed. "Actually…yes. What have you got there?"

He set the tray holding the coffee and other dishes on the dresser and carried another to her, opening the small legs on the tray so it fit over her lap. "Gabe had just pulled some cinnamon rolls from the oven, so they're still hot. I thought you might like some."

"Gabe cooks?"

Sawyer handed her the coffee, then watched to make sure it was to her liking. Judging by the look of rapture on her face as she sipped, it was just right. "We all cook. As my mom is fond of saying, she didn't raise no dummies. If a man can't cook, especially in a household devoid of women, he goes hungry."

She'd finished half the cup of coffee right off so he refilled her cup, adding more sugar and cream, then gave her a plate with a roll on it. The icing had oozed over the side of the roll, and she quickly scooped up a fingerful, then moaned in pleasure as she licked her finger clean.

Sawyer stilled, watching her and suffering erotic images that leaped into his tired, overtaxed brain. His reactions to her were getting way out of hand. Of course, they'd been out of hand since he'd first seen her. And last night, when she kept kicking the covers away, he'd almost gone nuts. Pinning them down with his feet had been a form of desperate self-preservation.

He hadn't had such a volatile reaction to a woman in too many years to count. No, he'd never been entirely celibate, but he had always been detached. Now, with this woman who remained more a stranger than otherwise, he already felt far too involved.

He cleared his throat, enthralled by the appreciative way she savored the roll. "Good?"

"Mmm. Very. Give my regards to the chef."

She sounded so sincere, he almost laughed. "It's just a package that you bake. But Gabe really can do some great cooking when he's in the mood. Usually everyone around here grabs a snack first thing in the morning, then around eight they hit Ceily's diner and get breakfast."

"If they can cook, why not eat here?"

He liked it that she was more talkative today, and apparently more at ease. "Well, let's see. Gabe goes to town because that's what he always does. He sort of just hangs out."

Her brows raised. "All the time?"

With a shrug, he admitted, "That's Gabe. He's a handyman extraordinaire—his title, not mine—so he's never without cash. Someone's always calling on him to fix something, and there's really nothing he can't fix." Including her car, though Sawyer hadn't asked him to fix it. Not yet. "He keeps busy when he wants. And when he doesn't, he's at the lake, lolling in the sun like a big fish."

Gabe stuck his head in the door to say, "I resent that. I bask, I do not loll. That makes me sound lazy."

Sawyer saw Honey gulp the bite in her mouth and almost choke as she glanced up at his brother. As a concession to their guest, Gabe had pulled on frayed jean shorts rather than walking around in his underwear. He hoped Jordan and Morgan remembered to do the same. They each had more than enough female companionship, but never overnight at the house, so they were unused to waking with a woman in residence.

Gabe hadn't shaved yet, and though he had on a shirt, it wasn't buttoned so his chest was mostly bare. Sawyer shook his head at his disreputable appearance. "You are lazy, Gabe."

Gabe smiled at Honey. "He's just jealous because he has so much responsibility." Then to Sawyer, "Now, if I was truly lazy, would I plan on fixing the leak in your office sink this morning?"

Sawyer hesitated, pleased, then took a sip of coffee before nodding. "Yeah, you would, considering you can't go to the lake because it's raining."

"Not true. The best fishing is done in the rain."

He couldn't debate that. "Are you really going to fix the sink?"

"Sure. You said it's leaking under the cabinet?"

Sawyer started to explain the exact location of the leak, but Honey interrupted, asking, "Where is his office?"

Gabe hitched his head toward the end of the hallway. "At the back of the house. He and my dad built it on there after he got his degree and opened up his own practice. 'Course, I helped because Sawyer is downright pathetic with a hammer. He can put in tiny stitches, but he has a hell of a time hitting a nail or cutting a board straight."

Honey carefully set down her last bite of roll. "Your dad?"

"Yep. He's not a military man, like Sawyer's dad was, but he is a pretty good handyman, just not as good as me."

Standing, Sawyer headed toward Gabe, forcing him to back out of the doorway. He could see the questions and the confusion on Honey's face, but it was far too early for him to go into long explanations on his family history. "Go on and let her drink her coffee in peace."

Gabe put on an innocent face, but laughter shone in his eyes. "I wasn't bothering her!"

"You were flirting."

"Not that she noticed." He grinned shamefully. "She was too busy watching you."

That sounded intriguing—not that he intended to dwell on it or to do anything about it. Likely she watched him because he was the one most responsible for her. "I'll be at the office after I've showered and gotten dressed."

"All right. I'll go get my tools together."

Sawyer stepped back into the room and shut the door, then leaned against it. Just as Gabe had mentioned, Honey watched him, her blue eyes wide and wary. He nodded at her unfinished roll. "You done?"

"Oh." She glanced down at the plate as if just remembering it was there. "Yes." She wiped her fingers on the napkin he'd provided and patted her mouth. "Thank you. That was delicious. I hadn't realized I was so hungry."

Eating less than one cinnamon roll qualified as hungry? He grunted. "More coffee?"

"Yes, please."

Her continued formality and good manners tickled him. Here she was, bundled up in his bed, naked except for his son's jersey, and with every other word she said *please*. She still sounded like a rusty nail on concrete, but she didn't look as tense as she had last night. Probably the need for sleep had been more dire than anything else. As he refilled her cup, emptying the carafe, he said, "I have spare toothbrushes in my office. If you'd like, I can give you one. I'd go get yours, but I'm not sure which box it's in."

"I'm not sure, either."

"Okay, then. I'll fetch you one in a bit." He finished his own coffee while leaning on the dresser, looking at her. "Before I start getting ready for my day, you want to tell me who you are?"

She went so still, it alarmed him. He set down his empty cup and folded his arms over his chest. "Well?"

"I think," she muttered, not quite meeting his gaze, "that it'll be simpler all around if I don't involve you."

"You don't trust me?"

"Trust a man I've known one day?"

"Why not? I haven't done anything to hurt you, have I?"

"No. It's not that. It's just...Sawyer, I can't stay here. I don't want to endanger you or your son or your brothers."

That was so ludicrous he laughed. And her lack of trust, regardless of the time limits, unreasonably annoyed him. "So you think one little scrawny woman is better able to defend herself than four men and a strapping fifteen-year-old?"

Her mouth firmed at his sarcasm. "I don't intend to get into a physical battle."

"No? You're going to just keep running from whatever the hell it is you're running from?"

"That's none of your business," she insisted.

His jaw clenched. "Maybe not, but it would sure simplify the hell out of things if you stopped being so secretive."

She pinched the bridge of her nose and squeezed her eyes shut. Sawyer felt like a bully. Just because she'd sat up and eaten a little didn't mean she was up to much more than that. He sighed in disgust—at himself and her—then pushed away from the dresser to remove the tray from her lap.

She glanced at him nervously. "I...I don't mean to make this more difficult."

He kept his back to her, not wanting her to see his frown. "I realize that. But you're going to have to tell me something sooner or later."

A heavy hesitation filled the air. Then he heard her draw in her breath. "No, I don't. My plans don't concern you."

Everything in him fought against the truth of her words. "You landed in my lake."

"And I offered to pay for the damages."

He turned to face her, his muscles tense. "Forget the damn damages. I'm not worried about that."

She looked sad and resolute. "But payment for the damages is all I owe you. I didn't ask to be brought here. I didn't ask for your help."

"You got it anyway." He stalked close again, unable to

keep the distance between them. "No respectable man would leave a sick, frightened woman alone in a rainstorm. Especially a woman who was panicked and damn near delusional."

"I wasn't—"

"You slugged my son. You were afraid of me."

She winced again, then worried her bottom lip between her teeth. His heart nearly melted, and that angered him more than anything else. He sat on the edge of the bed and took her hands in his. "Honey, you can trust me. You can trust us." She didn't quite meet his gaze, staring instead at his throat. "The best thing now is to tell me what's going on so I know what to expect."

She looked haunted as her gaze met his, but she also looked strong, and he wasn't surprised when she whispered, "Or I can leave."

They stared at each other, a struggle of wills, and with a soft oath Sawyer stood and paced away. Maybe he was pushing too fast. She needed time to reason things through. He'd wear her down, little by little. And if that didn't work, he'd have Morgan start an investigation—whether she liked it or not.

One thing was certain. He wasn't letting her out of his sight until he knew it was safe.

With his back to her, his hands braced on the dresser, he said, "Not yet."

"You can't keep me here against my will."

"Wanna bet?" He felt like a bastard, but his gut instincts urged him to keep her close regardless of her insistence. "Morgan is the town sheriff, and he heard everything you said. If nothing else, he'd want to keep you around for questioning. I'm willing to give you some time. But until you're ready to explain, you're not going anywhere."

He could feel her staring at his back, feel the heat of her anger. She wasn't nearly so frail as he'd first thought, and she had more gumption than the damn old mule Jordan kept out in the pasture.

Despite the raspiness of her voice, he heard her disdain when she muttered, "And you wanted me to trust you."

His hand fisted on the dresser, but he refused to take the bait. He pulled open a drawer and got out a pair of shorts, saying over his shoulder, "I need to shower and get dressed before patients start showing up. Why don't you just go on back to sleep for a spell? Maybe things'll look a little different this afternoon."

He saw her reflection in the mirror, the way her eyes were already closing, shutting him out. He wanted to say something more, but he couldn't. So instead he walked away, and he closed the door behind him very softly.

SHE SLEPT the better part of the day. After taking more medicine and cleaning up as much as she could using the toothbrush he provided and the masculine-scented soap in the bathroom, she simply konked out. One minute she'd been disgruntled because he was rushing her back to bed, and the next she was sound asleep. Sawyer roused her once to take more ibuprofen and sip more water, but she barely stirred enough to follow his directions. He held her head up with one hand, aware of the silkiness of her heavy hair and the dreamy look in her sleepy eyes. She smiled at him, too groggy to remember her anger.

Fortunately for him, since he couldn't stay by her side, she hadn't kicked off her blankets again. He'd worried about it, and gone back and forth from his office to her room several times during the day, unable to stay away. After Casey had finished up his chores, he promised to stay close in case she called out.

She hadn't had any lunch, and it was now nearing dinnertime. When Sawyer entered the room, he saw his son sitting on the patio through the French doors. He had the small cat with him that Jordan had brought home. Using a string, he enticed the cat to pounce and jump and roll.

This time Honey was on her back, both arms flung over her head. He could see her legs were open beneath the covers. She was sprawled out, taking up as much room as her small body could in the full-size bed. In his experience, most women slept curled up, like a cat, but not Honey. A man would need a king-size bed to accommodate her.

He was still smiling when he stepped outside with Casey. "She been sleeping okay?"

"Like the dead." Casey glanced up at him, then yelped when the cat attacked his ankle. "She looks like someone knocked her out, doesn't she? I've never seen anyone sleep so hard. The cat got loose and jumped up on the bed and before I could catch her, she'd been up one side and down the other, but the woman never so much as moved."

"She's a sound sleeper, and I think she was pretty exhausted, besides. Thanks for keeping a watch on her."

Sawyer saw a movement out of the corner of his eye and turned. Honey was propped up on one elbow, her hair hanging forward around her face, her eyes squinted at the late afternoon sunshine. Most of the day it had continued to drizzle, and now that the sun was out, the day was so humid you could barely draw a deep breath.

Honey looked vaguely confused, so he went in to her. Casey followed with the cat trailing behind.

"Hello, sleepyhead."

She looked around as if reorienting herself. The small cat made an agile leap onto the bed, then settled herself in a semicircle at the end of Honey's feet, tucking her bandaged tail in tight to sleep. Honey stared at the cat as if she'd never seen one before. "What time is it?"

"Five o'clock. You missed lunch, but dinner will be ready soon."

Casey stepped forward to retrieve the new pet, but Honey shook her head. "She's okay there. I don't mind sharing the bed."

Casey smiled at her. They all loved and accepted animals, thanks to Jordan, and it pleased his son that their guest appeared to be of a similar mind. "You want something to drink?"

She thought about that for a moment, then finally nodded. ''Yes, please.''

Sawyer was amused by her sluggish responses and said, ''Make it orange juice, Case.''

''Sure thing.''

Once Casey was gone, Sawyer studied her. She yawned hugely behind her hand, then apologized.

''I can't believe I slept so long.''

He resisted the urge to say, *I told you so,* and stuck to the facts instead. ''You've got bronchitis, which can take a lot out of you, not to mention you're just getting over a concussion. Sleep is the best thing for you.''

She sat back and tucked the covers around her waist. After a second, she said, ''I'm sorry about arguing with you earlier. I know you mean well.''

''But you don't trust me?''

She shrugged. ''Trust is a hard thing. I'm not generally the best judge of character.''

This sounded interesting, so he pulled up a chair and made himself comfortable. ''How so?''

She gave him a wary look, but was saved from answering when Casey came back in. He handed her the glass of iced orange juice and a napkin.

''Thank you.''

''No problem.'' He turned to Sawyer. ''I'm going to go down and do some more work on the fence.''

''Only for about an hour. Dinner will be ready by then.''

''All right.''

As Casey started out, Honey quickly set her glass aside and lifted a hand. ''Casey!''

He turned, his look questioning.

''I noticed your shoulders are getting a little red. Have you been out in the sun much lately?''

''Uh...'' He glanced at his father, then back to Honey. ''Yeah, I mean, I've been outside, but there's hasn't really been much sun till just a bit ago.''

''I know it's none of my business, but you should really

put on a shirt or something. Or at least some sunscreen. You don't want to burn.''

Sawyer frowned at her, then looked at Casey. Sure enough, there was too much color on his son's wide shoulders and back. Casey looked, too, then grimaced. ''I guess it was so cloudy today, I didn't think about it.''

She looked prim as she lectured. ''You can burn even through the clouds. I guess because I'm so fair, I'm especially conscious of the sun. But I'd hate to see you damage your skin.''

Casey stared at her, looking totally dumbfounded. Too much sunshine was probably the last thing the average fifteen-year-old would have on his mind. ''I'll, uh...I'll put some sunscreen on. Thanks.''

Sawyer added, ''And a shirt, Case.''

''Yeah, okay.'' He hurried out before he drew any more attention.

Sawyer looked at Honey. She was smiling, and she looked so sweet, she took his breath away. He didn't like her interference with his son, but since she was right this time, he couldn't very well lecture her on it.

''You have a wonderful son.''

He certainly thought so. ''Thank you.''

''He doesn't really look like you. Does he take after his mother?''

''No.''

She looked startled by his abrupt answer, and Sawyer wished he could reach his own ass to kick it. He didn't want her starting in on questions he didn't want to answer, but his attitude, if he didn't temper it, would prompt her to do just that.

''I got your clothes washed. If you're feeling up to a bath, we can get that taken care of before dinner, then you can change.'' Not that he wanted her trussed up in lots of clothes when she looked so enticing wearing what she had on. But he knew it'd be safer for his peace of mind if she at least had panties on.

Except that he'd already seen the tiny scrap of peach silk she considered underwear, and knowing she wore that might be worse than knowing she was bare, sort of like very sweet icing on a luscious cake.

Luckily he'd done the laundry while no one else was around. He didn't want his brothers envisioning her in the feminine, sexy underwear. But he knew they would have if they'd seen it. He could barely get the thought out of his mind.

"I'm definitely up for a bath. I feel downright grungy."

She looked far from grungy, but he kept that opinion to himself. "We'll use the hall bath. Morgan's room opens into it, but he isn't home yet. I think he's on a date. And Gabe only uses the shower in the basement."

Her eyes widened. "Good grief. How many bathrooms do you have?"

She looked confused again, and he grinned. "As many as I have brothers, I guess. Little by little we added on as everyone grew up and needed more room."

"It's amazing you all still live together."

He lifted one shoulder in a lazy shrug. "My father left us the house, and my mom moved to Florida after Gabe graduated. Morgan stays here in the main house with me and Case, but he's building his own place on the south end of the property. It should be done by the end of the summer."

"How much property do you have?"

"Around fifty acres. Most of it's unused and heavily treed, just there for privacy, or if any other family decides to build on it. Morgan'll have his own acreage, but still be close enough, which is the way we all like it. Jordan's settled into the garage. He converted it to an apartment when he was around twenty because he's something of a loner, more so than the rest of us, but with his college bills, he couldn't really afford to move completely out on his own. Now he could, of course, since there's even more call for a vet in these parts than there is for a doctor, but he's already settled. And Gabe has the basement, which runs the entire length of the house. He's got it fixed up down there real nice, with his own kitchen and bath and living room, and his own entrance, though he usually just comes through the house unless he's sneaking a girl in.''

''He's not allowed to have women over?''

''Not for the night, but that's not really a rule or anything now, just something my mother started back when Gabe was younger and kept trying it.'' Sawyer grinned, remembering how often he and his brothers used to get in trouble. ''Gabe has always attracted women, and sometimes I think he doesn't quite know what to do with them. Dragging one home for my mother to get rid of seemed to be a favorite plan of his.''

Honey chuckled, and he could tell by her expression she didn't know he was serious. He grinned, too. She'd get to know Gabe better, then she'd realize the truth.

''Keeping women out is just something that we've all stuck to. Especially with Casey around. He's old enough now not to be influenced, but he was always a nosy kid, so you couldn't do much without him knowing. He has a healthy understanding of sex, but I didn't want him to be cavalier about it.''

She pulled her knees up and rested her crossed arms on them. Smiling, she said, ''I guess your wife wouldn't have liked it much, either, if a lot of women had been in and out of the house.''

Annoyance brought him to his feet, and he paced to the French doors. The topic shouldn't be a touchy one, and usually wasn't. But Honey didn't know all the circumstances, all the background. He said simply, ''My wife never lived in this house.''

She didn't reply to that, but he knew she now felt awkward when that hadn't been his intention. He glanced over his shoulder, saw her worried gaze and grimaced at his own idiocy. He'd opened a can of worms with that confession, and he didn't know why. He never discussed his ex-wife with anyone except his family, and then only rarely.

"I got divorced while I was still in medical school. In fact, just a month after Casey was born. She was still pretty young and foolish and she wasn't quite up to being a mother. So I took complete custody. My mother and Gabe's father really helped me out with him until I could get through medical school. Actually, everybody helped. Morgan was around nineteen, Jordan fifteen and Gabe twelve. In a lot of ways, Gabe and Casey are like brothers."

She looked fascinated, almost hungry for more information. He walked over to her and sat again. "What about you? You have much family?"

"No." She looked away, then made a face. "There's only my father and my sister. My mother passed away when I was young."

"I'm sorry." He couldn't imagine how he'd have gotten through life without his mother. She was the backbone of the family, the strongest person he knew and the most loving.

Honey shrugged. "It was a long time ago. I'm not very close with my father, but my sister and I are."

"How old's your sister?"

"Twenty-four."

"How old are you?"

She looked at him suspiciously, as if he'd asked for her Social Security number. After a long hesitation, she admitted, "I'm twenty-five."

He whistled. "Must have been rough for your father, two kids so close in age and your mother gone."

She waved that away. "He hired in a lot of help."

"What kind of help?"

"You know, nannies, cooks, tutors, pretty much everything. My father spent a lot of time at work."

"Didn't he do anything with you himself?"

She laughed, but there wasn't much humor in the sound. "Not a lot. Dad wasn't exactly thrilled to have daughters. I think that's what he hated most about Mother dying—she hadn't given him a son yet. He thought about remarrying a lot, but he was so busy with his business, and he worried that someone would divorce him and get part of it. He was a little paranoid that way."

Sawyer looked her over, searching her face, seeing the signs of strain. She'd put up a brave front, but he could see the hurt in her blue eyes and knew there was a lot about her life that hadn't always been satisfactory. "Sounds like a hell of a childhood you had."

Color washed over her cheeks, and she ducked her face. "I didn't mean to complain. We had a lot more than most kids ever do, so it wasn't bad."

Except it didn't sound like she'd had a lot of love or affection or even attention. Sawyer had always appreciated his family, their support, the closeness, but now he realized just how special those things were. They came without strings, without restriction or embarrassment, and were unconditional.

She was still looking bashful over the whole subject, so he decided to let it drop. At least for now. "I guess if you're going to take that bath, we should get on with it or you'll miss dinner. And Jordan really outdid himself tonight for you."

"Now Jordan's cooking?"

He shrugged. "We take turns. Nothing fancy. I told him to make it light since I wasn't sure what you'd feel up to. He's got chicken and noodles in the Crock-Pot, and fresh bread out of the bread machine."

She shook her head. "Amazing. Men who cook."

Laughing, Sawyer reached for her and helped her out of the bed. She clutched at the top blanket, dragging it off the mattress and disturbing the cat, who looked very put out over the whole thing. Honey apologized to the animal, who gave her a dismissive look and recurled herself to sleep.

"You'll have cat hair in the bed."

"I don't mind if you don't. It's your bed."

"You're sleeping in it."

They stared at each other for a taut, electric moment, then Honey looked away. Her hands shook as she busied herself by wrapping the blanket over and around her shoulders. It dragged the ground, even hiding her feet.

He supposed that was best; even though the jersey covered her from shoulders to knees, he didn't want his brothers ogling her—and they would. They were every bit as aware of an attractive woman as Sawyer, and Honey, in his opinion, was certainly more attractive than most. His brothers might not comment on the sexy picture she made with her hair disheveled, her feet bare and her slender body draped in an overlarge male shirt, but they'd notice.

She seemed steadier now, but he kept his right arm around her and held her elbow with his left hand, just in case. She was firmly in his embrace, and he liked it.

To get his mind off lusty thoughts and back on the subject at hand, he asked, "Don't you know any men who cook?"

She sent him an incredulous look. "My father's never even made his own coffee. I doubt he'd know how. And my fiancé took it for granted that cooking was a woman's job."

They'd almost reached the door, and Sawyer stopped dead in his tracks. His heart punched against his ribs; his thighs tightened. Without even realizing it, his hands gripped her hard as he turned her to face him. "You have a fiancé?"

Her eyes widened. The way he held her, practically on her tiptoes, pulled her off balance, and she braced her palms flat against his chest. He saw her pupils dilate as awareness of their positions sank in. "Sawyer…"

Her voice was a whisper, and he barely heard her over the roaring in his ears. He pulled her a little closer still, until her body was flush against his and her heartbeat mingled with his own. "Answer me, dammit. Are you engaged?"

She didn't look frightened by his barbaric manner, which was a good thing since he couldn't seem to get himself in hand. That word *fiancé* was bouncing off his brain with all the subtlety of a bass drum. If she was going to be married soon…

"Not…not anymore."

"What?" He was so rattled, he wasn't at all sure he understood.

"I'm not engaged, not anymore."

Something turbulent and dangerous inside him settled, but in its place was a sudden blast of violent heat, an awareness of how much her answer had mattered to him.

He looked down at her mouth, saw her parted lips tremble, and he went right over the edge. He leaned down until he could feel her warm breath on his mouth, fast and low, and the vibrancy of her expectation, her own awareness.

And then he kissed her.

CHAPTER FIVE

HONEY CLUTCHED at him, straining to make the contact more complete. Her blanket fell to the floor in a puddle around her feet. She barely noticed.

She didn't think about what was happening, and she didn't think about pulling away. Overwhelmed by pure sensation, by heat and need she'd never experienced before, she wanted only to get closer. She'd thought the attraction was one-sided, but now, feeling the faint trembling in Sawyer's hard body, she knew he was affected, too.

Sawyer's mouth was warm and firm, and he teased, barely touching her, giving her time to change her mind, to pull back. Until she groaned.

There was an aching stillness for half a heartbeat, then his mouth opened on hers, voraciously hungry, and his hands slid around to her back, holding her so tightly she could barely breathe. She felt the hot slide of his tongue and the more brazen press of his swollen sex against her belly. A delicious sensation of yearning unfurled inside her, making her thighs tingle and her toes curl. Her fever was back, hotter than ever.

A knock sounded on the door.

They both jumped apart, Sawyer with a short vicious curse, Honey with a strained gasp. She almost fell as her feet tangled in the forgotten blanket, and would have if Sawyer hadn't reached out and snagged her close again. He stared down into her face, his expression hard, his gaze like glittering ice, then called out, "What?"

The door opened and Jordan stuck his head in. He took

one look at them, made a sheepish face and started to pull it shut again.

Sawyer caught the doorknob, keeping the door open. "What is it?"

Honey fumbled for the blanket, wishing she could pull it completely over her head and hide. It was so obvious Jordan knew exactly what he'd interrupted. Yet she'd only known Sawyer a day and a half, less if you counted how much she'd slept.

It didn't matter to her body, and not really to her heart.

"Dinner'll be ready in about ten minutes." Jordan glanced at her, gave a small smile at her fumbling efforts to cover herself and again tried to sidle out.

"Can you make it twenty?" Sawyer asked, apparently not the least uncomfortable, or else hiding it very well. "She was just about to bathe."

Jordan slanted her an appraising look, and Honey wanted to kick Sawyer. She was off balance, both emotionally and physically. That kiss...wow. She'd never known anything like it. How the hell could he stand there and converse so easily when she could barely get the words to register in her fogged brain? And how could he manage to embarrass her like that?

Firmly, but with a distinct edge to her croaking voice, she said, "I don't want you to hold up dinner on my account." She made a shooing motion with her free hand, trying to be nonchalant. "Just go on and eat. Really."

Jordan caught her fluttering hand and grinned. "Nonsense. We can wait. Morgan is running a little late, anyway. He had some trouble in town."

She felt Sawyer shift and tighten his arm around her. "What kind of trouble?"

"Nothing serious. A cow got loose from the Morrises' property and wandered into the churchyard. Traffic was backed up for a mile."

Honey tilted her head, thrilled for a change of topic. "The cow was blocking traffic?"

"No. Everyone just stopped to gawk. Around here, a cow on the loose is big news." Then, with a totally straight face and a deadpan voice, Jordan added, "Luckily, the cow wasn't spooked too badly by all the attention."

Honey bit back her smile.

At that moment, the cat leaped off the bed to twine around Jordan's ankles. Without even looking down, he scooped up the small pet and cuddled her close, encouraging the melodic, rumbling purr. To Honey, he said, "Go on and take your bath. There's no rush."

They stepped into the hallway en masse, two powerful men, an ecstatic cat and a woman wrapped head to toes in a blanket. They nearly collided with Casey, who was liberally caked in mud. He'd removed his shoes so he wasn't tracking anything in, but mud was on his legs clear to his knees. The shirt he'd worn, thanks to her interference—she still didn't know what had come over her—was dirt and sweat stained. He looked more like a man than ever.

Holding up both hands, Casey said, "Don't come too close. The fields are drenched and muddy as hell...uh, heck. And half that mud is on me."

Jordan clapped him on the back. "Well, you'll have to use Gabe's shower, because the little lady wants a bath."

Casey stared at her.

Honey deduced that the phenomenon of having a female bathing in the all-male household warranted nearly as much attention as a cow on the loose.

Her face was getting redder by the second. If she didn't have a fever, she soon would. Never in her life had bathing been such an ordeal, or been noted and discussed by so many males.

The front door slammed, and not long after, Morgan rounded the hall, already stripping his shirt off with frustrated, jerky movements. Powerful, bulky muscles rippled across his broad shoulders and heavy chest as he stamped around the corner of the hall. He had his hands on the button to his tan uniform slacks when he realized he had an audience.

He didn't look the least discomforted at being caught undressing in the middle of the day, in the middle of the house, in front of a crowd.

"Sorry," he grumbled without an ounce of sincerity, and yanked his belt free. "I'm just heading for the shower. It must be ninety out there, and the damn humidity makes it feel like a sauna." He pointed an accusing finger at Jordan. "It was only the thought of a cool shower that kept me from kicking that damn ornery heifer, who no matter what I tried, refused to budge her big spotted butt."

Jordan laughed out loud, gleefully explaining, "Your shower will have to wait because—"

Honey, knowing good and well he intended to announce her bath once again, pulled loose from Sawyer and stomped on Jordan's toe. Since he had on shoes and she didn't, he looked more surprised than hurt. He stared down at his foot, but then so did the rest of the men. They all looked as if they expected to see a bug to account for her attack. When no bug was found, all those masculine gazes transferred to her face, and she lifted her chin. Just because they were men didn't mean they had to wallow in insensitivity.

Jordan blinked at her, one brow raised high, and she quickly stepped back to Sawyer's side.

Her bravado wilted under Jordan's questioning gaze. Oh, God, she'd assaulted him! In his own home and in front of his family. Sawyer chuckled and put his arm around her.

Morgan stared at her with bad-tempered amusement. "Wanting a long soak, huh? I suppose I can use Gabe's shower..."

Casey stepped forward. "After me. I claimed it first."

"I'm older, brat."

"Doesn't matter!" And then Casey took off, racing for the shower. With a curse, Morgan started after him.

Honey wanted to slink back to bed and hide. The bath, which had sounded so heavenly moments before, now just seemed like a form of public humiliation. She was tired and her throat hurt and her head was beginning to ache. She turned to Sawyer, stammering, "I can wait."

Sawyer stared at her mouth.

Jordan stepped up and steered them both down the hall as if they were nitwits who needed direction. "Nonsense. Go take your soak. You'll feel better afterward." He limped pathetically as he walked, and Honey had the sneaking suspicion he did it on purpose, just to rattle her, not because she'd actually hurt him.

They were a strange lot—but she liked them anyway.

WARM WATER covered her to her chin, and she sighed in bliss. Finally, she felt clean again.

Where Sawyer had found the bubble bath, she didn't know, but she seriously doubted any of his brothers would lay claim to it. She smiled, wondering what they all thought of her. From the little bit she'd seen of them, they had a lot of similarities, yet they were each so different, too.

Of course, that might make sense considering their mother was evidently remarried. Honey couldn't imagine marrying once, much less twice. After the way her fiancé had used her, she wanted nothing to do with matrimony.

"You all right in there?"

"I'm fine. Go away."

"Just checking."

She smiled again. Sawyer had been hovering outside her door for the entire five minutes she'd been in the tub. He was something of a mother hen, which probably accounted for his chosen profession. He was meant to be a doctor. Everything about him spoke of a natural tendency to nurture. She liked it; she liked him. Too much.

The ultra-hot kiss... Well, she just didn't know what to think of it. Her lips still tingled and she licked them, savoring the memory of his taste. She'd almost married Alden, yet *he'd* never kissed her like that. And she'd certainly never thought about him the way she thought about Sawyer.

She'd known Alden two years and yet had never really wanted him. Not the way she wanted Sawyer after less than two days.

What would have happened if Jordan hadn't interrupted? Anything, nothing? She simply wasn't familiar enough with men to know. Not that familiarity would have helped, because she knew, even in her feverish state and even without a wealth of experience, Sawyer was different from most men. He was unique, a wonderful mix of pure rugged masculinity and incredible sensitivity.

He'd run the bathwater for her, placed a mat on the floor and fresh towels at hand and stacked her cleaned jeans and T-shirt on the toilet seat. All without mentioning the kiss and without getting too close to her. After he'd gotten everything ready, he'd looked at her, shook his head, then left with the admonition she should take as long as she liked, but not so long she got dizzy or overtired herself.

She intended to linger just a few minutes more. In all likelihood, the brothers would hold dinner for her. From all indications they enjoyed the novelty of having a woman underfoot and wouldn't pass up this opportunity to make her the center of attention again, as if she alone was the sole entertainment. She wasn't used to it, but she supposed she'd manage. For now, they were probably still organizing their own bath schedule, but how long would that take? Alden had always taken very short showers, his bathing a business, not a pleasure, whereas she'd always loved lingering in the water, sometimes soaking for hours.

She drained the tub and stepped out onto the mat. The steamy bath had relieved her throat some, and her muscles felt less achy after the soak. The towel Sawyer had provided was large and soft, and she wrapped herself in it, wishing she could just go back to bed and sleep for hours but knowing she wouldn't. She wanted to learn more about the brothers, she wanted to see the rest of the house and she needed to decide what to do.

She saw the edge of her peach panties showing from under the shirt, and she blushed. Somehow, the fact that Sawyer was now familiar with her underwear made their entire situation even more intimate, which meant more dangerous if she was honest with herself. How long would it take someone to figure out she was here? In a town this small, surely news traveled fast. Any strangers in town would have no problem finding her.

If she were smart, she'd forget her attraction to Sawyer, which weakened her resolve, and hightail it away as soon as possible.

"You about done in there?"

There was a slightly wary command to Sawyer's tone now. She grinned and called out, "Be right there. I'm getting dressed."

Silence vibrated between them, and Honey could just imagine where his thoughts had gone. She bit her bottom lip. Sawyer was too virile for his own good.

She heard him clear his throat. "Do you need any help?"

She almost choked, but ended up coughing as she finished smoothing her T-shirt into place. She pulled the door open and said to his face, "Nope."

His gaze moved over her slowly, from the top of her head, where she had braided her long hair and then knotted it to keep it dry, to her T-shirt and down her jeans to her bare feet.

She bit her lip. "I don't know what happened to my sandals."

"Gone."

"Gone?"

He shook himself, then met her steady gaze. "Yeah. One fell off in the lake and sank. The other might still be in your car—I dunno. At the time, I wasn't overly worried about it, not with an unconscious woman in my arms."

"Ah."

"You're not wearing a bra."

"You can tell?" She quickly crossed her arms over her

chest and started to go back into the bathroom to look for herself in the mirror. Sawyer caught her.

He slowly pulled her arms away and held them to her sides. She didn't stop him. Everything she'd just told herself about staying detached faded into oblivion under his hot, probing gaze.

There they stood in the middle of the hallway, only a foot apart, and somehow fear, sickness and worry didn't exist. All she could think of was whether or not he'd kiss her again, and if he found her satisfactory. She'd always been pleased with her body, but then, she wasn't a man.

In a hoarse tone, he noted, "You have goose bumps." Gently, his big, rough hands chaffed up and down her bare arms.

"The...the house is cold."

He lifted one broad shoulder. "We keep the air-conditioning pretty low this time of year. Men are naturally warmer than women. Especially when the woman is so slight. I'll get one of my shirts for you to put on."

Excitement at the way he watched her made it impossible to speak. She nodded instead.

"You two going to stand there all day gawking? I'm starved."

Sawyer swiveled his head to look at Gabe. He still held Honey's arms. "How can you be starving when you didn't do anything all day?"

"I cooked rolls this morning, fixed your leak, then visited three women. That's a busy day in anyone's book." He grinned, then asked, "Should I just drag the table in here so we can all gather in the hallway? Is that what we're doing?"

Sawyer narrowed his gaze at his brother, but there was no menace in the look. "I have an appointment with Darlene tomorrow so she can get her flu shot. Maybe I'll mention your fondness for Mississippi mud pie. I hear Darlene's quite a cook."

Gabe took a step back, his grin replaced with a look of pure horror. "You fight dirty, Sawyer, you know that?"

Honey was amazed at the amount of grudging respect in Gabe's tone, as if fighting dirty impressed him. And then he stomped away. Sawyer laughed.

She wondered if she would ever understand this unique clan of men. She looked up at Sawyer. "What in the world was that all about?"

A half smile tilted his mouth. "Darlene has the hots for Gabe and she's looking to get married. She's been chasing him pretty hard for awhile. Gabe has this old-fashioned sense of gallantry toward women, so he can't quite bring himself to come right out and tell her to leave him alone. He remains cautiously polite, and she remains determined."

"So if you mentioned a pie..."

"She'd be here every day with one." He grinned again and gently started her on her way. He moved slowly to accommodate her. The bath had tired her more than she wanted to admit, even to herself. Being sick or weak wasn't an easy concept to accept. Not for Honey.

"Why doesn't Gabe like her?"

"He likes her fine. She's a very attractive woman, beautiful even. Gabe went through school with her. I sometimes think that's the problem for him. He knows all the women around here so well. Gabe doesn't want to get serious about anyone, so he tries to avoid the women who are too obvious."

"Darlene's obvious?"

Sawyer shrugged. "Where Gabe's concerned, they all are. Darlene was just the first name to come to mind."

"Then she won't really be here tomorrow?"

"Nope." He put his arm around her waist and offered his support. "Come on, let's get that shirt and get to dinner so the savages can eat. If I leave them hungry too long, they're liable to turn on each other."

SAWYER WATCHED HER nibble delicately on her meal. And he watched his brothers watch her, amused that they were all so distracted by her. She looked uncomfortable with all the notice, but she didn't stomp on any more toes.

He doubted she had the energy for that. Her face was pale, her eyes dark with fatigue. Yet she refused to admit it. She had a lot of backbone, he'd give her that. As soon as she finished eating, he planned to tuck her back up in bed where she belonged.

He sat across from her—a deliberate choice so he *could* watch her. Gabe sat beside him, Casey sat beside her, with Morgan and Jordan at the head and foot of the table.

She'd been all round eyes and female amazement as she'd looked at the house on the way to the kitchen. Her appreciation warmed him. Most women who got through the front door were bemused with the styling of the house, all exposed pine and high ceilings and masculine functionality. The house wasn't overly excessive, but it was certainly comfortable for a family of large men. It had been his father's dream home, and his mother had readily agreed to it. At least, that's how she liked to tell it.

Sawyer grinned, because in truth, he knew there were few things his mother ever did readily. She was a procrastinator and liked to think things over thoroughly. Unlike his guest, who'd barreled through his fence and landed in his lake and then proceeded to try to slug him.

Sawyer noticed Morgan staring at him, and he wiped the grin off his face.

He returned his gaze to Honey and saw her look around the large kitchen. They never used the dining room, not for daily meals. But the kitchen was immense, one of the largest rooms in the house, and the place where they all seemed to congregate most often. For that reason they had a long pine table that could comfortably seat eight, as well as a short bar with three stools that divided the eating area from the cooking area. Pots hung on hooks, accessible, and along the outside wall there was a row of pegs that held everything from hats and jackets to car and truck keys. The entire house had black checked curtains at the windows, but the ones in the kitchen were never closed. With the kitchen on the same side of the house as his bedroom, there was always a view of the lake. His mother had planned it that way because, she claimed, looking at the lake made the chore of doing dishes more agreeable. After they'd gotten older and all had to take their turn, they'd agreed. Then they'd gotten a dishwasher, but still there were times when one or more of them would be caught there, drinking a glass of milk or snacking and staring at the placid surface of the lake.

Honey shifted, peeking up through her lashes to find a lot of appreciative eyes gazing at her. She glanced back down with a blush. She was an enticing mix of bravado and shyness, making demands one minute, pink-cheeked the next.

He liked seeing his shirt on her, this one a soft, worn flannel in shades of blue that did sexy things for her eyes. And he liked the way her heavy hair half tumbled down her nape, escaping the loose knot and braid, with silky strands draping her shoulders.

She didn't look as chilled, and he wondered if her nipples were still pebbled, if they pressed against his shirt.

His hand shook and he dropped his fork, taking the attention away from Honey. To keep his brothers from embarrassing him with lurid comments on his state of preoccupation, he asked Honey, "How come your car was filled with stuff, but no clothes?"

She swallowed a tiny bite of chicken and shrugged. She'd drunk nearly a full glass of tea but only picked at her food. "I left in a hurry. And that stuff was already in my car."

Sawyer glanced around and saw the same level of confusion on his brothers' faces that he felt.

Morgan pushed his empty plate away and folded his arms on the edge of the table. "*Why* was the stuff already in your car?"

She coughed, drank some tea, rubbed her forehead. Finally she looked at Morgan dead on. "Because I hadn't unloaded it yet." She aligned her fork carefully beside her plate and asked in her low, rough voice, "Why did you decide to become a sheriff?"

He looked bemused for just a moment, the customary scowl gone from his face. "It suited me." His eyes narrowed and he asked, "What do you mean you hadn't unloaded it? Unloaded it from where?"

"I'd just left my fiancé that very week. All I'd unloaded out of the car were my clothes and the things I needed right away. Before I could get the rest of the boxes out, I had to leave again. So the stuff was still in there. What do you mean, being a sheriff suits you? In what way?"

Her question was momentarily ignored while a silence as loud as a thunderclap hovered over the table. No one moved. No one spoke. All the brothers were watching Sawyer.

He drew a low breath. "She's not engaged anymore."

Gabe looked surprised. "She's not?"

"No."

"Why not?" Morgan demanded. "What happened?"

Before Sawyer could form an answer, Honey turned very businesslike. "What do you mean, being a sheriff suits you?"

A small, ruthless smile touched Morgan's mouth as he caught on to her game. He leaned forward. "I get to call the shots since I'm the sheriff. People have to do what I say, and I like it. Why did you leave your fiancé?"

"I found out he didn't love me. And what makes you think people have to obey you? Do you mean you lord your position over them? You take advantage?"

"On occasion. Did *you* love your fiancé?"

"As it turns out...no. What occasions?"

Morgan didn't miss a beat. "Like the time I knew Fred Barker was knocking his wife around, but she wouldn't complain. I found him drunk in town and locked him up. Every time I catch him drinking, I run him through the whole gambit of sobriety tests. And I find a reason to heavily fine him when I can't stick him in jail. He found out drinking was too expensive, and sober, he doesn't abuse his wife.'' He tilted his head. ''If you didn't love the guy, why the hell were you engaged to him in the first place?''

''For reasons of my own. If you—''

''Uh-uh. Not good enough, honey. What reasons?''

''None of your business.''

His voice became silky and menacing. ''You're afraid to tell me?''

''No.'' She stared down her nose at him. Even with dark circles under her red-rimmed eyes and her hair more down than up, the look was effectively condescending. ''I just don't like being provoked. And you're doing it deliberately.''

Morgan burst out laughing—a very rare occurrence—and dropped back in his chair. The way Jordan and Gabe stared at him, amazed, only made him laugh harder.

Sawyer appreciated the quick way she turned the tables on his dominating brother. It didn't happen often, and almost never with women. Evidently, Morgan had been amused by her, too, because he could be the most ruthless bastard around when it suited him. Sawyer was glad he hadn't had to intervene. He wouldn't have let Morgan badger her, but he had been hoping Morgan could get some answers.

He found Honey could be very closemouthed when it suited her. It amazed him that she could look almost pathetically frail and weak one moment, then mean as a junkyard dog the next.

Gabe waved his fork. ''Morgan does everything deliberately. It's annoying, but it does make him a good sheriff. He doesn't react off the cuff, if you know what I mean.''

Jordan looked at Sawyer. ''Not to change the subject—''

Morgan snorted. ''As if you could.''

''—but do we have anything for dessert?''

''Yeah.'' Sawyer watched Honey as he answered, aware of her new tension. She wasn't crazy about discussing her personal life, but he had no idea how much of it had to do with her claimed threats or the possibility of a lingering affection for her ex. His jaw tightened, and he practically growled, "Frosted brownies."

Jordan sat back. "They're no good?"

"They're fine. And in case none of you noticed, there's a new pig in the barnyard."

Honey started, the tension leaving her as confusion took its place. "A pig?"

"Yeah." Casey finished off a glass of milk, then poured another. He was a bottomless pit, and growing more so each day. "Some of the families can't afford to pay cash, so they pay Dad in other ways. It keeps us Adam's apple high in desserts, which is good, but sometimes we end up with more farm animals than we can take care of. We have horses, and they're no problem, but the goats and pigs and stuff, they can be a nuisance."

Jordan looked at Sawyer. "The Mensons could use a pig. They had to sell off a lot of stock lately to build a new barn after theirs almost collapsed from age."

Sawyer continued to watch Honey, concerned that she was pushing herself too hard. At the moment, she didn't look ill so much as astonished. He grinned. Buckhorn was a step back in time, a close community that worked together, which he liked, but it would take some getting used to for anyone out of the area. "Feel free, Jordan. Hell, the last thing I want is another animal to take care of."

"They'll insist on paying something, but I'll make it real cheap."

"Trade for some of Mrs. Menson's homemade rock candy. Tell her I give it away to the kids when they come, and I'm nearly out."

"Good idea."

Honey looked around the table at all of them as Casey went to the counter to get the brownies. Her face was so expressive, even before she spoke, he knew she was worried. "You know everyone around here?"

With a short nod, Sawyer confirmed her suspicions. "We know them, and most people in the surrounding areas. Buckhorn only boasts seven hundred people, give or take a couple dozen or so."

Suddenly she blurted out, "Have you told anyone about me?" and Sawyer knew she was talking to everyone, not just him. What the hell was she so afraid of?

Casey dropped a brownie on the side of her plate, but she barely seemed to notice. Her hands were clenched together on the edge of the table while she waited for an answer.

"Dad told me not to say anything to anyone," Casey offered, when no one else spoke up. "So far, I'd say no one knows about you."

"Why do you care?" Sawyer waited, but he knew she wouldn't tell him a damn thing. "Is it because you think these people you claim want to hurt you might follow you here?"

Morgan, still lounging back in his chair, rubbed his chin. "I could run a check on you, you know."

She snorted over that. "If you can, then you already have. But you didn't find anything, did you?"

He shrugged, disgruntled by her response to what had amounted to a threat. She didn't threaten easily.

Jordan leaned forward. "You say someone is after you. Could it be this fiancé of yours?"

"Ex-fiancé," Sawyer clarified, then suffered through the resultant snorts and snickers from his demented brothers.

"I thought so at first. He...well, he wasn't happy that I broke things off. He was actually pretty nasty about it, if you want the truth."

"Truth would be nice."

She glared at Sawyer so ferociously, he almost smiled. But not quite.

"I think it wounded his pride or something," she explained. "But regardless of how he carried on, my father is certain it couldn't be him."

"Why?"

"If you'd ever met Alden, you'd know he doesn't have a physically aggressive bone in his body. He'd hardly indulge in a dangerous chase. He's ambitious, intelligent, one of my father's top men. And my father pointed out how concerned Alden is with appearances and that he'd hardly be the type to cause a scene or run the risk of making the news.'' She shrugged. ''That's what my father likes most about him.''

Sawyer curled his lip, more angered at her father's lack of support than anything else. ''Alden? He sounds like a preppy.''

''He *is* a preppy. Very into the corporate image and climbing the higher social ladder, though I didn't always know that. My father scoffed at the idea that Alden would chase me because regardless of his temper, I wouldn't be that important to him in his grand scheme of things.''

He watched her face and knew she was holding something back, but what? Sawyer pushed her, hoping to find answers. ''Even though you walked out on him?''

''I left, I didn't walk out.''

''What the hell's the difference?''

She sighed wearily. ''You make it sound like I staged a dramatic exit. It wasn't like that at all. I found out he didn't care about me, I packed up my stuff, wrote him a polite note and left.''

Her body was tense, her expression carefully neutral. Sawyer narrowed his gaze. ''Why did he ask you to marry him in the first place if he didn't care about you?''

She closed up on him, her face going blank, and Sawyer knew she still didn't trust him, didn't trust any of them. It made him so angry his hands curled into fists. He wasn't the violent type, but right now, he would relish one of Morgan's barroom brawls.

Sawyer surged to his feet to pace. He wanted to shake her; he wanted to pull her up against his body, feel her softness and kiss her silly again until she stopped resisting him, until she stopped fighting. He tightened his thighs, trying for an ounce of logic. ''How in hell are we supposed to figure this out if you won't even answer a few simple questions?''

Morgan leaned back and stacked his hands behind his head. Jordan propped his chin on a fist. Gabe lifted one brow.

''You're not supposed to figure anything out.'' Honey drew a deep breath, watching him steadily. ''You're just supposed to let me go.''

CHAPTER SIX

SAWYER'S DARK EYES glittered with menace, and his powerful body tensed.

Watching him with an arrested expression, Morgan murmured, "Fascinating."

Jordan, also watching, said, "Shh."

Honey turned to Gabe, ignoring the other brothers, and especially Sawyer's astounding reaction to her refusal of help. She couldn't look at him without hurting, without wishing things could be different. She'd known him almost no time at all, yet she felt as if she'd known him forever. He'd managed, without much effort, to forge a permanent place in her memory. After she was gone, she'd miss him horribly.

Gabe grinned at her. It seemed they all loved to be provoking, but she wasn't up to another round. All the questions on Alden had shaken her. She'd tried to answer without telling too much, juggling her replies so that Sawyer might be appeased but at the same time wouldn't learn too much. Alden had been so vicious about her refusal to come back to him, to continue on with the marriage, she didn't dare involve anyone else in her troubles, especially not Sawyer, until she better understood the full risk, and why it existed in the first place.

She'd been looking blankly at Gabe for some time now, and she cleared her throat. "Does your handyman expertise extend to cars?"

"Sure."

Jordan kicked him under the table. Honey knew it, but in

light of everything else they'd done, it didn't seem that strange or important.

While Gabe rubbed his shin and glared daggers at Jordan, Sawyer stalked over to her side of the table. With every pump of her heart, she was aware of him standing so close. She could feel his heat, breathe his scent, unique above and beyond the other brothers, who each pulsed with raw vitality. But her awareness, her female sensitivity, was attuned to Sawyer alone. Her skin flushed as if he'd stroked those large, rough hands down her body, when in fact he'd done no more than stand there, gazing down at her.

When she refused to meet his gaze, he propped both hands on his hips and loomed over her. "Gabe can fix your car, but you're not going anywhere until I'm satisfied that it's safe, which means you're going to have to quit stalling and explain some things."

Honey sighed again and tilted her head back to see him. Sawyer was so tall, even when standing she was barely even with his collarbone. Since she was sitting, he seemed as tall as a mountain. She really was tired of getting the third degree by overpowering men. "Sawyer, how can I explain what I don't understand myself?"

"Maybe if you'd just tell us what you do understand, we could come up with something that makes sense."

Leave it to a man to think he could understand what a woman couldn't. Her father had always been the same, so condescending, ready to discount her input on everything. And Alden. She shuddered at her own stupidity in ever agreeing to marry the pompous ass. Now that she'd met Sawyer and seen how caring a man could be…

With a groan she leaned forward, elbows on the table, and covered her face with her hands.

She was getting in too deep, making comparisons she shouldn't make. Morgan was right, he could start tracking her down. And since she didn't know what the threat was, only that it was serious, it was entirely possible he'd accidentally lead the threat to her—and to this family. She couldn't have that.

Car keys hung accessible on the wall by the back door. Sawyer wouldn't be sleeping in the same room with her tonight; there was no need. She'd have to take advantage of the opportunity. She'd borrow one of their vehicles, go into town and then get a bus ticket. She could leave a note telling Sawyer where to find his car.

Just the thought of leaving distressed her on so many levels, she knew she had to go as soon as possible, whether she felt up to it physically or not.

Sawyer evidently wanted her for a fling; he'd made his interest very obvious with that last kiss. He'd also indicated he found her to be a royal pain in the backside, and no wonder, considering she'd wrecked his fence and left a rusted car in his lake, along with taking his bed and keeping him up at night. When he wasn't watching her with sexual heat in his dark eyes, he was frowning at her with unadulterated frustration.

She felt the same incredible chemistry between them, but she also felt so much more. He had the family life she'd always wondered about, the closeness and camaraderie, the sharing and support that she'd always believed to be a mere fairy tale. So often she'd longed for the life-style he possessed. And he was that special kind of man who not only accepted that life-style, but also contributed to it, a driving force in making it work for everyone.

She found Sawyer very sexually appealing, but he also felt safe and comforting. Security was a natural part of him, something built into his genetic makeup. And after the way her engagement had ended, she would never settle for half measures again, not when there was so much more out there.

She heard the shifting of masculine feet, a few rumbling questions, then Sawyer leaned down, his hand gently cradling the back of her head. "Honey?"

With new resolution she pushed her chair back, forcing

Sawyer to move. ‘‘You’re not going to let up on this, are you?’’

Morgan snorted. Sawyer shook his head.

‘‘All right.’’ With an exaggerated sigh, she looked down, trying to feign weary defeat when inside she teemed with determination. ‘‘I’ll tell you anything I can. But it’s a long, complicated story. Couldn’t it wait until the morning?’’

She peeked up and caught Sawyer’s suspicious frown. With a forced cough that quickly turned real, she said, ‘‘My throat is already sore. And I’m so tired.’’

Just that easily, Sawyer was swayed. He took her arm and helped her away from the table. ‘‘The morning will be fine. You’ve overdone it today.’’

By morning, she’d be long gone. And once she got to the next town, she’d contact her sister and let her know she was all right, then she could go with her original plan. She’d hire a private detective and pay him to figure out what was going on while she stayed tucked away, and those she cared about would stay safely uninvolved. She’d never forget this incredible family of men...but they would quickly forget her.

‘‘Sawyer...’’ Morgan said in clear warning, obviously not pleased with the plan. Honey knew that particular brother couldn’t care less if she was sick. Even though she wasn’t really *that* sick, not anymore. But he didn’t know it.

‘‘It’s under control, Morgan.’’ Sawyer’s tone brooked no arguments.

Morgan did hesitate, but then he forged on. ‘‘I know Honey’s still getting over whatever ails her, but we really do need—’’

With a loud gasp, she froze, then stiffened as his words sank in. Slowly, she turned to face Morgan. ‘‘You know my name.’’

There was no look of guilt on his hard, handsome face, just an enigmatic frown.

Sawyer shook his head in irritation while glaring at Morgan. ‘‘Around here, everything female is called honey.’’

Casey nodded. ‘‘We’ve got an old mule out in the field that Jordan named Honey because that’s all she’d answer to.’’

She almost laughed at the sincerity on Casey’s face, but instead she pulled free of Sawyer’s hold and blazed an accusation. ‘‘He wasn’t using an endearment. He was using *my name.*’’

Morgan shrugged. ‘‘Honey Malone. Yeah, I went through your purse.’’

Her eyes widened. ‘‘You admit it? Just like that?’’ She nearly choked on resentment and coughed instead.

While Sawyer patted her on the back and Casey hurried to hand her a drink, Morgan said, ‘‘Why not?’’ He rolled his massive shoulders, not the least concerned with her ire. ‘‘You show up here under the most suspicious circumstances and you claim someone is trying to hurt you. Of course I wanted some facts. And how could I run that check on you if I didn’t have your name? I thought you’d already figured that out.’’

Her mouth opened twice, but nothing came out. She should have realized he’d already gone through her things, only she’d been so busy trying to hold her own against him, and she’d taken his words as an idle threat, not a fait accompli. She was making a lot of stupid mistakes, trusting them all when she shouldn’t.

Tonight. She had to leave tonight.

Then she remembered her bare feet and wanted to groan. She couldn’t very well get on a bus without shoes. Maybe she could swipe a pair from Casey. She glanced at his feet and saw they were as large as Sawyer’s. Good grief, she was in a house of giants.

Sawyer tipped up her chin. ‘‘He only looked in your wallet to find your name. He didn’t go through every pocket or anything. Your privacy wasn’t invaded any more than necessary. Your purse is in the closet in my room, if you want to check and make sure nothing is missing.’’

She ground her teeth together. ‘‘It isn’t that.’’ The last

thing she was worried about was them stealing from her. She had little enough with her that was worth anything.

"Then what is it?"

She thought quickly, but trying to rationalize her behavior while the touch of Sawyer's hand still lingered on her face was nearly impossible. Everything about him set her off, but especially his touch. No matter where his fingers lingered, she felt it everywhere. "I...I don't have any shoes."

He frowned down at her bare feet for a long moment. "Are your feet cold?"

She wanted to hit him, but instead she turned away. Her brain was far too muddled to keep this up. If she didn't get away from him, she'd end up begging him to let her stay. "I'm going to bed now. Jordan, thank you for dinner."

He answered in his low, mesmerizing voice, no less effective for the shortness of his reply. "My pleasure."

She glanced at him. "I'd offer to help with the dishes, but I have the feeling—"

"Your offer would definitely be turned down." Sawyer released her, but added, "I'll be in to check on you in a few minutes."

The last thing she needed was to be tempted by him again. "No, thank you."

He stared at her hard, his gaze unrelenting. "In a few minutes, Honey, so do whatever it is you feel you have to do before going to bed. I left the antibiotics and the ibuprofen on the bathroom counter so you wouldn't forget to take them. After you're settled, I want to listen to your chest again."

There was a lot of ribald macho humor over that remark. Jordan choked down a laugh, and this time Gabe kicked him.

With a glare that encompassed them all, Honey stalked off. She was truly weary and wondering where in the world she was going to find shoes for her feet so she could steal a car and make her getaway from a group of large, overprotective, domineering men whom she didn't really want to leave at all.

Gads, life had gotten complicated.

HE KNOCKED on the door, but she didn't answer. Sawyer assumed she was mad and ignoring him, not that he'd let her get away with it. He opened the door just a crack—and saw the bed was empty. *She was gone.* His first reaction was pure rage, tinged with panic, totally out of proportion, totally unexpected. He shoved the door wide and stalked inside, and then halted abruptly when he saw her. His gut tightened and his heart gave a small thump at the picture she presented.

Honey sat on the small patio outside his room. She had her feet curled up on a chair, her head resting to the side, and she was looking at the lake. Or maybe she wasn't looking at anything at all. He couldn't see her entire face, only a small part of her profile. She looked limp, totally wrung out, and it angered him again when he thought of her stubbornness, her refusal to let him help her.

No one had ever refused his help. He was the oldest, and his brothers relied on him for anything they might need, including advice. Casey got everything from him that he had to give. Members of the community sought him out when they needed help either with a medical problem or any number of others things. He was a figurehead in the town, on the town council and ready and willing to assist. He gave freely, whatever the need might be, considering it his right, part and parcel with who and what he was. But now, this one small woman wanted to shut him out. *Like hell.*

Her physical impact on his senses was staggering. But it was nothing compared to the damn emotional impact, because the emotions were the hardest to fight and to understand. If it was only sex he wanted, he'd drive over the county limits and take care of the need. But he wanted *her* specifically, and it was making him nuts.

Being summer, it was still light out at eight o'clock, but

the sun was starting to sink in the sky, slowly dipping behind a tree-topped hill across the lake. The last rays of sunshine sent fiery ribbons of color over the smooth surface of the water. A few ducks swam by, and far out a fish jumped.

Sawyer went back and closed the bedroom door silently, drawn to her though he knew he should just walk away. As he passed the bathroom, he noticed her toothbrush, still wet, on the side of the sink, along with a damp washcloth over the spigot, and his comb that he'd lent her. Those things looked strangely natural in his private domain, as if they belonged. She'd evidently prepared for bed, then was lured—as he often was—by the incredible serenity of the lake.

Though the house had a very comfortable covered deck across the entire front and along one side by the kitchen, he'd still insisted on adding the small patio off his bedroom. In the evening, he often sat outside and just watched the night, waiting for the stars or the clouds to appear, enjoying the way mist rose from the lake to leave lingering dew on everything. The peacefulness of it would sink into his bones, driving away any restlessness. Many times his son or one of his brothers would join him. They didn't talk, they just sat in peace together, enjoying the closeness.

He'd never shared a moment like this with a woman, not even his wife.

He approached Honey on silent feet. She looked melancholy and withdrawn, and for a long time he simply took in the sight of her. He'd seen her looking fatigued with illness and worry, and he'd seen her eyes snapping with anger or panic. He'd watched her cheeks warm with a blush, her brow pucker with worry over his son. He'd even seen her muster up her courage to embrace a verbal duel with Morgan. Sawyer had known her such a short time, but in that time, he had truly related to her. Whereas hours might be spent on a date, her health had dictated they bypass the cordial niceties of that convention, and their relationship had been intimate from the first. The effects were devastating.

He'd already spent more time in her company than most men would through weeks of dating.

Every facet of her personality enthralled him more than it should have. He wanted to see her totally relaxed, without a worry, finally trusting him to take care of her and make things right.

And most of all, he wanted to see her face taut with fierce pleasure as he made love to her, long and slow and deep.

He slid the French door open, and she looked at him.

There were two outdoor chairs on his private patio, and he pulled one close to her. He spoke softly in deference to the quiet of the night and the quiet in her blue eyes. "You look pensive."

"Hmm." She turned to stare back out at the lake, tilting her head at the sound of the crickets singing in the distance. "I was...uneasy. But this is so calming, like having your problems washed away. It's hard to maintain any energy out here, even for irritation."

"You shouldn't be irritated just because we want to help."

Her golden brown lashes lowered over her eyes. "Dinner with your family was...interesting. Around our house, there was only my sister and me. It was always quiet, and if we talked, it was in whispers because the house was so silent. Dinner wasn't a boisterous event."

"We can take a little getting used to."

She smiled. "No, I enjoyed myself. The contrast was wonderful, if that makes any sense."

That amused him, because meals at home were always a time to laugh and grouse and share. She'd probably find a lot of contrasts, and he hoped she enjoyed them all. But it also made him sad, thinking of how lonely her life must have been. "It makes perfect sense," he assured her.

"Good."

Because it had surprised him, he added, "You held your own with my brothers."

She laughed, closing her eyes lazily. "Yes. Morgan is a bully, but I have the feeling he's fair."

Sawyer considered her words and the way she'd spoken them. "Honorable might be a better word. Morgan can be very unfair when he's convinced it's for the best. He's a no-holds-barred kind of man when he's got a mission."

Her long blond hair trailed over her shoulder all the way to her thigh, catching the glow of the setting sun as surely as the lake did. She tilted her chin up to a faint warm breeze, and his blood rushed at the instinctively feminine gesture and the look of bliss on her face. "It was so cold inside," she whispered, "I wanted to feel the sunshine. I came out here to warm up, then couldn't seem to make myself go back in."

They did keep the air low, but not so much that she should be uncomfortable. He reached over and placed his palm on her forehead, then frowned. "You could be a little feverish again. Did you take the ibuprofen I left in the bathroom?"

"Yes, I did. And the antibiotic." She blinked her eyes open and sighed. "Did I thank you for taking such good care of me, Sawyer?"

A low thrumming started in his veins, making his body throb. He could feel his own heartbeat, the acceleration of his pulse—just because she'd said his name. "I don't know, but it isn't necessary."

"To me it is. Thank you."

He swallowed down a groan. He wanted to lift her onto his lap and hold her for hours, just touching her, breathing in her spicy scent, which kept drifting to him in subtle, teasing whiffs. Right now, she smelled of sunshine and warmth and the musky scent of woman, along with a fragrance all her own, one that seemed to be seeping into his bones. It drove him closer to the edge and made him want to bury himself in the unique scent.

But beyond that, he wanted to strip her naked and settle her into his bed. He wanted to look his fill, to feel her slender thighs wrap tight around his hips, her belly pressed to his abdomen, her body open and accepting as he pushed inside for a nice long slow ride, taking his time to get her out of his blood.

He wanted to comfort her and he wanted to claim her, conflicting emotions that left him angry at his own weakness.

He was aware of her watching him, and then she said, "Can I ask you a few questions?"

He laughed, and the sound was a bit rusty with his growing arousal. "I'd have to be a real bastard to say no, considered how my brothers and I have questioned you tonight."

She sent him an impish smile. "True enough." She curled her legs up a little higher then rested her cheek on her bent knees. "Why did Morgan really become a sheriff?"

That wasn't at all what he'd been expecting, and her interest in his brother brought on a surge of annoyance. "You think there's a secret reason?"

"I think there's a very personal reason." She shooed a mosquito away from her face, then resettled herself. "And I'm curious about him."

Sawyer felt himself tense, though he tried to hide it. "Curious, as in he's a man and you're a woman?"

She looked at his mouth. "No. Curious as in he's your brother, and therefore a part of you."

Satisfied, his twinge of unreasonable jealousy put to rest, Sawyer turned to look at the lake. "There's no denying our relationship, is there? Morgan and I share a lot of the same features, even though he is a bit of an overgrown hulk. Except I have my father's eyes, and he has my mother's."

"You look alike more so than the other two."

"We had a different father. Our father died when Morgan was just a baby."

"Oh." She shifted, unfolding her long legs and sitting upright. She reached over and touched his arm, just a gentle touch with the tips of her fingers, lightly stroking, but the effect on his body was startling. He felt that damn stroke in incredible places.

"I'm sorry," she whispered. "I had thought your mother just divorced."

He covered her hand with his own to still the tantalizing movement. "She was that, too."

"But..."

To keep the emotions she evoked at bay, he launched into a dispassionate explanation. "She married Jordan's father when I was five, and divorced him shortly after Jordan was born. I barely remember him, but he lost his job after the marriage and he started drinking. It became a problem. At first my mother tried to help him through it, but she would only tolerate so much in front of her children, and he couldn't seem to help himself, or so she's said. So she left him. Or rather, she divorced him and he took off and we never hear from him. My mother never requested child support, and he never stayed around long enough to offer it."

"Oh, God. Poor Jordan."

"Yeah. He wasn't much more than an infant when they divorced, so he didn't know his father at all. He's never mentioned him much. He was always a quiet kid. Morgan loved to beat up the boys who gave Jordan any grief. We both used to try to protect him. We sort of understood that he was different, quiet but really intense."

"He's not so quiet now." She made a face, wrinkling her nose, probably remembering the way Jordan had teased her about her bath. "He's not as demanding as Morgan, but I wouldn't exactly call him shy."

"No. He's not shy." Sawyer smiled, thinking of how she'd stomped on Jordan's foot. "None of my brothers are. But Jordan isn't as outgoing as the others, either."

"When did he change?" An impish light twinkled in her eyes. "After his first girlfriend?"

She was teasing, and Sawyer liked that side of her, too. "Actually, it happened when he was only ten. He found some kids tormenting a dog. He told them to leave the dog alone, and instead, one boy threw a rock at it. The dog, a really pitiful old hound, let out a yelp, and Jordan went nuts on the boys.'' Sawyer chuckled, remembering that awesome day. ''He was like a berserker—impressed the hell out of everyone who watched.''

Honey shook her head. ''Males are so impressed by the weirdest things.''

Sawyer glanced at her. ''This wasn't weird! It was life-altering stuff. Sort of a coming-of-age kinda thing. My mother had always taught us to be good to animals, and Jordan couldn't bear to see the old dog harassed. The boys were two years older than Jordan, and there were three of them. Morgan and I were on the sidelines, waiting to jump in if we needed to, but being so much older, we couldn't very well start brawling with twelve-year-olds.''

''Too bad they weren't older.''

He heard her impudent wit, but pretended she was serious. ''Yeah. Neither of us is fond of idiots who abuse animals. We wouldn't have minded a little retribution of our own. But Jordan held his ground and did a good job of making his point. He ended up with a black eye, a couple dozen bruises, and he needed stitches in his knee. My mother liked to have a fit when she saw him. And Morgan and I got lectured for hours for not stopping the fight. But no one messed with Jordan again after that. And anytime an animal was hurt or sick, someone would tell Jordan. I swear, that man can whisper an animal out of an illness.''

''So that started him on the road to being a vet. What made Morgan decide to be a sheriff?''

Sawyer turned her hand over and laced his fingers with hers. Her hands were small, slender, warm. Along the shore of the lake, a few ducks waddled by then glided effortlessly into the water, barely leaving a ripple. Peonies growing on the other side of the house lent a sweet fragrance to the air, mixing with her own enticing scent.

He was horny as hell, and she wanted to talk about his brothers.

"Morgan is a control freak," he managed to say around the restriction in his throat.

"I noticed."

Since she'd been a recipient of his controlling ways, he supposed she had. "He used to get into a lot of scrapes, sort of a natural-born brawler. Give him a reason to tussle and he'd jump on it. He got in trouble a few times at school, and my mother was ready to ground him permanently. Gabe's dad was a good influence on him."

Honey started. "Your mother was married three times?"

Sawyer didn't take offense at her surprise. No one had been more surprised by that third marriage than his mother herself. "Yeah." He smiled, dredging up fond memories. "I was eight years old when Brett Kasper started hanging around. My mother wanted nothing to do with him, and I'd ask her why, since he was so obviously trying to get in good with her and he was a nice guy and *we* all liked him—even Morgan. Brett would offer to clean out her gutters, play baseball with us, run to open doors for her. But he was always honest about why he did it. He'd tell us he was wooing our mother and ask for our help." Sawyer laughed. "We'd all talk about him to her until finally she'd threaten to withhold dessert if we mentioned his name again. I now understand how burned she felt, losing her first husband in the military, divorcing her second husband as a mistake."

"Because you went through a divorce, too?"

He wouldn't get into that with her. The divorce hadn't bothered him that much, unfortunately. It was all the deceit that had changed his life.

Sawyer shrugged. "My mother worked damn hard to keep everything going, raising four sons, working, keeping up the house. My father's pension helped, even paid for a lot of my college. And we all pitched in, but it wasn't easy for her."

"She must be incredible."

"Brett used to say she was as stubborn as an aged mule and twice as ornery."

"What a romantic."

Sawyer laughed. "He didn't cut her any slack, which is good because my mother is strong and she wouldn't want a man who couldn't go toe to toe with her. Brett wanted her and he went after her, even though she was gun-shy and didn't want to take another chance. Sometimes she was rude as hell to him. But Brett was pushy and he kept hanging around until he finally wore her down."

Honey gave him a dreamy smile. "A real happy ending."

"Yeah. They've been married twenty-eight years now. Brett's great. I love him. He's always treated us the same, as if he'd fathered the lot of us. Even Morgan, who can be so damn difficult."

"You said he helped Morgan?"

"He helped redirect Morgan's more physical tendencies by signing him up for boxing. And he set up a gym of sorts in the basement, which we all used until Gabe moved down there. Now there's just a weight room in what is supposed to be a den. My mother frets every time she sees it."

Honey laughed again, a low, husky sound that vibrated along his nerve endings and made him acutely aware of how closely they sat together, their isolation from the others, the heaviness of the humid summer air. He reacted to it all and kissed her knuckles before he could stop himself.

Just that brief touch made him want so much more.

Trying to regroup, he said, "Morgan chose to be a sheriff because he likes control, and for him, that's the ultimate control. But regardless of what he says, it isn't control over other people, it's control of himself. He knows he's more wild than not, that he'll always be more aggressive than most people. Choosing to run for sheriff was his way of forcing himself to be in control at all times."

She gave a very unladylike snort. "I think he's a big fraud."

Her misperceptions prompted Sawyer to grin. He could just tell she and Morgan would butt heads again and again if they spent much time around each other.

Of course, that was iffy, with her planning to leave and him planning to eventually let her.

"The hell of it is, Morgan never starts fights, he just finishes them. With that scowl of his, he can bring on a lot of attitude that men, especially bullies, generally object to. And to be fair, he always gives the other guy a chance to back off, but there's that gleam in his eyes that taunts. Morgan's always had an excess of energy and he gets edgy real quick. So to burn up energy, he either fights or he..." Appalled at what he'd almost said, Sawyer stemmed his ridiculous outpouring of personal confidences, wondering if he'd already stepped over the line. He was so comfortable with her, a fact he'd only realized, and she was so damn easy to talk to, he'd completely forgotten himself.

She tilted her head, her eyes alight with curiosity. "Or what?"

"Never mind."

"Oh, no, you don't!" She shook her head even as she fought off a yawn. "No way. You can't just tease me like that and then not tell me."

She looked sleepy and warm and piqued, all at once. Again he felt that unfamiliar rush of lust and tenderness and knew he was reacting to her when he shouldn't. But he just couldn't help himself. She drew him in without even trying.

Caught by her gaze, he admitted in a hoarse tone, "Morgan either fights...or he makes love. Either way, he burns off energy."

Her cheeks immediately colored and her eyes widened. "Oh. Yeah, I guess...I guess that could work."

Having caught her uncertainty, Sawyer leaned forward to see her averted face. "You don't sound certain."

She cleared her throat. "Well, it's not like...that is..." She peeked at him, her brow furrowed in thought. "Is it?"

Sawyer stared at her, blank-brained for just a moment, then he surged to his feet. Damn, if she was asking him if sex was really all that vigorous, he didn't think he could suffice with a mere verbal answer. Surely a woman as sexy, as attractive as she would already know! Damn her, she plagued his brain with her contradictions, her looks earthy and sensual, her behavior so modest. Bold one minute, timid the next.

He stared down at the lake for long moments, trying to get himself together and fight off the surge of lust that swamped him. He heard her stand behind him.

"Sawyer?"

"What?" He didn't mean to sound so brusque, but it felt as if she were killing him and his resolve by small degrees. Torturous, but also extremely erotic.

"Can I ask you something?"

Her tone was hesitant and shy, and he prayed her question wouldn't be about sex. He was only human, and she was too much temptation.

He looked at her over his shoulder and tried to dampen his frustration. "What is it with all these questions? I thought your throat was sore."

"It is. But your family is so different, so special. It's the way I always thought families should be. I've enjoyed hearing about them. And I have had a few things vexing my mind."

A grin took him by surprise; she sounded so worried. "Vexing you, huh?"

"Yes."

"All right." Turning, he gave her his full attention. The setting sun did amazing things to her fair hair and her blue eyes while making her skin appear even smoother. It was still hot and humid outside, even though it was evening, and she'd removed his shirt. He could visually trace the outline of her breasts beneath the T-shirt, the full shape of them, the roundness, even the delicate jut of her nipples. His abdomen pulled tight in an effort to fight off the inevitable reaction in his body, but he still felt himself harden. He could see the narrowness of her midriff, the dip of her waist. She hadn't tucked the T-shirt in, and still the flare of her hips was obvious and suggestive.

She shaded her eyes with a small hand and blurted, ''Why did you kiss me?''

Taken completely off guard, he blinked at her. After a moment, he said, ''Come again?''

''Earlier.'' She bit the side of her mouth and shifted nervously. ''When you kissed me. Why'd you do it?''

She had to ask? He was thirty-six years old, had been kissing females since he was twelve, and yet none of them had ever asked him such a thing. Trying to figure out what she was thinking, he countered her question with one of his own. ''Why do you think I did it?''

She looked so young when she turned bashful. He wondered at the man who'd given her up, who hadn't really loved her, as she'd put it. Sawyer had already decided he was a damn fool. Now, seeing her like this, he was glad. She deserved better than a fool, better than a man who'd be stupid enough to let her go.

He stepped closer, so tempted to kiss her again, to show her instead of tell her about her appeal. But he knew it wasn't right, that he was taking advantage of her situation and confusion. She stared down at her bare feet. ''My sister always told me I was pretty.''

He wanted to see her eyes, but no matter how he willed it, she wouldn't look up. ''You're very pretty. But I hardly kiss every pretty woman I see.'' And in truth, he'd known women much more beautiful. They simply hadn't interested him; they didn't draw him as she did. ''Besides,'' he added, trying for some humor, ''your face is bruised, and your lips are chapped, and there's dark circles under your eyes.''

''Oh.'' She touched her cheeks, then let her hands drop away with a frown.

He waited while she thought about that. ''Alden used to tell me I was shaped...okay.''

''Okay?''

She gave a grave nod. ''Men can be...enticed, by physical stuff, I know.''

She was attempting to sound blasé, and he barely held

back his laugh. Alden must have been a complete and total putz. She was much better off without him. "Honey, you're sexy as hell, and sure, to some men that's all that matters, but again—" He gave a philosophical shrug.

"You don't kiss every sexy woman you see?"

"Exactly."

She licked her lips, and her expression was earnest, if reserved. "So then why did you?"

Very softly, he admitted, "I shouldn't have."

"That doesn't answer my question."

Her cheek was sun-warmed beneath his palm as he tilted up her face, determined to see her eyes, to read her. Besides, he couldn't seem to *not* touch her. "What's your real question, sweetheart?"

Her eyes darkened, and the pulse in her throat raced, but she didn't look away this time. She fidgeted, shifting from one foot to the next. "Did...did you think since I was available, but determined not to be here too long, you could just...you know. Have a quick fling?"

He couldn't remember the last time he'd smiled so much. But she amused and delighted him with her every word—when she wasn't provoking him and pricking his temper. She was both the most open, honest woman he'd ever met, sharing her feelings and emotions without reserve or caution, and the most stubbornly elusive, refusing to tell him any necessary truths. "Anyone who knows me could tell you I'm hardly the type for a quick indiscreet fling, or any kind of fling. But certainly not with someone who didn't want the same."

She looked startled. "You think I don't want—"

Interrupting that thought seemed his safest bet. "I don't think you know what you want right now. But it surely isn't to be used."

Her eyes narrowed in suspicion. "Meaning?"

"Meaning I'm human, and I get restless like any other man. But I have a reputation here, and a lot of people look up to me. I have to be very circumspect."

She stared at him, her expression almost awed that such sanctimonious words had escaped his mouth. He felt like an idiot. "Honey, I'm sorry, but I just can't—"

She took an appalled step back. "I wasn't asking you to!"

His mouth quirked again, but he ruthlessly controlled it. "When I get too restless, there are women I know *outside* of town who feel just as turned off by commitment as I do. They're content with physical release and no strings."

Her mouth formed an O.

Feeling aggrieved, he explained, "They're *nice* women, who are content with their lives, but they get lonely. The world being what it is, it's not easy to find someone respectable who isn't looking for marriage. We suit, and it's simple and convenient and—"

Her face was bright red. He couldn't believe he'd gotten into this.

"I see. So you…indulge yourself with these women you don't really care about. But I don't fall in that category?"

His teeth clicked together. He wanted to shake her. He wanted to haul her up close and nestle his painful erection against her soft belly. He shook his head, as much for himself as for her. "You most definitely don't fall into that category. You're young and confused and scared. You're not from around here and you don't know me well enough to know I have no desire to remarry. And that's why I said I shouldn't have kissed you." He shoved his hands into his pockets and took a determined step away. "It won't happen again, so you don't have to worry about it."

She drew a long, considering breath. "I wasn't worried. Not really. I just wasn't sure…" She bit her lip and then blurted, "Most of the time you don't seem to like me very much. You feel responsible for some dumb reason, and you're kind enough, but…I just wasn't sure what to think about the kiss."

She obviously had no experience with aroused men, to mistake his personal struggles for dislike. And no sooner did he have that thought than he tried to squelch it. It was dangerous territory and would lead him into more erotic thoughts of what he'd like to show her, and just how much he liked her. Instead of explaining, he said, "I'd like you a whole lot more if you'd stop keeping secrets."

She got her back up real quick, turning all prickly on him. "We agreed we'd talk in the morning."

"So we did." He was more than ready to let it drop before he dug himself in too deep. "Why don't you head on in." If she stood there looking at him even a minute more, he was liable to forget his resolve and gather her close and kiss her senseless—despite all the damn assurances he'd just given her. These uncontrollable tendencies had never bothered him before; now he felt on the ragged edge, like a marauder about to break under the restraint. The things he wanted to do to her didn't bear close scrutiny. "You look ready to drop," he quickly added, hoping she wouldn't argue.

Sighing, she turned to go in. "I feel ready to drop."

Sawyer followed her through the door. The cold air-conditioning was a welcome relief as it washed against his heated skin. It may be evening, but summer in Kentucky meant thick humidity and temperatures in the nineties, sometimes even through the night.

Honey came to an abrupt halt beside the bed and stared at the fresh linens. "Someone changed the bed."

"I did. I figured you'd want clean sheets."

She gave him a querulous frown for reasons he couldn't begin to fathom, then sat on the edge of the mattress and reached for the cat. Until she did so, Sawyer hadn't realized the cat was back. Her calico coloring made her blend perfectly with the patchwork quilt.

Honey lifted the cat onto her lap and stroked her, being especially careful with her bandaged tail. "So I know you won't kiss me again, but I still don't know why you did in the first place."

Watching her pet the cat mesmerized him—until she

spoke, breaking the spell with her unsettling question. He didn't want to answer her because he knew it would somehow complicate things further. But she had that stubborn, set look again, and he figured she wouldn't go to bed until he satisfied her curiosity. He crossed his arms over his chest and studied her while searching for the right words. "I kissed you because I couldn't seem to stop myself."

"But why?"

He growled, "Because you're quick-witted and sweet and you have more courage than's good for you. And you're stubborn and you make me nuts with your secrets." Almost reluctantly, he admitted, "And you smell damn good."

She stared up at him, bemused. "You kissed me because I annoy you with my stubbornness and...and my *courage?*"

He gave a sharp nod. "And as I said, you're smart and you smell good. Incredibly good."

"But I thought—"

"I know what you thought." She'd complained about smelling like the lake when to him, she'd smelled like herself, a woman he wanted.

He started to ask her why she'd kissed him back, because she had. She'd nearly singed his eyebrows with the way she'd clung to him, how her mouth had moved under his, the way she'd greedily accepted his tongue, curling her own around it.

He shuddered, then headed for the door, escape his only option. Somehow he knew he'd be better off not knowing what had motivated her. "I won't sleep in here tonight, but if you need anything just let me know. I'm using the front bedroom."

She rushed to her feet. "I hadn't thought...I didn't mean to chase you out of your own room!"

There was so much guilt in her face, he slowed for just a heartbeat. "You didn't chase me out. I just figured since you were already settled..."

"I'll switch rooms." She took an anxious step toward

him. ‘‘You shouldn’t have to be inconvenienced on my account.’’

He hesitated a moment more, caught between wanting to reassure her and knowing he had to put distance between them. ‘‘It’s not a problem. Good night.’’

She started to say something else, but he pulled the door shut. Truth was, he liked knowing she was in his bed. He didn’t know if he’d ever be able to sleep there again without thinking of her—and dreaming.

CHAPTER SEVEN

THE HOUSE was eerily quiet as she slipped the bedroom door open, using only the moonlight filtering in through the French doors to guide her way. Though she hadn't lied about being exhausted, she hadn't slept. The clean sheets no longer smelled of Sawyer's crisp, masculine scent. She'd resented the loss.

She listened with her ear at the crack in the door, but there was nothing. Everyone was in bed, as she'd suspected, probably long asleep. She pictured Sawyer, on his back, his long body stretched out, hard, hot. Her heart gave an excited lurch.

He'd kissed her because she was smart.

And sweet and stubborn and... She'd wanted to cry when he'd given those casual compliments. She'd almost married a man who'd never even noticed those things about her, and if he had, he wouldn't have found them attractive. For him, her appeal had been based on more logical assets, what she could bring him in marriage, her suitability as a partner, the image she'd project as his wife.

Occasionally he'd told her she was lovely, and he'd had no problem using her body. But nothing he'd ever done, not even full intimacy, had been as hot, as exciting, as Sawyer's kiss. God, she'd been a fool to almost marry Alden.

Her father had once claimed she could have any husband she wanted based on her looks and his financial influence, neither of which she'd ever considered very important. Sawyer couldn't be interested in her father's influence, because he didn't know about it and didn't need it, in any case. And from what he'd said, he didn't find her all that attractive. She smiled and touched her cheek. She was a wreck, and she didn't even care. He'd kissed her, and he'd told her she smelled good, and he liked her wit and stubbornness and courage. Such simple compliments that meant so much. Without even realizing it, he'd given her a new perspective on life, a new confidence. She'd no longer doubt her own worth or appeal, thanks to his grudging admission.

She knew she had to leave before she threw herself at him and begged him to pretend she was one of the women from outside of town. Every time she was around him, she wanted him more.

She'd left a note on the bed, made out to Sawyer and sealed in a bank deposit envelope she'd found on his dresser. It was a confession of sorts, explaining how she felt and part of the reasons she had to leave. It was embarrassing, but she felt she owed him that much, at least. She knew he wouldn't be happy with her furtive defection, but from what he'd said, he'd be even less happy if she lured him into an intimacy he was bound and determined to resist.

Her purse had been in the closet, as the brothers had claimed, and all her credit cards and I.D. were still inside. She was ready to go.

The door was barely open when the small cat leaped off the bed to follow her out. When Honey reached for the cat, meaning to close her back in the bedroom so she wouldn't make any noise, the cat bounded out of reach. Honey wasn't sure what to do, but it was certain she couldn't waste time hunting for the animal in the dark. She'd been through the house, but she wasn't familiar enough with the setup to launch a search; odds were she'd knock something over.

She was halfway down the hallway, moving slowly and silently though the blackness, when the cat meowed. Every hair on her body stood on end while she waited, frozen, for some sign she'd been discovered. Nothing. The brothers slept on.

Honey glared behind her, but could only see two glowing

green eyes in the darkness. Again she reached for the cat; again it avoided her. She felt the brush of soft fur as the cat moved past, then back again, always just out of reach. Honey cursed silently and prayed the cat would be quiet, and that she wouldn't trip on it and knock anything over.

The house was so large, it took her some time to make her way to the kitchen, especially with the cat winding around her ankles every few steps. She'd always liked cats, but now she was thinking of becoming a dog woman.

A tiny, dim light on the stove gave scant illumination across the tiled kitchen floor. She could barely see, but she knew the keys were hanging on a peg on the outside wall, close to the door, so she used the stove light as a compass of sorts, helping her to orient herself to the dark room. Shuffling her feet to avoid tripping on unseen objects, including felines, she made her way over to the door, trying to avoid the heavier shadows of what she assumed to be the table and counter. Once her searching hand located the keys, she had another dilemma. There were too many of them!

Her heart pounded so hard it was almost deafening. Her palms were sweaty, her stomach in a tense knot. The damn cat kept twining around her bare feet, meowing, making her jumpy. She had no idea where the pet food was kept and had no intention of trying to find out.

Finally, knowing she had to do something or she'd definitely faint, she ignored the cat and decided to take all the keys. When she found one that operated the closest vehicle, she'd drop the rest in the grass, leaving them behind.

She tucked her purse under her arm and wiped her sweaty palms on her jeans. Carefully, shuddering at every clink and rattle, she lifted the various key rings. There were five sets. She swallowed hard and, clutching the keys in one hand, her purse in the other, she reached for the kitchen door. The cat looked up and past her, meowed, then sprinted away. Honey turned to see where the cat was headed and barely caught sight of a large, looming figure before a growling voice took her completely off guard.

"You were actually going to steal my car!"

She jerked so hard, it felt like someone had snapped her spine. At first, no sound escaped her open mouth as she struggled to suck in air, then her heartbeat resumed in a furious trot, and she shrieked involuntarily. Shrill. Loud. The cat took exception to her noise, and with a hiss, darted out of the room. Honey seriously thought her heart might punch right through her chest, it was racing so frantically. It didn't matter that the voice was familiar; she'd been sure she was all alone, being incredibly sneaky, and then he was there. The sets of keys fell from her limp hand in a clatter on the tile floor. Her purse dropped, scattering the contents everywhere.

Sawyer was there in an instant, his hands clasping her shoulders and jerking her around to face him, hauling her up close on her tiptoes again. Her body flattened against his, and she could feel his hot angry breath on her face, feel the steel hardness of his muscles, tensed for battle.

"You were going to steal my goddamn car!"

"No..." The denial was only a whisper. She still couldn't quite catch her breath, not after emptying her lungs on that screech.

He took one step forward, and her back came up against the door while his body came up against her front. "If I hadn't been sitting there in the shadows, you'd be sneaking out right now." He shook her slightly. "Admit it."

She swallowed, trying to find her tongue. Instead, the damn tears started. He'd been there all along? She'd never stood a chance? She sniffed, fighting off the urge to weep while trying to decide what to say, how to defuse his rage.

She trembled all over, and she couldn't find the willpower to explain. She felt Sawyer practically heaving, he was so angry, and in the next instant he groaned harsh and low and his hands were on her face, his thumbs brushing away the tears, his mouth hungrily searching for hers. The relief was overwhelming.

She cried out and wrapped her arms around him. He'd

said it wouldn't happen again, that not only didn't he want her for a fling, he didn't want her for anything. She'd told herself that was for the best. She'd told herself she hadn't cared. But inside, she'd crumbled.

Now he wanted her, and she was so weak with fear and excitement, all she could do was hold on to him.

One of his hands slid frantically down her side, then up under her shirt. He bit her bottom lip gently and when she opened her mouth, his tongue thrust inside, just as his long, hot fingers closed over her breast.

She jerked her mouth away to moan at the acute pleasure of it—and the kitchen light flashed on.

Blinded, Honey shaded her eyes while Sawyer jerked her behind him and turned to face the intruder.

''Just what the hell is going on?'' There was two seconds of silence, then, ''Ah. Never mind. Stupid question. But why the hell is she screaming about it?''

Morgan's voice. *Oh, my God, oh my God, oh, my God.* Honey peeked around Sawyer, then yelped. Good grief, the man was buck naked and toting a gun!

Sawyer shoved her back behind him again with a curse. ''Damn it, Morgan, put the gun away.''

''Since it's just you, I will. That is, I would if I had any place to put it.'' Honey could hear his amusement, and she moaned again.

Sawyer muttered a low complaint. ''You could have at least put some shorts on.''

''If I'd known you were only romping in the kitchen I would have! But how the hell was I supposed to know? She *screamed,* Sawyer. I mean, I know you're rusty and all, but damn. You must have completely lost your touch.''

Honey clutched at Sawyer's back, her hot face pressed to his bare shoulder. This couldn't be happening.

Sawyer crossed his arms over his chest. ''She screamed because I caught her trying to steal the car keys.'' He kicked a set toward Morgan. The sound of them skidding over the floor was almost obscene. Honey didn't bother to look to see if Morgan picked them up. The man was blatantly, magnificently naked, and didn't seem to care. She shuddered in embarrassment and burrowed closer against Sawyer, pressing her face into his hot back, trying to blot the vision from her mind.

Morgan gave a rude grunt. "I see. She was stealing one of our cars. And so you kissed her to stop her?"

"Don't be a smart ass."

Suddenly she heard Casey say, "What's going on? I heard someone scream."

Honey thought if there was any luck to be had for her, she would faint after all. She waited, praying for oblivion, and waited some more, but no, she remained upright, fully cognizant of the entire, appalling predicament she'd gotten herself into.

Sawyer's body shifted as he gave a heavy sigh. "It's all right, Casey. Honey was just trying to sneak off in the night. She was going to steal a car."

"I was not!" Honey couldn't bear the thought of Sawyer's son believing such a thing about her. She cautiously peeked around Sawyer and saw Jordan and Gabe amble into the room. *Just what she needed.* Morgan, bless his modest soul, had sat down behind the bar. All she could now see of him was his chest. But that was still more than enough, especially since the gun remained in his hand, idly resting on the bar counter.

Gabe held up a hand. "I already heard the explanations. Damn, but she has a shrill scream. I had to scrape myself off the ceiling, it startled me so bad."

Jordan held the cat in the crook of one arm, gently soothing it. "I even heard her all the way out in the garage. When I got here, the poor cat was nearly hysterical."

Ha! Honey eyed them all, especially that damn traitor feline, and tried to muster up a little of that courage Sawyer claimed she had. At least they weren't *all* naked, she told herself, then shuddered with relief. Casey had pulled on jeans, and Gabe had on boxers. Jordan had a sheet wrapped around himself, held tight at his hip with a fist.

She felt remarkably like that damn cow in town who'd drawn too much attention.

"I wasn't stealing the car." They all stared at her, and the accusing look on Casey's face made her want to die. She wiped away tears and cleared her throat. "I left a note on the bed, explaining. I just wanted to get to town and I thought it'd probably be too far to walk. I would have left the car there for you to pick up."

Jordan frowned. "What'd you want in town that one of us couldn't get for you?"

"No, you don't understand. I was going to take the bus."

Morgan shook his head in a pitying way. "We don't have bus service in Buckhorn," he explained with little patience. "You'd have gotten to town and found it all closed up. Around here, they roll the sidewalks up at eight."

Her heart sank. "No bus service?"

Gabe pulled open the refrigerator and pulled out the milk. He drank straight from the carton. "The only bus service is in the neighboring county, a good forty miles away."

Honey watched him with a frown. "You shouldn't do that. It's not healthy."

Sawyer turned to glare down at her, his face filled with incredulous disbelief. She shrugged, feeling very small next to him. In a squeak, she said, "Well, it isn't."

Gabe finished the carton. "I knew it was almost empty."

"Oh."

Sawyer flexed his jaw. "What about your car? Your stuff? You don't even have any shoes, remember?"

He was still so furious, she took a step back. And even though Casey had looked wounded by what she'd attempted to do, he came to her side. He didn't say anything, just offered his silent support by standing close. She sent him a grateful smile, which he didn't return.

She shifted. "After I got things taken care of, I'd have sent for my stuff."

"Taken care of how?"

She'd known Sawyer was large, but now he seemed even bigger, his anger exaggerating everything about him. There was no warmth in his dark eyes, no softness to his tone. She wasn't afraid of him, because she knew intuitively that he'd never hurt her. None of the brothers would hurt a woman; that type of contemptible behavior just wasn't in their genetic makeup. But she was terribly upset.

She opened her mouth, hoping to put him off until she wasn't quite so rattled, and he roared, *"No, God dammit, it will not wait until the morning!"*

She flinched. Silence filled the kitchen while she tried to decide how to react to his anger. Jordan stepped over to her, flanking her other side. "For God's sake, Sawyer, let her sit down. You're terrorizing her."

Sawyer's eyes narrowed and his jaw locked. With a vicious oath he turned away, then ran a hand through his dark hair. Just then Honey noticed Sawyer wore only boxers himself. Tight boxers. That hugged his muscled behind like a second skin.

Her lips parted. Her skin flushed. Blinking was an impossibility.

She stood there spellbound until Jordan set the cat down and started to lead her away. He held her arm with one hand and his sheet with the other and tried to take her to the table. Belatedly she realized his intent and held back because that would put her alongside Morgan, and she knew no one had thrown him any pants yet.

"I'm all right," she whispered, wishing Sawyer would look at her instead of staring out the window at the pitch black night.

Jordan released her with a worried frown. She went back to the door and began picking up the keys and the contents of her purse. No one said anything, and when she was done, she carefully replaced the keys where they belonged. With her back to all of them, she said, "I wanted to get to the next town. I have a credit card, and I could charge a room, then call my sister to let her know I'm okay.''

Jordan, Gabe and Morgan all asked, ''You have a sister?'' and, ''Does she look like you?'' and, ''How old is she?''

Honey rolled her eyes. She couldn't believe they could be interested in that right now. ''She's way prettier than me, but dark instead of fair, and she's a year younger. But the point is, she'll be worried. I told her I'd call her when I got settled somewhere. Then I'm going to hire a private detective to find out who's after me.''

Casey frowned at her. ''Why couldn't you do that from here?''

How could she tell him she was already starting to care too much about them all? Especially Sawyer? She tempered the truth and admitted, ''I want to make things as simple as possible. I don't want to involve anyone else in my private problems.''

Sawyer still hadn't turned or said a word, and it bothered her.

Gabe rooted through the cabinets for a cookie. ''Why not just go to the police?''

She really hated to bare her soul, but it looked as if her time had run out. She clutched her purse tightly and stared at Sawyer's back. ''My father is an influential man. Recently he decided to run for city council. He's been campaigning, and things have looked promising so far. When I broke off my engagement, he was really angry because he'd planned to use the wedding as a means to campaign, inviting a lot of important, connected people to the normal round of celebrations that go with an engagement. Our relationship was already strained, and we'd barely spoken all week. He...well, he hit the roof when I told him I thought someone was after me. He thinks I'm just overreacting, letting my imagination run away because I'm distraught over the broken engagement. When I said I was going to the police, he threatened to cut me off because he says I'm causing him too much bad publicity, and he's certain I'll only make a fool of myself and draw a lot of unnecessary negative speculation that will damage his campaign.''

Morgan started to stand, but when she squealed and covered her eyes, he sat back down again. ''Casey, go get me something to wear, will you?''

''Why me? I don't wanna miss what's going on.''

Morgan frowned at him. ''I'm not dressed, that's why. And she's acting all squeamish about it, so she'd probably rather I didn't get up and parade around right now. Course, if you don't care how she feels...''

Put that way, Casey had little choice. He looked thoroughly disgruntled, and agreed with a lot of reluctance. ''All right. But you owe me.'' He sauntered off, and the cat, apparently enjoying all the middle-of-the-night excitement, bounded after him.

Morgan folded his arms on the bar, looking like he'd made the most magnanimous gesture of all by offering to put on clothes. ''So since your daddy threatened to cut the purse strings, you ran off instead?''

Now, that did it! It was almost one o'clock in the morning; she was tired, frazzled, embarrassed and worried. The last thing she intended to put up with was sarcasm.

Honey slammed her purse down on the counter and stalked over to face Morgan from the other side of the bar. Hands flat on the bar top, she leaned over until she was practically nose to nose with him. ''Actually,'' she growled, forcing the words through her teeth, ''I told him to stick his damn money where the sun doesn't shine.''

Morgan pulled back, and astonishment flickered briefly in his cobalt eyes, mixed with a comical wariness. ''Uh, you said that, did you?''

''Yes, I did. My father and I have never gotten along, and money won't change that.''

Jordan applauded. ''Good for you!''

She whipped about and pointed a commanding finger at Jordan. ''You be quiet! All of you have done your best to bulldoze me, and I'm getting sick and tired of it. I don't take well to threats, and I couldn't care less about my father's money.''

Jordan chuckled, not at all put off by her vehemence. ''So what happened?''

Deflated by their eternal good humor, Honey sighed. Men in general were hard enough to understand, but these men were absolutely impossible. ''He threatened to cut off my sister, instead, and though she reacted about the same as I did, I can't be responsible for that. I had no choice except to leave.''

Sawyer spoke quietly from behind her. ''Except that you got sick, so you didn't make it very far. At least, not far enough to feel safe.''

She didn't turn to face him. Her gaze locked onto Gabe's, and he smiled in encouragement. As long as she didn't see the disappointment and resentment in Sawyer's eyes, she thought she'd be all right.

''Someone had been following me for two days. I wasn't imagining it. I know I wasn't.'' She spoke in the flatest monotone she could manage. She didn't want them to hear her fear, her worry. It left her feeling too exposed. ''The first day I managed to dodge them.''

''You say 'them.' Was there more than one person?''

She glanced at Morgan. ''It's just a figure of speech. I never saw inside the car. It was a black Mustang, and the windows were darkened. I noticed it the day after I ended things with Alden. When I left the bank where I worked, the car was in the parking lot, and it followed me. I'd promised my sister to stop at the grocery, so I did, and it was there when I came out. It spooked me, so I drove around a little and managed to lose it by jumping on the expressway into the heavy traffic, then taking an exit that I never take.''

Morgan rubbed his chin. ''Must not have been a professional if you lost 'em that easy.''

''I don't know if they're professional or not. I don't know anything about them.''

Gabe leaned against the countertop, ankles crossed, eating

cookies. "You know, I hate to say this, but you could have just been spooked. If that's all that happened—"

"That's not all! I'm not an idiot."

He held up both hands, one with a cookie in it, and mumbled, "I wasn't suggesting you are."

Totally ruffled, she glared at him a moment longer, then continued. "The car was there again the next day. And that's too much of a coincidence for me."

They each made various gestures of agreement, all but Sawyer, who merely continued to watch her through dark, narrowed eyes.

"This time it followed me right up until I pulled into my sister's house. The car slowed, waited, and I practically ran to get inside. Then it just drove away."

"I still think it's your ex," Jordan said. "If you left him, he probably wanted to know where you'd gone. I would have."

"Me, too," Gabe concurred.

"I thought it might be Alden at first. But it just doesn't fit." Honey watched Casey come back in with jeans and toss them to Morgan. Casual as you please, Morgan stood to put them on, and she quickly turned her back, but she could already feel the heat climbing up her neck to her cheeks. The man could improve with just an ounce of true modesty!

"So what changed your mind?"

Sawyer didn't look so angry now. Or rather, he didn't look so angry at *her*. He still seemed furious over the circumstances.

"I talked to Alden. He kicked up a fuss about me breaking things off, yelling about how humiliated he'd be since so many of his associates knew we were engaged. And he even threatened me some."

With cold fury, Sawyer whispered, "He threatened you?"

A chill went up her spine as she remembered again the lengths Alden had gone to just to punish her for breaking things off. And worst of all, she knew he wasn't motivated by love, but obviously by something much darker. "He used the same type of threats as my father. Alden told me he'd get me fired from my job, and he did. The bank claimed they were just scaling down employees, but Alden has a relative in a management position at the bank."

"You could sue," Jordan pointed out, and she saw he was now as angry as Sawyer. It was an unusual sight to see, since Jordan had always looked so serene. Now his green eyes were glittering with anger, his lean jaw locked.

"I...I might have," she admitted, dumbfounded by their support, "but that night when I was at my sister's house, someone broke in. She was out on a late date, so I was alone. I could hear them going through the drawers, the cabinets. I *know* it was the same people who'd been following me. They saw where I was staying and then they came back. They went through everything. I just don't know why, or what they were looking for. I'm ashamed to admit it, but I don't think I've ever been so afraid in my life. For the longest time I couldn't move. I just laid in the bed, frozen, listening. When I realized they'd eventually search the bedroom, I forced myself to get up. I didn't bother getting clothes, I just grabbed up my purse, slipped out the bedroom window and snuck to my car. I saw the curtain open in the front room as I started the engine, then I just concentrated on getting away. I was nearly hysterical by the time I got to my father's."

She lowered her face, embarrassed and shaken all over again. Masculine hands touched her, patting her back, stroking her head, and gruff words of comfort were murmured. She was caught between wanting to laugh and wanting to cry.

She pulled herself together and lifted her chin. After a deep breath, she continued, and the men all subsided back to their original lounging posts.

"My father took me seriously this time, at least for awhile. He sent some men over to check out the apartment, but they said nothing seemed to be out of place. The only thing open was the window I'd gone through, and there was no one there when they arrived. Again, my father thought I was just overreacting. He wanted to call Alden, thinking I'd feel better when we got back together."

Sawyer never said a word, but Morgan grunted. "Did you tell him the bastard had cost you your job?"

She shrugged. "My father said he was just acting out of wounded male pride."

"Hogwash." Gabe tossed the rest of the cookies aside to pace around the kitchen. Though he wore only his underwear, he made an awesome sight. "Men don't threaten women, period."

"That's what my sister said. My father had sent men to get her, also, before he decided there wasn't a problem, that I'd made it all up. Luckily she believed me. She promised not to go back to the house until after a security alarm was put in—a concession from my father, which my sister refused, saying she'd get her own."

Jordan grinned. "Your sister sounds a lot like you."

Why that amused him, she couldn't guess. "In some ways."

Gabe looked thoroughly disgusted. "Someone is following you around town, looting through your house with you in it, and the best your father could do was offer an alarm system?"

Honey held up her hands. She couldn't very well explain her father's detachment when the very idea would be alien to such protective men. Why, even now, they'd gathered in the kitchen, in the middle of the night, pulled from their beds, and no one was complaining. They just wanted to help.

Those damn tears welled in her eyes again.

Morgan flexed his knuckles, and the look on his face was terrifying. Even though she felt disturbed rehashing the whole story, Honey smiled. They were all so overprotective, so wonderful. She couldn't drag them into her mess. She had no idea how much danger she might actually be in.

"When I left my father's that afternoon, the car was there again, following me, and I *did* panic. I took off. But it followed, and even tried to run me off the road."

Jordan stared at her. "Good God."

"It kept coming alongside me, and when I wouldn't pull over, it...it hit the back of my car. The first time, I managed to keep control, but then it happened again, and the third time I went into a spin. The Mustang had to hit his brakes, too, to keep from barreling into me, and there was an oncoming car and the Mustang lost control. He went off the side of the road and crashed into a guardrail. The other car stopped to see if he was hurt, but I just kept going."

"And you've been going ever since?"

She nodded. "I left Alden a week ago. It seems like a year. I stopped once and traded in my car, which was a nice little cherry-red Chevy Malibu, not worth much with the recent damage in the back. I bought that old rusted Buick instead. But I've been so on edge. I stopped to get gas once, and saw the Mustang again. I have no doubt I'm being followed, I just don't know why. Alden didn't really care about me, so it seems insane he'd go to this much trouble to harass me. And harassing me certainly wouldn't make me reconsider marrying him."

Sawyer pulled out a kitchen chair then forced her to sit in it. He said to Jordan, "Why don't you put on some coffee or something? Casey, you should go on back to bed."

Casey, who'd been sitting at the table, his head in his hand, looking weary, said, "No way."

"Chores still have to be done tomorrow."

"I'll manage."

Honey, relieved to be off her feet, smiled at him. "Really, Casey. You should get some sleep. There's not anything else to hear tonight, anyway."

Sawyer crouched down beside her, his expression intent, his nearness overpowering. She couldn't be this close to him without wanting to touch him, to get closer still. And right now, he had all that warm, male skin exposed. She turned her face away, but he brought it back with a touch on her chin. "Now there's where you're wrong, sweetheart. You're going to tell me why you agreed to marry this bastard in the first place, and why he wanted to marry you. Then you're going to tell me what made you change your mind. And if we have to sit here all night to get the full truth, then that's what we'll do."

She knew she'd get no rest until he had his way, and she was limp from the nerve-racking experience of trying to steal away and getting caught in the act. She folded her hands primly in her lap and nodded. "Very well. But at least get dressed." She looked over her shoulder at the others. "*All* of you. If I'm to be forced through the inquisition, I demand at least that much respect."

Sawyer stared at her hard, and she couldn't tell if it was amusement, annoyance or sexual awareness that brought on that hardness to his features. His gaze skimmed over her, then lit on her face. "Fair enough. But Casey will stay here to keep an eye on you. Don't even think about running off again."

He walked away, and she admitted she'd been wrong on all accounts. It was distrust that had been so evident on his face. And she had to admit she'd deserved it.

CHAPTER EIGHT

WHEN SAWYER STALKED into his room to grab some pants, still angry and doubly frustrated, the first thing he saw was the rumpled bed where she'd lain. Heat drifted over him in waves, making his vision hazy. He wanted her so badly he shook with it, and he knew the wanting wouldn't go away. He hadn't even known that kind of lust existed, because it never had for him before. Unlike Morgan, and even Gabe, he'd always had a handle on his sexuality. He was, more often than not, cool and remote, and *always* in control.

And after the way his wife had played him, used him, after suffering such a huge disappointment, he'd made a pact never to get involved again. Yet he'd been involved with Honey from the second he'd seen her in the car. He'd lifted her out, and awareness had sizzled along his nerve endings. He wanted to rail against the truth of that, but knew it wouldn't do him any good. When he'd caught her stealing keys from the kitchen, his only thought was that she was leaving, not about the damn car, not about the danger she'd be in.

He hadn't wanted her to go.

He needed to get her out of his system so he could function normally again, instead of teetering between one extreme reaction and another. He didn't like it. He wanted his calm reserve back. But how?

And then he saw the note and remembered. She'd written a note to explain why she felt it necessary to sneak away from him. His fists clenched, and every muscle pulled taut as he struggled with his fierce temper—a temper he hadn't even known he had until he'd met Miss Honey Malone. Damn, but it filled him with rage. She didn't trust him at all, on any level. Curiosity and resentment exploded inside him, and he took two long strides to the mattress and snatched up the sealed envelope. His name was written across the front in a very feminine scrawl. He started to tear it open, but caught himself in time and carefully loosened the seal instead.

She'd written on a cash receipt, probably the only paper she could find on his dresser. All stationery was kept in his office. He drew a deep breath, ready to witness her lame excuses for trying to sneak out—and what he read instead made his knees buckle. He dropped heavily to the side of the bed as his heart raced.

Sawyer,
I know you won't be happy that I'm leaving this way, but it's for the best. I'm finding I want you too much to stay. Since you made it clear you'd rather not get involved, and I know it wouldn't be wise anyway, I have to leave. I can't trust myself around you.

His eyes widened as he read the words, amazed that she'd written them and even more so that she'd had the audacity to put a smily face there, as well, as if poking fun at herself and her lack of restraint around him. The little drawing looked teasing and playful and made him hard as a stone. She wanted him? And she thought he should be amused by that?

He swallowed hard and finished the note.

To be honest, you're just too tempting. Shameful of me to admit, but it's true. And I'm afraid I'm not sure how to deal with it, since I've never had to before. I hope you understand.

Please forgive me for taking your car. I'll leave it at

the bus station with the keys inside, so bring a spare set to open it. When I get things resolved, I swear I'll send you a check to pay for the damage to your fence, and your incredible hospitality. I won't ever forget you,

Honey

He wanted to go grab her and put her over his knee, not only because she would have risked herself in what he now realized was very real danger, but because she'd have been leaving for all the wrong reasons. And she'd offered him a check. He wanted to howl. He didn't want her money and he never had. How many times did he have to tell her that?

Morgan tapped on the door and stuck his head inside. "You found the note?"

Sawyer quickly folded it. Since he hadn't put pants on yet he had nowhere to put it. "Yeah. It, uh, it said she'd leave the car at the bus station with the keys locked inside, just like she told us."

Morgan crossed his arms and leaned against the door frame. He still wore only jeans, but he had at least put the gun away. "I don't suppose you'd let me see the note?"

"Why?"

"Idle curiosity?"

Sawyer grunted. "Yeah, right. More like plain old nosiness." Sawyer kept his back to his brother, more than a little aware of how obvious his erection was at this point.

His gaze met Morgan's in the mirror over the dresser, and he saw Morgan was struggling to contain his grin. "I gather you got something to hide there?"

Opening a drawer and pulling out a casual pair of khakis, Sawyer mumbled negligently, "Don't know why you'd think that."

"The way you're clutching that note? And acting so secretive and protective?" He laughed. "Don't worry. I won't say a word. Take your time getting dressed. I think I'll just go round up something to eat."

"Morgan?"

"Yeah?"

"Don't mention to her that I have the note."

"Whatever you say, Sawyer." Then he laughed again and walked away.

After carefully easing his zipper up and buttoning his slacks, Sawyer smoothed out the note, removing the wrinkles caused by his fist. He neatly folded it and slid it into his back pocket, making certain it was tucked completely out of sight. He'd talk to her about the note—hell, yes, he had a lot to say about it—but that could be taken care of after everything else was straightened out.

He didn't bother with a shirt or shoes, and when he entered the kitchen, he saw the rest of the men had felt the same. Gabe had on shorts; Morgan and Jordan wore jeans.

Honey was at the stove cooking.

His every instinct sharpened at the sight of her. She, too, was barefoot, her hair now pulled back in a long, sleek ponytail that swished right above her pert behind—a smooth, very soft behind he'd stroked with his palms. As he drank in the sight of her with new admiration, he felt like a predator, ready to close in. With that tell-all note, she'd sealed her own fate. He wanted her, and now that he knew she wanted him, too, he'd have her; he wasn't noble enough to do otherwise. After the other issues were resolved, he'd explain to her one more time how he felt about commitment, and then they'd deal with the personal issue of lust.

He glanced at his brothers who sat around the table like a platoon waiting to be fed, and he frowned. They shrugged back, each wearing a comical face of helplessness. Sawyer growled a curse and stepped up to Honey. "What the hell are you doing?"

Without raising her head, she barked back, "Cooking."

His brows lifted. He heard one of the brothers snicker. Crossing his arms over his naked chest, he said, "You wanna tell me why?"

She whirled, a hot spatula in her hand, which she pointed

at his chest, forcing him to take a hasty step back. "Because I'm hungry. And because they're hungry!" The spatula swung wildly to encompass the men, who quickly nodded in agreement to her fierce look. "And I'm tired of being coddled and treated like I'm helpless. You want me to stay, fine. I'll stay. But I'll be damned if I'm going to lay around and be waited on and feel like I owe the lot of you."

Sawyer leaned away from the blast of her anger, totally bowled over by this new temperament. Cautiously, he took another step back. "No one wants you to feel beholden."

"Well, I *do!*"

"Okay, okay." He tried to soothe her and got a dirty look for his efforts. "You want to cook, fine," he added with a calm he didn't feel.

"Ha! I wasn't asking your permission. And don't try that placating tone on me because Jordan already did. And he's much better at it than you are."

He glanced at his brother, only to see Jordan's ears turn red. She was intimidating his brothers! Sawyer crowded close again and opened his mouth, only to meet that spatula once more.

"And don't try bullying me, because Morgan has been at it since I met him, and I'm not putting up with it anymore. Do you know he told me I wasn't allowed to cook because I was sick? He tried to force me to sit down. Well, I'll sit down when I'm good and ready. Not before."

Sawyer had no idea what had set her off this time, but he almost grinned, anxious to find out. Now that he'd decided against denying himself, he wanted to absorb her every nuance instead of fighting against her allure.

"Am I allowed to ask what you're cooking, or will you threaten me with that spatula again?"

She tilted her head, saw he wasn't going to argue with her and nodded. "Grilled ham and cheese. Do you know Gabe was about to give that box of cookies to Casey? Or at least, the ones he hadn't already eaten. If we're going to do this interrogation, we might as well eat properly rather than shoving sugar down our throats.''

Sawyer looked at Gabe in time to see him sneak a cookie from his lap and pop it into his mouth. He laughed out loud.

''You think that's funny? And here you are a doctor. You should be telling them about healthy diets and all that.''

''Honey, have you looked at my brothers? They're all pretty damn physically fit.''

She tucked her chin in, and a delicate flush rose on her cheeks. ''Yeah, well, I noticed, but Casey is still a growing boy. He should eat better.'' She put another sandwich on a plate, and it was only then Sawyer noticed there were six plates, meaning she'd made one for him, too. The sandwiches were neatly cut, and there were pickle slices and carrot curls beside them. He honestly didn't think any of his brothers had ever in their lives eaten carrot curls.

She'd turned the coffeepot off and poured glasses of milk instead. Sawyer started carrying plates to the table, since his brothers had evidently been ordered to sit, given that none of them were moving much. They all looked uncomfortable, but then, they weren't used to getting waited on. Their mother hadn't been the type to mollycoddle once they'd all gotten taller than her, which had happened at the tail end of grade school.

''Casey gets more physical exercise than most grown men. And he gets a good variety of things to eat. My mother harped on that plenty when he was first born.''

Casey grinned. ''And they're all still at it. I get measured almost daily to make sure I'm still growing like I should be, and because Grandma calls and checks. She says the good part is, they all eat more vegetables and fruits because they keep the stuff around for me.''

Honey looked slightly mollified by their explanations. Sawyer held her chair out for her, and as she sat, he smoothed his palm down the tail of her hair, letting his fingers trail all the way to the base of her spine, where they lingered for a heartbeat. He imagined her incredible hair, so silky and cool, loose over his naked body as she rode him, his hands clamped on her hips to hold her firm against him. A rush of primal recognition made his breath catch. He wanted to pick her up from the table and carry her off to his room.

Of course he wouldn't do that, so he ignored the startled look she gave him and forced himself to step away.

Everyone waited until she'd taken her first bite, then they dug in with heartfelt groans of savory appreciation. It *was* good, Sawyer had to admit, even the damn carrot curls.

Sitting directly across from her, he couldn't help but watch as Honey took a small bite of her own sandwich. His thoughts wandered again to the note. *She wanted him.* He forgot to chew as he watched her slender fingers pick up a sliver of carrot, watched her soft lips close around it. He saw her lashes lower, saw soft wisps of blond hair fall over her temple.

Gabe nudged him, and he choked.

"I don't mean to drag you from whatever ruminations you were mired in, but don't you want to ask her some questions? I mean, that is why we're all up at two in the morning, gathered around the table eating instead of sleeping, right?"

Sawyer drank half his milk to wash down the bite of sandwich and nodded. "Come on, Honey. 'Fess up."

She sent him a fractious glare, but she did pat her mouth with her napkin, then folded her hands primly as if preparing to be a sacrifice. She didn't look at anyone in particular, but neither did she lower her face. She stared between him and Gabe, her chin lifted, her shoulders squared.

"I found out my fiancé had only asked to marry me to inherit my father's assets. All his stock, his company, the family home, is willed to my future husband, whoever the man might be."

There was a shock of silence as they all tried to comprehend such a mercenary act, but Sawyer was more tuned to her features. This was such a blow to her pride; he saw that now. He shouldn't have forced this confrontation, certainly not in front of everyone.

"Honey..."

"It doesn't matter." She still hadn't looked at him. Her fingers nervously pleated her napkin, but her chin stayed high. "My father and I never got along. I love him, but I don't like him much. I think he feels the same way about me. He's always resented having daughters instead of sons." Her gaze touched on each of them, and she gave a small smile. "He'd love the lot of you, a household full of big, capable men. But my sister and I never quite measured up."

"I have to tell you, I don't like your father much."

She laughed at Jordan. "Yeah, well, he's had hell putting up with me. We've butted heads since I was sixteen. When I refused to get involved in the business, which is basically electronics, new computer hardware and very state-of-the-art sort of things, he cut me out of his will. I knew it, but I didn't care. What I didn't know is that he'd changed the will to benefit the man I'd someday marry." Her mouth tightened and her eyes flickered away. Then in a whisper, she finished. "When Alden started pursuing me, I thought it was because he cared. Not because he had discovered my father's intentions."

There was, of course, the natural barrage of questions. Sawyer got up and moved to sit beside her but remained silent, letting his brothers do the interrogating. He no longer had the heart for it. He picked up her cold hand from her lap and cradled it between his own. She clutched at him, squeezing his fingers tight, but otherwise made no sign of even noticing his touch.

Gently, Gabe asked, "Why didn't you want to be in your father's business?"

She answered without hesitation. "It's a cutthroat environment. Company spies, takeovers, social climbers. It kept my father away from home the entire time my sister and I were growing up. I hate the business. I'd never involve myself in it. I wasn't even keen on marrying a man who worked for my father. But Alden led me to believe he was content with the position of regional manager, that he didn't aspire to anything more. It seemed...like a good idea."

She blushed making that admission, and Sawyer rubbed his thumb over her knuckles to comfort her. "Because your father approved of Alden?"

"Yes." She looked shamed, and he almost pulled her into his lap, then her shoulders stiffened and he saw her gather herself. In many ways, he was as drawn by her spirit and pride as he was by the sexual chemistry that shimmered between them.

She sighed. "I hadn't realized I was still trying to gain my father's approval. But then I went to see Alden at the office, to discuss some of the wedding plans, and his secretary was out to lunch. I heard him talking on the phone about his new status once the marriage was final. I listened just long enough to find out he was making grand plans, all because marrying me would put him in a better social and professional position. It hit me that I was angry and embarrassed over being so stupid, but I wasn't...I wasn't lovesick over learning the truth. In fact, I was sort of relieved to have a good reason to break things off, strange as that may sound. So I went back to his house, packed and left him the note."

Morgan rubbed his chin. "Company status seems like a pretty good reason for him to want you back, to possibly be following you."

She shrugged. "But why try to hurt me? Why try to run me off the road? Without me, there'd be no marriage and then he'd gain nothing. And when my sister's house was broken into, what were they looking for? That's what doesn't make sense. Alden is already in a good financial position. And as my father's regional manager, he's on his way to the top of the company. It's not like he *needed* to marry me to get anywhere. All that would accomplish was to speed things along."

"Maybe." Morgan finished his last carrot curl, then got

up to fetch a pencil and paper. "I want you to write down your father's name, the company name, addresses for both and for this Alden ass, and anything else you can think of. I'll check on some things in the morning." He hushed her before she could speak. "Discreetly. I promise. No one will follow you here from anything I say or do."

She tugged on Sawyer's hand, and he released her so she could write. Gabe stood up with a yawn. "I'll start work on your car tomorrow, as long as you promise you won't go anywhere without telling one of us first."

Absently, she nodded, her attention on making her list for Morgan.

"Good. Then I'm off to bed. Come on, Casey. You look like you're ready to collapse under the table."

Casey grinned tiredly, but rather than leave, he walked around the table and gave Honey a brief kiss on the forehead. She looked up, appearing both startled and pleased by the gesture.

Casey smiled down at her. "Thanks for the sandwich. It was way better than cookies."

Morgan gently clasped the back of her neck when he took the note from her. "I can see why you've been cautious, but that's over now, right?"

When she didn't agree quickly enough, he wobbled her head. "Right?"

She gave him a disgruntled frown. "Yes."

"Good girl. I'll see you in the morning. Saywer, you should hit the sack, too. You got almost no sleep the night before, and you're starting to look like a zombie."

Sawyer waved him off. He was anxious for everyone to get the hell out of the room. He had a few things he wanted to say to Honey that would be better said in private.

Jordan pulled her out of her chair for a hug. "Sleep tight, Honey. And no more worrying. Everything will be okay now. Sawyer will take good care of you."

She glanced at Sawyer, then quickly away. He wondered if his intentions showed on his face, given the timid way she avoided looking right at him. He didn't doubt it was possible. He felt like a sexual powder keg with a very short fuse.

Finally they were alone in the kitchen. Honey gathered up the plates and carried them to the dishwasher, her movements unnaturally jerky and nervous. Sawyer watched her through hot eyes, tracking her as she came back to the table for the glasses.

"You're feeling better?"

"Yes." She deftly loaded the dishwasher, as much to keep from looking at him as anything else. He could feel her reservations, her uncertainty. He stepped close enough to inhale her spicy scent, leaning down so his nose almost touched her nape, exposed by the way she'd tied her hair back. She stilled, resting her hands on the edge of the counter. She kept her back to him, and when she spoke, her voice was breathy. "My...my throat is still a little sore, but I don't feel so wrung out. I think all the sleep helped."

He crowded closer still and placed his hands beside hers, caging her in. Deliberately he allowed his chest to press against her shoulder blades. "I have patients in the morning, but in the afternoon I'll take you into town to get a few things."

"Things?"

"Whatever you might need." He nuzzled the soft skin beneath her ear. "More clothes, definitely shoes." His mouth touched her earlobe. "Anything you want."

"I'll pay for it myself."

"Not unless you have cash. Your credit cards can be traced." He kissed her skin softly, then added, "We can call it a brief loan if that'll make you feel better." He had no intention of letting her pay him back, but she didn't need to know that now. Fighting with her was the absolute last thing on his mind.

Her head fell forward. "All right."

He pulled his hands slowly from the counter, letting them trail up her arms to her sides, then down and around to her belly. He heard her suck in a quick, startled breath. His body throbbed; he nestled his erection against her soft behind, finding some comfort from the razor edge of arousal and intensifying the ache at the same time. His fingers kneaded her soft, flat belly, and when she moaned, he trailed one hand higher to her breast, free beneath the smooth cotton of the T-shirt.

Just as she'd done the last time he'd touched her there, she jerked violently, as if the mere press of his fingers was both an acute pleasure and an electrifying pain. His heart thundered at the feel of her soft weight in his hand. Her nipple was already peaked, burning against his palm. She'd instinctively pulled backward from the touch of his hand, and now she was pressed hard against him.

He adjusted his hold, one hand clamping on her breast, the other opened wide over her abdomen. In a growled whisper, he said, "I read your note."

As he'd expected, she exploded into motion, trying to get away. He held her secure with his firm hold and said, "Shh. Shh, it's all right."

She sounded panicked. "I...I'd forgotten!"

"I know." He didn't release her, adjusting his hold to keep her still, to keep her right where he wanted her. "I should let you sleep. I should give you time to think about this. But I want you too much. Now."

He could feel her trembling, the rapid hammering of her heart. He turned his hand slightly until his thumb could drag over her sensitive nipple, flicking once, twice. Her hands gripped the countertop hard, and she panted.

Opening his mouth on her throat, he sucked the delicate skin against his teeth. He wanted to mark her; he wanted to devour her. The primitive urges were new to him, but he no longer fought against them. She was his now, and there was no going back.

He caught her nipple between his rough fingertips and plucked gently. She moaned, then gave a soft sob, and all the resistance left her until she stood limp and trembling against him.

"You want me, Honey."

Her head moved on his shoulder, and her voice was faint with excitement. "Yes. That's why I had to leave. It's…too soon, but I was so disappointed when you said you didn't want me. I knew I couldn't trust myself…."

He pressed his erection hard against her and wondered what it would be like to take her this way, from behind, her plump breasts filling his hands, her legs quivering….

"It's only sex, sweetheart. That's all I can give you." The words emerged as a rough growl because he didn't want to say them, didn't want to take the chance she'd turn him away. But from somewhere deep inside himself, his honor had forced him to admit the truth to her.

To his surprise, she merely nodded, then repeated, "Only sex. That's probably for the best."

A surprising wash of indignation hit him, even as he admitted to himself the reaction was totally unfair. She'd only agreed with him, yet he'd thought she felt more. *He did.* Whether or not he admitted it, he knew it was true, and he hated it. He couldn't get involved. Never again.

He turned her around, then lifted her in his arms. "So be it. At least we're agreed."

She clutched at his shoulders and stared up at him with wide eyes. "What are you doing?"

He was burning up with urgent need, making his pace too rushed. He wanted to take his time with her, but as he looked down at her, seeing the same shimmering heat in her gaze, he wondered if he'd even make it to his room. It seemed much too far away.

"Sawyer?"

Her voice shook, and he bent to place a hard, quick kiss to her soft mouth. "I'm taking you to bed. Then I'm going to strip you naked and make love to you."

That sexy mouth of hers parted and she gasped. "But… It's late."

The bedroom door was already open and he walked in, then quietly shoved it closed with his heel. "If you think I'm going to wait one second more, especially after reading that note, you're dead wrong." He lowered her to the mattress, but followed her down, unwilling to have any space between them at all. In one movement he used his knee to open her slender thighs and settled between her legs. He wanted to groan aloud at the exquisite contact, at the feel of her soft body cushioning his. Damn, if he wasn't careful, he'd come before he ever got inside her.

He cupped her face to make certain he had her attention. "If you'd gotten away today, I'd have come after you." Her eyes turned dark, her pupils expanding with awareness. "There's something between us, and damned if I can fight it anymore. I don't think I could stand going the rest of my life without knowing what it'd be like to have you under me, naked, mine."

She stared up at him, her breathing fast and low, then with a moan she lifted while at the same time pulling him down. Their mouths met, open, hot, and Sawyer gave up any hopes of slowing down. He'd only known her a few short days, but he felt like he'd been waiting on her for a lifetime.

CHAPTER NINE

SHE WAS ALIVE with sensation, aware of Sawyer on every possible level, the hardness of his body, his heat, the way his kiss had turned commanding, his tongue thrusting deep into her mouth, stroking. She breathed in his hot, musky, male scent, felt the rasp of a slight beard stubble, and she moaned hungrily. Every touch, every movement, drove her closer to the brink. She'd never experienced this flash fire of desire before and probably would have argued over its existence. But now she was held on the very threshold of exploding, and all he'd done was kiss her.

Her hands moved over his bare back, loving the feel of hot flesh and hard muscle. She'd seen more male perfection in the past two days than most women experienced in a lifetime, but nothing and no one could compare to the man now making love to her. Desperately, she pulled her mouth free and groaned out a plea. *"Sawyer..."*

It seemed to be happening too fast. Her body was taut, her breasts swollen and acutely sensitive. And where his pelvis pushed against her, she ached unbearably.

"It's all right," he whispered against her mouth, the words rushed and low. "Let me get this shirt off you."

Before he'd finished speaking, the T-shirt was tugged above her breasts. He paused, staring down at her with black eyes, and one large hand covered her right breast. His fingertips were caloused, and they rasped over her puckered nipple, around it, pinching lightly. She cried out, her body arching hard. The pleasure was piercing, sharp, pulling her deeper. He soothed her with mumbled words, then bent, and his mouth replaced his hand.

With a gasp, her eyes opened wide. She couldn't bear it. His mouth was so hot, his tongue rough, and then he started sucking. Hard. All the while his hips moved in that tantalizing rhythm against her in a parody of what was to come. She lost her fragile grasp on control, unaware of everything but the implosion of heat, the wave of sensation that made her muscles ripple and her skin burn, the link between her breasts and her groin and the way he touched her, how he moved against her…

Without thought, she dug her nails into his bare shoulders and she tightened her thighs around his hard hips, sinking her teeth into her bottom lip and groaning long and low with the intensity of her orgasm.

After a moment the feelings began to subside, leaving her shaken and confused. Sawyer raised his head, his lips wet, his eyes blazing. He stared at her and whispered, "Damn."

She shared his sentiments. Shock mingled with sated desire. She hadn't even known such a thing was possible, much less that it would ever happen to her. She wasn't, in the normal course of things, an overly sexual woman, and gaining her own pleasure had always been an elusive thing, not a bombarding rush.

He kissed her gently, and all she could do was struggle for breath, unable to even pucker for his kiss. His hand trembled as he smoothed hair away from her face, now pulled loose from the string she'd tied it back with. "I didn't expect that," he admitted, still softly, with awe.

She swallowed hard, trying to gain her bearings. A pleasurable throb reverberated through her limp muscles. She could barely think. "Wh…what?"

He touched her cheek and a gentle smile lit up his face. Without a word, he sat up astride her thighs and pulled the T-shirt the rest of the way off, lifting each arm as if she were a child. "You are so damn sweet."

She covered her aching breasts with her hands, shyness

over what had just happened engulfing her. Sawyer ignored the gesture as he looked at her body with an absorption that left her squirming. His hands smoothed over her shoulders, down her sides. He touched her navel with his baby finger, dipping lightly, then flicking open the snap to her jeans.

"I want you naked. I want to look my fill."

What he said and the heat in his words made her entire body blush. He smiled, then moved to the side of her to wrest her jeans down her legs. "Lift your hips."

She swallowed her embarrassment and did as he asked, anxious to see what would come next. So far, nothing had been as she'd anticipated, or what she'd come to expect between men and women. Then he took her panties with her jeans, and as he looked at the curls between her legs, she squeezed her eyes shut.

They snapped open again when the bed dipped and she felt his mouth gently brush over the top of one thigh. "Sawyer!"

He reversed the position of his upper body so that he faced the foot of the bed; his arms caged her hips and again he kissed her, this time flicking his tongue out and tasting her skin. "Open your legs for me," he growled low.

She released her breasts to clutch at the sheet, trying to ground herself against the unbearable eroticism of his command. He didn't hurry her, didn't repeat his order. He merely waited and finally, after two deep breaths, she found the courage to do as he asked. She felt stiff with expectation and nervousness and excitement as she felt herself slowly exposed.

He made a low rasping sound of appreciation, then whispered, "Wider."

Shaking from head to toe, she bent one knee, and with a raw groan, he took swift advantage. She felt his hot moist breath, the touch of his lips on the inside of her thigh, then higher, until he was there, kissing her, nuzzling into her femininity. With a jolt of red hot lust, she lifted her hips, the movement involuntary and instinctive, offering herself to him completely.

"Easy, sweetheart." His hands slid under her, locking around her thighs, keeping her still. Keeping her wide open.

She felt the bold stroke of his tongue, then the seeking press of his lips before he found what he wanted and treated her to another, more gentle but twice as devastating suckle.

She was sensitive and swollen from her recent climax, and the feel of his mouth there was both a relief and a wild torment. She had a single moment of cognizance and pulled a pillow over her head to muffle her raw cries, and then she was climaxing again. And again. Sawyer reveled in her reactions, and she found he could be totally ruthless when he chose to be. He used his fingers, gently manipulating her. He used his tongue to make her beg, his teeth to make her gasp. And she gladly obeyed.

When he stood by the side of the bed, she no longer tried to cover herself. She doubted she could move. Her legs were still sprawled, her breasts trembling with her low, shallow breaths, but she didn't care. She felt replete and wrung out and willingly pliant.

Sawyer shucked off his jeans, his face dark with desire, his breathing labored. Honey let her head fall to the side so she could see him better, and through narrowed, slumberous eyes, she took in the gorgeous sight of his naked body. Though she didn't move, her heart gave a heavy thump at the sight he presented.

His shoulders and chest were wide, his stomach hard, his thighs long and muscled. The hair around his groin was darker, and his erection was long and thick, pulsing in impatience. She shuddered at the sight of it, wondering if she could bear taking him inside when everything else he'd done had already shattered her. She felt emotionally raw, unable to cope with the depth of what she'd experienced, of what he could so easily make her feel.

She watched as he opened the nightstand drawer and

pulled out a slim pack of condoms. He tore one open and deftly slid it on, then turned to stare down at her.

She whispered, ''I didn't know, didn't think...'' but she couldn't put into words the way he'd made her feel, how it both thrilled and alarmed her. She could tell by the grim set of his features he understood, and to some degree, felt the same. They both resented the strength of the desire between them. Mere sex shouldn't be so consuming, so uncontrollable.

''I can feel you everywhere,'' she added in the same low tone, almost fearfully because she'd never suspected sex could be so wild and forceful, to the point she was helpless against it. Her skin still tingled, her senses alive though her body was sated.

Remaining at the side of the bed, his eyes hot on her face, Sawyer reached down and cupped his hand over her sex. His fingers moved gently between her slick folds until they opened; he pressed his middle finger inside her, and his eyes closed on a groan. ''Damn, you're wet and tight.''

Honey bit her lip and tears seeped from the corners of her eyes as she struggled to accept this new onslaught of sensation. ''It's...it's too much, Sawyer.''

''And not enough,'' he rasped, then came into the bed over her.

She opened herself to him without reserve, lifting her face for his kiss. Though the hunger was still tightly etched in his features, his kiss was gently controlling. He took his time, making love to her mouth, bringing her desire back into full swing.

''Please.''

Sawyer cupped her face and stared into her eyes. ''Wrap your legs high around my waist. That's it. Now hold me tight.''

His voice was so low and gruff she could barely understand him. She felt him probing, his erection pressing just inside, burning and appeasing, and her heart swelled. She gave a shuddering sob and closed her eyes, but he kissed her and said, "Look at me, Honey."

It was so wonderful, it hurt. She cried while she stared at him, not out of sadness, but from inexplicable pleasure. She knew she'd probably fallen in love within the first hour of meeting him. She drew her palms down his chest to his small brown nipples and smoothed over them, determined to take everything she could. His expression hardened and he locked his jaw, rocking against her, entering her by excruciatingly slow degrees. She lifted her hips to hurry him along and was rewarded with his harsh groan. His muscles rippled and tightened, and then he thrust hard with a curse.

Honey held on to him, stunned by the shock of pleasure as he filled her. He tangled his fingers in her hair and locked his mouth onto hers and rode her hard. His chest rubbed against her stiffened nipples, his hips grinding into her with an incredible friction, his scent invading her.

She screamed as she climaxed, and Sawyer, still kissing her, swallowed the sound. He held her so close she felt a part of him. He held her and kissed her until she'd relaxed and then continued doing so even as he found his own release, his hold almost crushing it became so tight.

The kiss dwindled, turning light and soft and lazy as Sawyer sank onto her. His heartbeat rocked them both, and still he kept kissing her, easily, consuming her, soft lazy kisses that went on and on.

A noise in the hallway made him lift his head. He stared toward the closed door, and Honey couldn't remember if he'd locked it or not. After a second of squeaking floorboards, she heard Morgan call softly, "Sawyer?"

Sawyer dropped his forehead onto hers with a muffled curse. He swallowed, took two deep breaths and said with feigned calm, "Yeah?"

"Ah, I heard a scream. Again. But I'll assume you're… kissing her again." There was a slight chuckle. "Carry on." Then the sound of retreating footsteps.

Honey wanted to cover her face; she even wanted to

blush. She couldn't manage either one. She closed her eyes and started to drift off to sleep. Sawyer kissed her slack mouth, smoothed his rough hand over her cheek, then rolled to her side. He was silent for a few minutes, and she felt the weight of lethargy settle into her bones. Right before she dozed off, she heard him murmur, "God knows I got more than I bargained for, but I intend to keep taking it while you're here."

And how long would that be, she wondered? Two days, maybe three? With Gabe fixing her car and Morgan checking into things, she wouldn't have much time at all. But like Sawyer, she intended to make every minute count.

In the next instant, she was sound asleep.

SAWYER WATCHED HONEY with a brooding intensity. She'd been here two weeks now, and he'd made love to her at least twice a day. Yet it wasn't enough, and he'd begun to doubt there could ever be enough. She wasn't out of his system—far from it. It seemed the more he had her, the more he wanted her, to the point he could think of little else.

She'd integrated herself completely into their lives. She now took turns cooking and cleaning, regardless of how they all complained. Unlike the other women who on rare occasions had visited the house, Honey didn't suggest they should sit and let her do it all. She didn't excuse them from duty just because they were male. No, she willingly allowed them their fair share. But she wanted to do her own part, too.

Seeing her in his kitchen cooking made him want her.

Seeing her pulling weeds from the flower beds around the house made him want her.

And listening to her argue with his brothers or coddle his son really made him burn with lust. Dammit. This wasn't the way it was supposed to be.

It was late in the day, and a barrage of patients had kept him busy for several solid hours. He hadn't had a chance to visit with her as he usually did. Twice she had poked her head into his office to offer him lunch or a quick snack. Even seeing her for those brief moments had brightened his day, as if he'd grown accustomed to her and had been suffering withdrawal from her absence.

He didn't like the feeling. Never before had he felt annoyed by having so many patients, or having to deal with the occasional imaginary illness. He was known for his patience and kindness, not his lust.

But lust today had ruled him, just as it had since he'd first laid eyes on her.

Right now, Honey was hanging over Gabe's shoulder while he looked at her car engine. Gabe had done a fair job of taking his time on the car. He'd ordered unnecessary parts, replaced things that didn't need replacing and generally stalled as long as he could. But Honey was getting antsy. There'd been no sign of the men after her, and Morgan hadn't been able to turn up a damn thing, though he'd alerted several people in town to let him know of any strangers passing through. Now all they could do was wait, but Honey was done waiting. She'd gotten it into her head that she was taking advantage of them and therefore should get out from underfoot.

Sawyer grunted to himself as he leaned on the shed door, watching her and Gabe together. His hair was still wet from his recent shower, but the heat pounding down on his head and radiating from the lush ground would quickly dry it. Already his T-shirt was starting to stick to his back, and his temper felt precarious at best, in sync with the sweltering summer weather and his disturbing thoughts of a woman he shouldn't want, but did.

Honey had no way of knowing her presence here had been carefully staged. His brothers had manipulated things so that she had no reason, and no way, to leave. Between Gabe toying with her car and Jordan supplying her everything she could possibly need from town, she'd had no reason to step foot off his property, which was how his brothers had planned it.

He appreciated their efforts, but they couldn't know what it was costing him.

Honey suddenly straightened and put her hands on her shapely hips. She glared at Gabe suspiciously while a sunbeam slanting through a high window in the large shed got caught in her fair hair, forming a halo. "Are you sure you know what you're doing?"

Gabe grinned and touched the tip of her nose with a grease-covered finger, leaving a smudge behind. "Of course I know what I'm doing, sweetie. Relax."

They'd all taken to calling her *sweetie* since they insisted on using an endearment, and her name was just that—her name. Honey had laughed and said that at least this way she could be distinguished from the mule and the cat and the various other assorted animals wandering the land.

Today she had on shorts Jordan had brought her. He'd made the purchases to keep Sawyer from taking her to town, afraid that once she was there, she'd find a way to sneak off. And none of them wanted her to do that.

But to Sawyer's mind, Jordan's fashion sense left a lot to be desired. The shorts were *too* short, displaying the long length of her slim legs and emphasizing the roundness of her pert little butt. But when he'd suggested as much, he'd gotten jeered by his brothers, who seemed to take maniacal delight in commenting on his every thought these days.

He still thought the shorts were too short, but he now suffered in silence. Just as he did when she wore the new skimpy cotton tank tops, or the flirty sundresses, or the lightweight summer nightgowns and robe. Then again, he didn't completely approve of any of the things she now wore. Jordan and Gabe had gotten together and figured out a list of everything she'd need, including some very basic female items he'd never have considered in his lust-induced fog. They'd also shown her where to add neccessities to the list kept posted on the front of the fridge. So now, among the items of aftershave and car oil, face cream and fingernail files had been added.

Every day it seemed she became a bigger part of their lives, and he didn't know what he was going to do when she eventually left. Which she would. Because once she was safe, he wouldn't ask her to stay.

Honey, tired of watching Gabe fumble under the hood of her car, turned to flounce out of the shed. When she caught sight of him, her face lit up with a warmth that filled him to overflowing. "Sawyer! I didn't know you were here."

As usual, her eyes ate him up and sexual tension immediately vibrated between them. But she never touched him in front of anyone, too concerned with trying to keep their intimate involvement private. He didn't have the heart to point out his brothers were far from idiots and had already deduced more than he'd ever admitted even to himself. Besides, the fact she touched everyone *but* him was pretty telling, like the drunk who overenunciated to hide his state of inebriation. Honey was what Gabe called a touchy-feely woman, always hugging and patting people she cared about. And she cared about all of them, that was painfully obvious.

It was one of the main reasons his brothers insisted on prolonging her stay. Not that he'd let her leave anyway until the issue of her safety was resolved.

And that was the topic he brought up now. As she neared, he braced himself and said, "I think you should call your fiancé."

Just like that, the light died in her eyes and her welcome became wary, twisting at his heart. She stalled, her new sandals kicking up dust on the shed floor as she came to a standstill. She tried a sickly smile that made him ache. "My fiancé?"

"Ex-fiancé. This Alden idiot."

Gabe quickly wiped off his hands and strode over to them. "What the hell are you talking about, Sawyer?"

Sawyer rubbed his neck, trying to ease his growing tension. He didn't like the idea much himself. If he had his way, he'd never let her get within shouting distance of the bastard. But he couldn't take the pressure anymore, waiting for something to happen so they could act and put an end to it. And he couldn't seem to keep his hands off her.

To get things settled, they had to force the issue, and calling her ex was the only way he could think of to do it.

He stared down at her and resisted the urge to hold her close. "Morgan and I discussed it. We both still think Alden is involved somehow. You said yourself that his behavior was strange. The only problem is finding the link. If you call him, we can listen in and maybe we'll catch something you missed."

Her expression turned mulish, so he quickly clarified. "I'm not suggesting we're any better at this than you are. But at the time you left, you were upset. Now you're calm, and we're totally detached." Only he wasn't. He was in so far, he didn't know if he'd ever see daylight again. He cleared his throat and forged on. "Between us we might pick up a small detail that will make sense. I know the waiting is hard on you."

She nodded slowly, her eyes never leaving his face. "I was just telling Gabe that I think I should stop imposing on you all."

His stomach knotted. "And no doubt Gabe told you that was nonsense."

"Well, yes."

Gabe put his arm around her shoulders. "Damn right I did. She's not going anywhere until we know it's safe."

"And this is the best way to find out if it is or not," Sawyer replied, trying to ignore the way Gabe held her and the hot jealousy he couldn't deny. The only male who could touch her without setting off his possessive alarms was his son. And it was a good thing, since Casey seemed even more inclined than the rest to dote on her. Sawyer was almost certain Casey had his own agenda in mind, but unlike the others, Casey wasn't as easy to figure out. He'd always been a mature kid, proud and too smart for his own good, but he'd never been overly demonstrative with anyone but the family. In fact, he was usually more closed off, keeping his thoughts and feelings private. The way he'd so openly accepted Honey was enough to raise a few brows.

"You plan to set some bait?" Gabe asked, pulling Honey even closer as if to shield her. From Sawyer.

He scowled and nudged Gabe away, looping his own arm around Honey and hauling her up possessively against him, regardless of her chagrined struggle. "Not exactly bait. You know I wouldn't endanger her. But I want her to come right out and tell the bastard that she's been followed, that she's in hiding, that she damn well might go to the police despite her father's absurd edict if she doesn't get some answers. There's a good chance Alden will slip up and give something away."

Gabe gave a thoughtful nod. "It's not a bad plan. If he's innocent, we should be able to tell, don't you think?"

"I would hope."

Honey stepped away from both men. "Do I have any say-so in this?"

Sawyer looked at her warily. In the past two weeks he'd come to learn her moods well. Right now she was plenty peeved, and when Honey wasn't happy, she had no qualms about letting them all know it. The fact that she was one small woman in a household of five large men didn't appear to intimidate her one bit. "Uh...sure."

"Then *no*. I'm not doing it. What if Alden is at the heart of it all? What if he traces the call? He's certainly capable of doing that. Then the trouble could land right here at your own front door."

"And you still don't trust us to take care of you?" His temper started a slow boil; this was a constant bone of contention between them. "You think we're all so helpless we'd let someone hurt you? That *I'd* let anyone hurt you?"

In a sudden burst of temper, she went on tiptoes and jutted her chin at Sawyer. "I'm not thinking of me, dammit! *I'm thinking of you and your family!*"

Gabe glanced at Sawyer, a comical look of disbelief on his face. "She's trying to protect us?"

Sawyer crossed his arms over his chest and nodded, thoroughly bemused and annoyed. "Looks that way."

Throwing her hands into the air, Honey shouted, "You're not invincible!"

Sawyer rolled his eyes to the heavens. He wanted to shake her, and he wanted to take her back into the shed, slam the door on the world and make love to her again. Just that morning, right before dawn, he'd slipped into her bed and attempted to rouse her with gentle kisses and touches. But things always turned wild with Honey, no matter his resolve. When he'd left the room for his office shortly after seven o'clock, he'd been totally spent, and his legs had been shaking from the vigorous lovemaking they'd indulged in. Honey had gone soundly back to sleep. He'd never known a person who could sleep as hard and sound as she did. She'd be awake one moment, gone the next, especially after sex. A marching band could go through the room, and she wouldn't stir so much as an eyelash.

Now, it felt like months since he'd touched her. He turned away. "We're not dealing with organized crime, sweetheart. Buckhorn is a small county without a lot of need for reinforcements. It's natural for us to rely on ourselves to take care of problems whenever possible. But until we figure out exactly who is after you, we're helpless. Getting more information is the only sensible thing to do."

She looked ready to kick dirt at him, then she turned on her heel and stomped back to the shed. Gabe stared after her. She went to the back of the car and opened the trunk.

"I can't keep messing with her car much longer. She's starting to get suspicious. If I don't fix it soon, she'll figure it out, or else she'll decide I'm an inept idiot. I don't relish either prospect."

Sawyer's smile was grim. "Yeah, you must've changed everything that can be changed by now."

"Just about. Changing a few parts that had to be ordered

was a stroke of genius, if I say so myself.'' Gabe shrugged. ''I don't think she knows it's in better running order now than ever, but to be on the safe side, I took a few wires off in case she decides to give it a try. I'm still not willing to trust her to stay put.''

''We can't keep her here forever.''

Gabe rubbed some grease off his thumb, trying to look indifferent. But Sawyer heard the calculating tone to his words. ''I don't see why not.''

Sawyer sighed. ''Because this isn't her home. She has a sister who's dying to see her again, despite the reassurances Honey gave her over the phone.'' Honey had called her sister, Misty, the morning she'd accepted the fact they wouldn't let her leave while there was danger. Misty had been relieved that her sister was safe, and very curious about the men she was staying with. Sawyer had spoken a few words with her, trying to allay her concerns. Misty had a husky voice and a lot of loyalty. Sawyer had liked her instantly.

''She can call her sister again. That's not a problem. Or better yet, her sister could visit her here.''

All the brothers were curious about Misty Malone, much to Honey's amusement. Sawyer sighed. ''She also has some issues she needs to resolve with her father.''

''Ha! I personally think she'd be better off never laying eyes on the man again.''

''If everything she's told us is accurate, then I'd agree. But I've never met the man and I have no idea what motivates him.''

''You're defending him?''

Sawyer understood Gabe's disbelief. From what she'd said, Honey's father wasn't an easy man to like. ''You've met Honey. You've gotten to know her in the last few weeks. Do you honestly believe any male could be so immune to her, but especially her father?''

Gabe seemed to chew that over. ''I see what you mean.

She's such a sweetheart, she's hard to resist. No, I can't imagine a man, any man, not loving her on sight.''

Sawyer felt those words like a sucker punch in the solar plexis. It took his breath away. ''I wasn't talking about love, dammit.''

With a pitying look, Gabe shook his head. ''Be glad you staked a claim first, Sawyer, because just about anyone else would be more than glad to talk about love. Maybe you should remember that while you're being so pigheaded.''

It took two steps for Sawyer to be chest to chest with his youngest brother. Through his teeth, he growled, ''Just what the hell is that supposed to mean?''

Gabe didn't back down, but then Sawyer would have been surprised if he had. Instead, he took a step closer so they almost touched, and his eyes narrowed. ''It means, you stubborn ass, that she's—''

Honey suddenly shoved herself between them. She had a large box in her hands, and her scowl was hotter than the blazing sunshine. ''Don't you two start! I've got enough to worry about right now without having to listen to you bicker!''

Flustered, Sawyer glared one more time at Gabe then forcefully took the box from Honey. ''Men don't bicker.''

''Ha! You were both muttering low and growling and acting like bulldogs facing off over a meaty bone. It's absurd for brothers to carry on that way.''

Gabe blinked at her. ''We were just...uh, discussing things.''

''Uh-huh. Like what?''

Sawyer stared at her, stymied for just a moment, then he hefted the box. ''What the hell have you got in here?''

Sidetracked, she said, ''My stereo stuff. It's been in the trunk. Thank goodness nothing got wet when I went in the lake. Since I've had no reason to listen to music lately, I'd almost forgotten about it—until Casey and I decided to dance.''

Gabe muffled a startled laugh. ''You're going to *what?*''

She sniffed in disdain at his attitude. "Dance. To *my* music. What you men listen to is appalling."

Gabe trotted along beside them as Sawyer started toward the house with the box. "It's called country and it's damn good."

She made a face. "Yes, well, I prefer rock and roll."

"This oughta be good."

Her gaze turned to Gabe. "You plan to watch?"

"Hell, yes."

"If you do," she warned, as if she could make him reconsider, "you'll have to dance, too."

"Wouldn't miss it."

Sawyer marched through the back door, through the kitchen, down the hall and into the family room. The stereo was on a built-in shelf beside the huge stone fireplace centered on the outside wall. The speakers hung from the pine walls in four locations beneath the cathedral ceiling. This room wasn't carpeted, but instead had a large area rug in a Native American motif that covered the middle of the polished wood floor. Facing the front of the house, it had a wall of windows reaching to the ceiling, shaded by the enormous elms out front. Two comfortable couches, a variety of padded armchairs and some eclectic tables handmade from area denizens filled the room.

The first time they'd all gotten together and played music and chess and arm wrestled, in general goofing off and relaxing, Honey had looked agog at all the noise. Their boisterous arguments over the chess match, more intense than those over the wrestling, almost drowned out the country songs, and she had winced as if in pain. After half an hour she'd claimed a headache and said she was going down by the lake to sit on the dock and enjoy the evening air and quiet.

Sawyer had promptly followed her, ignoring the gibes of his brothers and Casey's ear-to-ear grin. Knowing he wouldn't be interrupted, not when they all worked so hard at conniving just such a situation for him, he'd made love to her under the stars. Dew from the lake had dampened their heated bodies, and Honey's soft moans were enhanced by the sounds of gentle waves lapping at the shore. Now, looking at her face, he could tell she was remembering, too.

He dropped the box and took a step toward her. Her eyes suddenly looked heavy, the pulse in her throat raced, her skin flushed. Damn, he was getting hard.

Casey hit him in the back. "Snap out of it, Dad. I'm too young to see this, and Uncle Gabe is about to fall down laughing."

Sawyer scowled at Gabe, who lifted his hands innocently even though his shoulders were shaking with mirth, then he turned to Casey and couldn't help but chuckle. "Where did you come from?"

"Well, according to you and that talk we had when I was seven—"

Sawyer put him a headlock and mussed his hair. "Smart ass. You know that wasn't what I meant."

The second Casey twisted free, laughing, Honey stepped forward and smoothed his hair back down. And he let her, grinning the whole time. Casey was a good head and a half taller than Honey, with shoulders almost twice as wide. Yet he let her mother on him. And every damn time she did, something inside Sawyer softened to the point of pain. He loved Casey so much, had loved him from the first second he'd held him as a squalling, red-faced infant, regardless of all the issues present, that anyone else who loved him automatically earned a place in his heart.

She finished with Casey's hair and gave him a hug of greeting. Sawyer felt ridiculously charmed once again—and he hated it.

"I brought in my music," she told Casey, as if any reprieve from country music was the equivalent of being spared the gallows. Casey hadn't yet told her he actually liked country. "You want to take a look, see if anything interests you?"

"That'd be great. I'll check them out as soon as I've washed up."

Gabe stood to stretch. "You get everything taken care of, Case?"

He nodded, then turned to Sawyer. "When Mrs. Hartley left here today, I saw she was limping."

Sawyer pulled his thoughts away from Honey with an effort. "She twisted her ankle the other day rushing in from her car when it was raining."

"She told me. So I followed her over there to help her out. I got her grass cut and did some weeding, then went to the grocery for her." To Honey, he said, "Mrs. Hartley is close to seventy, and she's real sweet. She's the librarian in town, and she orders in the books I like."

Honey laced her fingers together at her waist and beamed at Casey. "What a thoughtful thing to do! I'm so proud of you."

Casey actually blushed. "Uh, it was no big deal. Anyone would have done the same."

"That's not true." Honey's smile was gentle, warm. "The world is filled with selfish people who never think of others."

The men exchanged glances. They really didn't think too much of helping out, since it was second nature to them. But Sawyer supposed to Honey it did seem generous, given the men she'd known.

Gabe saved Casey from further embarrassment by throwing an arm around him and hustling him along. "Go get washed so we can put the music on. I'm getting anxious." He winked at Honey, and then they were gone.

The family room had open archways rather than doors that could be closed, so they weren't afforded any real privacy, but already Sawyer felt the strain of being alone with her. He looked at her with hot eyes and saw she was studying some of the framed photos on the wall. There were pictures of all of them, but the majority were of Casey at every age.

Sawyer came up behind her and kissed her nape. He felt desperate to hold her, to stave off time, and he looped his arms around her. "Mmm. You smell good."

He could feel her smile, hear it in her response. "You always say that."

"Because you always smell so damn good." He nipped her ear. "It makes me crazy."

She leaned against him, and her tone turned solemn. "You've done an excellent job with Casey. I don't think I've ever known a more giving, understanding or mature kid. He's serious, but still fun-loving, sort of a mix of all of you. He's incredible." She leaned her head back to smile up at Sawyer. "But then, he inherited some pretty incredible genes, being your son."

Sawyer's arms tightened for the briefest moment, making her gasp, then he released her. He shoved his hands into his back pockets and paced away. Maybe, considering he had insisted she call her fiancé tonight, he should at least explain a few things.

Honey touched his arm. "What is it?"

"Casey's not really mine." He no sooner said it than he shook his head. "That is, he's mine in every way that counts. But I didn't father him. I don't know who his father is—and neither did his mother."

CHAPTER TEN

"WHAT DID YOU SAY?"

Sawyer laughed at himself. He made no sense, so her confusion was expected. "My wife cheated. A lot. She didn't like my long hours studying, or my distraction with school in general. By the time Casey was born, I'd already filed for a divorce. It wasn't easy for her. She had no family, and she wasn't happy about the divorce. In fact, she was crushed by it. She pleaded with me not to leave her, but she...well, once I knew she'd been with other men, I couldn't forgive her. I understood it, but I couldn't forgive."

Honey wrapped her arms around him from behind, leaning her head on his back. She didn't say anything, just held onto him.

"I'd been sort of taking care of her for a long time, since high school even. Her parents died when she was seventeen, and an aunt took her in, but then she died, too, when Ashley was nineteen. She never had a job, and the idea of getting one horrified her. I just...I dunno. It seemed logical to marry her, to take care of her. We'd been dating forever, and I felt sorry for her, and there was no one else I wanted."

Honey kissed his back, showing her understanding. "Why did she cheat?"

Sawyer shrugged. "Hell, I don't know. She seemed plenty satisfied with..." He stalled, casting her a quick look.

"She seemed satisfied with you sexually? Of course she did. You're an incredible man, Sawyer." Her small hands were flat on his abdomen, making him catch his breath as she idly stroked him, meaning to offer comfort, but arousing him instead. All she had to do was breathe to turn him on; her touch made him nearly incoherent with lust.

"You're also an incredible lover," she added huskily, making his muscles twitch. "No woman would have complaints."

He looked away again. When she said things like that, it made him want to toss her on the couch and strip her clothes off. He reacted like an uncivilized barbarian, ready to conquer. Feeling a tad uncomfortable with that analogy, he rushed through the rest of his explanation. "She told me she felt neglected, so she cheated. And then she couldn't understand why I wouldn't forgive her, because in her mind, it was my fault. I filed for divorce, but then I found out she was several months pregnant. She was angry and taunted me with the fact it wasn't mine. But by then, I hardly cared. It was an embarrassment, but little else."

"Did everyone know?"

"Not at first. She got over being mad and just started pleading with me to take her back. She fought the damn divorce tooth and nail. I tried to be considerate with her, but I was also in the middle of med school and I had my hands full. When she went into labor, she begged me to go the hospital with her." He got quiet as he remembered that awful day, his guilt, his feelings of helplessness. His family had wanted to be supportive, but no one knew what to do. The entire town had watched the drama unfold, and it was painful.

"There was no one else," he murmured, "and I couldn't leave her there alone. So I went. And after they handed me Casey, Ashley told me she was putting him up for adoption."

He shook his head, once again feeling the utter disbelief. After holding Casey for just a few short hours, he knew he wouldn't let him go. It wasn't the baby's fault his mother had been discontent in her marriage, and while wonderful adoptions existed, he wouldn't put it to the chance.

He pulled away from Honey and went to stare blindly at a photo of Casey as a toddler. In a hoarse tone, he admitted, "I signed the birth certificate, claiming him as my own, and dared her to fight me on it." His throat felt tight, and he swallowed hard. "We're not without influence here. My family has been a force since my father's days, and Ashley knew in a battle she didn't stand a chance. She hadn't wanted Casey, and I damn sure did, so she reluctantly agreed. For awhile, she was bitter about it. I don't know who all she complained to, but everyone around here knew the whole private story within days. They knew, but they didn't dare say anything."

Honey didn't approach him this time. She kept her distance and spoke in a whisper. "Where's his mother now?"

"I'm not sure. She got ostracized by the town, not because of me, because I swear I tried to make it easy on her. But she was bitter and that bitterness set everyone against her. She moved away, and last I heard, she'd remarried and moved to England. That was years ago. Casey knows the truth, and I've tried to help him understand her and her decisions. And my own."

"You feel responsible."

He turned to face her. "I can't excuse myself from it, Honey. I played a big part in her actions. She resented my sense of obligation to others, and I resented her interference in my life. I *like* taking care of people, and I like being a doctor, yet that's what drove her away. She wanted more of my time, and I didn't want to give it to her, not if it meant taking away from my family and the community."

"And you don't ever want a wife to...interfere that way again?"

"I don't want to run the risk of another scandal. I haven't changed."

Her smile was gentle as she crossed the floor and hugged

herself up against him. "There's no reason you should. You accept the influence of your name, but also the responsibility of it, like a liege lord, and you handle that responsibility well. If Ashley didn't understand, it's not your fault."

"She was my wife."

"She was also a grown woman who made her own terrible decisions. I can only imagine how you felt, with everyone knowing the truth, but I'm sure no one blames you."

"I blame myself."

She burrowed against him, her small body pressed tight to his own. Damn, but he wanted her.

All his life he'd been surrounded by family and neighbors and friends. That wouldn't change, but he knew when Honey left, he'd feel alone. And for the first time in his life he felt vulnerable, a feeling he instinctively fought against.

He wrapped his fist in her hair and turned her face up for his kiss. She tried to dodge his mouth, wanting to talk, to instruct him on his sense of obligation, but he wouldn't allow it. With a low growl, he held her closer and roughly took her mouth, pushing his tongue inside, stemming any protest she might make.

Just as she always did, Honey kissed him back with equal enthusiasm. Her hands clutched his shirt, and she went on her tiptoes to seal the space between them.

Sawyer groaned. He pulled his mouth free and kissed her throat, her chin. "I hate feeling like this," he said, meaning the way his need for her consumed him beyond reason. There were so many other things to consider right now, and all he wanted to do was get inside her.

Honey pressed her fingers to his mouth, and though she smiled, her eyes looked damp. "You feel responsible for me, and you're trying to do the right thing, because that's who you are. You help people by giving. You take in strays, both people and animals."

"The animals are Jordan's."

"But they're accepted by you. By all of you. Your wife was a stray. I'm a stray."

He grasped her arms and shook her slightly. "Dammit, Honey, I care about you."

She gave a soft, sad chuckle. "You care about everyone, Sawyer. But I don't want or need anyone to take care of me. This time, you aren't responsible."

"I wasn't making comparisons, dammit." His frustration level shot through the roof as he tried to find a balance for the feelings.

"I know." Her hand cupped his jaw, her eyes filled with emotion. "I won't lie and tell you I don't want a family. I was willing to marry a despicable creep like Alden for it, and he couldn't offer half what you do with your nosy, domineering brothers and your incredible son and your unshakable honor. But I have no intentions of clinging to a loveless relationship. I tried that with Alden, and look where it got me." She smiled, then shook her head. "I've been thinking about it, and I decided I deserve to be loved. I deserve a family of my own, and a happily ever after. I would never settle for anything less now."

Her words left him empty, made him want to protect her, to ask her to stay forever. But the one time he'd tried marriage it had been for all the wrong reasons. Now, he wanted Honey horribly, but he just didn't know about love, not a romantic, everlasting love. All he knew for certain was the uncontrollable lust that drove him wild.

She looked up into his face, her eyes soft, her expression softer, then she sighed. "Don't look so stern, Sawyer. You haven't done anything wrong. You didn't make me any false promises, and you didn't take advantage of me." Her teeth sank into her bottom lip to stop it from trembling. "All you did was show me how men can and should be. And for that, more than anything, I thank you."

She stepped away and drew a deep breath. "So, now that

we've cleared that up, what do you say I make that phone call?''

He wanted to say to hell with it; he wanted to shake her for being so nonchalant about her own feelings.

Trying for a detachment he didn't possess, he glanced at his watch. ''Morgan should be home soon. Then we'll call.''

From the open doorway, Morgan growled, ''I'm home now.''

Sawyer looked up and saw his brother lounging there, arms crossed belligerently over his chest, his eyes narrowed and his jaw set. He looked like a thundercloud. How much had he heard? Obviously enough, given his extra-ferocious scowl.

First Gabe, and now Morgan. They didn't approve of his methods, his urgency in getting the issue resolved. Despite what he'd told Gabe and Honey, Morgan had argued with him over the idea of contacting Alden. Morgan had called him an ass for denying that he cared. Sawyer had countered that he'd only known her for a little over two weeks, which had made Morgan snort in derision. *You knew Ashley for a short lifetime, but that didn't make the relationship any better.* Truthful words that had been gnawing at him all day.

Sawyer abruptly headed for the doorway to call Gabe and Jordan in, determined to blot Morgan's warning from his mind. Once the brothers were all collected, Sawyer noticed Honey wouldn't quite meet his gaze. It was as if she'd shut him out, already removing herself from him. He hated it, but told himself it was for the best.

The brothers were setting up the extra phones in the room so they'd all be able to listen in the hopes of catching a clue. Casey had Honey's collection of music pulled toward him, idly thumbing through CDs and tapes. Sawyer doubted there'd be any dancing tonight, but he understood Casey's need for a distraction.

Then Casey nudged Honey. ''What's this?''

Absently, she glanced down, frowning at a plain tape with the word *Insurance* written on it. "I don't know."

Sawyer, hoping to ease her tension, said, "We'll be a few minutes yet if you want to check it out."

Casey carried the tape to the stereo and put it in. With the very first words spoken on the tape, a crushing stillness settled over the room. Murmured conversations and quiet preparations ceased, as slowly, everyone stopped what they were doing to listen.

Her gaze glued to the stereo as if transfixed, Honey whispered, "Sawyer," and he was by her side in an instant, taking her hand, as appalled as she.

The voices were unrecognizable to Sawyer, other than being male. But what they were discussing was painfully obvious: murder. And the fact that Honey knew the voices was easy to see by her horrified expression.

So you'll do it?

It won't be a problem. But we'll need some good-faith money upfront.

I can give you half now, the rest after she marries me and her father is gone. But remember, you have to wait for my instructions. If you kill the old man before the legalities are taken care of, I won't get a damn thing. Which means you won't get a thing.

How long are we talking?

A week or two. It's already in his will, but I want to make sure there won't be any mix-ups.

Honey turned wounded eyes to Sawyer. "That's Alden."

Sawyer pulled her closer, but her face remained blank, white with hurt and disbelief. One by one, his brothers and Casey gathered around her until she was listening to the tape from behind a wall of protective men.

You just make sure the wedding goes off without a hitch. I don't want to be wasting my time here.

I can handle the bride. Don't worry about that.

What if she objects to her daddy being snuffed? Will the conditions of the will alter if she divorces you?

No, she's completely clueless to my plans, so don't worry about her. She won't have any idea that I was behind it all. If anything, she'll want me to comfort her.

There was some masculine chuckling over that, and one of the men mumbled, *An added bonus, huh?*

Sawyer shot to his feet, his fists clenched, the corners of his vision clouded by rage. "I'll kill him."

Morgan grabbed Sawyer's shoulder. "Don't be stupid."

"Or so human," Gabe added, staring at him in fascination. "It shocks me. You're usually such a damn saint."

Honey slowly stood and faced them all. "I...I have to call the police."

Sawyer squeezed his eyes shut and tried to find his control. Gabe was right—he was acting out of character. He was the pacifist in the family, yet all he wanted to do was get Alden close enough to beat him to a pulp.

Morgan stepped around Sawyer. "Honey, I think you should still make that call."

She blinked owlishly, as if coming out of a daze. Feeling grim, Sawyer nodded. "We need to find out who the hell he hired."

Casey stood beside Honey, one arm around her waist. "He made the tape for insurance, just as it says, didn't he? He couldn't take the chance that the men he'd hired would go against him. Or maybe he planned to blackmail them later with it."

Morgan shrugged. "Who the hell knows. The man's obviously an idiot as well as a bastard."

"But why were they after me?"

She looked so lost, everyone was quiet for a moment, trying to find a gentle way to explain it to her.

Sawyer cleared his throat, taking on the duty. "Honey, when you left Alden, you fouled up all the plans. Not only did you make it impossible for him to recoup the money through the marriage, but when you packed up, you evidently took his tape by mistake.''

''It...it was with my things. I just sort of shoved everything into a box. I was angry and not really paying attention.''

''Exactly. I don't know why he would have hidden the tape among your things, but—''

''Oh, God, he didn't.'' She clutched at Sawyer, eyes wide. ''When I pulled the stereo out, there was a tape shoved up against the wall behind it. Alden only has CDs so I assumed it wasn't his, and I just threw it in with the others.''

''But now you have it, and it's evidence not only against the men after you, but against Alden, too. I imagine he had to tell them about it, knowing you'd find it sooner or later and they'd all go to jail. They have to get you, to get the tape.''

Honey covered her mouth with a hand, then turned for the phone. ''I need to call my father to make sure he's okay. And my sister—''

She looked so panicked, Sawyer gently folded her close, despite her struggles, and held her. ''Baby, listen to me. You spoke with Misty yesterday, remember? If anything had been wrong, she'd have told you.''

He felt her relax slightly, the rigidity seeping out of her spine. ''Yes, of course you're right.''

She drew a deep breath, and slowly, right before his eyes, Sawyer watched her pull herself together. She'd been given a terrible blow, but already her shoulders were squared, her expression settling into lines of determination. She stepped away from him. ''Let's get this over with. I want to talk to Alden, to find out what I can, and then we can have the police pick him up. The tape will be enough evidence, don't you think?''

Morgan gave one hard nod. ''Damn right, especially with the break-in at your sister's and the way you've been chased. But with any luck, he'll incriminate himself further on the phone, and we'll all be witnesses. Don't worry, Honey. It's almost over with. I have friends with the state police who can handle everything."

Sawyer didn't want to let her go, didn't want her to so much as speak to Alden, much less carry on a deceptive conversation, but she was adamant. When she turned her back and walked away from him, it was all he could do not to haul her back up to his side and tote her out of the room.

Honey took a seat by the phone, looking like a queen surrounded by her subjects, and she dialed Alden's number. It took several rings for him to answer, and when he finally did, Honey closed her eyes. "Hello, Alden."

There was a heavy pause. "Honey? Is that you?"

"Yes."

Another pause, then, *"Where the hell have you been?"*

Honey started, but in the next instant she scowled and tightened her hand on the phone. Sawyer felt a swell of pride for her courage.

"Have you been looking for me?"

"You're goddamned right, I've been looking for you. For God's sake, Honey, *I thought you were dead.*"

HONEY STARED at the phone, her entire body trembling with rage. "Why would you think that, Alden? I left because I didn't want to marry you. Didn't you read my note?"

Her calm tone seemed to sink in to him. She heard him breathing heavily in an effort to control himself. "Yes, I read it. Where are you, Honey?"

She stared at her hands on the desk, not at the men who watched her so closely. "I'm afraid, Alden. Someone has been chasing after me."

He muttered low, then said in sugary tones, "Have you spoken with anyone?"

"About what? Our breakup?"

"About... Dammit, never mind that. Where are you living now? I'll come get you."

"I'm not living anywhere." In a calculated lie, she said, "I've been so afraid, just running from whoever is after me. I haven't had a chance to unpack. My clothes were all left at my sister's, but everything else is still in boxes in my trunk. I shouldn't have left, Alden. My father doesn't believe someone is after me, so I can't go to him."

"I know," he answered in soothing tones. "He's never been overly concerned for you. But I am, sweetheart. You know that. I wanted to marry you long before I learned about his will. If you want, we'll make him change it. He can leave everything to your sister. I don't care about the money, I just want you back with me, safe and sound. Tell me where you are so I can come get you."

"I don't know...." She tried to put just the right amount of hesitation into her tone.

"Listen to me, damn you!" He made a sound of pain and cursed. "People *are* after you, and they're dangerous. I know because they already put me in the hospital once. I spent almost a week there and I can tell you it wasn't pleasant!"

Honey glanced at Sawyer and saw his dark eyes glint with satisfaction. She held no sympathy for Alden, either, but knowing they'd hurt him scared her spitless. She didn't want the men anywhere near Sawyer or his family. "Why would anyone hurt you, Alden?"

"I don't know. I think it might have something to do with a shady deal your father made to buy some inside corporate information."

Honey raised her brows. That was an excellent lie, because it was one she would have believed. She made sounds of understanding, and Alden continued. "They won't hesitate to do the same to you, Honey. Let me bring you home where I can protect you while we sort this all out."

Sawyer covered the mouthpiece. "Tell him to meet you

here tomorrow.'' He handed her a piece of paper that Morgan had slipped to him. Honey stared down at the address, recognizing that the location was an area on the outskirts of Buckhorn. Numbly, she shook her head, knowing he planned to put himself in danger. ''No.''

''No what?'' Alden tried cajoling. ''Listen to me, Honey. I know you feel betrayed. And I'm sorry. I really do care for you—''

''Let me think, Alden!''

Sawyer walked over to her and gripped her shoulder. He shoved the paper toward her again, then whispered low, ''Trust us, Honey. Tell him.''

They were all looking at her, waiting. How in the world could she do this to them? She loved each of them. Then Morgan gave her the most furious face she'd ever seen on a human. He reached into his pocket and pulled out his sheriff's badge, flashing it at her as if to remind her this was his job, as if her hesitation had insulted him mightily.

Jordan shrugged at her, and he, too, spoke in a faint whisper. ''Either you have him come here, on our own home ground where Morgan has some legal leverage, or we go after him. It's your decision.''

She narrowed her eyes at the lot of them. Bullies every one. They had the nasty habit of ganging up on her whenever it suited them.

Alden suddenly asked, ''Who's with you?'' and suspicion laced his tone.

Knowing she had no choice and hating Alden for it, she did as the brothers asked. ''I'm in a diner in a small town in southern Kentucky.'' She glanced at the note again, then said, ''You can meet me in Buckhorn at the town landfill at nine o'clock tomorrow morning. It's…it's deserted. There won't be anyone around.''

Sawyer nodded and whispered, ''Good girl,'' and she elbowed him hard. He rubbed his stomach and scowled at her.

''Can you give me directions, sweetheart?'' Alden

sounded anxious, and Honey's stomach knotted with dread even as she did as he asked.

"Just hang on until tomorrow morning, darling. You'll feel safer as soon as I get you home."

Though she nearly choked on it, she said, "Thank you," and after she hung up the phone, she glared at all the men, but concentrated most of her ire on Sawyer. "I hope you're happy," she meant to growl, but what emerged was a pathetic wail quickly followed by tears. The brothers looked appalled, and Sawyer, his face softening with sympathy, reached for her. Honey knew if he so much as touched her she'd completely fall apart, so she ran from the room.

She didn't want him to confront Alden. She didn't want him in danger. At the moment, she wished she'd never laid eyes on him. At least then she'd know he would stay safe, and because she loved him so damn much, even though he didn't feel the same, his safety was the only thing that seemed to matter.

She wanted to pretend sleep when Sawyer crept into the dark bedroom hours later, but she was shaking so bad, he knew right away she was awake. He sat on the side of the bed and smoothed his hand over her cheek.

"Are you all right, sweetheart?"

"Yes. Did you make all your plans?"

His hesitation was like an alarm, making her sit up. "Tell me, Sawyer."

"You'll stay here with Casey and Gabe."

"No. If you insist on doing this..."

"I do. Morgan has alerted the state police, and once Alden shows up, we'll grab him. There's no reason to worry."

"Like you wouldn't if you were left behind!"

"Honey..."

She hated acting like a desperate ninny, but she was choking on her helplessness, and she didn't like it. "If Morgan and the police have it in hand, why do you need to go?"

"Because he hurt you."

His quiet words nearly crumbled her heart. She launched herself at him and knocked him backward on the bed. "Sawyer."

He couldn't answer because she was kissing him, his face, his throat, his ear. Sawyer chuckled softly and tried to hold her still, but she reared back and tugged on the fastening to his pants. Surprised, but more than willing, Sawyer lifted his hips and helped her to get his pants off, removing his underwear at the same time. Honey stretched out over him, relishing the feel of his hot, hard flesh. She loved him so much, she wanted to absorb him, his caring, his strength and honor.

Sawyer groaned as she pressed against his pelvis, rocking gently. She felt the immediate rise of his erection along with his accelerated breaths. "Honey, slow down."

She had no intention of listening to him. Moving quickly to the side, she caressed him from shoulders to hip. His hands fell to the mattress, and his body stiffened. Honey bent and kissed his chest. "I love how you feel, Sawyer, how you smell, and how you…taste."

He caught his breath, then let it out in a whoosh when her mouth began trailing kisses down his chest to his abdomen. Both of his hands cupped her head, his fingers tangling gently in her long hair.

Her hand wrapped tightly around his erection, holding him secure, giving him fair warning of her intent. She heard a low growl and knew it was Sawyer.

Rubbing her face over his muscled abdomen, she whispered, "You know how you've done this to me?"

"This?" The word was a strangled gasp.

"Mmm, *this,*" she clarified, and lightly ran her tongue down the length of his penis.

"Damn." His entire body jerked and strained, his hands tightening in her hair.

"And…this." She gently raked her teeth over him, down and then back up again.

"Honey."

"And this." His body lurched as her mouth closed hotly around him. She'd had no idea that pleasuring him would pleasure her, as well, but her heart raced with the incredible scent and taste of him and the muttered roughness of his curses. He slowly guided her head, his entire body drawn taut, his heels digging hard into the mattress.

She had no real idea how to proceed—she'd never done this before—but it seemed he enjoyed everything, so she supposed her inexperience didn't matter. But before long he was pulling her away despite her protests.

"You're a witch," he growled, then tucked her beneath him after hastily donning a condom. He entered her with one solid thrust, and she bit back a loud moan of acute sensation. As he moved over, his rhythm smooth and deep, he watched her face. "You liked doing that, didn't you?"

The room was dark, but moonlight spilled over the bed through the French doors, and she could see the intent expression on his face, how his eyes seemed to glow.

She licked her lips and felt his thrusts deepen. "Very much." Smoothing a hand over his back, she asked, "Do you like doing it to me?"

He froze for a heartbeat, struggling for control, then with a vicious curse he wrapped her up tight, holding her as close as he could get her. "Hell, yes, I like it," he growled. His thrusts were suddenly hard and fast and frantic, and when she cried out, her entire body flooding with sensation, he joined her.

And through it all, his arms were around her, and she heard him whisper again. "I like it too much."

JORDAN STUCK his head in the door but kept his gaze judiciously on the ceiling. He spoke in a near silent murmur. "I hate to interrupt all this extracurricular activity, but you didn't hear my knock and we have visitors."

Sawyer immediately lifted away from Honey, and answered in the same quiet hush. "Who?"

"I don't know for sure. I was in my room about to bed down when I heard a noise. I looked out and saw someone in the shed. If I don't miss my guess, good old Alden called in the muscle. His bully boys are probably looking for the tape in her car."

"Goddammit," Sawyer hissed, angry at himself, "we should have thought of that." Sawyer was out of the bed in an instant and pulling on his pants.

Honey threw herself against his back, wrapping her arms tight around him. "No, Sawyer, just stay inside!"

"Shh." He took a moment to gently pry her hands loose and kiss her forehead. "It's all right, sweetheart."

Since she was barely covered by the sheet and evidently didn't care, it was a good thing Jordan had averted his face. He said without looking at her, "Morgan has called in the troops, sweetie, so don't get all frantic on me."

Sawyer had assumed as much, but he saw it didn't ease Honey at all. He glanced sharply at Jordan. "Casey?"

"I sent him to the basement. Gabe is with him, and they're waiting on her."

He nodded. "Come on, Honey. You need to get your robe."

"Don't do this, Sawyer."

Her pleading tone unnerved him, but he hardened himself against it. He'd do what he had to to protect her. "There's no time for this, babe. Come on, have a little trust, okay?"

She moved reluctantly, but she did scoot off the bed and put her arms into the robe he held for her. Wearing only his slacks, Sawyer followed Jordan out, keeping Honey safely at his back. "How did they know she was here?"

"Maybe Alden had the phone call traced, or maybe someone in town knows and spilled the beans. She's been here a couple of weeks now, and you've had a line of patients every day. And Honey, once you've seen her, isn't exactly a woman to forget.''

Sawyer grunted at that. She was so damn sexy she made his muscles go into spasms. Jordan was right; no one would forget her, and her description would be easy enough to peg.

When they neared the basement steps, Gabe was there waiting. ''You owe me for this one, Sawyer. You know how I hate missing all the action.''

''Keep her safe, and you can name your price.''

Gabe grinned at that. ''If you get a chance, punch the bastards once for me.''

He handed Honey over to his brother. She hadn't said another word, and she wouldn't look at him. Gabe gently put his arm around her. ''Come on, sweetie. Casey is looking forward to the company.''

''Gabe?'' Sawyer waited until his brother met his gaze. ''Don't come out, no matter what, until I come for you.''

''We'll be fine, Sawyer. Go, but be careful.''

Sawyer watched Honey disappear down the steps. She was far too passive to suit him at the moment, but he brushed it off. Morgan was already outside and no doubt could use their help. He closed the basement door, heard Gabe turn the lock, and he and Jordan rushed silently out the back door and across the damp grass. They kept low and in the shadows and they found Morgan just where Sawyer knew he would be, peering around the barn, the closest outbuilding to the shed, keeping the intruders in sight.

''You two sleuths sounded like a herd of elephants.''

Morgan's sibilant mutter was filled with disgust, but Sawyer didn't take exception. ''Did you see anything?''

''Two men, both big bastards. From the sounds of it, they're getting into Honey's car.''

''Looking for the tape.''

''I assume. And when they don't find it, they'll head for the house.''

''You see any weapons?''

Morgan grunted, but the sound was drowned out by the myriad night noises, crickets, frogs, rustling tree branches. An eerie fog, visible through the darkness, drifted over the ground. Morgan wiped his forehead, his gaze still trained on the shed. "They'd be total idiots if they weren't armed."

"Jordan said you put the call in to the state police?"

"Yeah." Suddenly he pressed himself back, then glanced at Sawyer. "I don't think they're going to make it on time, though."

Sawyer curled his hands into fists, easily comprehending Morgan's meaning. He was on his haunches, and he tightened his muscles, ready to move. There was no way in hell he was letting anyone near the house, not with Honey and Casey inside.

Morgan reached past him and thrust his gun at Jordan, a silent order for Jordan to be backup. Jordan accepted the gun with a quietly muttered complaint, then braced himself.

Shadows were visible first, then the dark, indistinct forms of two men creeping quietly across the empty yard. They mumbled to each other, then the one trailing slightly behind growled, "That little bitch has been more trouble than she's worth. When I get hold of her—"

Without a word, Morgan launched himself at the first man, who caught the movement too late to turn. Sawyer was right behind him. It gave him enormous satisfaction to hear the grunt of pain from the man who'd threatened Honey as he drove him hard to the ground. His fist connected solidly with a jaw, earning a rank curse before the man shoved him aside with his legs and struggled to his feet. Sawyer faced him, taunting, anxious, confident in his abilities.

And then he heard Gabe shout, and Honey was racing across the yard, distracting Sawyer for just a moment. The man swung, but she got in the way, and his fist clipped her, knocking her to the ground.

Sawyer erupted with blind fury. He stood there heaving

just long enough to insure Gabe had Honey in hand and that she was all right. He was barely aware of Morgan pounding a man into the dirt, or of Jordan standing silently in the shadows, the gun drawn. He didn't notice that his son had turned on the floodlights or that the man, knowing he was outnumbered, stood frozen before him, waiting. He'd been dealing with a clamoring swell of emotions all day, pushing him slowly over the edge. And now, seeing Honey hurt, he went into a tailspin. Sawyer felt himself exploding, and with a look of shock, the man raised his fists.

The bastard was large, but not large enough. He was strong, but not strong enough. And he fought dirty, but Sawyer had the advantage of icy rage, and after a few short minutes, Morgan wrapped his arms around Sawyer from behind and pulled him away. "Enough, Sawyer," he hissed into his ear. "The state guys are here and we don't need to put on a show."

He was still shaking with rage, his knuckles bloody, his heart pounding. Slowly, Honey approached him, and Morgan, using caution, released him.

She had a swelling bruise beneath her left eye, but it was the uncertainty in her gaze that nearly felled him. Sawyer opened his arms, and with a small sound she threw herself against him.

He hadn't wanted responsibility for another wife, but ironically, the more Honey insisted on taking care of herself, the more she agreed with his edicts, the more he wanted her. The fact she *didn't* need him, that she was strong and capable and proud, only made her more appealing and made him more determined to coddle her.

Noise surrounded them, questions, chatter. Sawyer heard Morgan giving directions for Alden to be picked up, but none of it mattered to him. He squeezed her tighter and tried not to make a fool of himself by being overly emotional. She'd been hurt so much already. He tipped her back and kissed the bruise on her cheek. "Are you okay?"

Her long hair fell forward to hide her face. ''Yes. I'm sorry I got in your way. Gabe told me you'd be likely to skin me for it, after he finished fussing over me.''

''What were you doing out here, sweetheart? I told you to stay safe in the basement.''

''I snuck out when Gabe wasn't looking.'' She peered up at him, her expression earnest. ''I couldn't stay down there, hiding, while you put yourself in danger for me. I couldn't.'' Her uncertainty melted away, replaced by a pugnacious frown. ''And you shouldn't have asked me to!''

Sawyer fought a smile. ''I'm sorry.''

She pulled away and paced. The small cat darted out of the bushes to follow her, keeping up with Honey's agitated stride. It was only then Sawyer realized she was wearing Jordan's shirt. Her housecoat, or what he could see of it beneath the shirt, looked nearly transparent under the bright floodlights. He glanced at Jordan, who lounged against the barn wall, his arms crossed over his bare chest. Casey stood beside him, looking agog at the men being handcuffed by a bevy of uniformed officers. Morgan was in the hub of it all, a tall figure of authority.

Gabe reentered the yard with an ice pack and came directly to Honey. ''Here, sweetie, put this on your cheek.''

Honey ignored him, still pacing, her bare feet now wet and her movements agitated. Sawyer took the pack from Gabe and corralled Honey and started the parade back into the house. They'd all be answering questions soon enough, but for right now, Morgan could handle things.

HOURS LATER, Honey once again found herself seated in the kitchen, the center of attention in the middle of the night. All the men were fussing around her, fretful over a silly bruise that she felt stupid for having. If she hadn't panicked, if she hadn't run into the way of a fist, she wouldn't have been hurt. And after seeing Morgan's and Sawyer's knuckles, her one small injury seemed paltry beyond compare.

She sighed. The men each jumped to her aid, taking that small sound as one of pain.

"Will you all stop hovering?" she groused. "You're making me nervous."

Gabe grinned, finally seeing the hilarity in the situation. "I kinda like doting on you, sweetie. You may as well get used to it."

Honey didn't dare look at Sawyer. She tried for a sunny smile that made her face feel ready to crack. "I don't think that'll be necessary. Thanks to you macho guys, my worries are over. There's no reason for me to keep imposing, or to hang around and get used to your domineering personalities. The police told me I could leave, that when they need me, I'll hear from them. And my sister was so anxious when I called her, I think I should be getting home."

It was as if they'd all turned to statues. Honey managed to eke out one more smile, though it cost her. "Since I don't have much to pack, I can be out of here in the morning. But in case I don't catch any of you before you leave for work, I wanted you to know..." Her throat seemed to close up, and she struggled to hold back her tears. Casey stared at her, his jaw ticking, and she wanted to grab him up and claim him as her own. She swallowed and tried again. But this time her voice was so soft, it could barely be heard. "I wanted you all to know how special you are, and how much I appreciate everything you've done for me."

Jordan and Morgan glared at Sawyer. Gabe got up to pace. Casey, still unflinching, said, "Don't go."

Honey stared down at her folded hands. "I have to, Case. It's safe now, and my family needs me."

Morgan made a rude sound. "Your sister, maybe. But your father? I can't believe you're so quick to forgive him."

"I haven't. But he is my father, and I almost lost him by marrying the wrong man. He was as shocked by it all as I was. He said his lawyers will take care of everything, but we still have a lot to talk about."

"You could stay just a little longer," Jordan suggested, and he, too, looked angry.

"I can't keep hiding here, Jordan. It isn't right."

Morgan walked past Sawyer and deliberately shouldered him, nearly knocking him over. Sawyer cursed and turned to face his brother, but Gabe laughed, diffusing the moment. "Down, Sawyer. The fight is over."

Sawyer stared at him, red-eyed and mean.

Honey didn't quite know what to think of him. He'd fought so...effectively. Yet the brothers claimed he was a pacifist. After the way he'd enjoyed punching that man, Honey had her doubts.

Gabe was still chuckling. "You know, Sawyer, it isn't Morgan's ass you're wanting to kick, but your own."

Sawyer glared a moment more, then pulled out a chair and dropped into it. The brothers seemed to find his behavior hilarious, but Honey couldn't share in their humor. She hurt from the inside out, and trying to keep that pain hidden was wearing on her.

Morgan crossed his arms over his chest. "What if she's pregnant?"

Sawyer's narrowed gaze shot to Honey. She sputtered in surprise. "I'm not pregnant!"

"How do you know?"

"Dammit, Morgan, don't you think a woman knows these things?"

"Sure, after a while, but not this early on."

There was no way she would explain with four pairs of masculine eyes watching her, just how careful Sawyer had been. Through her teeth, she growled, "Take my word on it."

Sawyer stood suddenly, nearly upsetting his chair, and he leaned toward Honey, his battered hands spread flat on the tabletop. He looked furious and anxious and determined. "Would you be opposed to getting pregnant?"

Her mouth opened twice before any words would come out. *"Now?"*

He made an impatient sound. "Eventually."

Not at all sure what Sawyer was getting at, her answer was tentative, but also honest. "No, I wouldn't mind. I want to have children." She stared at him hard. "But only if a man loves me. And only if it's forever."

Sawyer straightened, still keeping his gaze glued to hers. "Would you be opposed to sons, because that seems to be the dominate gene among us."

Honey, too, stood. She bit her lips, feeling her heart start to swell. A laugh bubbled up inside her, and she barely repressed it. "I'm getting used to men and their vagaries."

"Your father would have to change his goddamned will, because I won't take a penny from him, now or ever."

"Absolutely. I already told him that."

"Do you love me?"

There was a collective holding of breath, and she smiled. For such big, strong, confident men, they were certainly uneasy about her answer. "Yes. But…but I don't want your pushy brothers to force you into anything."

That response brought about a round of hilarity, with the brothers shouting, "Ha," and, "Yeah, right," and, "As if we ever could!"

Sawyer rounded the table with a purposeful stride and the brothers got out of his way, still laughing. Casey whooped. Sawyer stopped in front of Honey and whispered, "Damn, I love you," which made her laugh and cry, then he scooped her up in his arms and turned so she faced everyone, and announced formally, "If you'll all excuse us, it seems Honey and I have some wedding plans to make."

Morgan clapped him on the shoulder as he walked past, and then winked at Honey. Jordan gave her the thumbs-up.

Casey yelled, "Hey, Dad, just so you don't change your mind, I'm calling Grandma to tell her!"

Sawyer paused. "Now? It's not even dawn yet."

Gabe smirked. ''And you know damn good and well she'd skin us all if we waited even one minute more.''

Sawyer laughed. ''Hell, yes. Go ahead and call her. But you can answer her hundred and one questions, because I don't want to be interrupted.'' He smiled down at Honey and squeezed her tight. ''I plan to be busy for a long, long while.''

MORGAN

PROLOGUE

IT WAS one of those sweltering hot weekend mornings when a man had nothing better to do than sit outside in his jeans, feel himself sweat and wait for a breeze that wouldn't come. The sky was the prettiest blue he'd ever seen, not a single cloud in sight. He loved days like this, and looked forward to viewing them from his own house once he finished it. If all went well, it would be ready for him to move in by the end of summer.

Morgan Hudson tilted his chair back and closed his eyes. Everyone was gone for the day, and the house seemed strangely quiet, not peaceful so much as empty. He hoped he didn't feel that way when he got moved in. Living with three brothers and a teenage nephew got a man used to chaos, especially with *his* brothers.

Sawyer, the oldest, was the only doctor for miles around, and he had patients coming and going through the back office attached to the house all day long—sometimes even through the night. It was one reason the brothers had all hung around together for so long. Sawyer was an excellent father, but when Casey was little, they'd all pitched in to cover dad duty so the rigors of med school, and later being the town doc, didn't overwhelm him. It had been a pleasure.

Jordan, his younger brother, was a vet, and that meant the house and yard were always filled with stray animals. Morgan didn't mind. More often than not he got attached to the odd assortment of mangy, abandoned or just plain homely critters. 'Course, he didn't tell Jordan that.

Gabe, the youngest brother, was a rascal, with no intention of settling down anytime soon. And why should he when half the female populace of Buckhorn County, Kentucky would be bereft if he ever did? The women had spoiled Gabe something awful, and he indulged them all. Gabe just plain loved women, young and old, sweet or sassy. And they loved him back.

Casey, Sawyer's son, was constant chatter. He was at that awkward age of sixteen, half man, half kid, when females fascinated him, but then, so did driving and stretching his independence. Casey, as well as the brothers, was thrilled when Sawyer decided to marry again, adding a female into the masculine mix. The adjustment to Honey Malone had gone surprisingly smooth.

Morgan smiled. Damn, but he liked Honey. Mostly because the woman had snared his brother with a single look. Sawyer had fought it, Morgan'd give him that, but it hadn't done him a damn bit of good. He'd gone head over arse in love with Honey almost from the first day. And once Casey had decided he loved her, well, that had put a bow on the package. Sawyer would do anything for that boy, so it was a good thing Casey had taken to Honey the way he had.

Morgan wanted to have a son just like Casey some day—if he ever found a woman he wanted to marry. At thirty-four, he figured he'd waited plenty long enough. He almost had the house done, and he sure as hell was settled enough now, despite what his brothers thought. He had a respectable job and plenty of money put away. It was time for him to get on with his life, his hell-raising days long over.

A bird landed on the porch, right next to where Morgan's bare foot was braced on the railing. He cocked an eye open, whistled softly to the bird, then watched it take flight again. Obviously the bird hadn't known he was human—or else it'd thought he was dead. With a grin, Morgan closed his eyes again. He was like that, so still sometimes it set people on edge. To Morgan, it was all about control, taking charge of his life and seeing that things fell into place. He had the future mapped out, and he had not a single doubt that things would be just as he wanted them. He controlled himself, he controlled his future.

Whenever possible, he controlled those around him.

THE MAN was sound asleep when Misty pulled up in front of the huge, impressive log house. It seemed to go on and on forever, sprawling over incredibly beautiful land. On the way in she'd seen a lake surrounded by colorful wildflowers, an enormous barn and several smaller outbuildings. In the distance, sitting atop a slight rise, was another house, but apart from that, the home was isolated.

Honey had told her a little about the property, but mostly she'd talked of her marriage. Sawyer, her husband-to-be, had rushed things through, and Honey was putting a wedding together in just under three weeks. It had taken Misty a few days to gather her things and join her sister so she could offer some last-minute help. The timing couldn't have been better, and Misty had given a silent prayer of gratitude that she actually had a place to stay for a short time. Otherwise, she'd have been homeless.

Honey had warned her that the testosterone level would be enough to strangle a frail woman, but still, Misty hadn't been prepared for the sight of the hard, dark man sitting on the porch. He wore tight faded jeans, the waistband undone—and nothing else. She gulped, seeing a flat, six-pack, slightly hairy abdomen.

Besides being massively built and layered in solid muscle, he was breathtakingly gorgeous. Not that it mattered to Misty, who was twice burned. She'd written men off, and they'd stay written off. But that didn't mean she couldn't look. And appreciate what she saw.

She inched closer, wondering exactly how to wake him or even if she should. She'd arrived a day early, so Honey might not be expecting her. But surely there was someone else in the house, and maybe if she knocked quietly…

She was right beside him, practically tiptoeing in her sandals, trying to decide what to do, when suddenly he opened his eyes.

Oh, Lord.

She felt snared, like a helpless doe in the headlights of a semi. She stared, swallowed and stared some more. The man seemed as surprised as she was, and then he suddenly moved, jerking upright. He lost his balance, and his chair went crashing backward with jarring impact.

The string of curses that emerged should have singed her ears, but instead it amused her. She smiled widely and leaned down to where he lay sprawled on the polished boards of the porch. ‘‘You all right?’’

Still flat on his back, he ran one hand through his dark, wavy hair, eyes closed, and Misty had the distinct feeling he was counting to ten. When he turned his head to face her, she prepared herself for the impact of his gaze again.

It didn't help. The man had the most sinfully beautiful blue eyes she'd ever seen.

‘‘Is there some reason why you're sneaking up on my porch?’’

The chuckle came without warning. She was nervous, damn it, and she couldn't be. She didn't want Honey to know of her troubles, not when Honey had just found so much well-deserved happiness. Misty had already decided to act as if nothing had happened, to resolve her difficulties—*what an understatement*—on her own. Having the invitation to stay with Honey for a little while was a reprieve from heaven, and hopefully would give her a chance to get her bearings and make some very necessary plans.

‘‘Now, I didn't sneak,’’ she lied easily. ‘‘You were just snoring so loud you didn't hear me.’’

His blue gaze darkened to purest midnight. ‘‘I don't snore.’’

‘‘No?’’

‘‘Any number of women can tell you so.’’

Uh-oh. She was on dangerous ground. This obviously wasn't the kind of man you could easily flirt with. He took things too seriously. And she sensed he wasn't exactly going to behave like a gentleman. Misty brushed her bangs out of her eyes and gave him a cocky grin. "I'll take your word for it. Must have been distant thunder I heard." She looked pointedly at the clear blue sky, and he scowled, quickly prompting her to add, "Did you break anything?"

Without her mind's permission, her gaze drifted over his big, hard, mostly bare body, and her pulse accelerated.

The man pushed himself into a sitting position off to the side of the chair. He let his arms dangle over his bent knees and narrowed his eyes in what she took to be a challenge. A very small, very sensual smile tilted his mouth. "You want to check me over to see?"

The idea of her hands coming into contact with all that exposed male skin made her fingertips itch. Distance became a priority, especially with the husky way he'd asked it. Misty came swiftly to her feet, but that just redirected his gaze to her legs, so close he could kiss her knee by merely leaning forward.

He looked as if he were considering it.

She quickly stepped back. Perspiration dampened her skin and caused her T-shirt to stick to her breasts. It had to be over ninety degrees, and the humidity was so thick you could choke on a deep breath.

Trying to lighten the suddenly charged mood, she asked, "How in the world can you sleep in this heat?"

He pushed himself to his feet and righted the chair. He was a good head taller than her, with sleek, tanned shoulders twice as wide as hers. She felt equal parts fascination and intimidation. She didn't like it. She would never let another man affect her in either way. When he looked down at her, his expression somewhat brooding, she gave her patented careless grin and winked. "Out all night carousing and now you're too exhausted to stay awake?"

He stepped forward, and she quickly stepped back—then had to keep stepping back until her body came into contact with the wood railing. He towered over her, not smiling, taking her in from head to toe. If Misty hadn't known for a fact that she had the right house, and if Honey hadn't assured her that all the men were beyond honorable, she'd have been just a tad more worried than she was. "Uh, is anyone else here?"

"No."

"No?" *Now* she was getting worried. "What about your brothers? And wasn't your mother supposed to be visiting, too?"

He frowned, but didn't back up a single pace. He was so close she could smell the spicy scent of his heated skin.

She held her breath.

"My mother had a slight emergency and she won't be able to make it after all. My brothers and my nephew are all in town together, enjoying a Saturday off."

They were alone! She could barely form a coherent sentence with him deliberately crowding her so. She had a suspicion that was why he did it. She swallowed and asked, "What about Honey?"

His gaze sharpened and his dark brows pulled down in a ferocious frown. "She's with them." He looked her over again, very slowly this time. To her, it seemed as if he was savoring the experience. Then he asked, "Just who the hell are you, lady?"

His expression was bland, but there was something in his tone, a mixture of heat and expectation. Misty bit her lip, then stuck out her hand, warding him off and offering a belated introduction. "Misty Malone." Her voice broke, and she had to clear her throat. "I'm Honey's sister."

His expression froze, then abruptly hardened as he stepped away without taking her hand. "Ah, hell." He glared an accusation, then added, "That wasn't at all what I wanted to hear."

CHAPTER ONE

JUST LOOKING AT HER MADE HIM SWEAT.

And in the damned tux for his brother's reception, sweating was more than a little uncomfortable. Even the air-conditioning didn't help. He should look away, but he couldn't seem to drag his gaze from her. The sensuous way she moved, her deep black hair swaying to the music, looking almost liquid it was so silky, her husky laugh, all worked to make him crazy and put a stranglehold on his attention. Morgan loosened the tie around his throat and undid the top two buttons of his white shirt. But that didn't help the restriction of his pants, and he just knew if he started loosening them up, his new sister-in-law would have a fit. And he'd sooner kick his own ass than upset Honey.

"If you stare any harder, you're liable to set her on fire."

Morgan jerked, then turned to glare at Sawyer. "Aren't you supposed to be with your bride?"

"Jordan's dancing with her."

Great. Just great. After meeting Misty that first day on the front porch, Morgan had done his best to avoid her. Hell, he'd almost seduced his new sister-in-law's sister. And worse, she'd egged him on. What kind of woman did a thing like that?

He felt infuriated every time he thought about it. All his lauded control seemed to be paper-thin these days, especially with the way Jordan and Gabe adored the woman. They doted on Misty, every bit as fascinated as Morgan had been by her sensual looks and careless smile, only they seemed genuinely interested in her, and that really put a crimp in his mood.

Morgan didn't particularly like her. She was so brazen, so sassy and unrestrained, it was almost impossible not to be drawn to her on a sexual level. But where her sister was discreet and gentle, Misty was bold and outgoing. It was no wonder he hadn't figured out who she was on the spot; he'd expected the sister to be more like Honey, not the exact opposite.

With her come-on lines and lack of inhibitions, Misty could put any male on edge, and that wasn't at all the type of woman he was determined to be interested in these days. No, he wanted a woman like Honey, one he could settle down with, one that was as interested in becoming domestic as he was. Not that he wouldn't indulge in a little dalliance here and there before he found the wife, just not with Honey's sister. No way. That would be crossing the familial line.

Trying to sound disinterested rather than disgruntled, Morgan said, "I'm surprised Jordan could pull himself away from Misty. He and Gabe have been crowding her all night." Then he shook his head. "Hell, they've both been dogging her heels like lovesick puppies all week."

"And that bothers you, does it?"

Morgan snorted. "Hell, no. Except that she's a far cry from Honey and I don't want to see them get stuck in an awkward situation."

That made Sawyer laugh out loud. "Jordan and Gabe? I hate to break it to you, Morgan, but they're grown men and they've been handling their fair share of female companionship for some time now. Hell, Gabe started earlier than you did."

"He lied."

Sawyer laughed again. "Nope, I caught him at it, out in the barn that first time, so I know exactly how old he was."

Diverted for the moment, Morgan turned to Sawyer with a grin. "You're kidding?"

"Don't I wish. I think that's what started him on the path of debauchery."

Morgan chuckled at that. The youngest brother was a regular Lothario, to the delight of the female population of Buckhorn. "Details?"

Shrugging, Sawyer said, "The girl was four years older than him, and since then, it's like he's irresistible to women."

"Honey resisted him."

Sawyer's grin was very smug. "Yeah. I was glad to see it. Good for his ego."

"'Course, he wasn't really giving it his all, seeing as you'd already staked a claim." Before Sawyer could object to that, Morgan turned to Misty. "Does it amaze you how two sisters can be so damned different? I mean, Honey is just so kindhearted and innocent."

Sawyer had just taken a sip of his champagne, and he choked, but when Morgan gave him a suspicious look, he just raised his brows, as if encouraging Morgan to continue.

"Misty is..."

"What?" Sawyer seemed intent on digging in. "Sexy?"

"Hell, yeah, she's sexy. But then so is Honey."

Sawyer blinked at that, then frowned ferociously. "I'm not at all sure I like—"

"Oh, give it a rest, Sawyer. I'm not blind. And I just appreciate the fact she's so sexy—for you."

After downing the rest of his champagne in one gulp, Sawyer demanded, "Your point?"

Sawyer was being damn entertaining again, but Morgan couldn't take advantage of it because he couldn't pull his gaze away from Misty. Gabe had just swept her up into a new dance. She complained for just a moment about her feet, and Gabe, the rascal, merely went down on one knee and pulled her shoes off, tossing them aside. Misty seemed charmed, and they began a rather heated, intimate dance. The floor cleared to give them room, and Misty behaved totally uninhibited. Gabe was no better, showing off, making the women cheer, but that was his damned brother and he wasn't interested in looking at Gabe.

Misty was something altogether different.

Morgan had to grind his teeth together. "Will you just look at her?"

"I'd rather look at you looking at her. More amusing that way."

"It's like, Honey is so sweet and gentle, and Misty's all spice and fire. What is it with her, anyway? Does she think she has to seduce every guy around her?"

"She's not seducing, she's dancing."

Morgan snorted. "The way she dances, it's the same damn thing."

Sawyer snickered. "For you, at least."

Just then, Jordan interrupted Gabe and stole Misty away. She laughed, as willing to partner him as Gabe, and Morgan nearly ground his teeth into powder. "It's not right, I'm telling you. She's playing with them both."

Deliberately adding oil to the fire, Sawyer said, "It seems to be a game they're enjoying." Then he clapped Morgan on the shoulder. "Relax, will you? She's just dancing, nothing more. Oops. Here comes Honey, so I better get this out quick. She's concerned because you're avoiding Misty. I was supposed to tell you to go dance with her."

"Ha." Morgan was positively appalled by that idea, but not for the reasons his brother would likely assume. "I'm not getting near her." He was afraid if he did, he'd explode. He couldn't recall ever wanting a woman quite the way he wanted this one.

She was staying with them at the house, so he saw her at breakfast, looking all sleepy but still full of smiles for his brothers. He saw her at bedtime, wishing everyone—but him—a good night's sleep. He even saw her in the afternoon, though he did his best to avoid it. She would be painting her toenails right out on the back patio, or puttering around the kitchen, giving the illusion of being domestic when he'd be willing to bet she didn't have a domestic bone in her entire lush little body.

It didn't matter what she did, he liked it—a little too much. And she knew it, which was why she avoided him as much as he did her. They were far too sexually aware of each other for comfort.

But it was all physical, and a fast, easy, physical relationship with his sister-in-law's sister would never do. Sawyer, damn him, had made the woman a relative with his marriage, and that put her off-limits for every single thing Morgan would like to do with her. And the things he'd like to do...

He almost groaned out loud. The vivid images of him and Misty together, naked, overheated, carnal, would amuse his brothers and shock the hell out of Honey. She was overprotective of Misty—why, he couldn't fathom. He had a feeling his sexual thoughts wouldn't shock Misty at all. He had the taunting suspicion she'd be with him every step of the way.

"Damn." Morgan felt the start of an erection and had to fight to control himself. Not easy to do when Misty was laughing and looking flushed from all that dancing. Jordan whirled her in a wide circle, and Morgan wanted to flatten him.

"Damn is right. You're in for it now."

Morgan turned to see what Sawyer was blathering on about and was met with Honey instead. She looked incredibly beautiful in her white wedding gown, her long blond hair loose and her face glowing. Morgan smiled at her. "Have I kissed the bride yet?"

"About a dozen times, I think." She grinned at him, and twin dimples decorated her cheeks.

"Morgan..." Sawyer's beleaguered tone didn't bother Morgan one whit. Annoying each other was the brothers' favorite pastime. And Sawyer, love-struck from day one though he fought it pretty damn hard, had made himself a prime target.

Honey laughed and patted her husband's chest. "Oh, Sawyer, relax. Your brother is just a big pushover."

Sawyer choked again.

Morgan, amused by her insistent misconceptions of him, grinned. Not another soul in Buckhorn, male or female, thought of him as a pushover—pretty much the opposite, in fact.

His grin fell flat with her next words.

"I want you to dance with Misty."

"Ah..."

"Morgan, it almost seems like you've been avoiding her. She told me just this morning at breakfast that you didn't like her."

They'd talked about him? Morgan wanted to ask exactly what had been said, but he didn't want to look too interested. "I don't dislike her."

"Of course you don't! But she thinks you do because you've spent so much time at work since she's been here, and you've barely said two words to her."

Morgan tugged on his ear, beginning to feel uncomfortable. He wanted to sock Sawyer, who stood behind his bride, smirking. "It's been really busy this week and being that I'm sheriff I can't just..."

"But you're not busy now. And look, she just finished a dance. It's the perfect time for the two of you to talk some more and get better acquainted."

Sawyer, ready to get back a little of his own, said, "Yeah, the timing is *perfect.* And with your, er, charm, you should be able to put her right at ease." Then he grinned, glancing at his wife. "You'd do that for Honey, wouldn't you, Morgan?"

Honey, playing along, gave him her most endearing smile.

He tried, but not a single rebuttal came to mind. "Well, hell." Morgan stomped away, resigned to his fate and unfortunately, in some ways, pleased to be forced into it. He saw Misty look up from across the room, as if she'd somehow sensed his approach. She did that a lot, seeming to know the second he entered a room. And then she'd get quiet and withdrawn—but only with him.

Her dark blue eyes, so bright and clear they still had the effect of making his heart skip a beat, widened. He saw her soft lips part, saw her cheeks darken with color. She turned, looking, he knew, for an avenue of escape. But she'd already been surrounded by every eligible bachelor in Buckhorn, and they were in no hurry to let her leave.

Morgan stopped right behind her. She didn't turn to face him, but she knew he was there; her shoulders stiffened the tiniest bit and her normally husky voice became a little bit shrill as she asked the men who would dance with her next.

Morgan looked at every man there, and he fashioned a grin. A very hard, unmistakable expression. Several of the men, eyeing him closely, began to back up, quickly making their excuses.

Morgan took advantage of their retreat. "I believe that'd be me, Malone."

She hated it when he called her by her last name. He'd found that out the first day they met. He'd been calling her by Malone ever since, because it helped to maintain the small distance necessary for his sanity.

"I don't think so, *Hudson.*" She reached for Gabe's hand. He was one of the few men who wasn't intimidated by Morgan's darkest stare. In fact, Gabe looked highly entertained. He was a gentleman and would have assisted her, if Morgan hadn't beat him to it, reaching around her and snatching her slim fingers in his own before she could get a solid hold on Gabe. The reach brought his chest up flush against her slender back. He could smell her, warm woman and sweet sexiness. Her scent was like an irresistible tonic to him, and like any basic male animal, he reacted strongly to it. Her hair, so silky and luxurious, brushed his chin, and it was like having fire lick down his spine. He caught his breath.

They both froze.

Gabe chuckled. ''You two going to stand there doing the statue imitation all night, or do you intend to dance? I have to tell you, Honey is frowning something fierce over the show you're giving the guests, and I think she's about to start this way.''

Morgan drew in a deep breath, searching for control. ''Get lost, Gabe.''

''No way. I don't get to see you this rattled too often.''

''I'm not rattled.'' He stepped back a safe distance but retained his hold on Misty. Trying to sound reasonable, rather than rattled, he said, ''Your sister wants us to dance.''

Misty's pink tongue darted out to lick nervously at her lips, and Morgan wanted to groan. He glanced at Gabe and saw that his brother was every bit as alert and fascinated as he was. *Damn.* He started backing out to the middle of the dance floor, tugging Misty along with him. Everyone could see she was a reluctant participant, and after the way she'd accepted every other partner, Morgan was peeved. ''Come on, Malone. I won't bite you.''

''Can I have that in writing?'' Gently, she tried to disengage her hand. Morgan stared at her, refusing to let go and refusing to respond to her sarcasm.

She sighed. ''Look, Morgan, this isn't a good idea.''

Perversely, he asked, ''Why not?''

''You don't like me! That was easy enough to figure out from the moment we met.''

She was so...lovely, he couldn't help but study her face, the narrow nose, the high cheekbones, her small rounded chin. If he looked any lower, he'd never survive the dance, so he brought his gaze to hers. ''I liked you well enough...at first.''

''All right. Then from the moment I introduced myself. I have no idea what you've got against me, and to tell you the truth, I really don't care.''

''You don't, huh?'' It was amazing how she went straight to the heart of the matter. Most women wouldn't have been so bold.

He wondered if she'd be that bold in bed.

"No, I don't," she said. "Truth is, I'm not at all crazy about you, either."

The grin took him by surprise. Strangely, Morgan realized he was enjoying himself. Beyond being turned on, he felt challenged, and that didn't often happen with women anymore. "Why not?"

Before she could reply, the music changed, turned sultry. Misty gave such a heartfelt groan of despair, he chuckled. "Oh, no. I'm outta here." Again she tried to pull loose, but Morgan swept her closer and wrapped one arm around her waist.

Near her ear, he whispered, "Quit fighting me, Malone. It's only one dance." One dance that felt closer to foreplay. Just holding her was making him nuts, and this close, he could see a few damp, glossy black curls clinging to her forehead and temple. Her upper chest, visible over the scooped neckline of her maid-of-honor gown, was dewy with perspiration. She was warmed up and flushed all over. The vigorous dancing, he thought, leaning subtly forward to breathe in her heated scent. The thought of any other man in the room, especially his damn younger brothers, being this close to her, being affected the same way, made him want to growl.

Misty frowned at him. "What's the matter with you, anyway? You look like a thundercloud."

She pulled back, putting a few more inches between their bodies, but Morgan could see the added color in her cheeks and knew she was feeling the effects of the closeness, same as he was.

When he didn't answer, just continued to stare at her, she sighed. "Don't pretend my honesty bothered you, Morgan. I won't believe it."

Going for the direct attack, he surmised, and smiled. "You haven't offended me." Then he made his own direct attack. "You wanna know what I don't like about you, Malone?"

"No."

Her naturally husky voice dropped another octave in her irritation. Where his hand rested on her back, he could feel the satin of the dress, warmed by her body, and the supple movement of her muscles. She was slim, but still stacked like a Barbie doll, with lush breasts and a narrow waist. Her legs seemed to go on forever, long and sleek and sexy. Her bottom, though small, was perfectly rounded and just bouncy enough to make him catch his breath whenever she walked away. He'd spent far too many hours obsessing over her bottom.

And those breasts. He could spend at least an hour enjoying her just from the waist up. Unable to stop himself, Morgan looked down at the pale, firm flesh and imagined the formal dress around her waist, her breasts naked for him to see, to touch and taste, to enjoy. He groaned. It was almost too easy to imagine his mouth on her, considering how much cleavage was showing, more so than any of the other women in the wedding party, though they were all wearing similar gowns in different colors. With the shape of the neckline there was no way she could be wearing a bra, or at least, not much of one.

Almost burning up, he growled, "You're Honey's sister."

She blinked, wary surprise evident in her expression. "So?"

"That puts you off-limits. And I don't like it."

Her eyes widened. "Good grief! You make it sound like if you decided to...to—"

"Yeah, all that you're imagining and more."

Her breath caught, and she choked on her anger. "Like I'd be agreeable! Well, let me put your mind at ease here, Morgan. The answer would be no!"

Annoyed all over again, he said, "I'm not buying it, Malone. You flirt all the damn time. Not just when you talk, but when you move, when you eat." He looked at her breasts again, which were trembling with her ire. ‘‘Hell, even when you breathe.’’

His words made her sputter before she managed to spit out, ‘‘That’s absurd!’’

‘‘Do you realize every guy here has been ogling your breasts?’’

Her mouth dropped open, then abruptly snapped closed. ‘‘You’re disgusting.’’

‘‘I’m not the one showing so much skin.’’

Through her teeth, she ground out, ‘‘Every woman in the bridal party is showing the same amount of skin, you idiot. Why don’t you go lecture one of them?’’

Easily, knowing it was true, he said, ‘‘None of them looks like you.’’ Then he pulled her closer despite her slight resistance. ‘‘And I don’t want any of them.’’

She looked flabbergasted. ‘‘Why, you…you arrogant bas—’’

‘‘Shh. Keep your voice down. I don’t want your sister’s reception ruined by a scene.’’ She glared at him and her eyes looked hot enough to roast him, her cheeks rosy with color. He wanted to kiss her, but had at least enough sense to hold back from that.

Actually, Morgan wouldn’t have been at all surprised if she’d socked him one, right there in the middle of the hall. And he was honest enough to admit he’d deserve it. He wasn’t sure why he goaded her, but he couldn’t seem to stop himself.

She huffed, then jerked against his arms. Very low, with clear warning, she said, ‘‘If you don’t want me to cause a scene, then kindly get your paws off me and leave me alone.’’

With relish, he said, ‘‘Can’t. Honey is determined to see us get acquainted.’’

She rolled her eyes. ‘‘Oh, for heaven’s sake… I’ll talk to her.’’

‘‘Why bother?’’ He stared into her incredible eyes and

felt a twisting in his guts as he muttered, "You won't be here much longer, and then it won't matter."

She quickly looked down and bit her lip.

Above the lust, suspicion blossomed. Morgan whispered, "Misty?"

Her gaze jerked to his face, and he realized he'd called her by her first name. Misty suited her, all dark and mysterious, except for those direct, intense blue eyes. "You *are* leaving soon, right?"

She swallowed, looking away once again. "I hadn't really thought about it."

Frowning, Morgan half danced, half steered them toward the patio doors. Misty didn't seem to realize his intent, she merely clutched at him to keep from losing her footing as he danced her first one way, then another, moving easily around the other couples.

When he opened the patio door and stepped outside, Misty started to hold back. Then he saw her square her shoulders and follow him. Evidently she'd decided they needed a showdown.

He thought she was exactly right.

He closed the door behind her, then said, "Come on."

The night was warm, heavy with humidity. Moonlight fell over her like a pale blush and formed a halo around her midnight hair. She tilted her head, ignoring his outstretched hand. "Where are we going?"

"Someplace more private. I know my brothers, and one or all of them will be out here in under two minutes to see what I'm doing."

"You won't be *doing* anything," she said.

He answered her with a shrug, then merely waited.

After a long moment, she sniffed, but took his hand and stepped cautiously forward. He realized then she was still barefoot. Irritation filled her tone when she said, "Obviously your brothers don't trust you any more than I do."

Morgan smiled in the darkness and stepped off the patio to head toward one of the gazebos decorating the back lawn of the town hall. ''Oh, they trust me, all right. They're just nosy as hell and can't ever pass up an opportunity to needle me.''

Misty paused outside the ornate gazebo, staring at it and breathing deeply of the scent of flowers, planted in profusion around the white wood and trellis structure. The entire county of Buckhorn was big on flowers. ''I love gazebos. I think they're so quaint.''

Morgan opened the door and cautiously entered the dim interior. ''Yeah, I guess Gabe feels the same because he built one—bigger and sturdier than this—down by the lake at home.''

''I saw it. Gabe really built that?''

''Yeah. He's a handyman of sorts, among other things.'' The door banged shut behind them, sealing them inside where the air suddenly crackled with awareness. Morgan refused to believe he was the only one who felt it.

Just enough moonlight filtered in to show the way to the white bench seats lining the inside. He stared hard, seeing the dull glimmer of Misty's eyes, the sheen of her white teeth. ''Would you like to sit down?''

''What I'd like is to find out what you want so I can get back to my sister's celebration.''

What he wanted? Now that was a loaded question. From the second she'd taken his hand, he'd had a throbbing erection. Morgan seated himself, stretching out his long legs on either side of her, caging her in. His eyes quickly adjusted to the darkness, and her pale skin and the light color of her dress made her visible. She didn't so much as move a muscle. He crossed his arms and considered her. ''You're different from Honey.''

''Night and day,'' she admitted without hesitation, then explained, ''we're also very close. So what's your point?''

''I wouldn't want to see her hurt.''

Misty stiffened again, but the rigid posture just caused her breasts to be more noticeable. ''Anyone who hurt her would have to answer to me.''

"Yet you think nothing of coming in here and flirting with my brothers, coming on to them—"

She suddenly inclined closer, and her voice was a near hiss. "I haven't *come on* to anyone! I danced, but then so did everyone else at the reception. It's what's expected at a—"

Morgan leaned forward and caught her shoulders in his hands, keeping her bent close. Her skin was silky and warm, and he flexed his fingers almost involuntarily. "You also parade around the house all day without a bra, and barefoot."

Her eyes narrowed, and he could feel her tremble. "It's ninety degrees outside, Morgan! Most every woman I've seen since I arrived has been wearing a sundress or tank top without a bra." She poked him in the chest, hard. "Maybe *you* should try wearing one to see how horribly uncomfortable they can be in this weather before you start judging me."

Morgan thought that was the most ludicrous thing he'd ever heard. He opened his mouth, but she quickly cut him off.

"And as for my bare feet, what of it? Don't tell me you have a foot fetish?"

He hadn't, not until he'd met her. He'd never even noticed a woman's feet before. But Misty had small, narrow feet, and she painted her toenails a bright cherry red. They looked sexy as hell, and every time he saw her pretty little feet, he imagined them digging into the small of his back while he rode her hard, making her scream with intense pleasure.

He also knew in his gut he wasn't the only male noticing. "You're entirely too comfortable around my brothers."

"Ha! I don't think it's your brothers you're worried about at all."

Because that was so close to the truth, even if he didn't want to admit it, Morgan slowly stood. Misty tried to back up, but he had hold of her shoulders and she didn't get far away from him. "You don't think so?"

She hesitated, going cautious on him now that he was so close and towering over her. But then she lifted her chin with her usual bravado. "No. I think it's...you."

He nodded, and his pulse thrummed in his veins. "You're right. It is me. But it's also you."

"No, I—"

He stepped so close her back came up against the smooth painted wall.

All the anger, all the frustration, abruptly shifted to pure sexual tension. Morgan couldn't resist one second longer. With his fingertips, he touched her cheek, then her lips, gently, barely brushing, savoring her softness and the way she trembled in response. Touching her felt so right and made him feel downright explosive. She went utterly still, not moving, not even breathing.

In a raw whisper, he said, "There is absolutely—" he leaned closer "—no possible way—" her eyes drifted shut and she panted for breath "—I'm feeling all this on my own."

"This?" The word was a mere whisper, sighed against his mouth.

"Lord, you make me hard, Misty." And then he kissed her.

She held herself stiff for all of about two seconds before her mouth opened and her hands fisted on the lapels of his formal jacket. She moaned, a low, hungry, needy sound.

Morgan, who'd been successfully avoiding her for an entire week, was a goner.

CHAPTER TWO

INSANITY, Misty thought, feeling the hot delicious stroke of Morgan's tongue, the slide of his large rough hands down her spine. He had her pulled so close, their bodies were practically fused together. She hadn't expected this, hadn't known *this* even existed. Lord, the man knew how to kiss, knew how to move his hands and his legs and his...hips. Everything he did, every place he touched her, made her too hot, too hungry. Made her want more. And so far he hadn't even let his hands wander that far.

But no sooner did that thought filter into her fogged brain than one of those large hands came up over her rib cage to close on her breast.

Her nipples immediately drew tight, and she pulled her mouth away to gasp at the incredible sensations his touch caused.

He groaned harshly, and a rough tremble traveled through his big body.

Stunned, somewhat disoriented by the unbelievable intensity, Misty whispered, "No..."

At that single word, not even said with much conviction, he froze. His hand opened slowly, as if it took great effort to get his fingers to obey. With his face pressed to the place where her shoulder and neck met, he struggled for air, and every muscle—pressed so closely to her—stiffened.

Then he stepped away.

The air positively throbbed between them, but still, he'd stopped the second she'd asked him to. The significance of that didn't escape her; he was a remarkable man, very much in control of himself. Misty did her best to catch her breath, to stop staring at him in the darkness. She should leave, right now, but she couldn't seem to get her feet to move. Every nerve ending in her body was still alive in a way she hadn't known was possible.

"I won't apologize."

He sounded breathless, frustrated, on the verge of anger, and she swallowed hard, trying to calm her galloping heart. "I...I didn't ask you to."

Still without moving, he added, "This is going to be a problem."

Again, she asked, "This?"

Several beats of silence passed, then suddenly he moved away from her and he actually laughed. "Come off it, Malone. You felt it as much as I did." He turned back, looking for verification.

It she assumed was the incredible sexual pull. "If you mean..."

Through his teeth, he said, "I mean I touched you and you got so hot I feel singed. I kissed you and you sucked on my tongue and rubbed up against me and it was like throwing a match on gasoline. There's enough goddamned heat in this room to start a bonfire."

Misty sucked in her breath, shocked at the words, at the harsh vehemence of his tone, but unable to deny them. Part of her new determination in dealing with men was to be brutally honest—with herself and them. Sugarcoating things, *faking* things, had caused at least half of her present problems. Being too timid, too naive, had caused the other half. In order to get on with her life, she had to start facing things head-on.

A rough warning growl rumbled from deep in his throat. "Malone—"

"You're right," she hurried to assure him, unwilling to let him shock her with more of his brutal honesty. "And I'm sorry. You took me by surprise."

"Bull." He propped his hands on his hips and glared at

her. "I've known from the day I met you how it'd be. Why the hell do you think I avoid you?"

Oh. That certainly explained a few things, she supposed. "I see. Well, I must not be as clever as you, because I thought you were a totally obnoxious, thoroughly unlikable jerk and I was thankful that you ignored me. I had no idea this—" she waved a hand, trying to come up with a word suitable to the loss of control and depth of sensation he'd sparked "—*chemistry* was between us. I wasn't even aware something like *this* existed."

He cursed again, but she didn't let him interrupt her. "Now that I do know, trust me, I won't let it happen ever again."

Morgan seemed to measure her words. And then she saw his eyes narrow, his expression darken. He looked at her breasts, and she knew her nipples were still painfully hard. Without a word, he reached out a hand and gently brushed the backs of his knuckles across one sensitive tip, gliding easily over the satiny material of the dress. Misty drew in a sharp breath and felt a small explosion of erotic stimulation throughout her body.

Morgan whispered, "Oh, it'll happen again, sweetheart, if you hang around. That's why you need to finish your little visit and hightail it out of town just as fast as you possibly can. My control only goes so far, and it seems you have no control at all."

The words were like a cold slap, reminding her of all her troubles, of how gullible she'd been, how utterly stupid.

She jerked away and bit her lip hard to keep herself from tearing up. No way would she let the big jerk see her cry. Much as she had hoped to regroup in Buckhorn, she could see that was now impossible. What she would do, she hadn't a clue. But he was right, leaving was imperative. She had absolutely no desire to get involved with a man again, for any reason. Especially not a domineering, bullheaded behemoth like Morgan Hudson, a man who didn't even like her, and in fact, seemed to disdain her.

Keeping her back to him, she drew a long, steadying breath. Then she reached for the door. "I'll leave first thing tomorrow morning." Despite her resolve, her voice quavered tenuously.

There was a slight pause. "Misty..."

He sounded uncertain, but she had no intention of discussing things with him. There was no one she could trust except Honey, and she wouldn't ruin her sister's current happiness for anything. After she got her life straightened out and made some plans that would hopefully carry her through the coming months, she could begin making confessions to her sibling.

The open door offered no relief from the heat; there wasn't a single breeze stirring. Misty stepped onto the dew-wet grass, then felt Morgan's hand settle on her shoulder. "Wait a minute."

She flinched at his tone but didn't bother trying to move away from him. Just that simple touch, his hand on her shoulder, made her acutely aware of him as a man. She almost hated herself. "What now?"

She turned to face him, trying to look irritated when she was actually breathless. The moonlight was brighter. She could see his every feature—the strong, lean jawline, the harshly cut cheekbones. He was by far the most impressive male she'd ever seen, but then, his brothers were nothing to sneeze at. There must have been a mighty impressive gene pool somewhere to create all that masculine perfection.

He stared at her, not answering at first. He shook his head, distracted, and just when he started to speak, another voice intruded.

"There you are."

Morgan looked up. "Casey. What in hell are you doing out here?"

Misty turned to see Sawyer's son. At sixteen, Casey already showed signs of his own masculine superiority. He was tall, nearly six feet, and had the bone structure that promised wide shoulders and long, strong limbs.

"Dad wanted someone to find you and haul you back inside."

Morgan shook his head. "And of course, you just naturally volunteered for the job."

Casey chuckled. "Actually, Uncle Jordan and Uncle Gabe beat me to it, and they did seem pretty anxious to come out here and fetch you in, but Dad told me to go instead, on account of he said you wouldn't slug me."

Morgan threw an arm around his nephew, held him in a brief headlock and then started them all toward the door. "Don't be too sure of that, boy. My affection for you is kinda thin at the moment."

With a laugh, Casey said, "I'm not worried. I can still outrun you."

"You think so, do you?"

"Yeah, 'cause I'm fast—and you're getting old." Casey ducked quickly under Morgan's arm and came to Misty's side. Walking backward, his grin wide, he said, "Dad also told me if you didn't want Honey to get after you, I should walk Misty in and you should come in after."

"He said all that, did he?"

"He said you wouldn't want to shatter Honey's skewed illusions, being as she doesn't know the real you, yet."

Casey was having a fine time of it, pestering his uncle. Misty smiled to herself, amused at their close camaraderie and a little wistful. Her own family consisted of Honey and her father, since her mother died when they were young. Her father had been overbearing and overcontrolling, cold, without the foundation of love that would have made those personality traits more bearable. If it hadn't been for Honey, she didn't think her childhood would have been at all tolerable.

Casey seemed to have a fantastic family foundation. It was easy to see why Honey had fallen in love with the whole clan.

Morgan stopped just out of reach of the patio, still in the shadows where the lights didn't reach. "You go on in, Casey, and tell your dad I expect him to control his wife. We'll be there in just a moment."

"Dad said you'd say that, and then I was supposed to tell you he's sending Uncle Gabe and Uncle Jordan out in two minutes."

Morgan made a playful grab for Casey, but he jumped back, laughing. Holding up his hands, he said, "Hey, it was Dad, not me!"

Morgan reached for him again and Casey hurried to the door. After he opened it, he yelled back, "Two minutes, Uncle Morgan!"

"Damn scamp."

Misty was still smiling, though she felt great sadness inside. "You're all very close."

"We helped to raise him. Sawyer got full custody when Casey was just a little pup, and between raising him and finishing med school, he would have been frazzled for sure if we hadn't all pitched in. Not that it was a chore. Hell, Casey's always been a great kid, even if his sense of humor is sometimes warped."

Misty stared at him, dumbfounded. "*You* helped raise him?"

"Yeah, sure. Along with my mother and the others. What'd you think, that I was too reprehensible to be around a youngster?"

Actually that was exactly what she thought, but she kept the words to herself. "I was just...surprised. The idea of four men raising a baby..."

"Yeah, well, like I said, my mother taught us what we needed to know. But she felt real strong about Sawyer being involved as the dad, and that meant the rest of us just kinda chipped in. I was...let's see. Nineteen at the time. I'll admit, the diaper thing threw me for a while there, and having formula spit up on me wasn't exactly a treat." Then he grinned. "But the whole uncle bit really turned the girls on. Hell, every time I took Casey into town with me, they'd come on like a mob."

Misty rolled her eyes. "What a lovely image."

Morgan laughed, but then his laughter died. "Look, about what happened..."

"You already made yourself pretty clear, Morgan. I don't think we need to beat it into the ground. I said I'd leave in the morning, and I will."

He ignored that and sighed. "Malone, I care a lot about your sister. I wouldn't want her upset."

She could only stare at him. "You're worried I'll say something to Honey? What? Am I supposed to go tattle on you, is that it?"

Even in the dim light she could see the way he locked his jaw. "She wanted us to be friends."

"Good God!" she exclaimed, and when he frowned she added, "All right, forget the disbelief. For your information, I happen to love my sister."

"Glad to hear it."

"I wouldn't do *anything* to hurt her, and that includes disillusioning her about her new family." She poked him in the chest, her frustration level going right out the window. Her entire life was presently in the toilet, and Morgan Hudson was worried about her discretion? Ha!

"As far as I'm concerned, Honey can think we got along like best pals. But until I can get out of here tomorrow morning, stay the hell away from me."

She turned and stalked in, but at the door, she couldn't resist looking back one last time at Morgan.

He stood there in the moonlight, head tilted toward the dark sky, eyes closed, jaw clenched. His big hands were knotted into fists on his hips. Misty felt herself shiver, even though the evening was oppressively hot.

She knew then that he was right. Tomorrow morning she would leave Buckhorn behind. Hopefully, she'd think of somewhere to stay in the meantime.

She'd spent all her savings fighting the criminal conviction, and lost. She was homeless, out of a job and with no prospects.

And that was the least of her problems.

IF MORGAN HADN'T been lying there awake, his body frustrated, his mind disturbed by sensual images, he might not have heard it. But he hadn't slept a wink all night, too busy remembering the sweet taste of Misty, the way she'd felt pressed against him. Perfect. Willing. *Hot.* Though his head told him things had ended when they should, his imagination had insisted on conjuring up a different ending to the tale, and he'd been rock hard and hurting for more hours now than he cared to admit. It was like suffering the curse of wretched puberty all over again, and he had Misty Malone to thank for it.

The squeak came again, and Morgan recognized the sound as the porch swing that hung in the huge oak at the back of the house. Throwing off the sheet that covered him, he stalked naked to the open window and listened. His room was at one end of the house, opposite to Sawyer and Casey's, with the entire living quarters in between so they all had privacy.

Morgan's bedroom faced the lake, as did Sawyer's. As did the porch swing.

Someone was out there and his gut instinct told him it was Misty. He felt it in his bones, by the way his heart beat faster, by the way his stomach knotted. Only Misty had ever had that intense effect on him, and he figured it was mostly because he had to deny himself. If she wasn't related by marriage, if he could have spent a long, hot weekend with her, indulging all his cravings, he'd be able to get her out of his system.

But he couldn't, and that was the only reason for his obsession. He was sure of it.

Morgan saw that the moon hadn't completely set, even while dawn was struggling to break. He glanced at the clock, surprised to see it was barely five-thirty. What was she doing up so early, hanging around outside? Looking for more ways to torment him?

It took him a mere two seconds to decide to go see her.

He knew all the reasons he shouldn't, but something overrode them all, some basic need to spar with her one more time before the rest of the family would be there to pull him back.

He was still buttoning his favorite pair of worn, comfortable jeans, and wearing nothing else, when he stepped out of his room. At the last minute, he stopped, went back into his bedroom and then into his bathroom. He brushed his teeth, giving a disgusted glance at his morning beard and disheveled hair, then decided to hell with it and headed out. But when he passed the kitchen, he halted again and concluded a cup of coffee was definitely in order, if for no other reason than to help him get his bearings before facing her again. She threw him off balance with just a glance, and set his teeth on edge with blinding lust.

As he hurriedly measured the coffee, being careful to be quiet so he wouldn't wake anyone else, he thought about Misty and how she would look so early in the day, her dark hair still tousled, her eyes soft and warm. He imagined her still in her nightgown, something thin and slinky, and he almost dropped the carafe of water. The anticipation he felt was ridiculous, but real.

For at least a few hours this morning, he'd have her all to himself.

Jordan had an apartment above the garage and would be oblivious to anything and everything until at least ten o'clock. He liked to sleep late on the weekends, his only chance to catch up from his busy week.

Gabe might not even be back yet. He'd been surrounded by the single women of Buckhorn when last Morgan had seen him. But if he was home, his rooms in the basement would insulate him from the normal busy-house noises.

As for Sawyer, he was no doubt occupied with his bride. Morgan wouldn't be at all surprised if he didn't leave the bedroom all day. He grinned at that thought, remembering how Casey had told his father to feel free to linger, that he'd take care of all the chores for him.

Morgan was still grinning and feeling a little too anxious when he silently stepped outside with two steaming mugs of coffee. His bare feet didn't make a sound on the wet morning grass as he walked to the swing. It was a bit chilly, a heavy fog hanging over everything, which turned his first sight of Misty, her back to him, curled up on the swing, into a whimsical, almost ethereal picture. He was only two steps away from her when he heard her give a delicate sniff.

Everything masculine in him froze, and he experienced that incomparable dread men suffered when women turned to tears. He didn't know what to do. He strained to hear, hoping he'd misunderstood the sound, hoping she had a cold.

She sniffed again, then dabbed at her eyes with a wadded tissue. *Oh, hell.* Morgan felt a hard, curling ache around his heart and closed his eyes for a moment. The fact that her tears bothered him so much was a sure sign that things were out of control. Just physical attraction, he insisted to himself, despite his burgeoning sympathy and concern. Shoring up his nerve, he announced himself by clearing his throat.

Turning around so quickly she nearly upset the swing, Misty stared at him. She had glasses on, which he'd never seen before, and her hair was tied back with a plain elastic rubber band, long tendrils carelessly escaping. Even in the gray predawn light, he could see that she blushed.

Truth was, she looked like hell, and he hadn't thought such a thing was possible. Her nose was red and her eyes were hidden behind the reflection of the glasses. His simmering lust died a rapid death, not because of how she looked, but because he knew she was upset, and he was horribly afraid that *he* was the reason.

Not knowing what else to do, he held out one cup of coffee, for the moment ignoring her distress. "I heard the swing and figured you could use this."

She glanced at the cup as if it might hold arsenic. Morgan

sighed. "It's coffee. Lots of sugar and cream. I figured since Honey drank hers that way, you likely did, too."

She took the cup, sipped, then quietly thanked him. Without another word, she turned her head to stare toward the lake, which could barely be seen through the fog. She had simply and plainly dismissed him. Her wishes couldn't have been any more clear than if she'd come right out and said, *Go away.*

Nettled, Morgan pretended not to notice.

He moved to sit beside her, never mind that there wasn't really enough room. She quickly scrambled to get her legs out of the way, and it was then he noticed she was wearing a soft old cotton housecoat. No belt, just fat buttons all the way down the front. It looked loose and comfortable, like something that his sixty-year-old mother would wear when she wasn't feeling well. All the buttons were done up except the top one, and Misty clutched that small span of material together with a fist.

Morgan pushed a bare foot against the ground, making the swing sway gently, mindful of the coffee they each held. He kept his gaze on her profile. "You wear glasses."

She didn't answer him.

"I guess that answers the mystery of your big blue eyes, doesn't it? I always figured the color was a little too clear, a little too good to be real. Colored contacts?"

Her shoulders stiffened and she turned to him. Over the rim of the glasses, she glared and gave him a view of those perfect, clear, startling blue eyes, unadorned.

Morgan stared into her eyes, then whispered, "I guess I was wrong."

She turned away again, but muttered, "It's not the first time."

Ignoring that, he touched the rubber band sloppily knotted in her hair. "Rough night?"

One hand clutched the coffee mug, the other a damp tissue and the top of her housecoat. She hesitated, then slanted him another look over her wire-framed glasses. "If that's what you want to think, why not? I mean, you left before me, so it's entirely possible that once you were gone, I staged an orgy in that nice little gazebo you showed me.''

Morgan sipped his coffee while keeping his gaze on her. His free arm rested over the back of the swing, his fingers almost touching her. *Almost.* ''I somehow doubt your sister would have tolerated that.''

She started to jerk to her feet, but Morgan caught her elbow. ''No, don't let me run you off. I didn't come out here to harass you.''

''No, you came to see if I was ready to leave. Well, don't worry. As soon as it's light, I'll get dressed and go. I packed last night so I could get an early start. I just wanted to watch the sunrise first.''

Her words made him feel almost as bad as that time Jordan needed help treating an ornery mule and it kicked him in the gut, breaking two of his ribs. Morgan rubbed a hand over his chest, which didn't do a thing to help this particular ache, then muttered, ''It's for the best and you know it.''

''I'm not arguing with you, Morgan.''

''Good, because I didn't come out here to argue.''

''No? Then why?''

Hell, why *had* he come out? Whatever warped reasoning he'd used to justify his actions, he couldn't remember it now. Because he didn't have an answer, he tried changing the subject. ''You look like you're...upset.''

She shook her head in denial. ''No, not at all.''

But there was that tissue clutched in her hand, and her red nose and watery eyes. His conscience bothered him, and that had to be a first. In the normal course of things, he didn't bother with a guilty conscience. He was always rock certain of his decisions. ''I don't have anything personally against you, Malone.''

She snorted.

Morgan clenched his jaw, but he was determined to have his say. ''It'll be best for all concerned if you leave soon.''

She sighed, then turned to stare at him. ''Yeah, well, you

seem to be the only one who thinks so. Gabe spent half the night trying to talk me into hanging around, and Jordan even offered me a job.''

In angry disbelief, he said, ''You told them I asked you to leave?''

His anger didn't faze her. ''No. But they knew I'd go sooner or later.'' Then she mumbled, ''Though sooner seems to be on your personal agenda.''

Morgan struggled to control his temper. ''What did you tell Jordan?''

''That I'd think about it.''

His muscles bunched in infuriated reflex. He wanted her gone. He did *not* want her hanging around his brother. ''Like hell.''

She shrugged nonchalantly, egging him on. She had a habit of doing that, deliberately pricking his temper—and his lust. Hell, half the time he was around her he didn't know for sure what he felt, just that he felt it too keenly and he didn't like it one damn bit.

Jealousy of his brothers was a unique thing, but he absolutely couldn't bear the thought of Misty being with one of them. Besides, he knew if she hung around, they'd eventually be involved, he had no doubt about that at all. Acting on gut instinct, he said, ''Forget the job with Jordan. I'll pay you to go.''

Her mouth fell open and she stared at him.

''How much do you want?'' he asked, forcing the words out through his teeth.

''You're not serious.''

''Why not?'' He felt goaded and angry and out of control. He absolutely hated it. ''You'd use Jordan, taking his infatuation with you to finagle a job. Well, why not use me instead? Hell, at least I know what I'm getting into. So name a price.''

Her lips pinched shut, her eyes narrowed and an angry blush rose from her neck up. Then, as he watched, she gathered herself, and anger was replaced by deliberate belligerence. "Hmm, well now, I know what it was Jordan wanted in exchange for the job. But...exactly what would you expect in return for cash, Morgan? Or do I even need to ask?"

Her innuendo goaded his temper, but more than that, it stirred his desire for her, sending him right over the edge. He broke out in a sweat, his gut clenched, his body hardened. He reached for her, not even sure himself what he would do once he had hold of her. But she surprised him by her reaction. She leaped to her feet with a gasp. The coffee mug fell from her hand to the soft ground with a dull thud, spilling the coffee and rolling a few feet away. Misty covered her mouth with both hands. Her face was pale, and she swayed.

Morgan stood also and caught her to him, ignoring her feeble struggles. "Damn it, are you all right?" He shook her slightly, his alarm growing. "What the hell is wrong with you? Answer me, Malone."

Staring at him in horror, she opened her eyes wide and then pushed away, ran several feet to a line of bushes and dropped to her knees.

Morgan was dumbfounded. He started after her, but halted when he heard the unmistakable sound of retching. Never had he felt like such a complete and utter ass. He'd been harassing her again, when that hadn't been his intent at all. He'd argued with her after telling her he wouldn't. And she was sick. He made a false start toward her, then pulled back, as uncertain of what to do as he'd been on his very first date.

He'd hated the feeling then; at thirty-four, he hated it even more.

She probably drank too much last night, he thought, staring at her slim back as she jerked and shuddered. Some people just couldn't hold their liquor—though he didn't remember seeing her imbibe. Mostly she'd just danced and laughed and driven him crazy with an inferno of lust.

When she was done being sick, sitting there on her knees

on the damp ground, her arms wrapped around her stomach, he inched closer. He felt totally out of his element, not quite sure what to say or do. But he knew he had to do something. She kept her back to him, no doubt mortified. He knew women could be unaccountably funny about such things. Finally, feeling like a fool, he knelt behind her. "You want me to go get you something to drink?"

She moaned and clutched herself a little tighter. "Just... go...away."

Morgan hesitated, then lifted one hand to her shoulder, gently rubbing. Touching her made *him* feel immeasurably better, whether it did anything for her or not. "I bet Sawyer has something he could give you for the hangover."

She laughed, a raw, broken sound that was close to a moan. "A hangover, Morgan? When I didn't drink a single drop?"

Way off base with that one, obviously. He nodded. "Okay, not a hangover."

She shook her head, and more silky strands of midnight hair escaped her rubber band to curl around her cheeks. A few tangled in the armature of her glasses, and he gently pulled them away.

Without looking at him, she said, "You always think the worst of me, don't you?"

He didn't know what to say to that.

"I should be used to it. God knows, men always... Oh, just go away." Her voice was thin, washed out; she sounded too tired to argue.

He couldn't stop his deep frown or his concern. "If you're sick, then—"

Her hands fisted on her thighs in a sudden startling display of frustration. Still without looking at him, she hissed, "Damn it, why can't you just leave me alone?"

He wouldn't let her rile him again. "Look, Malone, my mother would skin my hide if I left a sick woman wallowing out in the dew, without—"

"I am not sick!"

Her stubbornness annoyed the hell out of him, even as he continued to gently stroke her back. ''Oh, then I'm hallucinating? That wasn't you just puking your guts up in my bushes? Because I have to tell you, Malone, if you're hoping to be a martyr to get my sympathy, it's not at all necessary. Hell, I already—''

She turned to him with a feral growl, momentarily startling him, then practically shouted, ''I am not sick, you idiot! *I'm pregnant.*''

CHAPTER THREE

OH, GOD. Misty stared at Morgan, horrified by her statement, and ready to be sick all over again. She slapped a hand over her mouth and gulped air through her nose, determined to hold it back. She'd thought the fresh air would help, and it really had, but then Morgan had joined her....

She frowned, her queasy stomach almost forgotten. It was all his fault, and she said, without the demonic tone this time, "I don't suppose you'll just forget I said that?"

Dumbly, he shook his head, his eyes still wide, his jaw still slack. For once he wasn't scowling. He looked too stunned to scowl. "Uh, no. Not likely."

Her temper snapped. "Oh, of course not. That would be too easy, wouldn't it?" She frowned ferociously, wishing she could hit him over his hard head. "Well, it's none of your business, anyway. And if you tell my sister, I swear I'll make you regret it."

Morgan's expression hadn't changed. It was a comical mix of surprise, chagrin and helplessness. Something else, too, something bordering on anger, but she couldn't be sure. He blinked, but didn't say a word. With a sound of disgust, Misty rolled her eyes and started to get to her feet. "Look, I'm sorry about your bushes. Really. Do you think anyone will notice?" Before he could answer, she added, "But in a way, you're the one to blame. If you hadn't kept prodding me... But that doesn't matter now. I'm feeling much better, fine, in fact, so I'll just go get dressed and get on my way. Please thank your brothers for me. And tell Honey I'll be in touch."

She was rattled, which accounted for the way she was blathering on and on. She wanted to bite her tongue off. She wanted more coffee.

She wanted away from Morgan Hudson.

He'd slowly stood when she had, and now he stepped in front of her, blocking her attempt at a strategic retreat. "I don't think so, Malone. You're not going to make a confession like that and then just creep off."

She was too tired, too mind weary to deal with him now. As if speaking to an idiot, she said, "I didn't exactly have creeping in mind. I thought I'd dress, pick up my bags, walk out the front door and drive away. There's a big difference."

"You were crying. Your eyes are all puffy."

He said it like a heinous accusation. She waved a negligent hand, not about to explain herself to *him.* "Don't be silly. I always look like hell in the morning. Lucky for you, you won't have to get used to it."

She started around him again, and this time he picked her up. She would have screamed her head off, she was so exasperated, except she sure as certain didn't want the other brothers witnessing her this way.

Gabe was such a comedian, he'd probably start joking about the whole thing. And Jordan, with that mesmerizing voice Honey claimed could put a cow to sleep, would do his best to comfort her, which would make her cry again.

And Sawyer—she had no idea how he'd react to his new wife's sister showing up pregnant.

So instead of screaming, she held herself stiff and tried to ignore how easily Morgan carried her, his incredible strength, the delicious way he smelled this morning and her twinge of ridiculous regret when he sat her on the swing.

It had been so long since she'd been held, so long since she'd felt anything like caring or concern or gentleness, she was almost starving for it. Even Morgan's aggressive, demanding concern felt like a balm.

But she was also more savvy now, and she knew beyond

a shadow of a doubt that Morgan Hudson was not a man to take comfort from.

"Uh, Morgan..."

Hands on his thighs, he leaned down in front of her until their noses nearly touched. "I'm going to go get you some juice. If you move so much as your baby toe before I get back, you won't be happy with my reaction. I mean it, Malone."

He looked more serious than she'd ever seen him. Not that she was afraid of him and his threats, but again, a ruckus might wake everyone else.

She turned her head away. "Bully."

"Damn right."

He sauntered off, but as if he hadn't trusted her to stay put, he was back in less than a minute. Misty hadn't moved, only because she was so tired. For weeks now she'd been trying to come up with a solution, but the problems just kept adding up, and she hadn't a clue what to do. Finding a job was obviously top of the list. Then she could sell her car to make the first month of rent once she found a place she could afford.

Borrowing money from her father was out of the question. She wouldn't ask him for a nickel. They had never been close and she knew without approaching him what his reaction to her most recent problems would be. Probably even worse than his reaction to her pregnancy, which predictably had been disappointment. He'd give her money, but that's all he'd ever give, never understanding or emotional support. She had enough to deal with without his overwhelming condemnation on her shoulders.

No, she'd rather go it alone than go to her father.

She was still frowning, deep in thought, when Morgan handed her a tall, cold glass of orange juice. The juice looked wonderful, and she accepted it gladly. Sipping, she said, "I thank you—at least for the drink."

Morgan seated himself beside her and crossed his long arms over his massive chest. With his dark frown and set jaw, he looked belligerent and antagonistic. She didn't like his attitude at all.

She liked him even less.

Knowing he hated it when she acted brazen, and hoping he'd go away and leave her alone with her misery, she said, "You know, you really should show a little more decorum. Running around half naked is almost barbaric. Especially for a man built like you."

He blinked in surprise, and his brows smoothed out. "A man built like me?"

"Yeah, you know." She glanced at his hard, hair-covered chest, felt a shot of heat straight through the pit of her stomach and raised her brows. "All muscle-bound. You do that to attract the women? Because while I appreciate the sight of your sexy body, I'm not at all attracted."

He narrowed his eyes. "Are you trying to distract me, Malone?"

She sighed. "No, I'm being honest. You're an incredibly good-looking man, Morgan. And evidently a pushy one, too. But I'm not interested in any man, for any reason. I'm through with the lot of you—for good. Besides, I'm leaving today, and with any luck, you'll be long married with kids of your own and moved away before I ever visit again." She nodded at his chest once more. "You're wasting the excellent display on the likes of me."

"Oh, I don't know about that, considering most of what you just said was bunk. You are interested—at least in me." His voice dropped, and he looked her over slowly. She felt the touch of his gaze like a stroke of heat, from the top of her thighs to the base of her throat. "Last night proved that."

Misty swallowed hard, feeling a new sensation in her belly that wasn't at all unpleasant. "Last night was an aberration. I've had a lot on mind and you took me by surprise."

He let that slide without comment. "The part about me moving out is true enough, though. But I won't be far. The house on the hill? That's mine. It'll be ready to move into soon."

She couldn't see the house from here, but she remembered admiring it when she first arrived. It wasn't quite as large as this one, but it was still impressive. She wondered if he already had the wife picked out, too, but didn't ask. "Good for you."

Tilting his head, his look still far too provocative, Morgan said, "I'm curious about this professed disinterest of yours, especially considering your condition."

"My *condition?*" She hated how he said that—just as her father had, just as her fiancé had—with something of a sneer. She wanted the baby and she wouldn't apologize for having it, not to anyone, and certainly not to him. "It's not a disease, you know."

His gaze hardened. "When're you getting married, Malone?"

The words were casual, almost softly spoken, but they sounded lethal. And his stare was so intent, so burning, she looked at his chest instead of meeting his eyes. "None of your business."

"I'm making it my business."

The juice did wonders for settling her nausea and she finally felt more herself. Morning sickness was the pits, and she hoped she got past that stage soon, though now that the worst had happened and she'd been sick in front of Morgan, anything else had to be an improvement. "You do that a lot, do you? Butt in where you've got no business being? I bet that's why you took the position of sheriff. It gives you a legal right to nose around into other people's affairs."

He looked off to the distance, and Misty, following his gaze, saw that the sun was beginning its slow climb into the sky. It was a beautiful sight, sending a crimson glow across the placid surface of the lake, bringing a visual warmth that had her feeling better already. She sighed, knowing she'd never forget this place and how incredibly perfect it seemed.

Then Morgan spoke again, reminding her of a major flaw to the peaceful setting. Him.

"We can sit here until everyone else joins us if you want, but I got the impression you're keeping your departure a secret."

She sighed again, actually more of a huff. "You've got no right to badger me about something that is none of your damn business, Morgan."

"You're family now," he explained with a straight face. "That gives me all the rights I need."

Something that ludicrous deserved her undivided attention. She stared at him, almost speechless, but not quite. "*Family?* Get real."

He looked her over slowly, and she knew, even before he told her, that he was making a point. "Oh, you're family, all right, because if you weren't, we'd never have left that damn gazebo, that is, not until things ended in a way that we'd both have enjoyed. A lot."

The tone of his voice, both aggressive and persuasive, sank into her bones. Her stomach flip-flopped and her toes curled. Damn him, how could he do this to her now, when she'd just been sick, when she didn't like him, when he didn't much care for her? It wasn't fair that of all the men in all the world, Morgan Hudson had this singular effect on her.

But then, little in her life had been fair lately.

She shook her head, denying both him and herself. "You're twisting things around—"

"I'm stating a fact."

"The fact is that you want me as far from your family as you can manage!"

His shrug was negligent, but his gaze was hard. "As you pointed out, everyone else feels differently. Jordan even offered you a job."

"Which I refused."

His brows shot up. "You did?"

He sounded surprised, but then, she had been purposely

harassing him by letting him think otherwise. That had been childish, and not at all smart. She sighed. "Of course I did."

"Why?"

Exasperated by his suspicious tone, she explained, "This'll be a shock, I'm sure, but I'm not the party girl you seem to think I am, Morgan. I realize both your brothers were likely just fooling around, but I don't intend to take any chances. I'm not interested in fun and games, and as I already told you, I'm even less interested in being serious with someone. I didn't want to accidentally encourage either of them, so I thanked Jordan for the offer, but declined, and I told Gabe I had other responsibilities and couldn't hang around any longer. So you can relax your vigil. Both your brothers are safe from my evil clutches."

He didn't react to her provocation this time, choosing instead to hark back to his earlier question. "When are you getting married?"

He wouldn't give up, she could tell. He looked settled in and disgruntled and determined. She was so tired of fighting men, her ex-fiancé, her ex-boss, even the damn lawyers and the judge. Maybe once she told Morgan everything, he'd be glad to be rid of her. She slumped into her seat, all fight gone. "I give up. You win."

He didn't gloat, and he didn't sound exactly pleased with himself. He was simply matter-of-fact in his reply. "I always do." Then more quietly, "When are you getting married?"

"I'm not." She felt him studying her and she twisted to face him so she could glare right back. "I'm not getting married, okay? There's no groom, no wedding, no happily ever after. Satisfied now?"

There was a sudden stillness, then Morgan relaxed, all the tension ebbing out of him, his breathing easier, his expression less stern. She hadn't even realized he was holding himself so stiffly until he returned to his usual cocky self. He uncrossed his arms to spread one over the back of the swing, nearly touching her shoulder, and he shifted, all his big muscles sort of loosening and settling in.

In a tone meant to clarify, he asked, "You're *not* getting married?"

"What, do you want it written in blood? I'm not getting married. The very idea is repugnant. I have absolutely no interest in marriage."

"I see." The aggression was gone, replaced by something near to sympathy, and to Misty, that was even worse. "What happened to the father of the baby?"

Why not, she thought, fed up with fending him off. "He found out he was going to be a father and offered me money for an abortion." She wouldn't look at him. The humiliation and pain she'd felt that day was still with her. It had been the worst betrayal ever—or so she'd thought, until she'd lost her job. "I refused, he got angry, and we came to an agreement."

"What agreement?"

"I wouldn't bother him with the baby, and he wouldn't bother with me."

The swing kept moving, gently, lulling her, and though Morgan was silent, it didn't feel like a condemning silence as much as a contemplative one. Finally he asked, "How long have you been sick in the mornings?"

"Only for a few weeks. And before you ask, yes, I'll tell Honey. But not now. She has a tendency to worry about me, to play the role of big sister even though I'm only a year younger than her. She's so happy with Sawyer now, she doesn't need to hear about my problems just yet."

His fingers gently touched her hair, smoothing it. It was clearly a negligent touch, as if he did it without thought. When she glanced at him, she saw he was watching her closely.

"Will the baby be a problem?"

"No! I want the baby."

His gaze softened. "That's not what I mean."

Lifting her chin, she said, "If you're asking me if I'll be

a good mother, I hope so. I don't have much experience, but I intend to do my absolute best.''

''No, I wasn't accusing you of anything or questioning your maternal instincts.'' He smiled slightly. ''I just wonder if you know what you're getting into. Babies are a full-time job. How do you intend to work and care for it, too, without any help?''

She shook her head. Since she didn't even have a job at present, she didn't have an answer for him.

''Will you be able to get a leave of absence?''

The irony of that question hit her and she all but laughed. Instead, she turned her face away so he couldn't see how lost she felt.

Morgan touched her cheek. ''Malone?''

''Isn't this interrogation about over?''

''I don't think so. So why don't you make it easy on yourself and just answer my questions?''

''Somehow I don't think this conversation is going to be easy on me no matter what I do.''

He got quiet over that. ''I don't mean to make things difficult for you.''

''Don't you?''

''I didn't create this situation, Malone, and the attraction isn't one-sided. Will you at least admit that much?''

She didn't want to, but saw no point in denying it. ''Yeah, so? I think the fact I'm pregnant and without a groom shows my judgment to be a bit flawed, so don't let it go to your head.''

His large hand cupped the back of her skull, his fingers gently kneading. The tenderness, after his previous attitude, was startling. ''Everyone makes a mistake now and then. You're not the first.''

''Which mistake are we referring to? Me being pregnant, or my response to you?''

Again, he was quiet.

She decided to make a clean break, to finish her confessions and get away before she became morose again. She slapped her palms on her thighs, turned to him with a take-charge air and said, "Okay. You've worn me down. Besides, the sun is almost completely up. Everyone will be waking soon, and I hope to get out of here before that. I'd just as soon avoid the lengthy goodbyes if I can. So tell me, Sheriff, what other intrusive questions do you have for me before I'm formally dismissed?"

Again, he easily ignored her sarcasm. "How far along are you? You sure as certain don't look pregnant."

She laughed shortly. "Yeah, just think, if I did look pregnant we probably wouldn't be having this conversation right now!"

"Malone?"

"Three months." She gave him a crooked grin. "From what I understand, I may not start to show until my fifth, maybe even my sixth month. By then, I'll be a distant memory for you, Morgan."

"But you're sure you are—"

"Had the test, so yes, I'm sure. Besides, I feel the pregnancy in other ways."

His gaze went unerringly to her breasts, now thoroughly hidden beneath her sexless robe. Still, she practically squirmed with the need to shield herself with her hands. She resisted the telltale reaction. "Yep, I'm bigger now," she said, doing her best to sound flippant, unaffected. Trying not to blush. Her glasses slipped a bit, and she pushed them back up.

"What about your job?"

Hedging, she asked, "What about it?"

"It occurs to me that I don't know all that much about you."

Her eyes widened and she laughed. "Now there's a revelation for you. Of course, anytime you don't know something, you just fill it in with fiction."

He touched her cheek with the back of one finger and his expression was regretful. "I admit to making some pretty hasty assumptions. But you haven't helped, Misty, coming on the way you did."

"I didn't—"

"Yeah, you did." He smiled just a little, making her heart twist. "You flirt with everyone."

She sighed. "True enough. I was trying to act cheerful and worry-free so Honey wouldn't suspect anything. Maybe I overdid it just a bit."

"And maybe I want you bad enough that all you have to do is breathe and it seems like a seduction. At least to me."

Her gaze shot to his face; she was speechless.

"It's true, you know. I don't think I've ever wanted a woman the way I do you." His hand opened and his palm cupped her cheek. "Even now, with you looking like a maiden aunt and after you tossed your cookies in the bushes. Even knowing you're pregnant with another man's baby, I still want you."

She shook her head, words beyond her.

"I know. It's a damnable situation, isn't it?"

"No, it's not." She was resolute, driven by her emotional fear. "I'm leaving, this morning, right now if you'll just stop questioning me and let me leave without a fuss."

"It's not that easy, Malone, now that I know you're in trouble."

"Such an old-fashioned sentiment! Unmarried pregnant women are no longer in *trouble.* They're just...pregnant." She gave a negligent shrug.

"All right, if you say so." He looked far from convinced. "So quit hedging and reassure me. Where do you work?"

Knowing that, as sheriff, it would be easy enough for him to check, and not doubting for a moment that he probably would, she sniffed and said, "I only recently left Vision Videos."

"Vision Videos?"

"A small, privately owned video store. It's located in the town I...used to live in." She sincerely hoped he missed her small hesitation. The idea of being homeless was still pretty new to her. "It's very small scale, only three employees besides the owner, but the store did incredible business. He'd planned to open another location by the end of the summer and I was going to run it for him."

"But you're not now?"

"Now, I'm in the process of reevaluating my options."

He stared, and his softly stroking fingers went still. With disbelief ringing from every word, he said, "You're unemployed?"

"Momentarily, yes."

His eyes narrowed. "By choice? Because I'll tell you, if your boss fired you for being pregnant, that's against the law...."

"No, he didn't fire me for that."

Morgan's back stiffened, and his scowl grew darker. "But he did fire you?"

"Actually...yes."

"Why?"

"He...well, he accused me of doing something I didn't do."

"Damn it, Malone," he suddenly burst out, his irritation evident, his patience at an end. "It's like pulling snake teeth to get you to tell the whole—"

"All right!" She shot to her feet, every bit as annoyed as he was. Hands on her hips, she faced him. "All right, damn it. I was convicted of stealing from him. Three hundred dollars. But I didn't do it, only they believed that I did!"

Morgan stood, too, and now he looked livid. "They?"

She waved a hand. "The owner, the lawyer I had to hire, the despicable judge. Everyone."

Very slowly, Morgan reached out and took hold of her shoulders. "Tell me what happened."

Misty had no idea if he was angry with her or the situation. She tried to shrug his hands away, but he held on. Her temper was still simmering, though, and she was in no mood for his attitude, so she jerked away and then sat on the swing, giving a hard kick to make it move. Morgan grabbed the swing to stop it and sat beside her. "I'm waiting."

She crossed her arms over her breasts. He made her feel vulnerable and defensive when she had no reason to feel either one. "Not long after I found out I was pregnant and Kent, my ex, bailed out, I was at work and the cash came up short. The woman who'd worked before me had signed out and made her deposit, so the money had to have been taken during my shift. Only I didn't take it and I don't know where it went. I was in the bathroom—" She glanced at him. "Pregnant women spend a lot of time in the bathroom."

He made a face. "Go on."

"Anyway, there was no one in the store, so I made a quick run to the bathroom, and when I came back out, my boss and his girlfriend were just coming in. He was royally ticked that I'd left the counter, even after I explained that the store was empty and that I'd hurried. We argued, because he said I'd missed too much work lately, as well. See, I'd come in late twice, because of the morning sickness. Anyway, he was in a foul mood and being unreasonable, to my mind. I'd never been late or missed work before. Not ever. That's why he was going to make me a manager of the new store, because I was a good worker and dependable and all that."

"Get to the point, Malone."

She wanted to smack him. Instead, she said, "He checked the drawer and found out the money was missing. I still can't believe he accused me of stealing it. I'd been working for him for two years. I did everything, from inventory to decorations to promotion to sales to orders. I'm the one that helped that business do so well! I thought he trusted me."

"He called the cops?"

"Yes." The police had arrived, and she now knew firsthand the procedure used for thiefs. She shuddered with the memory, which wasn't one she intended to share with Morgan. "To make a long story short, the lawyer I hired said they had a good case against me. I was the only one in the store at the time the money was taken, and they found out I was pregnant, that the father of the baby had taken off. They painted me a desperate woman, with plenty of motive to take the money. He suggested I plead guilty to save myself a bundle in lawyer fees and court costs. I...I refused. So my lawyer suggested that I go with a trial to the bench, since that would get it over with quickly."

"I gather that wasn't the best decision possible?"

She shook her head. "A jury might not have been so autocratic or sexist."

"Sexist?"

"Yes. The judge was a stern-faced old relic who saw me as a femme fatale just because I'm young and I don't exactly look like a college professor."

One brow shot up, and his mouth quirked. "You mean because you're sexy as hell and he noticed?"

"That's not funny, Morgan."

"No, it's not. Sorry."

He still looked amused, though, which annoyed her no end. The judge's reaction to her had been salt in the wound. She could still remember how exposed she'd felt, standing before him.

She looked away and said quietly, "He gave me six months probation, made me pay back the three hundred dollars I hadn't even taken, as well as court costs and legal fees, then finished up with a scathing lecture about my responsibilities and morals and hoping I'd learned my lesson." She snorted. "The lesson I learned was that men see things one way, which is seldom the right or honorable way, and they sure as hell can't be trusted."

"Misty..."

"Don't use that tone on me, Morgan Hudson. You got what you wanted, all the nitty-gritty details. Well, now I'm done. I want to get out of here. I need to go find a job, and I'm just plain not up to fighting with you anymore, so if you'll excuse me—"

"No."

"No?" Incredulous, she turned to face him. "What do you mean, no?"

He stood, then caught her arm and pulled her to her feet. Still holding her, his gaze intent on her face, he said softly, "I mean you're not going anywhere, Malone. You're going to stay right here."

CHAPTER FOUR

MORGAN STARED at Misty, knowing that despite her outraged frown, there was no way he could let her go, not now. Her shoulders felt narrow and frail beneath his big hands, and he wished like hell she looked pregnant, so she'd be easier to resist. But she didn't. She looked soft and sexy, even with a red nose and those hideous glasses. He wanted her more than ever, but that was beside the point.

At least she wasn't planning on getting married. Though it wasn't any of his damn business, the very idea had set his teeth on edge. She could certainly do better than settling for some clown who didn't want his own child. He swore to himself that was the only reason it bothered him. Then he called himself a fool.

"You can't be off on your own right now. You said it yourself, you don't have a job, and you're sick."

She gave him a blank stare, as if he was a stranger.

"Damn it, Misty, you know I'm right!"

"I know you're nuts, that's what I know." He made a grumbling sound, and she said in exasperation, "It's morning sickness, Morgan, that's all. I'm fine the rest of the time. I'm perfectly capable of finding and working a job. Pregnant woman do it all the time, you know."

Actually, his mind was buzzing with possibilities. If she stayed—and she would because he didn't intend to give her a choice—he could give her a job. He'd long since figured they needed someone to answer the phones at the office, but more often than not folks just called him directly. It was a small county, and the crime level was amazingly low, so he'd been in no rush to hire a new deputy. But a secretary of sorts, someone to keep track of his schedule and forward calls and take notes, that'd be a blessing.

He'd put off the hiring for some time now. He hadn't really wanted anyone else mucking around his offices. But now…

He eyed her belligerent expression and winced. Better to tell her about the job later, when she wasn't so annoyed with him. He gave her a slight shake. "So what do you intend to do?"

"I intend to punch you in the nose if you don't stop manhandling me!"

His fingers flexed on her shoulders, very gently, and he saw her eyes darken. He hadn't hurt her, would never deliberately hurt her. No, her complaint was for an entirely different reason. "Manhandling, huh?" he asked softly. "And here I thought I was being all that was considerate and caring."

She bit her lip in indecision, then resolutely shook her head. "Not likely, Morgan. You're up to something, I just haven't figured out what yet."

Her opinion of him was far from flattering, with good reason, he supposed. He dropped his hands and turned to think, only to hear her stomping away. He caught the back of her robe and drew her up short. "Whoa. Now where are you off to? We have to finish discussing this."

Through gritted teeth, she said, "There's no *we* to it, and there's nothing to discuss." She swatted his hands away and jutted her chin toward him. "I'm going in to shower and dress, and then I'm leaving. You won't have to worry about me at all, and your precious brothers will be safe from my lascivious tendencies."

Damn it, she was trying to make him feel guilty—and succeeding. "You let me think the worst about that, Malone. Admit it."

"You always assume the worst," she argued. "I'm not responsible for the way your mind works."

"No, you're not. But in a way, it is your fault." She looked ready to erupt, so he added, "I get around you, Malone, and I can barely think at all, much less with any logic. In case you haven't noticed, I've got the hots for you in a really bad way."

Her face went blank for a split second, and he braced himself for an attack. Then suddenly her mouth twitched, and she burst out laughing. "Is that your way of saying you're sorry?"

Hearing her laugh was nice, even if she was laughing at him. "I suppose you think I owe you that much?"

"Nope." Her glasses slid down her nose and more hair escaped the rubber band. She looked disheveled and vulnerable and so damn female he felt rigid from his neck all the way down to his toes. "I don't think you owe me a darn thing, Morgan, except to butt out of my business."

Shrugging in apology, he whispered, "I can't do that."

"You," she said with emphasis, "have no choice in the matter."

"I can help you, Malone."

"You want to help?" She turned away from him, then said over her shoulder, "Leave me be."

Why, Morgan wondered as she stalked away, would she steal money from an employer, but not take money from him when it was freely offered? Especially considering the situation she was in. And not only had she refused the money, she'd been downright livid over the idea. Somehow it didn't fit, and he damn well intended to find out what was going on.

Later. Right now he was busy plotting. She had turned down the money, but maybe she'd accept his help in other ways once he talked her into staying. He wasn't raised to turn his back on a woman in her predicament, especially considering that she *was* part of the family. Whether she liked it or not, that excuse was good enough for him.

He picked up the coffee mugs and her empty juice glass, then headed into the kitchen. He had a few things to take care of before she finished showering, so he might as well get to them. First was that ragtag little car of hers. Removing a few spark plugs ought to do the trick. Getting his brothers out of bed would be a little harder, considering the night they'd all had, but they would rally together for a good cause, and he definitely considered Misty Malone a good cause. Given how all his brothers had doted on her the past couple of weeks, he had no doubt they'd feel the same.

Twenty minutes later, Morgan was sitting at the kitchen table with a bleary-eyed Casey when Misty walked in. The others hadn't quite made it that far yet, but Morgan knew they'd present themselves shortly.

Casey, with his head propped in his hand, glanced at her and yawned. "Morning, Misty. What're you doing up so early?"

Misty stopped dead in her tracks. Her hair was freshly brushed and twisted into a tidy knot on the top of her head that Morgan thought made her look romantic and amazingly innocent. Her glasses were gone—thank God—and she no longer had a red nose. She wore a yellow cotton camisole with cutoff shorts and strappy little sandals and she looked good enough to eat.

Morgan drew in a shuddering breath with that image and steered his wayward thoughts off the erotic and onto the essential.

Rather than answer Casey, her accusing gaze swung toward Morgan and there was murder in her eyes. He grinned. He'd rather have her fighting mad than looking morose any day. Leaning against the counter with his arms crossed over his chest, Morgan said, "What's with the suitcase, Malone?"

Casey, who hadn't noticed the luggage yet, sat up straight. His gaze bounced back and forth several times between the suitcase and Misty's face, and he looked more alert than he had only five seconds ago. "You're not leaving, are you?"

Misty ground her teeth, then whipped around to face Casey with a falsely bright smile plastered in place. "'Fraid so, kiddo. I have things to do. But I did enjoy my visit. Tell your dad thanks for me, okay?"

She started to move, but Casey jumped up, looking panicked, and all but blocked her way. "But Dad'll kill me if you leave without saying goodbye! I mean, Honey will be upset and that'll upset Dad. Just hang around for breakfast, okay?" He glanced at Morgan for backup. "Tell her, Uncle Morgan. Shouldn't she stay and have breakfast?"

Morgan nodded slowly. "I do believe you're right, Casey."

"Ah, no... It's better if I—"

The kitchen door swung open and Jordan dragged himself in. He was wearing a pair of unsnapped jeans and scratching his belly while yawning hugely. His hair was still mussed and he looked like he could have used another six hours of sleep, at least. The last Morgan had seen him last night, three of the local women were trying to talk him into taking each of them home. It was a hell of a predicament for his most reserved brother.

Morgan had not one whit of sympathy for him.

Because Jordan had taken the path from the garage—where he kept his apartment—to the kitchen, the bottoms of his feet were wet. When he saw Misty packed up and ready to go, he nearly slipped on the linoleum floor in his surprise.

Morgan caught him, then pushed him upright. If Jordan knocked himself out, he'd be no help at all.

In his usual mellow tones, Jordan asked, "What's going on here?" He dried his feet on a throw rug while quietly studying everyone in turn.

Morgan feigned a casual shrug. "Misty says she's leaving."

Casey crossed his arms, ready to add his two cents' worth. "She's not even going to tell anyone goodbye."

Looking from Casey's disapproving face to Misty's red cheeks before finally meeting Morgan's gaze, Jordan frowned. Not a threatening frown, as Morgan favored, but rather a contemplative one. Jordan was no dummy and caught on quickly that this was the reason he'd been summoned from his bed. He fastened his jeans now that he knew there was a lady present, then took several cautious steps forward, making certain not to slip again. Holding Misty's shoulders, he asked softly, "What's wrong, sweetheart? Why are you sneaking off like this?"

Morgan didn't like his brother's intimate tone at all. And he sure as hell didn't like Jordan touching her. He glowered at Misty as he said, "I don't think she wanted anyone to know she was going."

Jordan glanced at Morgan, then crossed his arms over his chest and regarded Misty with quiet speculation. "Is that true?"

After a long, drawn out sigh, Misty dropped her heavy bag and propped her hands on her hips. "I'm not sneaking, exactly. You all knew I was going to be leaving today."

Gabe spoke from the doorway where he'd negligently propped himself, unnoticed. "Not true." He gave Morgan a look, then came into the kitchen and dropped into a chair with a theatrical yawn. He, too, was bare-chested, but he wore loose cotton pull-on pants. "You said you couldn't stay, Misty, but you didn't say a damn thing about taking off today at six-thirty in the morning. Hell, the birds aren't even awake yet, so I'd definitely call that sneaking. What's up, sweetheart?"

Misty looked ready to expire. Morgan took pity on her and pulled out a chair. "Why don't you at least sit down, Malone, while you do your explaining?" He reached for her arm, but she sidestepped him. Breathing hard, she glared at them all, then said, "I'm leaving, that's all there is to it. I'm already packed and I want to get an early start. I'm not good at long goodbyes, so...if you'll excuse me?"

She picked up her bag and headed for the door. Her car was parked at the side of the house, close to the back door. There was a flurry of arguments from Casey, Jordan and

Gabe, but Morgan had expected no less of them. It was why he'd so rudely dragged them out of their warm, comfortable beds. Unfortunately, Misty wasn't going to be swayed by them.

She stormed out of the house in righteous fury, and they all trailed behind, talking at once. Morgan listened to their arguments for why she should stay and even commended his brothers for making some good points.

Misty did an admirable job of ignoring them.

When Jordan realized how serious she was, he took the suitcase from her hand while stabbing Morgan with curious looks, as if waiting for *him* to stop her somehow.

Morgan almost laughed. He'd known there was no way he'd be able to bring her around. If he wasn't missing his guess, he was the biggest reason she was so set on going. That was why he'd pulled the spark plugs, as insurance until he got her over her pique and could make her see reason.

After Jordan stowed her suitcase in the back seat, he reached for Misty and pulled her into a fierce hug. To Morgan, seething at the sight of Misty snuggled up against Jordan's bare chest, the embrace didn't look at all familial. He was just about to tear them apart when Jordan leaned back the tiniest bit to look at her.

"Where will you be staying?" Jordan asked. "Is there a number where we can call you?"

Misty appeared stumped for just a moment, which made Morgan very suspicious, then she brightened. "I'm sort of moving around at the moment. But I'll let you know when I get settled, okay?"

Morgan continued to study her. It was amazing, even to him, but he could read her like a book, and he knew without a doubt she didn't have any place to stay. He wanted to throttle her, and he wanted to hold her tight.

Gabe stepped up next for his own hug, and he even dared to kiss her on the cheek, lingering for what Morgan considered an inappropriate amount of time. Morgan gave serious thought to throwing Gabe back into the basement. "If you change your mind,'' Gabe said, ''promise you'll come back.''

''I promise. And thank you.''

Casey shook his head. ''My death will be on your hands, because Dad is still going to kill me.''

Morgan silently applauded Casey's forlorn expression, but Misty didn't buy it. She actually grinned. ''Your father wouldn't hurt a hair on your head, and you know it! Now give me a hug.'' With a crooked smile, Casey obeyed.

And even that made Morgan grind his teeth. Casey was a good head taller than Misty with shoulders much wider. Morgan didn't like it at all. Hell, so far they'd all touched her more than he had!

Misty didn't even bother looking at Morgan. He crossed his arms and waited until she'd gotten behind the wheel and pulled her door shut, then he leaned back against a tall oak tree. He considered himself patience personified.

Jordan stepped up to him with an intent frown. It was unlike Jordan to be so disgruntled, and Morgan raised a taunting brow. ''Sorry to see her go?''

Jordan didn't rile easily. ''You got me out of bed just to tell her goodbye? I figured you'd stop her somehow. Honey's going to be damn upset when she finds out we let her leave.''

Morgan eyed his brother a moment longer, decided he didn't see any signs of lovesickness, and turned to stare at Misty. ''She's not going anywhere.''

Misty gave one final cheery wave to them all and turned the key. The engine ground roughly, whined, but didn't quite turn over. Frowning, she tried again. The car still wouldn't start.

Satisfied, Morgan watched Gabe saunter over to him, Casey at his side. ''You tinkered with her car?'' He sounded faintly approving. Gabe was the mechanic and handyman in the family. If he'd thought of it or had had time, he likely would have done the same.

Morgan gave him a wounded look. ''Now, would I do a

thing like that? I'm the law around here, Gabe, you know that. Tampering with a car is illegal.'' He looked at Misty with a smile. ''I'm sure of it.''

Grinning, Gabe went to the driver's window and tapped on it. When Misty rolled down her window, he said, ''Doesn't sound like she's going to start, hon.''

Misty dropped her head onto the steering wheel and ignored Gabe, ruthlessly twisting the key once again. She looked so forlorn that Morgan almost couldn't stand it. He wanted to lift her out of the car, hold her, tell her everything would be okay. He wanted, damn it, to take care of her. To protect her.

Because she was family.

Because she was a woman in need.

Because it was the right thing to do.

Not because he cared for her personally. Wanting a woman and caring for her were two different things, and he was never one to confuse the issues. Yes, he wanted her, more so now than ever, which seemed odd in the extreme. But he could deal with that. What he couldn't deal with was the idea of her running off with no place to go, and the fact that she'd be alone at a time when she needed family most.

So maybe she'd gotten into some trouble? He wasn't completely convinced yet. But even if it was true, everyone made mistakes, and being a pregnant, unmarried woman was as good a reason for theft as any he'd ever heard. He didn't approve, but he did understand. She was still young, only twenty-four, and she'd found herself in a hell of a predicament.

From the sound of it, she'd more than paid for the crime, not only financially, but emotionally, as well. He didn't blame her for not wanting to own up to it if she was guilty. Few people tended to brag about their bad judgment.

Convinced that he was still in control of things, including his own tumultuous emotions, Morgan walked over to the car and opened the back door. He lifted out her bag then nudged Gabe aside. He pulled her door open and cupped his free hand around her upper arm. Gabe stood there grinning at him, while Jordan and Casey watched with satisfaction.

"C'mon, Malone," Morgan said. "Sitting out here moping isn't going to solve anything."

She smacked her head onto the steering wheel again. "I can't be this unlucky."

Morgan hesitated, but he knew damn good and well he'd done the right thing. He'd needed to buy some time to undo the damage he'd inflicted with his insistence that she should leave. Later, she'd thank him. "Rattling your brains won't help. Come inside and we'll figure something out."

She leaned back in the seat and stared at him. "I hope you're happy now."

His smile was only fleeting before he wiped it away. "I'm getting there." He urged her out of the car and kept hold of her arm even as they walked back in. He was pleased that she didn't pull away from him. That surely showed some small measure of trust, didn't it?

Unfortunately, something he *hadn't* figured on happened: they found Sawyer and Honey smooching in the kitchen, wrapped up together in no more than a sheet.

Morgan halted abruptly when he saw them, which caused Misty to stumble into his side and Jordan to bump into his back. Like dominoes toppling one another, they all ended up crammed into the tiny doorway, gawking.

Misty groaned at the sight of her sister, then turned her face into Morgan's side. "I'm cursed."

At her softly spoken words, Honey jerked away from her husband, looked up, then blushed furiously. "Oh, Lord." She clutched at the sheet, pulling it up to her throat and all but leaving Sawyer buck naked. "It's barely six-thirty! We thought everyone was still in bed!"

Sawyer grabbed for an edge of the sheet to retain his modesty in front of Misty, then turned to frown at his brothers. "What the hell is going on?" He noticed the suitcase

Morgan held, and his expression altered. ''You going somewhere, Morgan?''

Standing on tiptoe, Casey attempted to see over Morgan's shoulder, then stated, ''Misty was going to leave, but Morgan stopped her.''

Sawyer glanced at his wife, then blinked at his son. His confusion was amusing, if unfortunate. ''Leave where?''

''I don't know.'' Casey gave an elaborate shrug. ''Home, I guess, though she said she's in the middle of moving somewhere and she'd have to tell us where exactly after she got settled. I tried to stop her, Dad, honest, but she was determined—''

Morgan felt Misty tremble and said, ''That's enough, Case.'' Then to Sawyer: ''Just a misunderstanding. What are you two doing out here? We thought you'd...sleep in...till at least noon.''

Grinning like a rogue, Sawyer announced, ''We needed nourishment.''

Honey turned bright pink and elbowed her husband, who grabbed her and kissed her hard on the mouth. Morgan couldn't help but smile at them. Though Sawyer had fought it hard, he was so crazy in love with Honey, it was fun to watch them.

Morgan wanted a relationship like that. Then he thought of Misty beside him, the exact opposite of her sister, and he scowled.

Jordan shoved his way past the others. ''If you two newlyweds want to go back to bed, I'll bring you a tray in just a few minutes. Coffee and bagels?''

''Perfect.'' Sawyer tried to turn Honey around, but she wasn't budging.

''Misty?'' Honey looked oblivious to Sawyer's efforts. ''You were going to leave without telling me?''

There was no mistaking her hurt, and although Morgan wouldn't have put Misty through such an ordeal, he decided it was probably best to get it all out in the open at once.

The sooner Misty got through it, the sooner she could understand that she didn't need to leave.

He was surprised and pleased when he felt Misty's hand slip into his, and he squeezed her fingers tight, then answered for her. "Well, she's not going anywhere right now because her car won't start. You don't have to worry."

Honey's brows shot up. "Her car won't start?" She sent a suspicious look at Gabe. "Did you tamper with her car like you did mine?"

Gabe straightened from his sleepy, slouched position and crossed his heart with dramatic flair. "Never touched it. Hell, I just got up. I'm not awake enough to be playing with engines."

Jordan spoke before Honey could turn her cannons on him. "Same here. I didn't even know she was planning to leave until I saw her with her suitcase."

Misty stared at her sister, and Morgan could feel her tensing. "They tampered with your car?"

Honey shrugged. "I wanted to leave, because I thought I was intruding and putting them all in danger. But they weren't worried, and they thought it'd be better if I stayed here with them. They knew I couldn't very well leave without transportation, so they kept my car disabled. I thought Gabe was fixing it for me, but instead he was making sure it wouldn't run if I tried to sneak off." Honey smiled at her husband, then added, "Their intentions were good, so I forgave them."

Misty pulled her hand away and slowly turned to glare at Morgan. Her eyes were dark with accusation and anger. "Did you ..?"

Shrugging, he said, "You didn't exactly leave me a lot of choice."

Her gasp was so loud she sounded as if someone had pinched her. She drew back her arm and slugged him in the stomach, gasped again, then shook her hand and glared at him. "How dare you!"

He tried to rub the sting out of her hand, but she held it

protectively away from him. Morgan frowned at that. "You wouldn't listen," he said by way of explanation. He was more than a little aware of their rapt audience, but saw no way around it. Damn it, she was Honey's sister, and she'd been preparing to slip off without a job, without money....

He'd never heard a woman growl so ferociously before. Everyone was frozen, silent. Misty looked as if she might hit him again, then thought better of it. Her expression was angry but resolute. "Fine. I'm calling a cab. He can take me to the bus station."

Morgan glared at her. "Don't push me, Malone."

"You've done all the pushing, you—you...!"

"Bastard?" he supplied helpfully.

She growled again. "Fix my car!"

"No." He crossed his arms over his chest.

Sawyer, ever the diplomat, cleared his throat. "Uh, Morgan..."

Still matching Misty glare for glare, Morgan shook his head. "She can't leave, Sawyer, all right?"

"Why?"

Gabe spoke. "If she's that set on going—"

"I'd prefer she stay, too," Jordan added, "but—"

Morgan closed his eyes, trying to think of some way around the problems. Nothing too promising presented itself. When he met Misty's gaze this time, he knew she could read his purpose.

"Don't you do it, Morgan," she warned.

He touched her cheek and gave her a small, regretful smile. "I'm sorry, sweetheart." Then he turned to everyone else and announced, "I don't want her to go, because she's pregnant."

The reaction wasn't quite what he'd expected. Honey's mouth fell open, Gabe and Jordan both became mute, Casey's neck turned red, and Sawyer leaned on the counter with a sigh, holding tight to his share of the sheet.

Misty went ahead and hit him again. He took hold of her hands before she hurt herself. This time she didn't pull away, but chose instead to stare at him with evil intent. He supposed she'd rather look at him than face everyone else. If he could have thought of a way to spare her, he would have.

Then Morgan realized no one was looking at Misty. They were all staring at him—with accusation. It was almost too funny for words.

"*I'm* not the father," he said dryly. "Hell, I've only known her a couple of weeks, if you'll recall."

Sawyer coughed. "That's actually quite long enough."

"In this case, it wasn't!"

Everyone relaxed visibly. Honey said to Morgan, "Well, of course she can't leave, you're right about that. Hang on to her until I get back, okay?" Then she took off like a shot, dragging Sawyer along with her, given that they shared the sheet and he didn't want to be left bare-assed.

Gabe sat down at the table and relaxed, at his leisure. "All this excitement has made me hungry. Jordan, if you're fixing breakfast, make some for me, too."

Jordan nodded and began pulling out pans. "Might as well skip the bagels and go for pancakes. Casey, Misty? Either of you hungry?"

Casey glanced at Misty, then pulled out his chair. "I'm always hungry. You know that."

Misty's eyes were wide, as if she'd been prepared for an entirely different response to his statement, maybe something more dramatic than an offer of breakfast. Did she think he and his brothers were ogres? Morgan almost smiled at her. Had she expected to be stoned? To receive a good dose of condemnation? He chucked her chin, then said gently, "Didn't I tell you it'd be all right?"

Misty didn't bother answering. She looked like she'd turned to stone. Morgan held her gaze, trying to think of some way to smooth things over with her. "I don't suppose you'll believe me when I tell you that wasn't intentional?"

Her eyes darkened to navy and her lips firmed.

"Okay, the car part was," he admitted, just to rile her.

He couldn't bear seeing her look so lost. "And I admit I got Jordan and Gabe and Casey out of bed."

She mumbled under her breath, no doubt something insulting, but he just pretended he hadn't heard her. "I swear, I had no idea our newlyweds would be up. And I didn't plan to let the cat out of the bag about your pregnancy, either."

Her expression remained murderous.

Leaning close, crowding her against the cabinets so his brothers couldn't see her or hear him, Morgan whispered, "I have no intention of sharing your other secrets, so you can rest easy on that score, okay?" They were so close, her scent filled him with every breath he took. He braced his hands beside her hips on the counter; she braced her hands on his chest. She didn't quite push him away, and he saw her lips part. It amazed him the effect they had on each other. Even when she was likely thinking of ways to bring him low, she still responded to him. When they did finally come together—and he was certain it would happen sooner or later—he could only imagine how explosive it would be.

His heart thundered. "Misty?" She slowly looked up and met his gaze. "There's no reason for anyone to know about the rest unless you want to tell them, okay?"

Misty shivered, but before she could answer Honey came whipping into the room in her robe and skidded to a halt when she saw Morgan's nose practically in Misty's ear. "Hey, now, none of that. Get away from her, Morgan. I want to talk to my sister without you trying to intimidate either of us."

Morgan slowly straightened, wondering what Misty was thinking, if she'd believed him. "I've never intimidated you, Honey."

"Not for lack of trying." She caught Misty's arm and pulled her aside.

Morgan lifted the suitcase. "I'll just take this back to her room."

Misty shook her head to refuse him, while Honey gave

him her sweetest smile. "Thank you, Morgan. Misty and I will be in the family room, talking."

"I'll call you when breakfast is ready," Jordan said, and Misty seemed unaware of the concern in his tone.

After the sisters left, Morgan felt both his brothers watching him. He turned to glare at them. "What?"

"Not a thing."

"Didn't say a word."

Casey made a show of studying a bird outside the kitchen window.

"Damn irritants," Morgan muttered. He lifted the suitcase and carried it out of the room. He knew his brothers each had at least a dozen questions, wondering what he was doing mixed up in the middle of Misty Malone's affairs, and why he was the only one privy to her startling news. But he wasn't about to betray her trust any more than he already had. They could just go on wondering.

When Morgan got to the room Misty had been using, he found the bed neatly made and everything very tidy. He pictured her sleeping in that bed last night, or rather, not sleeping. Just worrying. He'd told her she should leave, and this morning she'd been crying.

His stomach cramped and he idly rubbed his hand over it, but the ache continued. He could easily imagine what she'd been thinking, how she'd felt—how he'd made her feel—and he hated it. She probably hadn't slept at all last night, worrying about what she'd do, worrying about finding a job and about the baby.

A baby, a little person that would look like Misty, with dark hair and big blue eyes... He smiled at the thought, then caught himself and scowled.

What kind of job could a woman with a record get? He didn't know the terms of her probation—he'd have to ask her about that—but he knew it wouldn't sit well with an employer, especially not when she'd supposedly stolen from the last guy who'd hired her. Would she be able to earn enough to take care of herself and a baby?

She was certainly stubborn enough to make it work somehow, but she had a hard road ahead of her. And that route wasn't even necessary.

Morgan considered things for a moment, then came to some decisions. He opened her suitcase, emptied it on the bed, took the case to his room and shoved it under his bed. If she wanted to try sneaking out again, he wouldn't make it easy for her. At least until he knew she had a decent plan. Then, he told himself, he'd let her go.

He also intended to do a little investigating. Getting the details of the theft wouldn't be hard, and then he'd make his own conclusions.

He felt like a warlord, holding her against her will, but damn it, it was only stubborn pride that had her wanting to leave in the first place. That and his big mouth. He had the feeling if he hadn't asked her about leaving, if he hadn't pushed her, she'd have stayed on for a while, using the time to make new plans. She had a lot to deal with, and until he'd started harassing her, she'd probably seen this as an ideal situation, a place to regroup and be with her sister without anyone knowing what had happened.

Except that she'd told him everything. He took immense satisfaction in that small success, discarding the fact that he'd bullied the information out of her. Misty wouldn't have told him if she hadn't trusted him at least a little.

He remembered stories of her father that Honey had shared. That man wasn't one to coddle or offer comfort, so Morgan had no doubt she hadn't even tried going to him for help. According to Honey, neither of them was overly close to the man, and with good reason.

Everything would work out, he was certain of it.

On his way to the kitchen Morgan passed the family room and was brought up short by a disgruntled, *''He hates me.''*

Morgan stalled, his heart jumping, his muscles pulled tight. He waited, eavesdropping like a maiden aunt to hear what Honey would say in reply.

Her soft voice was soothing, just as Morgan had known

it would be. ‘‘Morgan doesn’t hate you, Misty. He kept you here because that’s just how they all are. They’re a little on the gallant side, and Morgan wants to protect you.’’

There was a rough, disbelieving laugh. ‘‘Right. If you say so.’’

Morgan could tell she didn’t believe her sister and he pulled his hands into fists. Even his toes cramped. Hate her? Hell, no. What he felt was as far from hatred as it could get, and a whole lot steamier than that cold emotion. He wanted to devour her, to make love to her for a week so he could get her out of his system.

He hated the effect she had on him, but he didn’t hate *her.*

‘‘I do say so,’’ Honey insisted. ‘‘I know them all better than you do.’’

‘‘It doesn’t matter what Morgan thinks or how he feels about me, Honey. The point is, I didn’t mean to intrude on you. The last thing you need right now is to start worrying about me.’’

‘‘There, you see? I won’t worry as long as you’re around so I can see you’re doing okay. Morgan probably knew that, too.’’

Morgan lifted his brows. Sounded good enough to him, though thoughts of Honey hadn’t much entered into his mind while he was trying to think of ways to keep Misty around.

‘‘But…’’ Misty floundered, then insisted, ‘‘I need to get back to work. I can’t just stay here indefinitely.’’

Morgan hustled through the doorway before Misty could convince Honey that she should leave. He surveyed both women cozied up on the couch, and Misty’s eyes widened in alarm.

There was no way for him to reassure her right now, so he didn’t bother trying. He’d already given her his word that he wouldn’t tell about her stint with the law. It wouldn’t hurt her to trust him just a bit.

He got right to the point. "I heard you mention your job."

"Morgan." Her tone said she'd kill him if he said one more word.

The threat didn't worry him. After all, the woman had hurt her hand just smacking him in the stomach. And she had shared her secrets with him, which he chose to see as a sign of trust whether she realized it or not. "I have a solution."

Misty moaned again. He noticed she'd been doing a lot of that lately.

Undaunted, he held up his hands and pronounced, "You're going to come to work for me."

MISTY STARED at Morgan, wondering what he was up to now. Somehow, in the short time it had taken her to shower, he'd done something to her car so it wouldn't start, shaved so that he looked refreshed and ready to take on the day instead of looking like a dark savage, and he'd pulled on more clothes.

She was eternally grateful for the clothes part.

Even when he made her so mad she wanted to club him on top of his handsome head, she couldn't seem to ignore him. The man filled up the space around her with his size, his scent, his pushy presence. When he was there, he was really there, and she doubted any sane woman would be oblivious to him, especially not when he was flaunting his bare, muscled chest.

Morgan had the type of body that had always secretly appealed to her. He was tall and powerful and immeasurably strong—but he could be so gentle.

She shook her head. Just because he distracted her didn't mean she'd let him off the hook. What she'd most wanted *not* to happen he'd made sure *had* happened. Never mind that she was now in the situation she'd originally wanted, with a safe place to stay, close to her sister.

How the circumstance had come about was totally unfair—and all Morgan's fault. Honey deserved some carefree time, but now she'd worry endlessly. Honey had a horrible tendency to mother her, a habit she'd gotten into because their mother had died long ago and their father was so cold and undemonstrative. Though Honey was only slightly older, she'd taken the big-sister role to heart.

She'd have told Honey the whole story eventually, of course, because they didn't keep secrets from each other. But not now, not when Honey had just gotten married and found so much happiness. It wasn't fair to drop such a burden in her lap.

She should have choked Morgan instead of punching him in his rock-hard middle, she thought, surveying his dark frown. But judging by his thick neck, that wouldn't have done him much damage, either. The man was built like a pile of bricks and was just as immovable.

And now he'd offered her a job. Or more precisely, he'd demanded she take a job. *With him.*

He hadn't precisely told Honey that Misty didn't have a job anymore. No, he'd made it sound as if he was only offering her an alternative so she could stick around. Did that mean he'd been sincere when he'd promised not to tell anyone about the rest of her troubles? God, she hoped so. It was all too humiliating, and though she knew Honey would believe her innocent, she had no idea how the others would feel.

Being pregnant was one thing; she wanted the baby and couldn't really regret its existence. And the brothers had been very accepting about the whole thing—almost cavalier, in fact. But surely they wouldn't want a jailbird in their home. She felt sick at the idea of them finding out.

"I already have a job," she stated forcefully, when Honey gave her a nudge for sitting there and staring.

Morgan lifted one brow and proceeded to settle himself into the stuffed chair adjacent to the couch. Contrary to how Misty felt, he looked at his ease and without a care in the world. His dark blue eyes were direct, unflinching.

"Now Malone," he said easily, "you were just telling me that you hate that job, that you planned to look for something else. Why not look here, so you can be close to your...family?"

"I never—" Misty bit her lip, stopping her automatic protest in mid-sentence. How could she dispute his enormous lie without telling the actual truth? He'd cornered her, and he knew it.

After clearing her throat, she smiled sweetly. It always worked for Honey. "I never meant to imply *you* should give me a job."

Morgan waved his hand in dismissal. Apparently the big ape was immune to her smile. "Of course you didn't. I know that. You'd never hint around that way. You're much too...up-front and honest for that." His eyes glittered at her and he added, "But I want you to take the job."

She glanced at Honey, saw no help there and resolutely shook her head. "No."

"How can you refuse when you don't even know what the job is yet?"

Through set teeth, she growled, "What is the job?"

Morgan actually smiled, which put her even more on edge. "I need an assistant. Someone to act as sort of a secretary and a dispatcher, when necessary. No, don't look like that. You won't need special training. Buckhorn is a small county and we do things just a bit differently. You'd need to take calls, keep track of where I am and forward on the important ones, but make notes for the ones that can wait. Mostly just for mornings and afternoons. Your evenings will be free, and just think, you can spend more time with Honey."

Honey leaned forward in her seat, already excited by the prospect. "Morgan, that's a great idea!" To Misty, she said, "It only makes sense, Misty, for you to be with family now. This is no time to let your pride get in the way."

"Of course it isn't," Morgan agreed.

Honey sighed. "Didn't I tell you he was wonderful?"

Misty almost choked, especially when she glanced at Morgan and saw his amusement. She thought she might throw up again. She drew a deep breath and tried to sound reasonable. "I don't know anything about working for a sheriff..."

"I'll tell you everything you need to know, sweetheart."

There was only so much she could take and remain composed. "I am not," she said in lethal tones, "your sweetheart."

Honey patted her hand. "They all use endearments, so you might as well get used to it. I swear, at first I thought they knew my name before I'd even given it to them. Then I realized everything female is a sweetheart or a honey to these guys, even the hodgepodge of animals Jordan keeps around." Honey gave Morgan a fond smile. "They're very old-fashioned in a lot of ways."

Under her breath, Misty muttered, "You mean they're overbearing, macho, autocratic—"

"What's that, Malone? I couldn't quite hear you." Morgan looked ready to laugh.

"Not a thing." She stood, and both Honey and Morgan came to their feet, too, as if they thought she might topple over at any moment. Good grief, she wasn't even showing yet. "I'll think about the job, Morgan."

He gave her a slow nod, looking at her from his superior height in a way that made her feel downright tiny. "That's fine. But make it quick, okay? I need you to start tomorrow."

Her eyes widened. She didn't want to start tomorrow! She didn't want to start at all. If anything, she hoped to make some solid plans tomorrow that would appease everyone so she could be on her way. "But..."

"Will you, Misty? Please?" Honey hugged her close, and Misty had no choice but to return the embrace. Since meeting Sawyer, her sister was deliriously happy and she wanted everyone else to feel the same. Over Honey's shoulder,

Misty glared at Morgan. He winked at her, the obnoxious brute.

Misty pushed her sister away slightly and drummed up a reassuring smile. "Why don't you go have breakfast with that new husband of yours? I want to discuss this…job, with Morgan."

"But you haven't even told me about the baby yet, or how far along you are, or anything!"

Misty thought about moaning again, but with Morgan watching her so closely, she held it in. To her surprise, he took Honey's arm and said, "One thing at a time, hon, okay? If she takes the job and sticks around, you'll have all the time in the world to chat."

It was obvious Honey didn't want to, but she finally agreed to leave. She gave Morgan a warning look on her way out that had Morgan chuckling in a deep rumble.

Misty saw nothing funny in the situation, but he didn't give her a chance to light into him. No sooner was Honey gone from the room than he walked to her and said, "I told you I won't say a word about the job or the conviction. You have my word on that."

It was as if he'd deliberately taken away her steam. But Misty had more than one grievance and she was nowhere near ready to give up her anger. "Why should I believe you?"

His hesitation was plain before he lifted a hand and smoothed her cheek. He was so gentle, so warm, she couldn't get her feet to step out of his reach. "I didn't want to hurt you, Malone. You must know that."

She managed a rude laugh. "You couldn't hurt me."

Her disdainful tone never fazed him. His mouth tilted in a wry, regretful smile. "I think you're wrong about that. I think you've been through a hell of a lot and you're vulnerable right now."

Because he was right, she felt twice as determined to deny it. "Don't get all mushy on me, Morgan. My stomach can't take it."

He lifted his other hand so that he framed her face. "You're so tough, aren't you, Malone? Ready to take on the world all alone. I admire that kind of courage, you know."

"So my insults aren't having the desired effect, huh? You must have a thicker skull than I figured."

Morgan whistled. "You really are ticked, aren't you?"

"Ticked? I'm a whole lot more than *ticked.* What you did was reprehensible."

"What I did," he said, his thumbs gently smoothing her cheeks, "was try to keep you here since I was the one who had run you off."

Misty blinked at him. He felt guilty? Is that what this was all about? Caught between disbelief and annoyance, she struggled with her fading anger. She really hadn't wanted to go, but neither had she wanted her personal business sallied about for the entire family to hear. Facing them again was going to be incredibly tough. She already knew there'd be dozens of questions, most importantly about the absent father.

As if he'd read her mind, Morgan made a tsking sound. "Come on, Malone, stop beating yourself up. There's no reason to be embarrassed, you know. My brothers won't judge you. If anything, they'll rightfully blame the guy who got you pregnant and then walked away. Like Honey said, we're old-fashioned about things like that. A guy should take responsibility for his actions."

She appreciated the sentiment, if not the interference. "Yeah, well, this guy didn't. And believe me, things are better with him out of the picture."

Morgan laughed. "I'm not disputing that. If he was around, I'd be tempted to beat him into the ground."

"Really?" That wasn't an altogether unpleasant thought. She'd felt the same many times after the way Kent had reacted to her news.

Morgan nodded, then said gruffly, "He hurt you. The least he deserves is a good beating."

Misty was speechless. Morgan had sounded almost like he cared, like he didn't despise her, after all. She said facetiously, "How...sweet of you."

Morgan's look was stern. "Look, Malone. The last thing you'd want is to be married to a loser."

"The last thing I want is to be married, period." Misty stared at his chest and muttered, "I've had my fill of dealing with men, thank you very much."

"I think you've just been dealing with the wrong men."

"Such an obvious truth." She looked at him pointedly.

He let her implication pass without comment, then leaned down until his forehead touched hers. She could feel his warm breath on her lips, his body heat seeping into her, his gentleness flowing over her. She sighed.

"It's also obvious," he said very softly, "that Honey loves you to death. Nothing will change that."

Oh, how could he make her feel like this when she was rightfully angry? "I know my sister loves me, Morgan. But telling her wasn't your decision to make."

"Maybe, but it was the right decision. You were just being stubborn, admit it."

"No, never."

He laughed. "At least this way you're with family, and I'm talking about all of us. We are family now, Malone, whether you like it or not. You don't have a job, you don't even have a place to stay."

Alarmed, she finally managed to dodge his soothing hands and move out of reach. She tried for a credible laugh, but it sounded more like a weak snicker. "Don't be ridiculous."

His eyes narrowed. "It's no good, Malone. I know you too well."

"You hardly know me at all!"

"But we're getting there." Then in a softer tone, "Just where the hell did you think you were going to go?"

The best she could come up with was a shrug.

"That's what I figured. So why not stay here?"

Misty felt like screaming in frustration. "For crying out loud, Morgan, you *told* me to leave!"

He shook his head. "Damn it, that was before."

"Oh, I see. A pregnant woman isn't so risky. You're no longer worried that I'll seduce your brothers? After all, I thought that was your overriding concern."

Morgan leaned against the wall by the fireplace and crossed his arms over his chest. Misty recognized that stance and the accompanying expression all too well.

"No, my overriding concern was the chemistry between us. And your pregnancy doesn't change that much. You're still too damn sexy, and only a dead man wouldn't be tempted."

She wished she hadn't brought it up. "That's ridiculous."

He very slowly shook his head. "It's true. You have to know how gorgeous you are, how you make a man feel. But I have an idea on how to handle that."

The words, along with the way he'd looked at her as he spoke, made her skin flush and her belly tingle.

She didn't want to be attracted to him! He was arrogant and stubborn, but he was also very dedicated to his family, protective and so incredibly good-looking she imagined women had been chasing him for most of his life.

She mustered up a bored look to hide her reaction to him and asked, "So what's it going to be? Bundle me up in burlap? Paint a big red A on my forehead to ward off the innocent? What?"

"Nothing so drastic as that." He paused for a long moment, as if measuring his words, then he met her gaze and his eyes were hard...determined. "I'll just tell everyone that we're involved, so you're off-limits."

"What?"

He smiled at her reaction. "Believe me, Malone, that'll be enough to keep all other men away, which is what you wanted, right?"

CHAPTER FIVE

MORGAN WAITED until Misty looked at him, then snagged her gaze and refused to let her look away. There was a soft blush to her cheeks that about drove him crazy. He had a gut feeling that blush was a combination of anger, embarrassment and excitement.

He understood the anger and wished for some way to spare her the embarrassment. The excitement he relished.

"It's a good plan, Malone."

"For me to pretend to...to be your..." Her stammering ceased, and she stared at him blankly.

"My woman. Yeah, that's the plan." He wanted to walk closer to her, to touch her again, but he didn't dare. She looked skittish enough to jump out of her skin if he even breathed deeply. "Here's how I see it," he said, trying to sound reasonable. "You do need a job, but it won't be easy to find one without employers knowing you were convicted of stealing from the last place you worked. And once they know that, they'll be reluctant to hire you, right?"

"Maybe."

"And you're still on probation?"

She nodded hesitantly. "For a few more months."

"That's what I figured."

She gulped, and her hands fisted. In shame? In regret? He just didn't know, but he hated to see her feel either emotion. He intended to do what he could about her conviction as soon as possible. But for now, he had other things to contend with. "The job I'm offering gives county wages, which aren't great but neither are they piddling. And the fact you worked for a sheriff's office will have to look good on your résumé, and to your probation officer.''

She didn't appear quite convinced. She stared at her feet in deep concentration.

A niggling sense of panic seeped in. Misty had been very clear about her feelings on involvement of any kind. The only way Morgan could see around that was to wrangle his way into her life. Keeping her here, hiring her on, showing her she could trust him and rely on him was part of a great plan. He'd just have to make damn sure it worked. ''As I said, it's not a hard job—''

Her head shot up and she glared at him. ''I'm not afraid of hard work.''

''I didn't mean that.'' Sometimes Morgan wished he was as good at soothing frazzled nerves as his brother Jordan. Jordan could talk the orneriness out of a mule, whisper a baby bird to sleep. He was one hell of a vet, but his talents carried over to people, as well. Morgan, on the other hand, usually relied on rigid control to get his way. He managed things, taking on other people's problems and resolving them so they didn't have to worry. Most people appreciated that.

Only it didn't work with Misty. She bucked him at every turn, refusing to accept what he was best at offering.

''All I meant,'' he continued, ''is that you could easily do the job. You don't need any special training or skills. And by accepting it, you can stay here indefinitely, which rids you of the cost of room and board.''

She was already shaking her head before he'd finished. ''I can't just stay here free, Morgan.''

He straightened. ''Why the hell not? You hadn't been in a hurry to leave until I prodded you along.''

''That's not entirely true.'' She looked flabbergasted by his persistence, but he'd be damned if he'd back off. ''Sure, I had hoped to hang out for a week or two more while I figured out what to do next, but then I'd have left. I never intended to stay here any longer than that.''

He scowled at her. Everything had changed the moment she'd dropped to her knees in front of those bushes. She *should* stay, which meant he no longer had to fight himself for wanting her to stick around.

She'd said she wasn't as outgoing as she'd pretended. He wasn't buying that for a single second. She might not be such a real flirt, only using that as a way to cover her worries. But she was brazen and outrageous and beautiful. She was also strong and proud, qualities he'd always admired in men and women alike. But for right now, he wished she wasn't quite so proud.

"Honey wants you to stay." That was the only argument he could think of that might convince her. Telling her *he* wanted her to stay didn't seem to be such a great idea. She'd ask him why, and beyond telling her he wanted to ravish her senseless, he'd have no excuse. Even knowing she was pregnant by another man, now that she'd admitted she wouldn't be marrying that man, hadn't dampened his lust. In fact, he admired her courage, which seemed to add a keen edge to his feelings.

In a mumble totally unlike her usual decisive tone, Misty said, "My sister is new here. This is Sawyer's house and—"

"Honey is new, but permanent. She can invite anyone here that she wants." Misty had a lot to learn about them, first and foremost what *family* meant. When Honey became Sawyer's wife, she became an equal member of that family.

Actually, Morgan thought, smiling a little inside, she'd been an accepted member of their family as soon as they'd all realized Sawyer loved her.

"But Sawyer might not care for—"

"Sawyer will love having you here. But truth is, the house belongs to all of us. My father built it back when he and my mother were married. When she and Gabe's father retired, they decided to move to Florida, and we took over the upkeep of the house. Since grown men need some privacy, Gabe converted the basement into an apartment, and Jordan did the same with the rooms over the garage.''

She looked him over as if trying to figure him out. ''But you still live in the house.''

''Yeah.'' He could see the questions in her eyes and grinned. ''I don't, however, bring women here for overnight, if that's what you're asking. Casey is almost sixteen now, and *he* thinks he's all grown up, but I still wouldn't flaunt lovers in front of him. I remember being sixteen. Guys that age don't need any help in the raging hormone department.''

She looked startled for a moment, then frowned. ''Being raised in a house full of males must be ideal for a boy his age.''

Morgan shrugged. ''We've done the best we could. But I know Casey loves the idea of having Honey around. Just as he'll love the idea of you sticking close, too.''

''I don't know, Morgan. I mean, the others...''

''It won't be a problem. The only problem would be if I let you get away.''

She still didn't look convinced, then she harked back to what he'd said earlier. ''Gabe is your half brother?''

Morgan grinned, suddenly knowing how he'd reassure her. ''Come here, Malone. I have a nice long tale to tell you.''

She snorted at that, but she did go ahead and seat herself—in a chair so he couldn't sit beside her. He chose the couch, and realized they'd switched positions from earlier. He couldn't remember ever grinning so much, but damn, she amused him with her constant advance and retreat. She was a mix of bravado and prudence, and he realized it was a potent combination, guaranteed to drive any man crazy.

''My father died when I was just a baby.'' Her eyes widened and he laughed. ''I know. Tough to imagine me as a squalling infant, huh?''

''The squalling part I can believe, but the idea of you ever being little boggles the mind. You're just so—'' her gaze skimmed his chest, his shoulders, then down to his thighs "—massive now."

Because he had her attention, Morgan settled back and stretched out his long legs, then laced his fingers together on his stomach. Misty swallowed and slowly closed her eyes, so she didn't see his grin. "I was still little when my mom remarried and had Jordan. But things didn't work out and she divorced him."

Her eyes snapped open. Looking more fascinated by the moment, Misty said, "After she had Gabe, you mean?"

"Nope." He laughed outright at her confusion. "My father died in the war. He was my mother's first real love, and she had a hard time getting over him. Then she met Jordan's father. She was lonely and she had two sons to raise. She thought she loved him and married again. But not long after that he lost his job and started to drink. Things went from bad to worse. It wasn't easy for her to work a job, care for three kids and put up with the small-town stigma of being a divorced widow with three sons."

"I don't imagine it would be." Misty picked at a thread on her shorts, then admitted, "Even in this day and age, being a single mother has its problems. Not to mention being a mother of three. She must have a lot of courage."

He said softly, "You have your own share of courage, sweetheart. Deciding to have the baby shows a lot of guts and determination."

She changed the subject, or rather got it back on track. "Do you remember much of Jordan's father?"

"Not really. I was only two when she married him, and I've never heard my mother complain much about those times. All she says is that he gave her Jordan, so she doesn't regret a moment of it. But I've lived here my whole life and lots of people talk, mostly about how strong she was and how she'd gone off men completely after losing one and divorcing another." He watched her closely. "I guess sort of like you claiming you don't want anything to do with men now. A woman gets hurt like that, and it's hard to ever trust again.''

He stared at her until she slowly lifted her gaze to meet his.

''I'm not hurt, Morgan. I keep telling you that. I'm just a little wiser, is all. My priorities right now are a job and security for the baby. I don't need a man for that.''

But he wasn't just any man, and he damn well wanted her to realize it. He went on with his story as if he hadn't been sidetracked. ''You know what I do remember? Sitting with her in the evening and reading books, coloring pictures or sometimes making cookies. She worked damn hard, but she was never too tired to talk with us or to give us hell if she caught us fighting.''

Misty gave him a pointed look. ''Us, meaning *you* most likely. Somehow I don't see the others getting into as much mischief as you likely did.''

Morgan shrugged. ''True. I've always been a bit of a hell-raiser—something Mom claims I inherited from my father's side of the family, though I've seen her riled a few times so I'm not buying it. As to the others, Sawyer's always been serious and a bona fide overachiever. There aren't too many men I know who could have cared for a baby and finished up med school without missing a beat. Even with our help, he had his hands full, but he never complained.''

Misty sighed. ''Sawyer is the exception. Most men would run from that kind of responsibility.''

For some reason that observation irritated Morgan beyond all reason. ''You haven't known enough good men to make that judgment.''

Her laugh was a little sad. ''That's true enough, I suppose.'' Then she smiled at him, a real smile that affected him like a stroke in just the right place. ''I think it's wonderful that you're all so close. My father isn't that way at all. If it wasn't for Honey...''

''I know. She's told me a lot about him, and about how close you both are because of it.'' Morgan wished she'd open up a little with him, but her smile was gone and she now had that closed look on her face that he recognized all too well. He said carefully, "Being that you are so close, aren't you just a bit pleased by the idea of having her nearby?"

She ignored his question to ask one of her own. "So what about Gabe? I gather he wasn't found under a rock?"

"Sometimes I wonder. But my mother is still married to Brett Kasper, and he's Gabe's father."

She studied him closely. "You all look different, but I never realized.... I mean, well, you and Sawyer do have similar looks, except that you're an imposing hulk and he's not."

"Gee thanks."

She waved that away. "You have the same dark hair, and there's something about the shape of your jaws. Stubborn, you know?"

"I've heard that, yes."

"But now Gabe, with that blond hair and those incredible electric blue eyes—"

"Malone," he said in warning.

"And Jordan has brown hair and green eyes and his voice is so—" she shivered "—seductive."

"You're pushing me again, Malone."

Misty started laughing, and Morgan realized she'd been deliberately baiting him. He smiled with her. "Do I need to start worrying about my brothers' virtue again?"

"Ha! None of you have any virtue left, and you know it."

"Not true. Virtue and chastity are not the same thing at all."

She chuckled again, shaking her head in feigned disbelief. Whether she realized it yet or not, she liked him, and she'd like being with him. Morgan spoke his thoughts aloud without even thinking about it. "Hearing you laugh is much nicer than hearing you cry."

Just like that, she stiffened up on him. Color darkened

her cheeks, and her eyes narrowed. "If you hadn't been sneaking around this morning, you wouldn't have been subjected to hearing me cry."

Embarrassing her hadn't been his intent. He lowered his voice to a soothing growl. "I wasn't complaining, Malone, except that I don't like seeing you unhappy."

She sat forward, her brows lifted in mock surprise. "Oh, I see. That's why you announced to everyone that I'm pregnant, because you thought it would somehow make me happy?"

"No. But I knew going off on your own wouldn't make you happy, either. If anything, it would've made you more miserable."

"I am *not* miserable."

He raised his hands in surrender. "I stand corrected. And before you run away in a huff, do you want me to tell you the happy ending to my mother's story?"

"With your idea of *happy,* I'm not at all sure."

In a persuasive tone, he suggested, "Try trusting me just a little, Malone."

"No, never."

She was determined not to give an inch, and it frustrated him beyond measure. "You're awfully fond of that particular saying."

"Only when I'm around you."

He gave a drawn-out sigh at her stubbornness, then went on. "It took a long time, and Brett Kasper had to work real hard to get around my mother's resolve after losing one man and divorcing another, but he finally won her over. You never saw a more dedicated man than Brett. When my mom gave him the cold shoulder, he cozied up to us boys instead. Mom didn't stand a chance."

"You mean he manipulated events like you're trying to do with me?"

"Whatever works, Malone." When she growled, he gave her a small smile. His mother had supposedly been as against involvement as Misty, but she'd gotten turned around by the right man. He liked to think the same could be true of Misty. "I'll have you know, they've been married for some time now. You'd have met them at the wedding except Brett had a few health problems and couldn't travel, and my mom wouldn't leave him. He's okay now, nothing serious, but the doc still wants him to rest and Sawyer seconded that, so they missed the wedding. As soon as they can, though, they'll come for a visit."

"She sounds...incredible."

"She's as stubborn as a pit bull when you get her nettled, which luckily doesn't happen often. But for the most part, she's a woman who likes to laugh and isn't afraid to show how much she cares. She's going to love Honey. She's been waiting for one of us to give her a daughter by marriage. I think she's hoping for lots of granddaughters, too." He grinned. "She says I was such a trial, she's ready for something easier—like girls."

"I can believe that!"

Morgan leaned forward and caught her hand. "Do you see the point, Malone? You aren't the first person to make a mistake, but in time, you'll forget your reservations about men."

She started to speak, but he cut her off, already knowing what she would say. Her insistence that she wanted nothing to do with men was almost more than he could take. "So what do you say we join the others?"

She closed her eyes and groaned. "I don't know. The thought of facing your brothers again is enough to make my stomach jumpy."

Morgan considered that, then shrugged. "So don't face them. At least, not for long, and not today. Tell me you'll take the job, then we can go into town and get things set up for you. It's a good excuse and you can have a few hours to get used to the idea before sitting down with them all at dinner tonight. I can show you around town, and all in all, we can waste most of the day."

She bit her lip while scrutinizing him. ''You don't have anything else you need to do?''

''Nope. Sunday is my day off. If anything comes up, someone will call, otherwise I'm free.''

She still hesitated. ''I don't know. It seems pretty fishy to me that this job just suddenly came available.''

He still held her hand, and now he smoothed her knuckles with his thumb, marveling at how such a stubborn and defensive woman could feel so soft and delicate. He could just imagine those small hands on his body, and it made him crazy. He cleared his throat. ''The job was always there, only I didn't want to hire anyone for it.''

''Why?''

''Too many women were applying just to get close to me.'' She laughed hilariously and he waited, pretending to be affronted. When she finally quieted, he cocked a brow. ''It's true. I'm considered something of a catch, only I'd rather do the catching for myself.''

''That's right. You said you're looking for a wife.''

Her bald statement gave him pause. She didn't seem particularly bothered by the idea. ''Not actively,'' he muttered, ''just giving it some thought.'' The idea of a wife wasn't something he wanted to discuss with Misty, especially since he'd all but forgotten that plan since meeting her. She kept him far too preoccupied for rational contemplation of the future. ''And the last thing I need while I'm trying to work is a woman who's set on seducing me.''

''I suppose if she breathes, you'd consider it a come-on?''

''Ah, you have no faith in me, Malone. I told you, the effect you have is totally unique. Contrary to your dirty little mind, I don't run around jumping every woman in the area. Hell, I have to live here, and I'm the sheriff—a respected position, you know. I have to set an example.'' He squeezed her hand. ''Unfortunately I can't seem to remember that around you.''

His honesty had her pink-cheeked again. He loved how she blushed, how her eyes turned bluer and her lips pressed together in a prim line. She was bold, and she gave as good as she got, but any talk of intimacy flustered her.

Damn, but he wanted to kiss her silly.

"If all that's true, Morgan," she fairly sputtered, "if I really affect you like that, why in the world would you want me around the office?"

"Because it solves a dilemma for both of us." He used his in-command tone, the one that made people sit up and take notice of his official position as sheriff. "You need a job, and I need a worker who won't be jumping my bones, interfering with my schedule and causing a scandal. You've made it pretty clear you plan to resist my bones, so..." He didn't admit his hope that her resistance wouldn't last long. "It's an ideal trade-off."

She considered that for a long moment, then finally nodded. "Okay. I can try the job, I suppose. On one condition."

The restriction in his chest immediately lightened, though he hadn't even noticed how tight it felt until she said she'd stay. "Let's hear it."

"I want you to fix my car. I will not be left here without transportation."

She stared at him defiantly until he nodded. "I can do that, but I have a condition of my own."

"Why am I not surprised?"

He tugged her slightly closer, holding her gaze. "I want your promise that if you decide to leave, you'll tell me."

Her eyes narrowed. "You can't keep me here against my will, Morgan."

"I'm all too aware of that unfortunate fact. And I won't even try. But if you decide to leave I want to know it."

"I wasn't really sneaking this time—"

"Malone."

"Oh, all right. I promise. But fix my car today."

He nodded. "And my other suggestion?"

"What other suggestion?"

He looked at her mouth, so sweetly lush and very kissable, then at her full breasts pressing against the pale yellow camisole—just as kissable. He saw how she tucked her long slender legs beneath her, how smooth her thighs were, lightly tanned. Even her shoulders were sexy, making his tongue nearly stick to the roof of his mouth. "I'll stake a claim for all to see, and that'll keep interested males at bay."

Dark lashes swept down over her eyes to avoid his gaze. She subtly tugged her hand away from his and stood. "I don't know, Morgan."

He got up and stood very close behind her. "We will be involved, Malone, in an arrangement." She stiffened and he caught her shoulders before she could move away. "The type of arrangement is nobody's business but our own. I'm not coercing you into bed."

"As if you could."

"Is that a challenge?"

"No!"

He smiled at her anxious tone. "We'll be partners of a sort. You said you were through with men."

"Completely."

"Well, pretending to be mine ought to take care of other men hitting on you, and I'll have some much needed help at the office."

She shook her head while he stared at her nape, exposed by her upswept hair. He imagined kissing her there, watching her tremble. He couldn't push her now or she'd walk out the door, and she was right, there wasn't a damn thing he could do to stop her.

"That attitude is archaic, Morgan."

His newfound possessive streak was archaic, but he was dealing with it. Barely.

He rubbed her shoulders, relishing the warmth of her skin. His thumbs brushed the back of her neck to the base of her skull, lulling her, soothing her. "Look at it this way, Malone," he added in a whisper, "all your problems will be temporarily solved. And if you think this would be hard on you, just think of what it'll do to me."

"What?"

She sounded intrigued, and he hid his smile. "I want you, so you can figure it out, I'm sure. Given that you seem to take sadistic delight in making me miserable, the idea ought to appeal to you."

The torment would be worthwhile, he thought. He could spend a good deal of his time shoring up their ruse by getting closer to her. He knew, even if *she* didn't, that they'd eventually end up in bed. The chemistry between them was just too strong, no matter how hard she tried to deny it.

And he was tired of even trying.

With a wide, impish smile, she turned to face him. "Well, since you put it that way..." She patted his chest. "Making you miserable does hold a certain attraction."

He caught her hand and flattened it against his body. "So you agree?"

"You've convinced me."

Morgan stared at her, his heart thumping so heavily in his chest he thought for sure she'd felt it. He leaned toward her and saw her eyes widen. "Why don't we seal it with a kiss?"

MISTY BRACED HERSELF for a sensual assault. The memory of his last kiss in the gazebo was still fresh in her mind. But instead of being overwhelmed, she felt Morgan's mouth, warm and dry, brush very lightly over her own. She opened her eyes slowly and looked at him. His dark blue eyes were filled with heat, but also with tenderness, and she almost melted.

For a man of his size, he could sometimes be so remarkably gentle. She gave him a slight smile that he returned.

"Am I interrupting?"

They both jumped apart, she in guilty surprise, Morgan with a curse. He turned to face Jordan, leaning in the doorway with a contented smile.

Jordan tipped his head. "Breakfast is getting cold."

"Did you ever hear of knocking?"

"What fun would that be?"

Morgan turned his back on his brother and faced Misty. His wide shoulders completely blocked her from Jordan's view. Using the edge of his hand, he tipped up her chin, then asked, "What's it to be, Malone? Breakfast with the family, or do you want to go into town?"

"I'm not really hungry." She saw Morgan's understanding and quickly added, "I'm not being a coward. I really just don't have an appetite. I'll go in with you, though. No reason you should do without food, and I have to face them all sooner or later. It might as well be now."

"Get it over and out of the way, huh?"

His frown was back, but she had no idea why. "Something like that."

He glanced at Jordan over his shoulder. "We'll be right there."

Accepting the dismissal, Jordan chuckled and ambled off. The moment he was gone, Morgan framed her face and kissed her again. Before she could say much about it, if indeed she could have gathered her scattered wits to offer a protest, he took her hand and hustled her from the room.

Everyone was in the kitchen when they strolled in, still hand in hand. Like the audience at a Ping-Pong match, all eyes moved in unison to their entwined hands, to their faces, then to each other. Brows climbed high.

Morgan shook his head. "The lot of you remind me of monkeys in a zoo—not you, Honey. The masculine lot."

Honey frowned. "Is everything okay, Misty?"

"Everything is fine." She tried subtly to take her hand from Morgan, but he wasn't letting go, and shaking him off might bring on more speculation. She knew he intended to announce their involvement, but did he mean to do it right now? At this rate, no announcement would be necessary!

There was no way she could continue to stand there and let everyone stare at her with concern. She had to get hold of herself and the situation. She glanced at Sawyer, then

Jordan and Gabe. "Morgan insists it'll be all right if I stay here for a little while longer—"

"Absolutely."

"Of course!"

"You know you're welcome here."

Misty smiled at their combined assurance and even felt a little teary over it. "That's very generous of all of you."

Sawyer, with his arm draped over the back of Honey's chair, said, "You're family now, Misty. Family is always welcome for as long as they want to be here. Remember that, okay?"

Honey squeezed him in a tight hug. "Didn't I tell you they were all incredible?"

Gabe laughed. "Nothing incredible about welcoming beautiful women into your home." He eyed their clasped hands and added, "In fact, if you want some privacy, Misty, I have extra room in the basement." He bobbed his eyebrows at her.

Jordan looked mildly affronted. "I was going to offer to share my apartment with her. With Morgan always looming over her, it's for certain she won't get any peace and quiet around here."

Casey, looking like an imp, turned to the side to face his uncles and said, "Hey, if you guys have extra room, I'll move in with you."

Sawyer reached over and clapped his laughing son on the back. "They'll both strangle you for that, Case." Then to Morgan: "Stop letting them bait you. You look ready to do bodily harm, and then what will Misty think of you?"

"She'll think I'm possessive."

"And you have the right to be?"

"Damn right." Morgan released her hand and put his arm around her, hauling her up so close she felt her ribs protesting. "We've come to an agreement."

She gave Honey a helpless look, but Honey just rolled her eyes, as if she'd expected nothing less from Morgan.

In between bites of pancake, Gabe asked, "Is the baby's

father aware of this *agreement,* or is he likely to show up here any time soon, demanding to know what's going on?"

Jordan scoffed. "If he has any sense, he'll show up. I know I would. 'Course, I wouldn't have let her get away in the first place." Then he eyed Morgan, and added, "Not that it's likely to do him any good if he does come here."

Misty had never felt so overwhelmed in her life. Not only did they seem to accept her pregnancy without hesitation or condemnation, but they also championed her and complimented her and apparently welcomed her involvement with their brother. There were no prying questions.

She was totally speechless.

Morgan was not. "He's out of the picture, and I say good riddance. But if he does ever show his face here, believe me, I'd love to have a minute or two alone with him."

"He doesn't know where I am," Misty pointed out.

Morgan gave her a level look. "Perhaps you could tell him."

"Oh, for heaven's sake." Honey shook her finger at Morgan. "You're always looking for a reason to pound on somebody."

"Sometimes you don't have to look for a reason."

Honey turned to Misty. "Don't pay any attention to his threats. It's like a dog growling, all for show. He's actually very sweet."

A round of masculine grunts disputed Honey's description. Obviously nobody else thought Morgan to be sweet.

"He is!" Honey protested. "At least, once you get to know him better—" She stopped and laughed. "But I guess you know him well enough already, huh?"

Morgan paid them no mind. "I think I do a pretty good job of not pounding on people most of the time, which is why I was elected sheriff." He grinned. "Total control of my temper."

"As I remember it," Jordan said, "it was your ability to take control of everyone else that gave the townsfolk assurance you could handle just about any situation."

"I don't seem to have control over your mouth, brother."

"No." Jordan chuckled. "But then, I've been fighting with you all of my life and lived to tell about it."

"Can we get back to the subject at hand?" Gabe asked. "What's this agreement you two have? I'm dying of curiosity."

Misty held her breath, uncertain as to what Morgan might come up with by way of explanation. None of them seemed particularly surprised that they were supposedly involved, which to her was no less than amazing. All they'd done since they first met was antagonize each other. Or at least that's all any of his family had seen. If anything, they should have believed that they despised each other. But of course, his brothers knew Morgan better than she did, and maybe grousing and growling was part of his normal temperament.

Heaven knew, he seemed to wear a perpetual frown when he wasn't laughing with her or trying to kiss her. She glanced at him and saw that indeed, his brows were pulled down and his expression was dark. It irritated her. She moved away from his side and gave him a look to let him know that if he spelled out their agreement completely, there'd be hell to pay.

To her surprise, he laughed, then kissed her loudly, right there in front of everyone. "Quit scowling, Malone. You're going to get wrinkles."

"Yeah. Or worse, you'll start looking so forbidding, we'll confuse you with Morgan." Gabe ducked when Morgan reached for him, then laughed as he resettled himself in his seat and went back to work on his pancakes.

"Misty is going to help me out around the station."

Sawyer sat back in his seat. "I thought you didn't want to hire a woman because she might get ideas."

"In this case, it's a moot point. The ideas are mutual." He looked at each brother in turn. "Any objections?"

Jordan lifted his glass of milk and said mildly, "With the two of you competing for the darkest frown, who would dare?"

Casey stood and took his empty plate and glass to the dishwasher. "I think it's great. So can I be excused? I want to go into town today."

Sawyer glanced at his son. "A date?"

"Sorta."

Morgan snagged Casey and roughed up his hair. "You're taking after your uncle, boy."

With a twinkle in his eyes, Casey asked, "Oh, yeah? Which one?"

Gabe held out his arms. "If she's gorgeous, then obviously me!"

Honey reached over and slapped Gabe's arm. "Thanks a lot!"

The moment Misty had dreaded seemed to have come and gone without much notice. She was a tad bemused at that.

"No offense, Honey," Gabe said after blowing her a kiss, "but you're married into the family now so I can't make lecherous jokes about you."

Still holding Casey in a way that made Misty wistful over the easy familiarity, Morgan said, "We can give you a ride. Misty and I are going into town ourselves."

Misty, a little surprised that he'd even suggest it, thought she'd have a slight reprieve from Morgan's isolated attentions until Casey shook his head. "Thanks, but I'd rather ride Windstorm. Jordan said she needs the exercise and I was planning on cutting across the field."

Morgan explained to Misty, "Windstorm is a new horse. Jordan brought her home not too long ago."

"I'm meeting up with friends, then we're all going to the lake for a little while."

"Anybody I know?" Morgan asked.

Casey struggled to hide his grin. "Just some girls, mostly."

Sawyer took one look at his son's innocent expression and groaned. "Lord, he is like Gabe."

At that, Casey laughed. "We're just going to swim. We won't get into any trouble."

Gabe sent mock glares around the room. "I didn't always get into trouble, you know."

"Just often enough," Jordan said with a raised brow, "to keep everyone on their toes."

Sawyer raised a hand. But before he could interject anything into the conversation, Honey stood and took Casey's arm.

"Never mind your overbearing, interfering uncles." She slanted her gaze toward Gabe. "You're *nothing* like them, except for the good looks, of course. Go and have a good time, but be careful, okay?"

Casey lifted her off her feet in a bear hug. "I'll be home by three o'clock."

"That's fine." And once he left the room, she glowered at Sawyer. "Quit comparing him to your disreputable brothers. You'll put ideas in his head."

"Would you all quit talking about me like I was the scourge of the area? Disreputable, indeed."

Honey pointed at Gabe. "And proud of it, from what I can tell."

To Misty's surprise, Sawyer didn't look at all put out by Honey's audacity toward his son. Instead, he grinned. "You're turning into a rather ferocious mother hen."

"Oh, no," Misty said, "she's always been that way. Even when she was just a little girl."

There was a round of laughing comments on that, all teasing Honey until she blushed.

Morgan pulled up a chair next to Misty and propped his head on his fist to stare at her. "You look a little numb, sweetheart. You okay?"

She shook her head, watching Sawyer nuzzle on Honey, then Jordan and Gabe roughhousing. She didn't know what to think. "The way you all carry on, it amazes me, and now here I am right in the middle of it."

Honey's lips curled into a big smile. She said to the brothers, "It takes some getting used to, since we were from such a small family. And all our meals were very formal. No one gathered in the kitchen just to chat, and there was never this much joking around."

"I wasn't complaining," Misty said, not wanting them to misunderstand. "It's...nice."

"Of course it is." Honey cuddled against Sawyer's side, and he kissed her ear. "You know, you can't get around it, so now I just chime in, too. You'll get used to it."

Misty hadn't planned on being around long enough to get used to them. But now she was having fun. It had been a while since she'd felt the honest urge to laugh.

Morgan nudged her. "You want some pancakes or do you still want to head straight to town?"

Misty thought about it. Most of her anxiety was gone, and her stomach was starting to rumble. There was still a platter of lightly browned pancakes sitting in the middle of the table, with warmed syrup and soft butter beside it.

She grinned at Morgan, feeling more at ease than she had in ages. "Let's eat."

CHAPTER SIX

IT WAS ALMOST an hour before they finally left the house. Though she'd never have imagined it, she'd enjoyed breakfast immensely. No one said too much about her pregnancy other than to try to force an extra pancake on her along with a tall glass of milk. And no one pressured her for information on the father of the baby. They seemed to simply accept that she was there, unmarried, and that they wanted her to stay.

True to his word, Morgan played the part of an interested party, holding her arm, opening the door for her. But then she thought about how all the brothers did the same, for both her and Honey, and she realized Morgan likely wasn't playing at all. He was flat out mannerly, no way around it, and she had to admit she rather liked it.

"Are you sure I don't need to change clothes?" She wore her camisole and cut-offs, but Morgan had insisted she looked fine. The way he'd stared at her, though, giving her such a slow, thorough perusal, made her uncertain. She wore what most women wore on such hot days, but they were going to his office, and she'd likely meet a few townspeople.

"You look sexy as sin, which makes me nuts wanting to take you, but I can handle it. When you actually work tomorrow, you'll need to wear something more… conservative. Maybe jeans and a plain blouse or something. And definitely a bra. I won't get any work done if I know you're not wearing a bra."

Morgan took three more steps before he finally realized she'd stopped. He turned to face her, hands on his hips in an arrogant pose. He lifted one brow. ‘‘What’s the problem now, Malone?’’

As if he truly didn’t know. Amazing. Even more amazing was that she felt equal parts furious and aroused. After all the condemnation she’d received from men of late, his open admiration was a balm, whether she admitted to liking it or not.

It was unnerving that of all the men she’d ever known, this particular man could make her feel such depths of excitement at such a rotten time. She didn’t want to want him. She didn’t want to want any man, but definitely not one who was so bold and…potent. There’d be no way to control Morgan Hudson, or to control her own erratic heartbeat in his presence.

‘‘If this is going to work,’’ she said, carefully enunciating each word, hoping to hide her trembling, ‘‘you have to stop being so…outspoken.’’

‘‘Getting to you, is it?’’

He blocked the sun with his big body, leaving long shadows to dance around her. ‘‘Annoying me, actually.’’

His slow smile was provoking. He strolled over to stand directly in front of her. ‘‘Is that why you’re all flushed?’’ he asked. His gaze dropped to her chest and he groaned. Misty looked down, and she wasn’t surprised to see that her nipples were pressed hard against the soft material of her camisole. She ached all over, and she couldn’t stop her body from reacting.

Desperate, she turned to leave, and Morgan gently clasped her shoulders, halting her. They stood silent, motionless, for several heartbeats and then he sighed. ‘‘Give me a break here, Malone. I’m doing my best.’’

His best to seduce her? His best was actually pretty darn good. She turned slowly to face him and stared him in the eye, refusing to let him intimidate her.

Morgan hesitated, then ran a hand over his face in frustration. He ended with a rough laugh, taking her off guard. ‘‘You want the truth?’’

"No!"

"I'm not used to women pushing me away."

"Oh, please." But she could easily believe it. Morgan had an incredible body, sensual eyes and a devastating smile that he generally hid behind a frown. She imagined any woman he looked at was more than willing to look back—and more.

"I've never known such a contrary woman," he muttered. "You want me, but you keep saying no. You make me crazy, Malone."

He looked so endearing, as if he were baring his soul, she had to fight to keep from smiling at him. She huffed instead. "You were crazy long before I stepped into the picture."

"Nope. I was in control, one hundred percent. Now I'm walking around with a semierection."

She gave a groan of frustration. "That's exactly what I'm talking about, Morgan. Your…masculine discomfort is of no concern to me."

"Well, it should be since you're the cause." She would have groaned again, but Morgan added, almost to himself, "You've shot all my well laid plans to hell."

Misty sputtered, both hurt and insulted. It was the hurt that made her sarcastic, because she knew exactly what plans he referred to. "Please, don't let me get in your way! I'll even help in the wife hunt if you want." He looked surprised, then disgruntled.

"No." He leaned over her. "I don't need your help."

"Why not? Tell me what qualities you're looking for and I'll keep my eyes open."

Morgan leaned closer, then lifted her chin with the edge of his fist. "Right now, I don't want a wife. I want you. And if you were honest, you'd admit you want me, too."

She met his gaze just as intently, determined to make him understand before she broke down and proved him right. "Sorry, Morgan, but I've sworn off men."

His hand opened, cradling her face. "That's the hell of

it, Malone. You're not giving me a chance.'' His gaze touched on her everywhere—her eyes, her lips, her breasts. His thumb moved softly over her bottom lip. ''It could be perfect, sweetheart. I'd make sure of it.''

Misty wondered if she looked in the dictionary for the word *temptation* if it would feature a picture of Morgan Hudson. She could feel herself shaking inside, could feel her nerve endings all coming alive at his sensual promise—a promise she felt sure he could keep. The man was as seductive and searing as the bold stroke of a warm hand.

Wanting to give him equal honesty, she wrapped her hand around his wrist and shared a melancholy smile. ''I have no doubt you…know what you're doing, Morgan. But I already feel a little used. I don't relish feeling that way again.''

His fingers slid over her head to the back of her neck, cupping her warmly. ''Oh, babe.'' His fingers caressed, kindled. His sigh was warm, his words soft. ''I would never hurt you.''

When she started to speak, he hushed her. ''No, don't give me all your arguments. You'll make me morose.''

She laughed at that. Morgan was so brutally honest, so different from the other men she knew. He didn't try to whitewash what he wanted, which was sex. He made it clear he intended to find a wife soon and that she didn't fit the role—a fact she knew only too well. He kept her aware of what he thought about things, and while she did consider him far too forward and pushy, it was nice not to have to guess about ulterior motives and hidden agendas.

Compared to Kent, a man who'd sworn undying love then dropped her the moment he found out she was pregnant, Morgan's honesty was refreshing. It was still alarming, but she'd trust it over insincere promises any day.

He released her, then rubbed the back of his neck. ''You should know I'm not going to quit trying. I figure sooner or later I'll wear you down and you'll admit you want me.''

''Why don't you try holding your breath?''

He wagged a finger at her. ''Play nice, Malone.''

"But you're the one who told me I could make you miserable, right? That's why I agreed to this farce in the first place."

She grinned at him, which made him laugh and shake his head. "Witch."

Misty wasn't offended. Somehow he'd made the name sound like an endearment.

He took her hand and started them on the way again. "Speaking of this farce...I should also point out that the job has nothing to do with your continued rejection." He glanced at her. "I'm not going to fire you if you keep saying no. I won't like it, and I'll do my damnedest to change your mind, but the job is yours as long as you're fulfilling it."

"No blackmail, huh?"

"No. I just wanted to make sure we understood each other."

For some reason, she'd never once doubted that. The way Morgan interacted with his family, treating Casey almost like a son, Honey like a sister, she knew he was too honorable to try forcing her hand. And he'd already proven that night in the gazebo that all it took was a soft, simple no to make him back off. She wasn't afraid of him. She was only afraid of herself when she was with him.

She was still pondering that when Morgan opened the garage door and she got a good look at the official car he expected her to ride in.

She backed up two steps. Granted it wasn't a typical law enforcement vehicle, but it had the lights on the roof and the word Sheriff emblazoned on the side in yellow and blue. Memories flooded back, and she winced.

To stall, she asked Morgan, "What type of sheriff are you?"

He looked up, saw her expression, then glanced at the shiny black four-wheel-drive Bronco. "Just a regular run-of-the-mill county sheriff, why? You don't like my transportation?" He wore a devilish grin.

"I've never seen anything like it." She walked around

the truck, looking at it from all angles. "I thought officials drove sedans, not sport utility vehicles."

"It's for off-road driving, but there's no sport to it. There're a lot of hills in these parts. And though we don't have much in the way of big crime, just about anything that happens involves those damn hills. Last fall, a little girl got lost and we spent two days on foot looking for her. A four-wheel-drive would have made all the difference on some of the off-road searches. After that, the townsfolk got together and donated the Bronco."

Misty felt a little sick as she asked, "The child?"

"I found her curled up real tight under an outcropping of rock." His hands curled into fists and his jaw locked. "Her father had given up looking and was back at the station, drinking coffee and letting people dote on him."

He sounded thoroughly disgusted, not that Misty blamed him.

"Sawyer had rounded up about fifty people and we'd been at it all day and through the night. When I found her late the following afternoon, she was terrified, cold and crying for her daddy."

Misty put her hand on his arm, aware of the bunched muscles and his tension. Knowing Morgan as well as she did now, she could imagine how difficult that would have been for him, trying to console a child, hurting when that wasn't possible. "Her father should have been with you."

"He was a damn fool, visiting these parts and camping out when he didn't have a clue as to what he was doing. The weather was too cold for it and he didn't exactly pick the best spot to pitch his tent. The little girl wandered off because he wasn't watching her close enough."

"But she was all right?"

"Other than being a little dehydrated and scared silly, she did great. Cutest little thing you'd ever seen. About five years old." His eyes met hers, diamond bright, and he added, "I know if it had been my kid, I wouldn't have quit looking until I found her."

"I think," Misty said, studying his intent expression, "you wouldn't have let her out of your sight in the first place."

Morgan kissed her nose. "No, I wouldn't have."

Misty wondered if he'd slept at all during those two days, and seriously doubted that he had. She gave him a tremulous smile. The man was proving to be entirely too easy to like.

Morgan stared at her mouth, groaned, then pulled the door of the Bronco open. "Let's go, Malone, before I forget my good intentions."

She clasped a hand to her heart. "You have good intentions? Toward me? I had no idea."

Suddenly his eyes narrowed. "Why are you stalling? What's up?"

"Don't be ridiculous." She eyed the truck again, then with a distinct feeling of dread, hefted herself into the seat. Morgan gave her a long look before he slammed the door.

When he climbed in on his own side, he said, "You wanna tell me about it?"

"I have no idea what you're talking about." She stared with feigned fascination at the control panel, the radio. Behind her was a sturdy wire-mesh screen separating the cargo area from the front seat—for prisoners, she knew. Unable to help herself, she shuddered.

Morgan started the engine, then reached for her hand. "When you were arrested, they cuffed you?"

"I don't want to talk about that." She tried to pull away, but he held her hand tight and rubbed his thumb over her knuckles. He did that a lot, grabbing hold of her and not letting her go. This time she appreciated the touch. She curled her fingers around his.

"I imagine you were," he said, speaking about the arrest in a matter-of-fact way. "It's pretty much policy these days, for safety reasons."

She chewed her lip, then slowly closed her eyes, giving up. "It was the most degrading moment of my entire life. It was bad enough when Mr. Collins accused me of stealing the money, and I couldn't believe it when he actually called the cops."

"Mr. Collins?"

"My boss at Vision Videos. I kept thinking somehow things would get straightened out, that they'd realize there'd been a mistake."

"They didn't find the money on you?"

"No, because I didn't have it." She glared at him, then asked, "You think I'm guilty, don't you?"

Morgan was silent as they pulled onto the main road. He drove with one hand, still holding onto her with the other. Finally he muttered, "To be honest, I have serious doubts."

"Really?"

He glanced at her. "But if you did do it, I'd understand, okay?"

There was that damn honesty again; he wasn't convinced of her innocence, but he'd allow for the possibility. She almost laughed. For a man who wanted to get intimate with a woman, he wasn't going about it in the usual way—with lies and deceptions that would soften her up. "Even the lawyer I hired didn't believe me, not really."

"The evidence must have been pretty strong."

"Yeah, the fact that I'm a pregnant, supposedly desperate female was proof positive that I'd steal from a man I'd worked with for two years, even though I'd never been in trouble before in my life."

"Your boss knew you were pregnant?"

"Morning sickness kind of gives you away. That and the fact that I suddenly had more nights free." Misty was only vaguely aware of the beautiful scenery as they drove down the long road. The sun was bright, the day hot, but the air-conditioning in the truck had her feeling chilly.

Or maybe it was the dredging of memories that made her feel so cold inside. "I wasn't dating Kent anymore, and I knew that with the baby coming I needed to save up more money, so I'd offered to work more overtime." She slanted Morgan a look. "That made me seem guilty, too, by the way. My boss said small amounts of money had been missing several nights in a row, which was the first I'd heard of it, but he claimed that was why he'd come in unexpectedly to check on me that day, and found the money missing."

"When exactly did this all take place?"

She told him the exact day she'd been arrested.

Morgan surprised her by lifting her hand to his mouth and then turning it to gently kiss her palm. "I wasn't thinking. I didn't mean to make you uncomfortable riding with me."

Misty held her breath as his mouth moved against the sensitive skin of her palm. That, added to the gentle way he had of speaking to her somtimes, left her feeling vaguely empty and jumpy inside.

She swallowed hard. "After everything I've been through, it's silly to let a little ride get to me. But you just can't imagine what it was like. There were tons of people gathered outside the video store when I was arrested. They led me out in handcuffs and I just wanted to die. I thought I'd be glad to get in the car, where people couldn't see me, but instead, it seemed we hit every red light and folks in the other cars would stare."

Morgan slowed for a deer that ran across the road, distracting Misty for the moment. He spoke quietly, holding her hand on his thigh. "Sweetheart, people are always going to stare at you, no matter what, because you're beautiful. That's something you just ought to get used to."

Laughing helped to wash away the melancholy. "You may find this hard to believe, Morgan, but no one has ever carried on so much about my looks. Honey was the one the guys were always after. Men prefer blondes, you know."

"Sawyer certainly does." He turned to give her a lazy grin. "But I'm not Sawyer."

"You've got me there."

"You know what I prefer?"

She started whistling, which only made him chuckle. "I

prefer dark-haired women with long sexy legs and incredible..."

"Morgan—" she warned.

"—smiles." He laughed at her expression. "Such a dirty mind you have, Malone. What did you think I was going to say?"

She reached over and smacked him for that, then couldn't help laughing again. "I figure I'm only slightly better than average looking—and I'm giving you the slightly better based on all this praise you've heaped on me lately."

He didn't look at her, just made a sound of disagreement. "You can ask any man and he'll tell you the same. Hell, just hearing you talk makes me hard, even when I don't like what we're talking about."

Of course she looked, then immediately jerked her gaze away. "If you don't stop being so shameless—" She sighed, unable to think of a threat that might carry any impact. It annoyed her that he'd once again gotten her to stare at him in a totally inappropriate way.

"You'll what? No, don't answer that. And for your information, I can't seem to help it."

She tugged her hand free, tucking it close so he couldn't retrieve it. "Keep your lips to yourself. That might be good for starters."

"Malone, I swear, one of these days you're going to take back those words."

She laughed again. "You're incorrigible."

"And a distraction?"

She blinked, realizing that he had, indeed, distracted her. She nodded, giving him his due, but felt it necessary to point out the obvious. "My ride then was a little different. I was in the back, handcuffed, and the officers were in uniform—and armed."

Morgan grinned at her. "The county insists the Bronco is partly for my personal use, sort of a perk, so you're not the first woman to be seen in it."

"Did I ask for that information?"

"I just wanted you to know that if anyone stares this time, it'll be with a different kind of curiosity. And I do wear a uniform when I'm on duty, which I'm not right now. As to being armed, it's a habit." He made that statement, then shrugged.

"What do you mean?" Misty turned slightly in her seat to face him. "You carry a gun around with you?"

"All the time."

Once again she looked him over, then cocked an eyebrow. "Must be a good hiding place."

"Want to search me, Malone?"

Yes, but she wouldn't tell him that. "I'm waiting."

"You're no fun at all, but we'll work on that." He leaned down and lifted the hem of his jeans. "Ankle strap. I wear a belt holster when I'm on duty."

She'd seen him in uniform, and the sight had been impressive indeed. He looked nothing like Andy Griffith, that was for sure. When Morgan got decked out in his official clothes, he looked like a female fantasy on the loose. His shirt fit his broad shoulders to perfection, and his slacks emphasized his long, strong legs. The holster around his waist gave an added touch of danger to his dark good looks. She imagined the females of Buckhorn County would continue to elect him sheriff just to get to see him in uniform each day.

Not that he didn't look great today in his jeans and soft T-shirt.

Misty eyed the small handgun in a leather holster. It was attached to an ankle cuff with a velcro strap. Despite herself, she was fascinated. "Do the good citizens of Buckhorn know about that gun?"

"You kidding? They insist on me holding up my image. Why, if they thought I wasn't armed, they'd be outraged. They each consider me their own personal sheriff, you know."

"Especially the women?" *Ouch.* She hadn't meant to say that.

Morgan gave her a knowing look, but thankfully didn't tease her. "Men and women alike, actually. Half my job is spent letting them bend my ear and reassuring them that the corruption of outside communities hasn't infiltrated yet."

"If corruption hasn't infiltrated, then why do they want you to carry a gun?"

He shrugged a massive shoulder. "I told you. Image." Almost as an afterthought, he added, "And I have had occasion to use it now and then."

He had her undivided attention. "You're kidding?"

"Nope. Being that we're a small town, a few of the more disreputable sorts thought it'd be the ideal hideout. To date, I've apprehended an escaped convict, caught a man wanted for robbery, and another for kidnapping."

Her eyes were wide. "Did you…shoot anyone?"

His hands tightened on the wheel. "The kidnapper, in the knee. The son of a bitch held a gun to a woman. He's lucky that's all I did to him."

Misty fell back in her seat, amazed. "I never would have imagined." Morgan seemed dangerous in many ways, and he certainly held his own when it came to taking charge of any situation. But she'd never imagined him being involved in a possibly lethal situation. He could have been killed! "This is incredible."

Again, he shrugged.

"What would the good citizens think if they knew you were consorting with a known criminal?"

"You?"

"Do you know any others?"

"Sure." He didn't allow her to question that. He gave her a speculative look, then suggested, "You could get your name cleared, you know."

"I don't see how that's possible." She bit her lip. "Once something is on your permanent record…"

"I could get it taken care of. It's a lot of legal jumble, and I can explain it later, but if you really didn't take the money…"

Misty felt her heart beating faster. "I didn't take the money." She waited for his reaction, her breath held. She wanted Morgan to believe her. It had suddenly become important to her, and not just because he wanted to help.

Seconds ticked by, and then he nodded. "I'll see what I can do."

He said nothing else, and that, she supposed, was that.

They reached the center of town, which was really no more than a narrow street full of buildings. Misty hadn't paid much attention to it when she'd been at the hall for Honey's wedding. She'd still been too nervous about Morgan and too excited for her sister. But now she had the chance to take it all in, and she wasn't going to miss a single thing.

There were two grocery stores at opposite ends of the street, a clothing store that looked as if it had been there for over a hundred years, a diner and a hairdresser, a pharmacy... She eyed the pharmacy as they drove past, wondering how awkward it might be to get her prenatal vitamin prescription filled; she'd run out of them yesterday.

One thing she didn't see was a bus station, and she wondered just where the nearest one was. After her comment earlier that she'd take a bus home, she felt rather foolish to realize there wasn't a bus around. You'd think one of the brothers could have mentioned that fact to her.

There were people sitting outside their shops, others lounging against the wall or standing close chatting. There were even some rocking chairs sitting under canopied overhangs, to invite loiterers.

"This is like going back in time," she murmured as they drove to the end of the street then turned right onto a narrower side street. There were a few houses, a farm with some cattle moving around, and a funeral parlor, which was easily the biggest, most ornate structure she'd seen so far. Then Morgan pulled into the circular drive of a building that looked like an old farmhouse. It was two stories with a grand wraparound porch, white columns in the front and black shutters at every window.

"Why are we stopping here?"

"This is my office, darlin'." He chuckled at her as he drove right up close to the front door and stopped. The double doors wore a professional sign that read: Enter at Right. Evidently that didn't apply to the sheriff.

Morgan parked and turned off the engine. "The station used to be by the county courthouse, farther into town, but it was too small so years ago, long before I was elected, they moved it here. Makes for a bit of whimsy doesn't it?"

Morgan climbed out, and at that moment two men came around from the side of the house to greet him. "Hey there, Morgan! Didn't expect to see you today. Anything wrong?"

Morgan frowned, as if surprised to see them. "Nope, no problems. I was just showing the lady around." He opened Misty's door and handed her out of the vehicle. Close to her ear, he said, "Two of the biggest gossips around. They weren't supposed to be here today, but that never stopped them before. And since they're here, we might as well take advantage of it."

Misty leaned away to look at him. "I don't understand."

"Anything they see makes the rounds of Buckhorn faster than light. This'll be a good place to start letting folks know you're off-limits."

Misty froze just as her feet touched the ground. Surely, Morgan didn't mean to do anything in front of these nice old men! But then she met his hot gaze and knew that was exactly what he intended.

She started to shake her head but he was already nodding. And darned if he wasn't smiling again.

CHAPTER SEVEN

ALL IT TOOK, Morgan thought as he watched Misty's eyes darken and her lips part, was a nice long look from him. She could deny it all she wanted, but her hunger was almost as bad as his own. When he felt it, she felt it, and right now was proof positive.

Well aware of Howard and Jesse closing in behind him, their curiosity caught, he leaned down and kissed her. It was a simple soft touch. He brushed his mouth over hers, once, twice. She drew a small shuddering breath, and her eyes slowly drifted shut, but she didn't stop him. No, she'd raise hell with him after, he had no doubt of that, but for now, she was as warm and needy as he. Her small hand fisted in his shirt, trying to drag him closer, proved it.

"Misty?" He whispered her name, watching the way her eyelashes fluttered.

"Hmm?"

His own smile took him by surprise. All his life people had teased him about his ferocious frowns, but something about Misty made him feel lighthearted, joyful deep inside. He touched the tip of her nose. "Sweetheart, we have an audience, or I'd sure do better than one measly peck, I promise."

Her eyes flew open, then widened. She peeked around his shoulder cautiously, saw the two men, and her own version of a fierce frown appeared. Her fisted hand released his shirt, and she thumped him in the chest. "Of all the—"

Morgan grabbed her hand, threw one arm around her shoulders and turned, taking her with him to face Howard and Jesse. "I thought I told you two not to work on the weekend."

"Nothing better to do today. We figured we'd get it done and out of the way."

Morgan gave Jesse a good frown to show him what he thought of that, but he knew better than to start debating with him now. "So how's the work going?"

Jesse nodded quickly, a habit he had when he was nervous, and being around women always made him nervous, especially the really pretty ones. "It's getting there. I'll have the lot of it cleared out by midweek." Though he spoke to Morgan, his eyes didn't leave Misty's face.

Howard scratched his chin, watching Misty with acute interest. "It's looking real good."

Amused by their preoccupation, Morgan nudged Misty slightly forward and said, "This is Honey's sister, Misty Malone. She's here for an extended visit and she'll be helping out around the station. Misty, this is Jesse and Howard."

Both men did a double take at that announcement, but Morgan ignored their reactions, knowing why they looked so shocked. They'd obviously jumped to the wrong conclusion. He hid his grin and decided to explain things to them later.

Jesse tipped a nonexistent hat and muttered, "Nice to meet you."

Howard stuck out his hand, realized it was covered with dirt and pulled it back before Misty could accept it. With an apologetic shrug, he explained, "I've been digging out the weeds. Messy work, that. Nice to meet you, Miss Malone."

Misty smiled. "Call me Misty, please. What exactly are you doing back there?"

It was Jesse who answered. "There's been a ton of weeds growing in the gully out back for as long as the sheriff's been stationed here. It draws mosquitoes and gnats and it's just plain ugly. Morgan wants us to clear them out and plant a line of bushes instead. We don't have the bushes in yet, but we will soon."

"I love outdoor work." Misty stepped away from Morgan

and headed to the side of the house to check their progress. "I used to work with my father's gardeners when I was younger. It's hot work, especially on a day like today. But I always preferred that to being cooped up inside."

Morgan could just picture her as a little girl, hanging out with the hired help because her daddy ignored her and she had nothing better to do. It made his stomach cramp.

Howard nodded. "Know what you mean. Fresh air is good for you. I used to farm in my younger days. There's nothing like it."

She went around the corner of the house, Howard and Jesse trailing her like she was the Pied Piper. She kept chatting and they continued to hang on her every word.

Morgan was left alone with his disgruntled feelings. Odds were, he told himself, Misty had been as endearing as a wide-eyed child as she was now. The gardeners had probably loved having her underfoot. He shook his head. Gardeners, for crying out loud.

She made one simple statement about her youth and he got melancholy. It wasn't to be borne.

He heard Jesse's cackling laugh from way out back and frowned. They'd only just met her and she already had them mesmerized. He considered waiting until they came back, then changed his mind. He unlocked the front door, which only he and the deputy used, closed and locked it, then went through the converted house to the back. In what used to be the dining room, a space now housing all his file cabinets, he stared out the large picture window.

He could see Misty standing just outside the line of displaced weeds and dirt, her hands on her rounded hips as she conversed with the men. Her dark shiny hair glinted in the sunlight, and her bare shoulders and thighs appeared sleek. She looked over the still-packaged bushes while the two old codgers looked her over, eyeing the long expanse of her legs. Morgan felt like growling.

He knew he was in a hell of a predicament when two

elders made him jealous. What had happened to his acclaimed control?

He went to the soda machine in the hallway outside his office and fed in quarters. Seconds later he stepped into the yard with four icy cold cans numbing his fingers. Jesse and Howard accepted theirs with relish, popping the tops and guzzling the cola. Though he'd told the old men time and again to bring a cooler with drinks, they never remembered to do it.

Misty was more restrained, using the edge of her shorts to clean the top of the can then opening it cautiously and sipping. It was so hot and humid outside that the little wisps of her hair escaping her topknot had begun to curl around her face.

She squinted against the sun, wrinkling her small nose, and smiled at him. "The bushes will look great once they're in. It'll make the yard looked bigger, too, without the tall weeds breaking up the length."

Morgan nodded, content just to look at her and drink his soda and enjoy the feel of the sunshine.

He loved the old farmhouse—and had since the moment he'd been elected and moved his things into the desk. He forced his gaze away from her and surveyed the back porch. "She's a grand old lady, isn't she?"

"She's beautiful." Misty, too, looked at the porch with the turned rails and ornate trim. "You don't see that kind of detail very often any more."

"It's solid." Morgan finished off his cola, then crushed the can in his fist. "This house is partly what inspired me to build my own home. I was forever doing improvements to the station and finally decided I needed my own place to work on. But even with my house almost complete, I still love it here."

"Somehow, I think it suits you. Especially because you're in charge."

"It does," he agreed, ignoring her teasing tone. "You want to see inside where you'll be working?"

"Sure." She turned to the men and smiled. "Howard, Jesse, it was nice meeting you."

They each nodded, ridiculous smiles on their faces. Morgan could only shake his head in wonder. Was no man immune? As they walked through the back door, he saw her smile and raised a brow in question.

"They're very sweet."

He gave her an incredulous look. "Uh-huh. You go right on wearing those rose-colored glasses, sweetheart."

She gasped at him in disapproval. "You're such a cynic. They're very nice men who are working hard for you. I'd think you'd appreciate that a little."

Morgan led her into his office, which had once been the dining room. It had a large white stone fireplace, now filled with lush ferns instead of burning logs. He'd had the arched doorway framed and fitted so he could close the door for privacy. He'd never needed or wanted that privacy more than now.

He propped his shoulders against the mantel. "Jesse was picked up for fighting two weekends ago. He broke two pool sticks and several lights after a man accused him of cheating at a game. Jesse wouldn't cheat, but he does have a terrible temper."

Misty stared at him in blank surprise.

"Now Howard, he's cooler than that. You won't catch him causing a brawl."

"You're dying to tell me, so spit it out." She mimicked his stance, leaning against the opposite wall.

Grinning, Morgan said, "He slipped into the theater without paying—five times in a row. He loves the movies, but says the prices have gotten too high. Arnold kept kicking him out and Howard kept creeping back in. No one would have known, but during the last movie, he tried stealing a bite of popcorn from the woman sitting next to him."

"And she complained over that?"

Morgan winked at her. "The woman was Marsha Werner, and he'd recently broken off a relationship with her and was,

I imagine, trying to worm his way back into her good graces. She wasn't impressed, so she raised a ruckus and I finally had to arrest him. But it was Marsha who came and bailed him out, so who knows what's happening there?''

Misty tried to stifle a smile. ''It's a little hard to imagine him in a relationship.''

''That's only because you haven't met Marsha. Things soured between them when she wanted to get married, but they were a good couple, like the best grandma and grandpa you'd ever met.'' Morgan watched her smile widen and added, ''Marsha's real fond of the movies, too, but as she continually explains to me in rather loud tones, she's an upstanding citizen and she pays for her entertainment.''

Misty lost control of her twitching smile and laughed out loud. Morgan watched her, seeing the way the heat and humidity outside had made her shirt stick to her breasts. She'd smell all warm and womanly now if he could just get close enough to her to nuzzle her soft skin.

''So what kind of sentence did each of them get?''

He held her gaze and murmured, ''Community work. That's why they're fixing the yard. I bought the bushes and they agreed to do the work. In addition, of course, Jesse had to promise to stay out of the pool hall for a month, and Howard had to pay for the movies he'd seen.''

''Ah. They considered that a terrible punishment?''

''Not the yard work, but the other, yeah. With any luck, it'll make an impression this time. But I hate to see them in any real trouble. They're both pushing seventy, and even though they get around well enough to get into mischief, they don't mean any real harm. I think they're just lonely and a little bored, more than anything else.''

She twisted her mouth in a near grimace, then asked, ''When you arrested them…''

''No, I didn't handcuff them,'' he answered gently, able to read her train of thought. It hurt him to see her so hesitant, to know that her own memories ate at her. He'd fix things for her one way or another, he vowed. ''I didn't stick them in back of the Bronco, either. They both rode up front with me. That way, I could give them a stern talking-to during the ride. They hate that.''

Misty smiled at him for a nearly endless moment, then turned up her can of soda and finished it off. She set the can on his desk. ''I'm impressed, Morgan.''

''With what?''

''Your compassion. And the fact that you obviously have a soft side, which you hide pretty well, by the way.''

He wasn't at all sure he wanted her noticing his soft side, not that he had one, anyway. He frowned at the mere thought.

Misty gave a loud sigh. ''Now what are you scowling about? I insult you and you laugh, I compliment you and you start glowering at me.''

Morgan didn't move. She had an impish look about her that intrigued him. ''Come closer and I'll tell you why I'm frowning.''

''Oh, no, you don't.''

''Afraid of me, Malone?''

She made a rude sound, refusing to be drawn in by his obvious challenge. ''Not likely. You're as big as an ox and built like a ton of bricks, but you don't beat up on women.''

He made his own rude sound. ''That's not what I meant, and you know it.'' He lowered his voice to a suggestive rumble. ''You're afraid if you get too close, you won't want to move away again. But this is my office and I don't do hanky-panky here. At least, not any serious hanky-panky. So you're safe enough.''

''And what constitutes the serious stuff?''

He looked at her breasts and felt his heartbeat accelerate. ''Anything below the waist?''

She swallowed and he could see the thrumming pulse in her throat. ''Howard and Jesse are right outside.''

''Not for much longer. I only let them work for a few hours a day, mostly in the morning because the afternoon heat is too much for them.''

''Then why have them doing that job at all?''

She was bound and determined to distract him, so Morgan let her. The last thing he wanted was for her to be wary of him. "Their pride is important to them, and to me. Already they've told anyone who'd listen that I've given them such a hard, impossible job, then they come here and have a great time futzing around, proving that they can do it. In fact, they complain about the short days I insist on, because Jesse used to be in construction and Howard was a farmer. They say they're used to the heat, but—" He realized he was rambling and ground to a halt.

"You're pretty wonderful sometimes, Sheriff, you know that?"

He unfolded his arms, letting them hang at his sides. In a rough whisper, he said again, "Come here."

She took one step toward him, then halted. "This is crazy."

Morgan nodded in agreement. Crazy didn't even begin to describe the way she made him feel.

She looked undecided and he held his breath, but she turned away. She pretended an interest in the office. Her voice shook when she started talking again. "This is your desk?"

She picked up a framed school picture of Casey and studied it.

"You know it is. My office is the biggest room. The cells are in the basement, though they seldom get used—and yes, I'll take you on a tour in a bit. The kitchen has been rearranged into a lobby of sorts, and there's always coffee there for anyone who wants it. The family room faces the kitchen through open doorways across the hall, and that'll be where you work. There's a lot of office equipment in there. I'll have my deputy, Nate Brewer, show you where he keeps things and how to use the file system. The upstairs has been turned into conference rooms for different community events."

He watched her inch closer to him to look at a plaque hanging on the wall. Not wanting to scare her off now that she was almost within reach, he said, "That's my mission statement."

"Mission statement?"

"My intent for holding office as sheriff. The community got to read it prior to the election." He was thankful she didn't read the whole thing. His patience was about run out and he just wanted to taste her.

"You had the plaque made?"

"Nope. The advisory board did." He saw her start to ask and said, "They're a group of citizens that bring concerns to me. Sort of a community awareness system."

She leaned closer to the plaque. "It says here that you founded the advisory board during your first term in office."

He shook his head. "I was the one who suggested a voice in the community, so they'd all feel more involved in decisions. But they're the ones who organized the board and set up the structure for it. Now they have these big elections to decide who gets to serve in the various advisory board positions."

She moved closer still, examining a trophy on the mantel beside him. Morgan tried to block it with his shoulders, but she inched around him until she could see it clearly. "What's this for?"

Feeling uncomfortable with her inquisition, Morgan cleared his throat. "That was given to me by the student council at the high school."

"It says, outstanding community leadership."

"I know what it says, Malone." He glared, but she glared right back, and he gave up with a sigh. "I started a program where the students can interact with the elders in the community, helping out with chores and such. I'd hoped to give the kids some direction and the elders some company, that's all. But now participation is recognized by the governor for qualifications to state scholarships."

She looked at him. "That's remarkable."

Morgan shifted to face her, determined to satisfy her curiosity so he could get her mind on more pleasurable topics.

"Naw. The students took it a lot further than I did, making it a hell of a program. That's why I thought it deserved to be brought to the governor's notice."

She glanced at the writing on the base of the trophy. "It says here that you help supply scholarship funds, as well."

Morgan rubbed his ear and bit back a curse. "Yeah, well, that's just something I sort of thought would help...."

Misty reached up and took his hand, enfolding it in both of her own. Her blue eyes were filled with amusement and something else. He was almost afraid to figure out what. "Don't be modest, now, Sheriff."

"I'm not!"

"And don't be embarrassed, either."

He gave her his blackest scowl. "That's just plain foolish. Of course I'm not embarrassed. No reason to be. It's all just part and parcel of my job."

Misty shook her head as if scolding him, and it rankled. "I can't quite figure you out, Morgan."

Slowly, so she wouldn't bolt, he slipped his hand free and trailed his fingers up her bare arm to the back of her neck. He'd always loved the feel of women, the smoothness compared to a man's rough angles. But for whatever reason, he loved the feel of Misty more.

Just touching her arm made his heart race, his groin throb. He could only imagine how it would be once he had her naked beneath him, able to touch and taste and investigate every small part of her. He shook with the thought.

Goose bumps appeared where he'd touched her, and she gave a small shiver. "I'm as clear as glass, sweetheart." He was aware of how husky his voice had gone, but damn, he felt like he was burning up. Gently rubbing the back of her neck, he urged her a tiny bit closer, then closer still. He stared at her thick eyelashes, resting against her cheeks, at the warm flush of her skin. "I'm just a man who wants you."

She answered in a similar husky whisper. "*That* part has been plain enough." Staring at his throat, her small hands restless, she refused to meet his gaze. "It's the rest that confounds me."

"But anything else is unimportant." And then he kissed her.

MISTY KNEW her joke about making Morgan miserable had backfired in a big way. She was the one suffering, not him. She realized she actually liked the big guy, and almost cursed. He was so cavalier about all he did, all the responsibility he accepted.

And she seemed to have no control around him at all. He was just so big and so strong and so incredibly handsome. But it was more than that.

Morgan was a nice man.

He was also an honorable man who took his job very seriously and cared about people, not just the people he called family, but all the people in his community. Like an overlord of old, he felt responsible for their safety and happiness. And that made him almost too appealing to resist.

A soft moan escaped her when Morgan touched his mouth to hers and she felt his tongue teasing her lips.

"Open up for me, Malone."

Her hand fisted in his shirt over his hard chest. She felt the trembling of his muscles, the pounding of his heartbeat—and her lips parted.

Morgan let out his own groan only seconds before his tongue was in her mouth. She'd never known kissing like this, so hot and intimate and something more than just mouth on mouth. Maybe it was because Morgan was unique, but being kissed by him seemed more exciting than anything she'd ever done.

Beneath her fingers she could feel his labored breaths, and she opened her palm, amazed by the way his hard muscles shifted and moved in response to her touch. She felt powerful—no man had ever made her feel that way before.

As if he'd known her thoughts, he caught her other hand,

which had been idly clasped at his waistband, and dragged it up to his chest. "Damn, I love it when you touch me."

Misty tucked her face beneath his chin and tried to take a calming breath. Instead, she inhaled his hot male scent and renewed desire. Rather than pushing his advantage, Morgan looped both arms around her and rocked her gently.

"It's almost too much, isn't it?" he growled against her temple.

Words were too difficult, so she nodded, bumping his chin. She felt like crying and hated herself for it. She'd never been a woman who wept over every little thing, so she assumed it must be the pregnancy making her so weak.

Then again, Morgan wasn't a little thing. He was a great big hulking gorgeous thing, and how he made her feel was enough to shake the earth.

His fingertips smoothed over her cheek. "I'm trying to give you time, sweetheart. I know you've been through a lot and until this morning, I've done nothing but push you away. But it's not easy." He gave a shaky laugh and admitted, "It's damn near impossible, if you want the truth."

His words prompted a new thought, but there was no way she could look him in the eyes right now. Morgan would see everything she felt and he'd stop trying to be so considerate. If he pushed even the tiniest bit, she'd give in to him and she knew it. As much as she wanted him, she didn't know if it was the right thing to do. She needed more time.

Hiding her face close to his chest, she did her best to sound casual when she spoke. "It was a rather quick turnaround for you."

"No." He kissed her ear, then nipped her lobe, making her jump. "I wanted you something fierce the first second I saw you. I just figured it'd be too complicated if we got involved."

"Because you're looking for a wife?"

He stiffened slightly, then deliberately began rubbing her back. "Because you're Honey's sister, so you were off-limits for a fling."

It felt like her heart broke, his honest words hurt so much. Her throat was constricted, and she swallowed hard so he wouldn't know how strongly he'd affected her. "But now, since it's obvious what type of woman I am, my relationship to Honey no longer matters?"

"What the hell are you talking about?" Morgan tried to tip her back to see her face, but she held onto him like a clinging vine and he finally quit trying. His mouth pressed warmly to her temple and his arms tightened. "I don't think you're easy, Malone, if that's what you're getting at."

"No?" She forced herself to unclench his shirt. The man would wear wrinkles all day thanks to her. And his brothers would probably take one look at him and know why. "I'm pregnant, with no husband, no job. I'm a convict, for crying out loud. What's your definition of easy?"

He took her off guard, thrusting her back a good foot with his hands wrapped securely around her upper arms. His scowl was enough to scare demons back to hell. Misty held her breath, not afraid of him physically, really, but very uncertain of his mood.

He started to say something, then paused. "Damn it," he growled, "don't look at me like that. I would never hurt you."

She nodded. "I know it."

"Then why are you shaking?"

"*You're* shaking me."

He looked poleaxed by that observation, then dropped his hands to shove them onto his hips in a thoroughly arrogant stance. Misty wrapped her arms around herself and watched him cautiously.

He didn't apologize. "And you deserve it, too."

"For asking a question?" Now that he wasn't touching her, she could regain her edge.

"For suggesting something so stupid." He took a quick step toward her, leaned down in a most unnerving way and practically shouted, "I do not think you're easy!"

Misty blinked.

"Hell, woman, you're about the most difficult female I've ever run across. You fight me at every damn turn."

For some reason, Misty felt like smiling. She bit her lip, knowing Morgan wouldn't appreciate it one bit. "That's not true."

"No? I go crazy for you, and you ignore me, then flirt outrageously with every other male in the county."

That got her good and mad. "I did no such thing! And you ignored me first." She hadn't meant to bring that up; it made her sound spiteful, as if she'd ignored him to get even. She frowned at him for making her say too much.

"I tell you to leave, you argue about it. I all but beg you to stay, you argue about it."

"I did not argue about leaving."

"You got snide, I remember that well enough." He rubbed his neck and groaned. "Hell, it was all I could do to keep my hands to myself, to put up with having you in the house until Sawyer's wedding, and you just kept sniping at me, and for some fool reason that only made me want you more."

"How could I have ignored you and sniped at you at the same time? That doesn't make sense, Morgan."

His eyes narrowed. "You'd snipe with silence, by being there, making me want you, then chatting with one of my disreputable brothers as if I wasn't in the room when I knew damn good and well you were aware of me. Admit it, Malone."

This time she gave in to the grin; she couldn't help herself. "Admit I was aware of you? Sure. You're a mite hard to miss, Morgan, being so big and all."

He took another step toward her, and she backed up. In soft tones that sounded like threats rather than compliments, he said, "I admire your pride, sweetheart, I really do. But that pride is misplaced when you cut off your nose to spite your face."

"What is that supposed to mean?"

"It means you wanted to stay here, but stubbornly refused just because I'd been a pigheaded fool and asked you to go."

"I agreed to stay, Morgan," she said, feeling it necessary to point that out.

"And you refused a good job, just because you thought it was created for you."

"Uh...I took the job, too, remember?"

"I remember that I had to practically get down on my hands and knees, as well as resort to every lamebrained scheme around, to get your agreement! And you dare to say I think you're *easy?*"

"Will you stop shouting at me?"

He halted. Misty had her back to a bookcase, and Morgan was only a scant inch away. "Yeah, I'll stop shouting. As long as you promise to never again put words in my mouth."

Because he looked so sincerely put out over it, she agreed. "I'm sorry."

With his hands on the bookshelf level with her head, he caged her in. "Listen good, Malone, because I don't want to have to repeat this." His gaze dipped to her mouth, then came back to her eyes, pinning her motionless. "I do not think you're easy. I think you're a beautiful woman who got involved with the wrong guy and ended up in some trouble because of it. And no, I'm not talking about the pregnancy, because you're right, that's not real trouble. If you want the baby, then everything else will work itself out. I was talking about being blamed for the theft."

He drew a long breath, then squeezed his eyes shut. "And I'll have you know that even arguing with you makes me hot. I'm so damn hard right now I could be considered lethal."

A startled laugh burst out of her, making Morgan scowl all the more. She looked at his face, then doubled over in laughter, making an awful racket but unable to help herself.

Morgan waited patiently, crossing his arms over his chest and blocking her so she couldn't move away. His reaction made her laugh harder, and she fell against him until he was forced to prop her up.

When she finally quieted, Morgan was rubbing her back

and smiling at her. "You want to tell me what brought that on?"

"You're priceless, Morgan."

"How so?"

He was such a reprobate. She smiled at him as she explained, aware of his hands drifting lower, almost to her behind. "You have absolutely no consideration for my modesty or my sensibilities. You talk about the most personal things—"

"Like what?"

"Like the fact you seem to have a problem with control."

He shook his head very slowly. "Not usually. Everyone will tell you I maintain absolute control."

She quirked a brow and stared at his fly.

With a grin, Morgan said, "That's an aberration, an involuntary reaction that can't be controlled around you."

She almost started laughing again. "Well, whatever it is, you show no hesitation in talking about it, shocking me all the time, embarrassing me."

His hands slid over her bottom completely, and he lifted her to her tiptoes so she fit against him. She caught her breath as his voice went husky and deep. "I want you to know how much I want you, sweetheart."

Contentment swelled inside her. She knew it was dangerous to make herself vulnerable to him, but at the moment, she was too touched to care. "That's just it," she said softly, "you show no hesitation about making me blush, but you're so considerate of my feelings otherwise. Thank you."

Morgan's fingers contracted on her backside, caressing and exciting. "You want to know how you can thank me?"

Misty was ready to start laughing again when a tentative knock sounded on the door. She jumped, bumped her head on the bookcase, then shoved him away. "Good grief, my first time in your office and look what happens."

With a wry look, Morgan turned and headed for the door. "Unfortunately, not a thing happened." He stepped into the hallway. Misty went to the office door to peek out and see who it was. When she saw Howard and Jesse stomping to remove the dirt from their boots, she stepped out to greet them.

"Are you all done for the day?"

Jesse shook his head. "Just taking off for lunch. Is this your first day?"

"No, Morgan was just showing me around today. I'll start tomorrow."

Jesse frowned at Morgan. "How long does she have?"

Misty didn't understand the question, and Morgan didn't help by grinning at her. "I'm not sure yet. What do you think?"

"I think it'd be nice to keep her on for good, but I don't suppose that'd be fair."

Howard agreed. "Can't imagine what she could've done—not that I'm prying, you understand. But to be here in the first place..."

Misty frowned in confusion. "I'm here because Morgan said he needed someone to answer the phone and take messages."

Jesse nodded. "That's a fact. Just about every day one woman or another comes here insisting just that. But I always wondered if it's really work they have on their minds." He gave her an exaggerated wink. "Ought to put an end to that now, what with Misty here, though."

"That," Misty said while trying to hide her annoyance at the thought, "is entirely up to Morgan."

"Yes, it is," Morgan agreed, smiling at her, "but it so happens I think Jesse is right. One female in the office is more than enough."

Misty clamped her lips together to keep from replying.

Morgan looked disappointed at her restraint. He turned his attention to the men. "You both have lunch with you?"

"Naw, we're going to the diner. Ceily promised me meat loaf today."

He glanced at his watch. "Is the diner open yet?"

"She'll slip us in through the kitchen."

Howard added, "You take it easy on the little lady, now, you hear?"

"I should explain something, here, guys—" Morgan began, and Misty knew he was going to blurt out something stupid, about how they were involved.

She rushed to his side and nudged him playfully with her shoulder, trying to act like a pal instead of an almost lover. "Morgan is a big pushover. Don't you worry, I can handle him."

Both the men stared at her in awe. Morgan rumbled, a sound between a laugh and a growl. "Malone—"

"Behave, Morgan," she snapped, giving him a telling look before forcing a smile on the men. "They're hungry. Let them go eat."

"But—"

Misty ignored him. "Run on, now. You both look famished to me. Everyone knows big healthy men need to eat a lot to keep up their strength. Especially when they're working as hard as you two are."

Jesse and Howard puffed up like proud roosters.

Misty waved them off, and after Morgan had shut the door, he said with amusement, "You certainly wrapped them around your little finger."

She didn't appreciate that comment at all, considering she'd barely managed to keep him from embarrassing her again. "They're very sweet men."

Morgan choked on a laugh. "They feel the same way about you. That's why they were trying to find out why you're here."

She didn't understand his humor at all. "Is it so uncommon for you to hire someone?"

Morgan pursed his mouth, but ended up chuckling anyway. "Actually, yeah, it is. And Malone, they don't think you were hired."

"What's that supposed to mean? Do they think I coerced the job out of you? I swear, Morgan, if people are going to talk because I'm working here..."

He leaned a shoulder against the wall, and even though his mouth wasn't smiling, she saw the unholy glint in his blue eyes. "Oh, they'll talk, all right. You see, at this moment Jesse and Howard are probably telling anyone they can find that you're serving out your time working here—same as they are."

She felt her eyes nearly cross. "That's ridiculous!"

Shrugging, he said, "That's usually why I bring someone in underfoot. Because they got into mischief and have to do community work."

"But..." She couldn't think of anything to say, then her temper flared. "You could have set them straight!"

"I believe I tried to. But you were too intent on telling them how you could handle me to let me finish."

Misty moaned and covered her face. "So now, even though no one here knows I was actually arrested, they're all going to think the same about me anyway."

Morgan pulled her hands down and kissed the end of her nose. "Let me show you around the office, explain your duties, then we'll go to the diner and set them straight."

"We will?"

He brushed his thumb over her bottom lip. "Believe me, Malone, no one is going to have any doubts as to why I'm keeping you close, I promise. So quit your worries."

Misty followed him into the office, but his promise, and the way he'd given it, left an empty ache inside her.

Morgan was slowly getting under her skin, and that left her feeling far from reassured.

CHAPTER EIGHT

"OUCH." Misty bumped her head as she knelt and crawled beneath the desk. "You're sure she went under here?"

Jordan sounded slightly strangled as he said, "Yeah, she's under there."

In the farthest corner, against the back wall, Misty saw a curled calico tail. "Ah, I see her. She's a little thing."

"I found her abandoned." Anger laced Jordan's tone, and that was unusual because Misty had never heard this particular brother sound anything but pleasant. "I brought her home to heal, and your sister sort of bonded with her. Usually she's in bed with Honey, but today, well, I think she knew it was a day for shots and that's why she's running from me."

Misty bumped her head again when she tried to look at Jordan. All she could see was his feet. He'd been chasing the cat to take it to his clinic when they'd run into each other in the hallway. The cat had scurried away while Jordan kept Misty from falling on her behind.

Misty had been hoping to leave the house before Morgan. According to Honey, he'd been looking for her last night and had been disgruntled when he couldn't find her. But she wasn't yet ready to tell him where she'd been. Dodging him this morning was the only way she could think of to buy herself some time.

"So do you like your new job?" Jordan asked her as she crawled deeper beneath the desk.

"Actually, I do." She reached out her hand and the small cat, hissing at her, managed to inch a little farther away.

"That's good. I gather Morgan is behaving himself?"

"Morgan is Morgan. He never really behaves. You know that."

"Uh, yes, I see your point."

Morgan was the most forward, outspoken man she'd ever known, but he kept her smiling and sometimes even laughing. And he always made her very aware of her own femininity. The man could scorch her with a look, and in the short time she'd spent with him, she'd become addicted to the feeling.

But the entire week had been a series of near misses. Though she worked in his office, he was seldom there. She'd had no idea he kept such a horrendously busy schedule. After hours wasn't much better. When Morgan was free, she was gone. When she was free, Morgan got called away. His plan to make them look like a couple wasn't quite working out as she'd assumed. She hated to admit it, even to herself, but she'd been looking forward to his outrageous pursuit. And she missed him.

Jordan coughed suddenly, then suggested, "Uh, maybe you should just come on out of there?"

"No, I've almost got her. She's worked herself into a tiny little ball. Let me just scrunch in here a bit more."

"No, wait. I'll pull the desk out."

Misty was sure she heard repressed laughter in Jordan's voice, but the sound was muffled because most of her upper body was wedged into the seating area of the desk. "No, if you do that she'll just run off again. At least this way I have her cornered."

Jordan made a strangled sound.

"What?"

"Never mind."

Misty tried wiggling her fingers at the cat. She had hoped to be gone already, out the door before Morgan awoke. Working with him was more enjoyable than she'd thought it would be. She liked getting to know everyone in the town, and it was so obvious to her how they all adored their sheriff. He was treated with respect and reverence and a bit of awe.

"So your arrangement with Morgan is working out?"

She snorted, wondering which arrangement Jordan referred to. The work or the personal relationship. "Yes, things are fine. Although Morgan does like to complain a lot."

"Well, as to that," Jordan said cautiously, "I think he complains because things aren't going quite the way he planned."

"Things aren't going quite how I planned, either." She laughed, then added, "Morgan gripes because it's a habit, just like scowling at everyone." Misty thought of all she'd learned about Morgan in the past week, how he reacted with the various community members who liked to stop by and offer suggestions or complaints or idle chitchat. His patience was limitless, and why not? He usually controlled everything and everyone without anybody even realizing it. He was careful not to offend, strong and supportive, understanding. But the final word was his, and they all respected that about him. In fact, she often got the impression that they brought their minor gripes to him so he *would* take charge, saving them the hassle.

Overall, she admitted he made a pretty wonderful sheriff.

"You know, Jordan, Morgan would like the world to think he's a real bear, but Honey's right. Deep down he's just a big softy."

There was a choked laugh, then a loud thump. Jordan cursed under his breath.

"Now don't tease, Jordan. You know I'm right. Even though you all harass each other endlessly, you know your brother is pretty terrific."

Jordan's voice was lazy. "I think you and Honey are sharing that particular delusion. She's as misguided about him as you are." Then: "Just think. With you two singing his praises, Morgan will be known as a real pussycat in no time at all."

Laughing, Misty said, "I wouldn't go that far!"

Her laugh startled the cat, and when she tried to run, Misty reached out and scooped her up. "I've got her." She started crawling backward, inching her way out. The cat didn't fight her. Instead, it purred loudly at the attention.

Misty held the small calico close to her chest and scooted until she bumped into a pair of hard shins. Startled, she turned and looked up to see what Jordan was doing, and was met with Morgan's blackest look. He had his big feet braced, his hands on his hips and his jaw locked. He didn't move.

Jordan stood behind him, grinning.

For some fool reason, Misty felt her face heating. How long had he been there? What had she just been saying about him? She pulled her gaze away from his and frowned at Jordan. "You could have warned me."

"Warned you about what?" Jordan asked innocently.

Morgan reached down and caught Misty's elbow. "Come on, Malone, quit abusing my brother."

Judging by the way Jordan rubbed his shoulder, Misty had the suspicion Morgan had already done enough abusing, but she had no idea why. Jordan didn't seem bothered by it, though. He looked entertained. She frowned at Morgan. "What do you want?"

He didn't appear to like her question. "We need to get to work."

Misty stood, attempting to ignore Morgan's nearness and Jordan's attentive presence. "We've got a few minutes."

Crossing his arms over his chest, Morgan said, "Is that so? Then why were you trying to hightail it out of here so early?"

She couldn't very well explain with Morgan's brother standing there, so she turned to Jordan and handed him the cat. "Hang onto her this time."

"Thanks, sweetie." Jordan leaned forward and kissed her cheek, grinned at Morgan one more time, then left them. Misty could hear his soft crooning voice as he spoke with the cat.

She had a feeling Jordan had kissed her just to provoke Morgan, and seeing the way Morgan clenched his jaw, it must have worked. They stared at each other for a long, silent moment. Finally, Morgan shook his head. "You've been avoiding me all week."

"That's not true! We've just had conflicting schedules, that's all."

"Your only schedule is working with me. Yet I haven't had one single second alone with you. That's avoidance."

She didn't want to admit that she'd missed him, too, or that she did, in fact, have another schedule. "It's not my fault that you work all the time."

"I knocked at your door at six yesterday." His gaze softened. "I expected to find you in bed still, all warm and sleepy. But you were gone already."

Misty wondered what he would have done if he'd found her in bed, and the thought wasn't at all repulsive. She cleared her throat. "Maybe it was a good thing I wasn't there."

"There you go with those lecherous thoughts again, Malone. I was just going to offer to take you to breakfast."

She winced at the very idea. "If you'll recall, Morgan, mornings are a little rough for me. I like to walk down and sit by the lake. The fresh air settles my stomach some."

He scowled over that, and his voice sounded gruff, more with concern than annoyance. "I'd forgotten. Has the morning sickness been bad?"

Oh, when Morgan was being so sweet, it was all she could do to resist him. She wasn't even sure she wanted to anymore. Thoughts of being with him had consumed her lately. When he was around, she could barely take her eyes off him, and when he wasn't, her thoughts centered on him.

Misty realized he was watching her, and she coughed. "Actually," she said, deciding to give him a small truth, "it's been better lately. Usually, as long as I don't eat, my stomach settles down fairly quick."

"So you've been skipping breakfast?"

"I was never much for big morning meals, anyway."

His frown was back, more intense than ever. "You weren't at dinner last night, either." He looked her over, then shook his head. ''You know how important it is for you to eat properly right now. ''

''I have enough mothering from Honey. You don't need to start, too.'' And before he could protest that, she added, ''Besides, I'm not starving myself. I ate in town last night.''

He went still, then he flushed and growled, ''With who?''

This was exactly the subject Misty had hoped to avoid, but now it looked as if she had no choice but to tell him. Exasperated, she pushed past him and headed down the hall. Morgan followed. ''If you must know,'' she said over her shoulder, ''I was working.''

''You got off work at three o'clock, Malone. I watched you leave.''

Yes, he had. She shivered just remembering. Morgan had been watching her with a brooding frown as she'd gathered her things. He was stuck talking with an elderly woman who claimed her neighbor mowed his grass too early in the morning to suit her. Misty had known by the look on Morgan's face that his patience was about at an end. If she hadn't been required to be elsewhere, she very well might have hung around just to see what he'd do. ''I left the station at three o'clock. But then I went to the diner.''

''To meet someone?''

Her temper snapped. Did he always have to think the worst of her? ''That's none of your concern.''

She kept walking, but he had stopped. She didn't mean to, but when she turned to face him and saw his expression, her heart almost melted. He looked angry and frustrated and...hurt.

She'd never thought she'd see a look like that on the inimitable sheriff's face.

She didn't like it at all.

She stomped down the hall to glare at him, thrust her chin up and said, ''No, I wasn't meeting anyone. I went there to work.''

His confusion was almost laughable. ''You're working at the diner? Since when?''

"Since yesterday. Ceily hired me." His mouth opened and she said, "Before you ask, yes, I told her about my record."

"Misty." He said her name so softly, like a reprimand, and she felt a lump gather in her throat. He took both her arms, his thumbs rubbing just above her elbows. "I hadn't even thought of that."

"Bull. You had that look on your face."

"What look?"

"The one that's full of doubt."

"That was just me trying to figure you out." His mouth tipped in a small smile. "What did Ceily have to say?"

"I told her the truth, that I was innocent but couldn't prove it, and that the whole thing had cost a lot so I needed to save up more money now. She believed me." Misty twisted her hands together, once again caught in a worry. Ceily was a very pretty, petite woman with long golden brown hair and big brown eyes. She looked to be around Gabe's age. She'd been very warm and welcoming to Misty from the onset. "She didn't strike me as the type to carry tales. She even warned me about telling any secrets to Howard or Jesse. She said they're both horrible gossips."

Morgan laughed. "She would know. Jesse is her grandpa."

"I hadn't realized. They don't look anything alike."

"Considering Jesse is old and cantankerous and Ceily is young and cute, I'm not surprised you didn't see the family resemblance. But you're right about Ceily, she doesn't gossip. You don't have to worry about that."

Without meaning to, Misty frowned at him. "You know her well?"

He shrugged. "As well as I know anyone here. Ceily and Gabe went through school together, and she used to hang out at the house when they were younger. They're both water fanatics. She's a good kid."

Misty relaxed the tiniest bit. It appeared her secrets were safe with Ceily, which had been her only concern.

Morgan asked, "Do you mind telling me how you figure on doing both jobs?"

"I knew you wouldn't understand," she muttered. He was strong and capable and respected...and it would have been so easy to lean on him and let him help her, to follow suit with the entire town and let Morgan handle her problems. But she wanted to regain what she'd lost on her own. It was the only way she could think of to restore her self-respect.

He let her go reluctantly and fell into step beside her as she headed for her room. "Tell me what I don't understand, babe."

She shook her head. "What I do for you can barely be considered part time, Morgan. It's only six hours a day."

"I didn't want you to overdo."

Why, oh why, did he have to say things like that? "I'm not breakable, you know."

"I would never suggest such a thing." He kept pace with her easily, then paused when she reached her door. "No one would ever doubt your strength or determination, Malone. If that's what this is about..."

Flustered, Misty shrugged. "There's no reason I can't work for the diner in the evenings, right? Ceily agreed to put me on at four. That gives me time to grab a bite to eat and then get in four or five more hours. Last night, I made fifty bucks in tips. It's a good job."

Morgan propped his hands on his hips, dropped his head forward and paced several feet. When he finally faced her again, he looked grim. "I'm going to let all that go for now."

"How magnanimous of you."

He didn't appreciate her dry wit. "I want to talk to you about something else. Will you ride into work with me?"

She regretted the need to refuse him. "I can't. I'll be going to the diner again after we finish at the station. I'll need my car to get home."

"I'll pick you up when you get off."

"That doesn't make sense, Morgan. You never know when

you might get a call, and I don't want to interrupt things for you."

He did a little more jaw locking. Misty wondered why he didn't have a perpetual headache.

"All right. Then let me take you to my house tonight. I've been wanting to show it to you, anyway."

The idea was tempting. From afar, his house looked wonderful. It wasn't quite as large as the house he shared with his brothers, but it had just as much character. The exterior appeared to be cedar, and few of the mature trees had been displaced during the building. Every morning when she went to the lake, she looked at his house. Its position on the hill would prove a stunning view. "Why do you want to go there?"

He shrugged. "I just want your opinion, to see if you like it. No other woman has seen it yet, except for Honey. But the two of you are so different, I thought it'd be nice to get your reaction, too. The house will be done before much longer. Gabe works on it off and on, and I get up there whenever I can. All the major stuff is done, now it just needs the finishing touches."

Misty chewed her bottom lip. She wasn't stupid; she knew if she was alone with Morgan for any length of time, they'd probably end up making love. She'd honestly believed no man could ever tempt her again, but she hadn't counted on a man like him. She'd thought him incredibly sexy from the moment she saw him, and since then, she'd also discovered what a wonderful man he was, inside as well as out.

He was always honest with her, and she knew deep in her heart she'd never meet another man like him. She was through with lasting relationships, and as soon as she could save up a little money, she was going to move away. By the time she returned for a visit, Morgan might well be married and on his way to having his own children.

She shook her head, saying mostly to herself, "I don't know...."

His hands cradled her face. "I won't lie to you, Malone.

I want some time alone with you. I want to be able to talk to you without one of my damn brothers nosing in, or someone at the station staring at us." He looked at her mouth. "And I want to kiss you again. We've barely seen each other all week. At this rate, no one is going to believe we're involved. Already I've had people questioning our relationship."

He said the last with a growl, and she almost laughed at him. "What people?"

His frown deepened. "No one you need to know about. I made it clear you weren't free—like we agreed, right?"

"Uh, right." Morgan was in a very strange mood, she decided. It was almost as if he was...jealous.

"It's Nate's fault. He's running around telling people we hardly talk, much less act involved."

"Nate, your deputy?"

"Yeah." Morgan looked suspicious. "And that reminds me, has Nate been flirting with you?"

Startled, Misty shook her head. She'd met Nate her first day on the job. He was a good-looking young man, not a whole lot taller than she was, with brown hair and green eyes and full of smiles. He'd asked her to lunch during her break, but she'd declined, choosing instead to eat at her desk—an apple and a peanut-butter sandwich she'd packed. After that, Nate usually brought a bagged lunch, too, and visited with her while they ate.

Morgan generally had appointments during that time and ate on the road. The amount of community work he did astounded her.

Morgan gave her a long sigh. "Are you sure?"

She scoffed at him. "He's only a boy, Morgan."

"He's twenty-two years old, Malone, old enough to be my deputy, and only two years younger than you." Morgan's tone was exasperated. "Would you even realize it if Nate *was* flirting?"

"Well, I assume so."

Morgan put one arm on the wall beside her head. "For

some reason, I think you're just oblivious to the way you affect men."

"Maybe that's because, so far, you're the only one claiming to be affected. That only makes you the oddity, Morgan, not the norm."

He didn't look at all insulted by her comment. His large hand spread out over her middle, making her suck in her breath as a shock of awareness rolled through her. His fingertips, angled downward, nearly touched her hipbones. His palm was hot and firm against her.

Very softly he asked, "Now, how can that be true, when I know for a fact at least one other man chased you down? You didn't get pregnant all by yourself."

She couldn't reply. So many feelings swamped her at once, it was difficult to sort them out. In the past, every relationship she'd shared had started because she wanted someone to call her own, because she'd believed women were supposed to share their lives with men. It wasn't because she found a man irresistible and craved his company.

She no longer felt she needed or wanted a man in her life, and she'd decided she was better off on her own. But how she felt around Morgan was so different from those other relationships. She *did* crave him, and ignoring Morgan was like trying not to breathe—impossible.

By reflex, she put her hand over his, intending to pull it away, but instead, she held it tighter to her. "Kent...Kent was like most men, saying the right things to get my attention. I wanted to believe that he cared, so I did. But he never really wanted me, not like—" She stammered into silence and blushed.

Morgan gave her a satisfied smile. "You mean, like I do?"

How could he expect her to answer that? "All he really wanted," she said, ignoring his question and her embarrassment, "was the convenience of being with one woman. He never really cared about me."

"He was obviously a goddamned fool."

She looked up at him, then felt snared in his gaze. "Men

flirt by nature. It doesn't mean anything. And it doesn't matter who the woman is or what she looks like."

"There's flirting, and then there's flirting." Morgan gave her a small smile. "You can believe I've never disabled another woman's car, or dragged her into a gazebo."

Misty managed a laugh. "No, probably it was the women dragging you into private places."

Morgan's fingers on her abdomen began a gentle caress that made it difficult for her to remain still. "Let's try this from another angle, okay? Forget Kent—he's not worth mentioning. And he's hardly a good example of the male species. Agreed?"

"Agreed."

"So. Has Nate been hanging around your desk? Talking to you a lot? Has he asked you out?"

She could barely think with his palm pressed so intimately to her body. Her khaki slacks weren't much of a barrier. And she could feel his breath on her cheek, could smell the delicious scent of cologne and soap and man. His wrist was so thick where she held him, her fingers couldn't circle it completely. "Um, yes, yes and no."

He nuzzled his nose against hers. "Yes and no what?"

"Yes, he talks with me, and yes, he stops by my desk. Just about everyone who comes into the station does."

Morgan dropped his forehead to hers. "I need to put a paper sack over your head. I hadn't realized it, but I'd have been better off hiding you away here at the house."

Misty couldn't help but smile. "No, he hasn't asked me out. He invited me to lunch once, but that hardly counts as a date. That was just a friendly visit between employees. I think he gets lonely at lunchtime, because now he usually eats at the station with me."

Morgan looked at her like she was a simpleton. "He's *flirting*, Malone."

"No, he's not."

Morgan drew an exasperated breath and shook his head at her. "I'm going to put a stop to it."

"Jesse and Howard are always there. And don't you dare suggest they're flirting, too."

He tipped his head back and groaned. "I'm surprised every single male in the area isn't there hanging on your damn desk. From now on, I'm going to make sure I'm around to take you to lunch. And stop shaking your head at me!"

"Morgan, you're being unreasonable." But deep inside, she was pleased by his jealousy. She had to admit that maybe, just maybe, she was fighting a losing battle.

"I want to make sure you eat right."

"Uh-huh. I can tell that's your motivation." Misty quit denying him. "If you want to take me to lunch, that's fine with me."

"Then it's settled." Triumph shone in his gaze. "And about damn time, too."

"You know, Morgan, if everyone found out I was pregnant, that'd likely put an end to any interest—imagined or otherwise."

Morgan kissed her brow, then her nose. "Don't count on it. It didn't do a damn thing to make me want you less."

He was about to kiss her again, and she was about to let him, when Sawyer emerged from his bedroom and glanced at them.

"A little rendezvous in the hall?" he asked.

Misty felt like kicking Morgan. How did she always end up in these awkward situations when he was around? "Did we wake you?"

"Nope, I had early appointments this morning. The honeymoon is over now that a flu bug has started making the rounds."

That sounded innocuous enough, and Misty sighed. "Well, I need to get going, anyway. I was just on my way out."

Morgan tipped his head. "Didn't you need something from your room?"

She closed her eyes. She'd come to her room just to escape him, but she wouldn't admit that in front of Sawyer, who showed no signs of giving them any privacy. With a weak smile, she said, "Whatever it was, I've forgotten."

She darted around Morgan and made a beeline past Sawyer. She was almost out of hearing range when Sawyer said, "You've got her on the run, Morgan. I just wonder if that was your intent."

MORGAN GLARED at his brother. "I know what I'm doing."

"And what exactly is that?"

They both left the hall in the direction of the kitchen. The smell of coffee was tantalizing, and Morgan needed a shot of caffeine to boost him. Unfortunately, Jordan was still there, the cat on his lap.

"You," Morgan said, effectively distracted, "were ogling Misty when I walked in."

Jordan shrugged, then said to Sawyer, "She'd climbed under the desk to get the cat for me." His grin was unholy. "She has a damn fine bottom."

Morgan felt ready for murder. "Keep your eyes off her bottom."

"Why? You sure didn't." He rubbed the cat and said in an offhand way, "Sawyer, I meant to mention it to you earlier. I think there's something wrong with Morgan."

Sawyer filled his coffee cup then sank into a chair. He blew on the coffee to cool it, showing no interest in Jordan's gibe.

Which of course didn't stop Jordan. "Yep, I think he must be sick. Half the time I see him, he's got this glazed look in his eyes. And once or twice, I've actually caught him smiling."

Sawyer laughed. "No! Morgan smiling? That's absurd."

Morgan came half out of his seat, and Jordan held up a hand, grinning. "No, don't throttle me. I'm on my way out the door right now. I just hung around to tell you... goodbye." He stood, the cat tucked under his arm, and grabbed his keys hanging by the door. "I'll see you all later."

As the door closed behind him, Morgan muttered, "Good riddance."

"Quit being such a grouch, Morgan. I survived, so I'm certain you will, too."

"Survived what? I don't know what you're talking about."

"Falling in love." Sawyer added quickly, "No, don't give me all your excuses. I've heard them all and even made up half of them. It'll do you no good."

Morgan felt like an elephant had just sat on his chest. He wheezed, then managed to say, "I am not in love."

"No? Then what would you call it? Lust?"

"What I'd call it is no one's business but my own."

"I think Honey might disagree with you there. She loves her sister more than you can imagine. I think they spent the longest time with no one but each other. Right now, Honey's convinced you're an honorable, likable gentleman. But if you hurt Misty, she'll take you apart. And I can tell you right now, there's not a damn thing I could do about it."

"I keep telling you that you should control your wife."

"Spoken like a true bachelor."

"Besides, I'd never hurt Malone."

"Oh? You think having an affair with you won't hurt her? She's been through enough, Morgan. Did you know she went to her father and he offered not an ounce of comfort? Honey told me about it. It seems he was more disappointed with her than anything else."

Which, Morgan assumed, pretty much guaranteed she wouldn't bother him with her arrest and conviction. She'd known without asking that her father wouldn't assist her, or even take her side. Morgan shook his head, feeling that damn pain again. Misty had come to the only person she could really count on: her sister. And thank God she had.

Sawyer frowned at him. "She needs some stability, Morgan, not more halfhearted commitments."

Morgan downed half his coffee, burned his tongue and cursed in the foulest of terms. Sawyer never said a word.

"Look, Sawyer, she doesn't want a commitment, all right? She told me that herself. She's sworn off men."

"Hate to break it to you like this, Morgan, but you're a man."

"That's not what I meant! What we feel—well, it's mutual. Only she doesn't want to get overly involved." Almost as an afterthought, he added, "Any more than I do."

"I thought you wanted to get married?"

He shook his head, wondering if Sawyer was rattling him on purpose. "I want a wife like Honey."

Sawyer spewed coffee across the table. Morgan gave him a look then handed him a napkin. "I said a wife *like* her, not Honey, herself. I want someone domestic and settled and sweet...."

"You don't think Misty fits the bill? What, she's not sweet? She's got a nasty temper?"

"I never said that," he ground out between clenched teeth. He thought Misty Malone was about the sweetest woman he'd ever met, even if her temper rivaled his own. Or maybe because of her temper. He almost grinned. "You keep forgetting, Misty doesn't want to get married. She's told me that plain as day."

Suddenly Sawyer's eyes widened. "Good God. You're afraid."

Morgan slowly stiffened, and he felt every muscle tense. In a low growl, he asked his brother, "Are you deliberately trying to piss me off?"

Sawyer waved a hand, dismissing any threat. "You're afraid you'll ask her and she'll turn you down."

Even his damn toes tensed. "You're a doctor of medicine, Sawyer, not psychology. There's a good reason for that, you know."

Sawyer started to laugh. "I don't believe this. Women have been chasing you for as long as I can remember, and now here's one you've got cornered, keeping her as close as you can get her, but you're afraid of her."

"Honey's not going to like you much with a bloody nose."

Morgan hadn't actually raised a hand in anger toward any of his brothers since his early teens. He assumed that was why Sawyer so easily ignored his warning.

Sawyer was still laughing, and Morgan decided it was time to change the subject. "She's taken another job."

That shut him up. "Misty quit working for you?"

"No, she took a second job. But should she be doing that in her condition?"

"Her condition isn't exactly debilitating," Sawyer pointed out, then with curiosity: "What job did she take?"

"She's working at the diner." Morgan knew he sounded disgruntled, but damn it, he didn't want her working two jobs. And he sure as certain didn't want her out there where anyone and everyone from town would be able to look her over. The woman didn't know her own appeal. Before she'd even be aware of it, she'd find herself engaged again. Morgan wasn't about to let that happen.

"From what she said, I gather she plans to work there an additional six or so hours, all in the evening. I think it's too much."

Sawyer frowned in thought. "She's a healthy young woman, and her pregnancy is still in the early stages, so it probably won't bother her right now. But when she gets further along, there's a good chance her ankles will swell and her back will hurt if she stays on her feet for that long."

"Maybe you should try talking to her." Morgan thought it was a terrific idea, and his mood lightened. "You're a doctor. She'd listen to you."

"I'm not *her* doctor, so it's none of my business. Come to that, it's none of your business, either."

"Hmm. She hasn't mentioned seeing a doctor at all. And shouldn't she be taking vitamins or something?"

Sawyer gave it up. "Why don't you ask her about it. I can give her the vitamins, but she should have regular checkups with an obstetrician. Being she's new in the area, I could recommend someone." As an afterthought, Sawyer asked, "How far along is she?"

"I think she said around three months. Why?"

Sawyer finished his coffee and stood. "No matter." He looked his brother over carefully. "I've got to get to work. Are you going to be okay?"

Morgan immediately frowned again. "I'm fine, damn it."

"Just asking." He turned to go, but hesitated. "Morgan? At least think about what I said, all right? If you wait too long to figure things out, you could blow it. And I can only imagine what a miserable bastard you'd be in that case."

Morgan watched him go, thinking that marriage had made Sawyer more philosophical than usual. Then he thought of Misty at the office, with Nate and Jesse and Howard all sucking up to her. He saw red.

Howard and Jesse were old enough to be her grandfathers, and she was right when she said Nate wasn't much more than a kid.

It was a sad day when he got jealous over the likes of them, but Morgan admitted the truth—he *was* jealous. Viciously jealous. He didn't want anyone looking at her, because he knew good and well that any red-blooded male, regardless of his age, would be thinking the same erotic things he thought.

Jealousy was new to him. He'd been dating women since before he was Casey's age, and never once experienced so much as a twinge. If a woman wasn't interested, he moved on. If she was, they set up ground rules and had some fun. The twist with Misty was that she was interested, but she'd rather deny them both because she'd been burned and she didn't want to get *involved.* Morgan had thought that the promise of an uninvolved relationship might suit her, but so far she'd turned that down, too.

Was Sawyer right? Was Misty only trying to protect herself from being hurt again? He knew having a record wasn't something she'd ever be able to accept, so he'd set things in motion on that front. He didn't believe she was guilty, but he had a hunch who was. He'd hired a few men to check into it, and now it was only a matter of waiting to see if he was right.

Maybe once that was taken care of, she'd stop holding back on him. If he could only get her to see how good things would be between them.... What? He'd get her to marry him?

Morgan thought about that, then nodded. Life with Misty would be one hell of a wild ride. He grinned with the thought. She was spicy and enticing and sweet and stubborn, and he wanted her so bad he couldn't sleep at night.

Morgan stood and picked up his hat, then snatched his keys from the peg on the wall. It was well past time he got a few things clear with her. Tonight, when he took her to his house, he'd stake a claim. He'd show her that they were a perfect match and when she got used to that, he'd reel her in for the permanent stuff.

In the meantime, he'd shore up his cause by showing her how gentle and understanding he could be. He'd even make a point of not frowning and maybe, just maybe, she'd stop fighting him so hard and then he could quit feeling so desperate, because he sure as certain didn't like the feeling one damn bit.

CHAPTER NINE

MORGAN'S better intentions were put on hold when he found a woman with a car full of kids and a flat tire waiting on the side of the road. She'd been on her way home from grocery shopping when the tire blew. Unfortunately, her spare wasn't in much better shape. Morgan called in to Misty, told her why he'd be late and asked her to postpone his morning meeting with the town trustees.

She'd sounded a little frazzled when he called, but he didn't have time to linger and find out why. He bundled the woman, her children and her flat, as well as her worthless spare, into the Bronco and drove to her house. The kids, ranging in age from one year to twelve, had screamed and yelled and generally enjoyed the excitement of being in the sheriff's car. Morgan wondered if he ought to make that a regular part of the Blackberry Festival. He and his deputy could take turns giving the kids a ride around the town square.

His thoughts wandered from that as the woman tried to thank him in her driveway, obviously embarrassed that her children were loud and that he'd had his day interrupted. Personally, Morgan thought the kids were pretty cute, three of them girls, the youngest two boys, and he told her so even as he juggled a bag of groceries and a tiny three-year-old. The mother had positively beamed at him then.

All in all, they'd acted like children, which they were, so he saw no reason for her to be uncomfortable about a little noise.

After Morgan helped her get her groceries inside, he called

Gabe. His brother met him at the garage where they got both tires repaired. After they'd driven back out to her car and changed the tire, Gabe drove the woman's car to her house while Morgan took the Bronco. Finally, they both went back to the garage.

"I appreciate your help, Gabe. Could you believe those tires she's driving on? And with five kids in the car." Morgan shook his head, wondering if there was any way he could help her. She and her husband were both hard workers, but her husband had suffered an illness and missed a lot of work in the past year.

Gabe rubbed the back of his neck. "What's her husband do for a living?"

"He's a carpenter, I think."

"Maybe we could barter with him. You still need some trim put on the back deck, and if he could—"

Morgan grinned. "—do the work on a weekend, I could give them some tires." He clapped Gabe on the back, almost knocking him over. "Hell of an idea."

Gabe shifted his shoulder, working out the sting of his brother's enthusiasm. "If you want, I could get hold of the guy, tell him I'm not able to do the trim and see if he'd be interested. It'd probably sound more authentic coming from me."

Morgan started to clap him again and Gabe ducked away. "I'll take that as your agreement and get in touch with him tomorrow. I'll let you know what he says."

Morgan left Gabe with a smile on his face. But when he pulled into the station, Ms. Potter, the librarian, hailed him. She wanted to know if he'd agree to take part in their annual read-a-thon, where a group of leading citizens would each pick a day to read to the preschoolers and anyone else who wanted to listen in. Morgan agreed, though it wasn't one of his favorite tasks. The books for that age group tended to rhyme, and his tongue always got twisted.

Next it was two shop owners who wanted to know if he was going to have the county take care of a massive tree limb that was likely to fall on their roofs if a storm hit. Morgan eyed the tree, agreed it needed a good trimming and made a note to get hold of the maintenance crew.

By the time he finally walked into the station he was hot and sweaty and frustrated. He looked forward to seeing Misty, to reassuring her, showing her what a great guy he could be and that she could trust in him. Little by little, he'd win her over. Then he'd talk to her again about her avoidance of commitments.

He walked into chaos.

The noise had reached him even before he opened the door. Laughter. Lots of male laugher and music and a banging noise. Morgan frowned and headed directly for the small desk that Misty occupied during her work hours. He found her sitting there—not in the chair, but on the edge of the desk, her long legs bare, crossed at the ankles. Casey was there, too, with a couple of his pals, and they had evidently supplied the music that was blasting from a portable CD player. Howard had pulled Misty's chair to the side of the desk and was seated in it. Jesse had his bony butt propped on the arm of the chair. Nate stood in front of Misty, dancing while she cheered him on.

Her tailored slacks had been replaced with shorts. Her white blouse was gone in favor of a loose T-shirt. She was barefoot, and of all damn things, she was licking an ice cream cone.

Morgan saw red.

No one had noticed him, and he watched silently while his temper seethed. When Nate made a turn, Misty shook her head, swallowed a large lick of ice cream and then handed her cone to Casey. Casey, the traitor, just laughed and held it for her.

Misty stood in front of Nate and executed the dance step herself.

Lord, she looked sexy.

Morgan glanced around at the other men in the room and saw his thoughts mirrored on all their faces. The last thin thread of his control snapped. "What the *hell* is going on here?"

His roar effectively stopped the dance. Nate nearly jumped out of his skin, Casey quickly handed Misty back the cone, and both Howard and Jesse jerked to their feet. The loud banging noise continued.

Morgan stalked into the room. His gaze slid over Misty, then shifted to Casey. "Turn that damn music off."

One of the kids with Casey hurried to obey. Nate stepped forward. "Uh, Morgan, we were just—"

Morgan cut him off with a glare. Nate stammered for a moment, then clicked his teeth together and went mute.

With a sound of disgust, Misty stepped forward. "For heaven's sake, Morgan. Stop trying to terrorize everyone."

Morgan stared at her and silently applauded her courage. No one else in the room would have dared call him to task. She obviously didn't realize quite how angry he was.

Her hair was mussed, her skin dewy, her eyes bright. She looked like someone had just made love to her. And she dared to stand there giving him defiant looks in front of everyone.

"Is this what I pay you for, Malone? To have a party?"

Her eyes narrowed. "We weren't having a party. If you'll just listen..."

The T-shirt clung to her damp skin, emphasizing her breasts and distracting him. Her cuffed walking shorts showed off her long, sleek legs. A pulse tapped in his temple, making his head swim. "Employees of this office," he said succinctly, "do not traipse around dressed like that."

She took a step closer to him and stared up, her brows beetled. "I had to change."

His gaze dropped to the large cone she held, now dripping on her hand. "Nor do they eat ice cream cones during business hours."

"Morgan." She said his name like a growl.

He ignored the warning, too angry to care that now she was angry, too. "I pay you to work, to answer the phone and take messages. It's little enough to expect that you might take those duties seriously."

Casey groaned, then mumbled, "Now you've done it."

Morgan paid no attention to his nephew. He was too fascinated by the way Misty's eyes darkened, turning midnight blue.

She went on tiptoe. "I'll have you know, I've worked my butt off today!"

He leaned to look behind her. "Looks to me like you've got plenty of ass left."

Her gasp was almost drowned out by the groans of the spectators. Misty turned around and snatched up a stack of notes scattered over the desk's surface. "These," she said, slapping them against his chest one by one, "are from your various girlfriends hoping for a date tonight." They fluttered to the floor to land around his feet. "They've been calling all day, tying up the damn phone."

"Malone—"

"And they were rather persistent that you reply right away." She gave him a sarcastic-sweet smile. "Before I leave, I'll be sure to let them all know you're most definitely free!"

"Malone..."

"And this," she said, throwing a yellow bill at his face, "is for the plumber, because everything backed up and soaked the floor. If it wasn't for Howard and Jesse helping me mop we'd still be six inches under."

He started to get a little worried. "Uh, Malone..."

"And that constant banging you hear," she practically yelled, "is the repair man working on the cooling system. In case you missed it, it's about ninety degrees in here."

So that was why she was all warm and damp. Not because she'd been playing so hard? His brow lifted, but she wasn't through yet. Morgan was aware of Howard and Jesse trying to slip out unnoticed. Casey's two friends had already slunk as far as the door. Nate was openmouthed beside him, not moving so much as a muscle. Casey, the rat, whistled.

"And finally," Misty snarled, in a voice straight out of a horror movie, "this is the first break I've had all day. The flooding water ruined my lunch, and with no air-conditioning I was too hot to eat, anyway, so Nate got me an ice cream cone to tide me over until dinner. But since you don't think I should be eating it, why don't *you* take it!"

And with that, she aimed the damn thing like a missile, ice cream first, into the middle of his chest. Morgan gasped as the chill hit him, then made a face when he felt the first sticky dribble soak under his collar and mingle with his chest hair.

Casey stopped whistling. "Uh-oh. The fat's in the fire now."

Howard and Jesse ran out the door, slamming it behind them.

Nate made a strategic turn and crept out.

Like a stiff, well-trained soldier, Misty tried to troop out after him. Morgan caught her by the arm, pulling her up short. "Oh, no, you don't." A clump of ice cream dropped to the floor with a plop. He dragged Misty closer.

He hated to admit it, but her temper turned him on.

He had an erection that actually hurt it was so intense, and every muscle in his body was pulled taut against the need to take her. He stared at her, aroused by the glitter in her eyes, by the way her chest heaved. "I think we should share the cone, Malone."

Misty reared back, but he caught her other arm, pulling her up close. She stared at his chest, covered in goo, and her lips twitched.

"You think it's funny?" But he fought his own smile. No, life with Misty would never be mundane.

"I think you got what you deserved." Her bare heels slipped on the floor as she tried to dig in. She giggled as another plop of ice cream fell loose. "Morgan, no! I mean it, Morgan. Don't you dare—"

Her words ended in a gasp of outrage as he squished her up against his chest. "Cold, isn't it?"

She tried to twist free, which only made her breasts slip and slide over his chest. Morgan groaned.

"You..." she started to say breathlessly.

Morgan kissed her. It was a funny kiss, since she was struggling so hard against him, but laughing, too, and they had the damn cone crunching between them, the ice cream fast melting with their combined body heat.

Casey cleared his throat. "I'll be on my way now. See you both later. No need to see me off."

Morgan lifted his head. "Get out of here, will you?"

Casey laughed. "I'm going, I'm going."

Morgan watched as Casey dragged his gawking friends out the door and quietly closed it behind them. Misty tried again to pull loose, and he tightened his hold. "Oh, no, you don't. I have a few things to say to you."

She twisted in his arms, realized she couldn't get free, and stopped squirming. "What?"

He kissed her again. Then against her lips, "I'm sorry."

"You should be."

"Mm." With her mouth open he deepened the kiss, tasting her, making love to her. He groaned when the banging noise suddenly stopped.

As he gasped for breath, she muttered, "You ruined my T-shirt. Now what am I going to wear to work?"

Morgan cradled her head in his palms and asked, "You were going to go to the diner dressed like this?"

"I'm perfectly decent, Morgan, so don't start again."

"Dear God, you'll start a riot."

"It was your plumbing that ruined my other clothes. Casey was nice enough to bring these to me when I called."

"I'll run home and get you something else, okay?"

When she hesitated, he waggled her head. "Have some pity on me, Malone! I'm not used to being jealous, and it's taking some getting used to here."

"You really were jealous?"

"What did you think? That I just enjoy making an ass of myself?"

She mumbled, "Well, you do it often enough." Then she glared at him. "You have some explaining to do, insulting me like that in front of everyone."

He swallowed hard, still very aware of her soft body lined up along the length of his. "You're not going to quit on me, are you, just because I yelled a little?"

"I can't." She gave him a sad smile. "I need the job."

Morgan kissed her again, this time gently, because he hated to hear that, to be reminded of her position. "I'm sorry."

"For embarrassing me?"

"Yeah, though you didn't seem all that embarrassed to me. More like raging mad."

"True. On top of everything else, I was suffering my own share of jealousy. I mean, *eight* calls from women, Morgan."

"You were jealous?"

She frowned at him. "That, and annoyed. You have very pushy girlfriends."

He tried to look innocent. "Some of them are probably just friends."

"Probably? You don't know?"

He bit his lip, then chuckled. "It doesn't matter anymore, anyway. I swear. Now tell me you forgive me."

"Are you sorry for what you said?"

"About your sweet tush? Hell, no. You do have a great—"

"Don't say it, Morgan!" She laughed. "And about ruining my clothes?"

"Come into the bathroom and I'll help you clean up." Then he frowned. "I gather we do have running water now?"

"Yes, but I can clean up without your help. You," she said, pointing to all the paper littering the floor, "have a lot of calls to return."

Morgan looked down and saw that he'd stepped all over the message slips.

"You know, Morgan, it suddenly occurs to me." Her frown was back, her mouth set in mulish lines. "You're running around insisting every male in the area believes we're involved, even to the point of putting on this caveman routine. But there seems to be an awful lot of females who don't know a thing about it.''

''I've been too busy mooning over you to give other women a thought. And that includes thinking about them long enough to update my status from available to unavailable.''

He loved how quickly her moods shifted, from mad to playful, from brazen to shy. Right now she looked uncertain. She stared at his chocolate covered chest. ''Are you considered unavailable now?''

Morgan tipped her chin up. ''For as long as you're willing to put up with me.''

She stared at him a moment, then pulled him down for a hungry kiss. Her hands were tight on his shoulders, her mouth moving under his. Morgan felt singed. It was the very first time she'd ever initiated anything, and he wanted so badly to strip her naked and sate himself on her, he was shaking with need.

A sudden hum and the kick of cool air let him know the repairs on the system were complete. And just in the nick of time. A few more seconds and he'd have burned up.

''Tonight, will you let me make love to you, Malone?''

She touched his mouth, gave him a small smile, then nodded. ''I do believe I'd like that.''

His heart almost stopped. He reached for her, but the repairman gave a brief knock and stepped in.

''All done.'' He drew himself up short as Morgan stepped away from Misty and he got a good look at the ice cream mess on their clothes.

Morgan grinned. ''Just leave me a bill.''

CHAPTER TEN

IT SEEMED TO BE Morgan's day for chaos.

The rain was endless, coming down in sheets, and he was relieved and thankful when he saw that Misty's car was already parked around back by the kitchen door, as was her habit. He'd worried endlessly about her driving home in the pouring rain. She'd worked all day and had to be exhausted. He'd hoped to follow her home, then immediately sweep her off to his house. But then he'd gotten held up and the storm had started. He put the truck in park, close to where she'd left her car. Normally he would have driven the Bronco into the garage, but he wanted to be as close to the back door as he could, so Misty wouldn't have as far to run in the rain.

He sighed as he picked up his small bundle in the front seat beside him, wrapping his rain slicker around it to keep it dry, then dashed the few feet through the downpour.

The kitchen door opened before he reached it, so he figured someone had been watching for him. Unfortunately, it wasn't Misty. No, she was engaged in what appeared to be a heated argument with Sawyer. It was Honey who had opened the door.

He kissed her cheek to thank her, then turned to see what the hell was going on.

Misty went on tiptoe and said to Sawyer's chin, "If you don't take the money, I can't stay!"

Sawyer threw his arms into the air, spotted Morgan and let out a huge sigh of relief. "She's worse than Honey, I swear."

Rain dripped down the end of Morgan's nose. His shirt

stuck to his back. He glanced around the kitchen and asked, "Where's Jordan?"

Sawyer looked surprised by his question, then said, "In his rooms, why?"

Slowly, so as not to startle the creature, he unwrapped his burden. A fat, furry, whimpering pup stared at them all, then squirmed to get closer to Morgan. He said to Honey, "Can you get me a towel? I found the damn thing under the front steps of the gym. He's been abandoned awhile, judging by how tight his rope collar was."

Morgan was still so angry he could barely breathe. Cruelty to an animal sickened him, and it was all he could do to hold in his temper, but he didn't want to scare the poor pup more than it already was.

Sawyer picked up the phone and called Jordan while Misty inched closer. Her eyes were large, and she was looking at him in that soft, womanly way she had. He'd get her alone tonight if he had to carry her through the damn storm.

Honey skittered into the kitchen with a towel.

The back door opened, and both Gabe and Jordan came in. They wore rain slickers that did little enough to keep them dry. Jordan was all business, taking the pup without asking questions, ignoring his own damp hair and shirt collar. Gabe shook his head. "It looks pretty young. What kind of dog do you think it is?"

Jordan murmured to the frightened animal as he gently toweled it dry. "A mixed breed. Part shepherd by the looks of him, maybe with some Saint Bernard. He'll be big when he's full grown." Jordan investigated the pup's throat and scowled where the too small rope collar had rubbed off much of the fur. "I'll need my bag."

Gabe turned to the door. "I'll get it." He pulled the hood of his slicker over his head and stepped into the rain without hesitation.

Misty started unbuttoning Morgan's shirt as if she did so every day. "You'll catch a cold if you don't get some dry things on."

Sawyer nodded. "Go change, Morgan. And take Misty with you. Maybe you can talk some sense into her."

Morgan stood still while Misty peeled off his wet shirt. "What have you been up to now, Malone?"

Sawyer didn't give her a chance to answer. He waved a few bills under Morgan's nose. "She wants to pay for staying here."

Morgan scowled. "I thought we had all that resolved."

Taking his hand, Misty tugged him from the room. "I won't be a freeloader. If I stay I have to contribute. I've been eating here almost every day...."

Morgan allowed her to lead him away from the others, but the second they were out of sight he pulled her around and pinned her to the wall, then gave her a deep, hungry kiss. Against her lips, he whispered, "Damn, I missed you."

She looped her arms around his neck and smiled. "I was starting to wonder. I thought you'd be home hours ago."

"I had to do a class, and one of the women got hurt, and then I found the pup." He groaned. "God, it's been a hectic day."

He knew his wet slacks were making her damp, too, but he couldn't seem to let her go. He'd thought about her all day long.

"What kind of class?"

Oh, hell. He hadn't meant to say that. He took her hand and now it was he leading—straight into his bedroom. He closed the door and turned the lock. "Let me change real quick and we'll run up to the house. I'll drive you straight into the garage so you won't get wet."

"Morgan." She crossed her arms and leaned against his door while he hunted for a towel to dry himself. "What class?"

Trying to make light of it, he said, "I teach some of the women self-defense two Fridays of the month. Especially the women who work as park guides for the mountain trails. Sometimes they end up alone with a guy, so they need to know how to defend themselves."

Eyes soft and wide again, Misty asked, "You said one of them got hurt?"

"Yeah, but not in the class. I'm careful with them, and the high school gym lets us use the mats. But she slipped on the front steps when she was leaving and twisted her ankle. She couldn't drive, so I took her to the hospital and then had to go fetch her husband because they only have the one car and it was still at the high school. The only good part is that I found the pup when she fell. If I hadn't bent down to lift her, I'd never have heard it whimpering."

"So you bundled them both up and did what you could?"

"Don't get dramatic, Malone. Anyone would have done the same."

"Obviously not, or that poor little puppy wouldn't have been there in the first place." She sauntered over to him and touched his bare chest, smoothing her hands over his wet skin. "I don't think you control things so much as you try to take care of everyone."

Morgan kicked off his wet shoes even as he bent to kiss her again. Her hands on his flesh were about to make him nuts. "Let me change," he growled, "so we can get out of here."

She nodded and stepped away, then sat on the edge of his bed. If she had any idea what that did to him, seeing her there, she wouldn't have dared test his control. Morgan opened a drawer and pulled out dry jeans and socks. He was just about to unzip his slacks when she asked, "Morgan, am I just another person you're trying to take care of?"

He halted, unsure of her exact meaning, but angry anyway. "You want to explain that?"

She shrugged, then quickly looked away when he jerked his pants open. Hands clasped in her lap, she said, "You wanted me gone until you thought I needed to stay. And you not only try to coddle me, you said you're trying to prove me innocent of stealing. I just wondered if I was…I don't know. Another project of sorts. Like the scholarship at the school, the puppy you just brought home, that other woman you helped today."

"What other woman?"

"Gabe told me about the woman with the flat. He said you do stuff like that all the time."

She looked at him with deep admiration again, when what he wanted was something altogether different. "Gabe has a big mouth."

His dry jeans in place, Morgan sat beside her on the bed. He bent to pull on socks and shoes, his thoughts dark. He could feel her looking at him as he hooked his cell phone to his belt and clipped his gun in place.

"You might as well save it, you know."

Startled, Morgan glanced at her. "Save what?"

"The look. I'm immune to it. You're not nearly as much of a badass as you let everyone believe. Ceily told me you haven't even been in a fight in ages, and the last one was over too quick to count."

Displeasure gnawed at his insides. "You were talking about me with Ceily?"

"Oh, quit trying to intimidate me." She waved a hand at him. "You got a reputation when you were a hotheaded kid, but even then, you were never a bully. I've heard plenty, and any fights you got into were because you were defending someone else. The last fight was in a bar in the neighboring town. Ceily said some guy tried to drag his girlfriend out of there and you stopped him. Rather easily, as a matter of fact, which I suppose only added to your reputation, right?"

Morgan decided that when he got hold of Ceily he'd strangle her. "Did she also tell you how that woman was most...grateful?"

Misty snorted. "Yeah, she did. But that's not why you did it, so don't even bother running that by me. You're the sheriff now because you hate injustice and abuse and you take a lot of satisfaction in setting things right and taking care of others. Admit it."

The hell he would. His reputation had worked to his advantage for most of his life, and he'd damn well earned it. He pulled a loose black T-shirt over his head then twisted to face her. "You still going to the house with me?"

Her dark, silky hair swung forward and hid her profile as she stared at her hands. She looked a tiny bit nervous. "If you want me to."

Morgan caught her chin and turned her face toward him. "What do *you* want?"

She bit her lip, took a deep breath, then smiled. "To be with you."

His heart punched up against his breastbone and his vision blurred. He stood up before he decided to forget about the tour and took her right now. They needed privacy, not for what he wanted to do, but for all the things he wanted to say. "C'mon."

Her hand caught securely in his, he led her out of the room. She looked cuddly in a soft, oversize sweatshirt and worn, faded jeans. Unfortunately, she wore sneakers, but he'd keep her feet dry. He looked forward to holding her close. When they got into the kitchen, everyone leaned over watching Jordan and the pup. Now that it was dry, the dog resembled a round matted fur ball with a snout and paws. A stubby tail managed to work back and forth, and it gave a squeaky bark at Morgan.

Morgan grinned. The dog was incredibly cute in an ugly, sort of bedraggled way. "Is it going to be okay?"

"*It* is a *he,* about three months old, I'd say, and yeah, he'll be fine. He just needs to be cleaned up and loved a little."

Morgan nodded. It was obvious the poor thing had been abandoned, and if he ever found out who'd done it, a very hefty fine would be presented. "I'll keep him. I was thinking of getting a dog anyway, for when I move into the house. This one'll do as well as any." At his pronouncement, Misty squeezed his hand.

Honey predictably grumbled about him moving out. She protested any time he mentioned it, saying she wanted him to stay, then went on to tell him how wonderful his house was and offered to help him decorate. He adored her.

Jordan watched as Morgan pulled two raincoats off the hooks. "I can keep him with me tonight if you want, since you appear to have plans to brave the storm again."

"Misty hasn't seen my house yet."

The brothers all grinned and cast knowing looks back and forth.

Sawyer handed Morgan the money Misty had tried to give him. "Make her take this back."

Misty held up her hands, palms out. "I can't continue to eat here if you won't let me pay for my share of the food and stuff. That's just tip money—I can afford it. Honest."

Sawyer's eyebrows shot up. "Tips? You made this much in tips already?"

"According to Ceily," Morgan grumbled, "every male that came in wanted to show her his gratitude, even if she hadn't done a damn thing for him. She said Misty kept the restaurant packed most of the night."

Misty blinked at him. "You talked to Ceily? When?"

He flicked the end of her nose. "Before I came home. She felt the need to page me and let me know how…successful you were. She even suggested she might want to lure you away from the station so you could work more hours for the diner. She claims she wouldn't even need to show up with you there drawing in customers and raking in the dough."

Gabe laughed, Jordan bit his lip and Sawyer rolled his eyes. Morgan didn't think it was the least bit amusing. "I told her you were going to continue working for me. That's right, isn't it, Misty?"

Her eyes narrowed. "As long as you all let me pay my way."

She was the most cursed stubborn woman he'd ever met. He caught her chin on the edge of his fist. "Most of the time, the food is *given* to us."

With a wholly skeptical look, she murmured, "Uh-huh."

"It's true, damn it. Sawyer barters with his less fortunate

patients. Hell, he gets paid more often with food than with money. That's why we're always overloaded with desserts and casseroles."

"You're serious?" When he nodded, she said, "I had no idea."

Sawyer looped one arm around Honey and added, "I have vitamins I can give her, too, so she won't have to go to the pharmacy, but of course she refused them."

And Honey piped in, saying, "I know for a fact she's embarrassed about getting them in town. Everyone will know she's pregnant if she does. Make her accept them, Morgan."

Morgan took one look at Misty's inflexible expression and laughed out loud. Were they all under the misguided notion that he had some control over the woman? Hell, she butted heads with him more than anyone else!

Knowing it would only prompt her stubbornness more, he said, "Yeah, sure, I'll take care of it."

Her brows snapped down, her mouth opened to blast him with invective, and Morgan kissed her—a quick, grinning smooch. She gave him a bemused look, and he dropped the coat over her head, then lifted her in his arms.

She fussed and wriggled, but he contained her with no effort at all and when she saw all the brothers watching intently, she made a face at them, but at least stopped struggling. "You have the worst habit of hauling me around."

"I don't want your feet to get wet going out."

"Oh."

Sawyer said, "Finally, he's listening to me."

Honey acted as if it was all par for the course. "Here, Misty, I packed a basket so you could both eat. I doubt if either of you have had dinner yet. Take your time. You'll love Morgan's house and maybe the rain will have stopped by the time you head back."

Morgan watched Misty balance the large basket with one arm while looping the other around his neck. "Don't wait up for us," he said to the room at large.

He darted out the door and made his way cautiously to the

Bronco. Misty opened the car door, and he slid her inside. The rain wasn't coming down quite so fiercely now, and Morgan hoped Honey was right, that it would stop soon. Too many wrecks happened in weather like this, and he didn't look forward to his evening getting interrupted. Already his anticipation was so keen he had to struggle for breath. He was semihard and so hot the windows started to steam the second he got behind the wheel.

"Will you accept the vitamins?" He drove from the driveway to the main road, hoping the conversation would work as a distraction. "Sawyer offered them because he wants to, you know."

With her arms around the basket, she grumbled, "He offered because I'm Honey's sister."

"Bull. If you'd just stumbled into our lives the way Honey did, he'd do the same. Sawyer cares about people and likes doing what he can. It has nothing to do with you being related. Except that he takes it more personal when you refuse."

She shook her head. "All right, fine. I'll take the vitamins, but I insist on paying my own way. I won't be swayed on that. Regardless of where the food comes from, I'm still staying there and taking up room."

Morgan smiled at her. "Stubborn as a mule." He pulled up in front of his garage and hopped out to open the door, then drove inside. "I'm going to have the driveway poured soon, and then we'll install a garage door opener, but that's stuff I can take care of after I move in."

Misty didn't wait for him to open her door after he'd turned off the engine. She hefted the heavy basket in her arms and climbed out. "I want to see the outside of the house, too. From down the hill, it looks gorgeous."

Morgan felt like a stuffed turkey, he puffed up so proud. "Let's go through the inside first and maybe the rain will let up." He opened the door leading into the house and reached in for a light switch. The first-floor laundry looked tidy and neat, a replica of the one in the house where he'd grown up, with pegs on the wall for wet coats and hats, a boot-storage bench and plenty of shelving. "All the fixtures aren't up yet, but there's plenty of light."

He turned to look at Misty and caught her wide-eyed expression of awe as she stared from the laundry room into the kitchen. "Oh, Morgan."

Like a sleepwalker, she went through the doorway and turned a circle. "This is incredible."

The kitchen had an abundance of light oak cabinets, high ceilings with track lighting and three skylights. Right now, the rain made it impossible to see anything but the blackness of the sky, but Morgan knew on a sunny day the entire kitchen would glow warmly, and in the evening, you'd feel like the stars were right on top of you.

"C'mon. I'll show you around." He took the basket from her and set it on the counter.

She kept staring at his cathedral ceilings. "I love the design. It's like you're in a house, but not, you know? Everything is so open."

"I don't like closed-in spaces." He laced her fingers with his own and said casually, "I figure it's easier to keep an eye on kids when they aren't behind doors getting into mischief. Other than the four bedrooms and the two baths, all the doorways are arches."

She stalled for a moment inside the dining room. He turned to look at her, and she shook her head. "How many kids do you plan on having?"

He held her gaze and said, "Three sounds about right. What do you think?"

Her fingers tightened on his and she said quietly, "I think I'll worry about raising this one before I even contemplate adding any more."

He wanted to tell her she didn't have to worry, that she wouldn't need to raise the baby on her own, but he had to bide his time. He didn't want to scare her off. "I don't have the dining-room furniture yet. I'm still working on that."

She went to a window and looked out. "The view of the lake is gorgeous."

"Yeah. Back here in the coves the lake is almost always calm, not like farther up where all the vacationers keep it churning with boats and swimming and skiing. It's peaceful, nothing more disturbing than an occasional fishing boat."

"I bet in the fall it's really something to see."

"Yeah. And in the winter, too, when everything is iced over. I figure I'll need to hire someone to keep all the windows clear, but what's the point of living on a hill with great scenery if you can't see it? The view from the master bedroom is nice, too." He slipped that in, then added, "The deck runs all the way around the house."

The next room was the living room and he watched her inspect his choice of furniture, wondering if she'd like it.

"Everything looks so cozy, but elegant, too."

Morgan rubbed the back of his neck. When he'd chosen the blue-gray sofa and two enormous cranberry-colored chairs, elegance hadn't entered his mind. It was the saleslady who'd suggested the patterned throw pillows to "pull it all together." He'd been going strictly for comfort. The softness and large dimensions of the furniture had appealed to him. "I'm glad you like it."

"You could fill this place up with plants. You know, like you did around the fireplace at the station."

Morgan watched her closely as he admitted, "One of the women I used to see on occasion brought in those plants. I'd never have thought of it. It's the cleaning lady that keeps them watered and healthy."

She sent him a narrow-eyed look over the mention of a girlfriend. "Well, I can just imagine a lot of plants really blending in here. With the stone fireplace and the light from the windows, it'd be great. What do you think?"

"I think maybe you should help me pick some out."

She blinked at him in surprise, then smiled. "I'd love to."

Satisfied on that score, he took her hand and continued on

the tour. He opened the first door they came to. "This is the hall bath."

Misty stuck her head in the door, and her mouth fell open. "It's...decadent."

Grinning, Morgan gently shoved her the rest of the way in. "Yeah. I kinda like it. Other than my bedroom, it's my favorite room. It turned out just the way I wanted."

Morgan watched her run her hand over the cream-colored tiled walls, the dual marble vanity. A large, raised tub took up one entire corner, looking much like a small pool. You could see the water jets inside the tub, and all the fixtures were brass. There was a skylight right above it and a shelf surrounding it for lotions and towels and candles—things he'd noticed Honey was partial to, so he assumed other women would be, too. In the adjacent corner was a shower with two showerheads, one on either side of the stall.

Honey was a hedonist when it came to her baths—the woman could linger for hours. He'd assumed most women were the same, but Misty tended to take quick showers, just as he did. He frowned with that thought, until he considered showering with her, and then his breath caught. He eyed the shower. It was plenty big enough to make love in....

"It's beautiful, Morgan."

He shifted his shoulders, trying to ease the sexual tension that had invaded his muscles. "I still have to get towels and stuff, but I figured there was no rush on that."

Tentatively, without quite looking at him, she said, "I could help with that, too, if you want."

Morgan stared at her, then swung her around and gave her a hard, quick kiss. "Thanks," he said in a gruff tone, his throat raw with some unnamed emotion that he didn't dare examine too closely. It was based on sexual need, but there was a lot of other more complicated stuff thrown in that he didn't understand at all.

Misty looked at his mouth, drew a slow broken breath and then licked her lips. Morgan was a goner. Backing her into the cool tile wall, he took her mouth again, this time more thoroughly, then didn't want to stop kissing her. She felt perfect, tasted perfect. She made him feel weak when that had never happened before, but she also made him feel almost brutal with driving need. He wanted to devour her, and he wanted to cherish her.

She arched against him and he cupped her rounded backside with a groan. "Damn, Malone."

In a husky, laughing tone, she asked, "Are you ever going to use my first name?"

She sounded a bit breathless, and he forced himself to loosen his hold. Sawyer was right; she'd been through a lot, and even the strongest woman in the world needed time to adjust. "Malone suits you. It sounds gutsy and sexy and a little dangerous."

She allowed him to lead her from the room, but she asked, "Dangerous? Me?"

With his arm around her shoulders, his heart still galloping wildly, he steered her to the first empty bedroom. "To my libido, yeah."

The first three bedrooms were empty, but still Misty oohed over the tall windows and the ultrasoft carpet and the oak moldings. Morgan felt as if he might explode by the time he got her to his room. There were no curtains yet on the French doors that flanked the tall windows, almost filling an entire wall. The doors led to a wide, covered deck. The overhang wasn't quite sufficient to shield them from the wind, and the rain blew gently against the glass. "Let me show you something."

Without hesitation she came into the room and went to the wall of windows with him. "Look at the lights on the lake. Isn't it beautiful?"

She stared into the darkness for long minutes, then finally nodded. "Yes."

"I've always enjoyed the lake, the way sunlight glints on every tiny ripple, and how the evening lights along the shore turn into colored ribbons across the water. Even on stormy days, it's great to watch. The waves lap up over the retaining wall and every so often the lake swells enough to cover my dock. The fish get frisky on those days and you can see them leaping up into the air and landing again with a splash. On my next day off I'll take you boating and we can swim in the cove. Would you like that?''

She continued to gaze into the rainy night. ''I've always loved being outdoors, and around water. When I was younger, we had a sailboat. My dad would take us out about twice a year, but mostly he used the yacht for entertaining his guests or business associates.''

Morgan hugged her from behind, knowing her relationship with her father had been far from ideal. ''I don't have a yacht, but I think you'll like our boat. Or rather boats—we have three. An inboard for waterskiing, which Gabe uses more than anyone else. He's as much fish as man. And a fishing boat with a trolling motor, which is so slow you could probably paddle faster. And a pontoon. My mother bought the pontoon and left it here, but whenever she visits she takes it out.''

Misty leaned her head back to look at him. ''I didn't know you had a gazebo.''

The gazebo was only barely visible in the darkening sky, a massive shadow on the level ground fifteen feet off the shore of the lake. He'd had electricity run down there so a bug light could hang inside the high ceiling, though it wasn't lit now.

Morgan kissed her temple and looped his arms around her middle so that his hands rested protectively over her belly. ''I had Gabe build it for me.'' His fingers contracted the tiniest bit, fondling her gently.

She sucked in her breath, and her hands settled over his. ''When?''

In a hoarse tone, he explained, ''After that night I kissed you at the wedding. In the gazebo.''

She twisted in his arms. ''But...you'd asked me to leave then.''

He searched her gaze. There was no accusation there, just

confusion. "I wanted you to stay." Very gently, he pulled her closer. "Damn, I wanted you to stay."

Her smile was shaky, and then she touched the side of his face. "I have to tell you something about me."

Morgan leaned forward and nuzzled the soft skin beneath her chin. He felt wound too tight, edgy and aroused and full to bursting. He tasted the silky skin of her throat, her collarbone. He didn't say anything, waiting for her to continue.

He felt the deep breath she took. "You're a special treat for me, Morgan."

He grinned at that and continued to put soft, damp kisses on her throat, beneath her chin, near her shoulder. He felt her tremble and held her closer.

"I want you to understand what this means to me."

He leaned back to look at her. She appeared far too serious and solemn to suit him.

"I know that an unwed pregnant woman sort of gives the impression of being experienced—"

"Damn it, Misty, I didn't—"

She pressed her fingers to his mouth. "Just listen, okay?" He nodded reluctantly and she continued. "Truth is, I haven't had much experience at all. Back in high school I got very curious, and we experimented a little. Very little, actually. Things didn't last long with him, but it was no big heartbreak."

Very carefully, Morgan pulled her earlobe between his teeth. She shuddered.

"And then there was Kent. I'd only been with him a few times, but we were careful. It's just that the condom broke—"

He squeezed her tight, cutting off her spate of confessions. "Enough."

Jealousy washed through him. The idea of her with a kid in high school was bad enough; his brain nearly overflowed with visions of her being groped in the back seat of a car, making him hazy with anger. But to think of her as a grown woman with a man she'd thought she loved... A man who had gotten her pregnant, then turned away from her. He could barely tolerate the idea.

"I don't need to have an accounting for past lovers, Malone." He growled those words against her ear, then added, "I don't care about any of that."

She wriggled loose so she could see him. "But that's just it. I don't have much of an accounting to give. Not because I'm so particular, and not because I think it's wrong. It's because no one ever really made me want him. Not the way you do."

Emotion nearly clogged his throat. Morgan hugged her right off her feet. "You don't have to worry, baby. I'll take care of you. I won't hurt you."

She pushed against his shoulders. "Morgan, you don't understand."

Morgan lowered her to the floor with him so that they faced each other on their knees. Misty's eyes were dark and wide and even in the dim light he could see her excitement. He slipped his hand under the hem of her sweatshirt and stroked her bare waist. Very softly, he said, "Explain it to me then."

Morgan hoped she was about to give him a clue to her feelings. She hadn't balked at the idea of helping him decorate, but neither had she seemed to realize why he wanted her help. And his comment about kids had gone completely over her head: in order for him to have those three kids, he'd need her cooperation, because no other woman would do.

She hesitated, her chest rising and falling in fast breaths, then she blurted, "I want to get my fill of you."

A wave of lust washed over him, making him tremble. That was not what he'd been expecting, or even hoping for. *But it might do.*

"You're so open about sex and how you feel," Misty explained, "that I don't have to worry about my old inhibitions or any of that stuff. I don't have to worry about what you'll think of me, or if I'll offend you." She touched his face with a trembling hand. "I want to do everything to you that I've been imagining doing. I want to let go completely."

Morgan swallowed hard, struggling to come up with a coherent reply.

It wasn't necessary. Misty launched herself at him, her hands holding his ears while she kissed him hungrily. He felt her small tongue in his mouth, felt her sharp little teeth nip his bottom lip. With a harsh groan, he rolled to his back, keeping her pinned against his chest, and she touched him all over, her hands busy and curious and bold.

He thought of all the things he'd meant to say to her, but at the moment, none of them seemed important.

Morgan made a sound somewhere between a groan and a laugh. She didn't care if she amused him. "I've wanted you for so long," she told him between kisses. "It's awful to want someone that bad."

"Tell me about it." He worked her sweatshirt up until he could pull it over her head. She lifted her arms to help him, not feeling a single twinge of shyness. Not with Morgan.

As soon as the shirt was out of the way, Morgan reached for her. His hands were so large and rough and hot, and she moaned as he cuddled her breasts in his palms. His thumbs stroked over her nipples and she felt wild at the sweet ache his touch caused. "This is almost scary."

"No." Morgan brought her back down for another kiss, but she dodged him.

"I want your shirt off, too." He was such a big hulk that there was no way she could get his clothes off him without his cooperation. She slid to the side and tugged his shirt free of his jeans. Morgan curled upward, making the muscles in his stomach do interesting things, and he threw the shirt off. She'd seen his chest many times, but now was different. Now she was allowed to touch and taste and have her way with him.

Misty attacked the snap on his jeans.

"Slow down, babe."

"No, I don't want to. I kept telling myself I couldn't do

this, but then I realized there was no way I could *not* do it. I want you too much. I doubt I'll ever meet another man who makes me feel this way."

"Damn right you won't." Morgan caught her hands and pulled them away from his zipper. "Kiss me again."

She gladly complied. And while she was kissing him, licking his mouth, tasting his heat and feeling the dampness of his tongue, the smoothness of his teeth, Morgan rolled her to her back. The plush carpeting cushioned her.

"I don't want to hurt you, Malone."

She pulled him closer, breathing deeply of his scent. "You won't."

"The baby…"

Everything seemed to go still with his words. Morgan loomed over her, heat pulsing off him, his dark blue eyes burning hot, his hair mussed. There was so much concern and tenderness in his gaze that she felt tears well in her eyes. Misty touched his cheek, then his wide, hard chest. She let one finger drift over a small brown nipple and heard his sharp intake. "I want you naked, Morgan."

His head dropped forward and he labored for breath.

"You won't hurt me, I promise." She watched the way his wide shoulders flexed, how the muscles in his neck corded. "I've been thinking about this all day, and if I'm going to do this—"

His gaze snapped to hers. *"You are."*

"—then I want to do everything. Why take a risk unless you make it worthwhile?"

The look on his face was almost pained before he deliberately wiped it away. "I'm not a risk, babe."

Misty didn't want to tell him that he was the biggest risk she'd ever taken. She loved him so much, even more than she desired him. Around him her heart felt vulnerable and soft and a little wounded because she wished so badly she could have met him months ago. He could break her so easily.

She shook her head, willing to tease him to chase her dark

thoughts away. This wasn't a time for wariness, but a time to break free. "I've never had an excellent lover, Morgan." She slipped her fingers down his side, over his hip. "I want you to be excellent."

His teeth flashed in the darkness and his hand smoothed over her hair, then tucked it behind her ear. "You know how to put on the pressure, don't you?"

"Are you intimidated?"

He snorted. After staring at her for a long moment, he shifted to sit up. His gaze strayed to her body again and again while he pulled off his shoes and socks and laid his cell phone aside. "So you want to see all of me?"

"Yes."

"Should I turn on some lights?"

Misty laughed. How she could recognize humor while burning up with need was amazing. Morgan made her hungry, and he amused her, and he made her feel special and cherished in so many ways.

But then, he did that for a lot of people.

"With no curtains on the windows?" she asked. "Don't you think that might be unwise? What if someone is out there and they see you prancing around in the buff?"

He chuckled, but the sound was strained as he stared at her breasts. "I don't prance, Malone. And there's no one out there on a night like this."

She pretended to consider his offer, then said, "No, let's leave the lights off." She'd definitely be more daring without too much illumination. She needed the shadows to enjoy herself fully. At least this first time.

Morgan shrugged. "Whatever you want."

"That's the spirit." Her laugh ended on a gasp when he came to his knees and carefully pulled down his zipper, easing it around a rather large, hard erection. She didn't want to laugh now. No, she just wanted to watch. And touch.

And taste.

Without any signs of modesty, Morgan slowly shucked his jeans and underwear down his hips, then sat back and pulled them the rest of the way off. "Now you," he rumbled, and leaned forward to do the job himself.

Misty stared at his naked body and felt the warmth build beneath her skin, felt her womb tighten, her breasts ache. His hips were a shade lighter than the rest of his sun-darkened skin, the flesh looking smooth and hard, taut with muscle. Crisp curling hair covered his chest and tapered into a downy line on his abdomen. She felt a little lecherous eyeing his swollen erection and wondered how it would feel to touch him there.

Belatedly, Misty remembered that she wanted to be a full participant, not a passive one. She toed off her sneakers, then came up onto her elbows as Morgan worked the button of her pants loose and started on her zipper. "Would you rather I strip? It'll be easier."

Morgan froze for a heartbeat, then shook his head. "I'd never live through it. The fact you're not wearing a bra is already more than any man should have to deal with."

"You *wanted* me to wear a bra."

His hand opened over her belly and caressed her lightly, smoothing over her skin, dipping quickly into her belly button, then sliding beneath her open jeans to palm her buttocks. She reached for his erection and wrapped her hand around him.

He was hard and hot and silky. He flexed in her hand, and she tightened her hold.

With a groan, Morgan hooked his fingers into the waistband of her jeans. His voice was gravelly and low when he spoke. "Unveiling you slowly would have been better for my system. Saving me the shock, you know?"

Misty ignored his words, enthralled with the velvety feel of him. "Do you like this, Morgan?" She squeezed him carefully, heard his rough gasp. "You'll have to give me some direction, okay?"

He had her jeans as far as her knees and he paused to tilt his head back and suck in deep breaths. "Harder."

Misty's heartbeat drummed at his growled command. She

tightened her hand and stroked him again. ‘‘Like this?’’ she whispered.

Morgan suddenly caught her wrist and pulled her hand away. ‘‘I’m sorry, but I can’t take it.’’ He kissed her knuckles and placed her hand next to her head on the floor. ‘‘You need to do some catching up, sweetheart, so keep those soft little hands to yourself for a few minutes, okay?’’

Nodding, Misty lifted her hips so he could pull her jeans the rest of the way off. Morgan pushed them aside, and immediately bent down to kiss the top of her right thigh. ‘‘Damn, you smell good,’’ he muttered as he nuzzled her hipbone, her belly, leaving warm damp kisses on her skin.

Misty shifted, not sure if she should protest or not. He’d taken the lead, but she loved how he looked at her, the husky timbre of his voice.

‘‘Open your legs.’’

‘‘Morgan…’’

‘‘Shh. Trust me, okay?’’

It seemed as though her heartbeat shook her entire body. Around her nervousness, her excitement, she whispered, ‘‘I do trust you. I always have.’’

Morgan looked down at her, making her feel exposed and agitated and eager. He wedged her thighs apart and settled between them. He stared into her eyes and cupped her breasts. His solid abdomen pressed warmly against her mound, making her arch the tiniest bit. Her thighs were opened wide around his waist.

Misty nearly choked on a deep breath when he lowered his head and sucked one nipple deep into his mouth. Her back arched involuntarily, but Morgan took advantage of the movement to slip his arm beneath her, keeping her raised for his mouth. He shifted to her other breast, making her moan with the sharp tingle of a gentle bite.

‘‘I could spend an hour,’’ he whispered, ‘‘just on your breasts.’’

Misty tangled her fingers in his hair. ‘‘I told you I wanted to do some things.’’

"We'll take turns."

He went back to her nipple, and true to his word, he seemed insatiable, tasting her, licking her, sucking her deep. Each gentle tug of his mouth was felt in her entire body. His tongue was both rough and incredibly soft on her aroused flesh. When he finally lifted himself away from her, she could barely keep still. Her nipples were swollen and wet, and she covered them with her own hands, trying to appease the throbbing ache.

Morgan growled at the sight of her touching herself and began kissing his way down her abdomen. When he reached her belly, he paused, then rested his cheek there. "I can't believe there's a baby in here," he whispered. "You're so slim."

Misty choked on an explosion of emotion, so touched by the way he accepted her and her condition. "I...I'm bigger than I used to be. I've gained seven pounds." It amazed her that he didn't seem the least put off by her pregnancy. Kent had been disgusted and repulsed by the idea, but Morgan seemed more intrigued and concerned than anything else.

He placed a gentle kiss on her navel, then slipped his hands under her thighs and opened her legs wide. "Bend your knees for me, sweetheart. That's it. A little wider."

She felt horribly exposed with her legs sprawled so wide, his warm breath touching her most sensitive flesh. He was looking at her, studying her, and it embarrassed her even as it excited her almost unbearably.

Knowing what would happen, overcome with curiosity and carnal need, Misty dropped her head on the carpet and stared at the heavily shadowed ceiling.

The first damp stroke of his hot tongue felt like live lightning. She jerked, but he held her still and licked again. She groaned. Morgan used his thumbs to open her completely and tasted her deeply, without reserve.

"Oh God."

"So sweet," he murmured, and anything else he said was lost behind her moans.

She couldn't hold still, couldn't think straight. His fingers glided over her wet swollen tissues, dipping inside every now and again, but not enough to make the building ache go away. His tongue did the same, lapping softly, then stabbing into her.

"Morgan, please..."

"Tell me if I hurt you," he murmured hotly, and even his breath made her wild.

But then she gasped as he began working two fingers deep into her. Moving against him, she tried to make him hurry, tried to make him go deeper.

"You're so tight," he murmured and she heard the repressed tension in his voice.

"Morgan."

His mouth closed over her throbbing clitoris, sucking gently while his fingers stroked in and out, and she was lost. She cried out, thankful that they were alone, that he'd had the sense to insure their privacy, because she wanted to yell, needed to yell. Nothing had ever felt like this, so powerful and sweet and so much pleasure it was nearly too much to bear.

Morgan moved up over her, settling his hips gently against hers. His hands cupped her face until her eyes opened. "I'm going to come into you now."

"Yes."

"Tell me if I—"

"You won't hurt me." If he didn't get on with it, she might be forced to rape him. A gentle pulsing from her recent climax still shook her, but she wanted more, she wanted it all, she wanted Morgan.

"Put your legs around me."

As soon as she'd gotten her shaky limbs to work, he smothered her mouth with his own and pushed cautiously into her. Her body bowed, trying to accommodate him, then wilted as he sank deep, entering her completely. His raw groan echoed her own.

A moment of suspended pleasure and building anticipation

held them both, then he began moving in deep, gentle thrusts. He stayed slightly propped up on his elbows rather than giving her his weight. Misty tried to protest, wrapping her arms tight around him and doing her best to bring him to her.

"No, sweetheart. I'm too heavy," he panted, his jaw tight, his shoulders bunched. His eyes blazed at her and he kept kissing her, as if he couldn't get enough; deep, hungry kisses and gentle, tender kisses.

Even now, he was being so careful with her. Her heart swelled painfully. "Please, Morgan."

He squeezed his eyes shut, his jaw clenched, and the sight of him, so strong, so powerful, and so gentle, added to the physical pleasure and made her climax again with a suddenness that took her breath away. She strained against him, her thighs tightening, her fingers digging into his powerful shoulders. The second her muscles tightened around his erection, Morgan cursed, then gave up the struggle.

He allowed her to pull him down and pressed his face into her throat, hugging her closer still, his big body straining and shuddering as he came.

For long moments he rested against her, dragging in air, his body gradually relaxing. She felt him kiss her throat…and she felt his smile.

Misty squeezed him again. She didn't know what she had expected, but the contentment, the happiness, the peace nearly overwhelmed her. "That was wonderful," she whispered to him, needing to say the words. "You were wonderful."

As though it took a great effort, Morgan slowly struggled up onto his elbows and smiled down at her. "So you're satisfied?"

She bit her lip, then slowly shook her head. "No, never."

Morgan blinked at her, then threw his head back and laughed. "Damn, Malone, I never thought I'd like hearing those two words leave your lips."

She touched his mouth with a finger. She no longer vibrated with need, but the curiosity was still there, and the love. "What you did to me, Morgan? I want to do that to you, too."

Morgan jerked. He breathed deep and he cursed and he shuddered. Finally he just laughed again, the sound low and rough. "From the moment I met you I knew on a gut level exactly how things would be with you."

"Did you?" When Morgan smiled, he made her want to smile, too.

"Yeah. Why do you think I've been going so crazy? I'm glad to see I wasn't wrong."

He rolled onto his back so that she was perched above him. His grin was so wicked and so lecherous, she almost blushed. "Now," he said.

And before she could ask him, "Now what?" his cell phone rang.

CHAPTER ELEVEN

IT WAS ALMOST two in the morning by the time he got home, and he felt exhausted down to his soul. A three-car mishap had dragged him out of Misty's arms. Luckily no one was seriously hurt, but he was still pissed off. A few idiots from the next county over drank too much and tried joyriding over their deeper roads. They'd taken out not only a length of fence along Carl Webb's property, but they'd also knocked over a telephone pole. Cows had wandered loose in the road and into the neighboring field, Carl had been infuriated—and rightfully so—and many people had been without phone service.

In the pouring rain, it was damn inconvenient trying to sort everything out. One of the fools had a concussion, the other a broken nose. Morgan thought they deserved at least that much, though they'd both whined and complained endlessly.

He hadn't had a chance to say anything to Misty. He'd made love to her, and he'd made her laugh, but he hadn't told her that he wanted her to stick around as a permanent member of the family. He hadn't told her that he wanted her to be with him forever.

And she hadn't said a thing about how she felt, other than that she'd enjoyed making love with him. That was just dandy, but it wasn't enough. Not even close.

He kicked off his muddy boots just inside the kitchen doorway and made his way through the silent house to his room. His wet clothes went into a hamper and a warm shower helped to relieve his aching muscles, but not his aching head. He needed some sleep, but as he threw back the top sheet, the thought of climbing into his big bed all alone didn't appeal to him one bit. He glanced at the door, thought of Misty all warm and snuggled up in her own bed, and it felt like that fat elephant was on his chest again.

He stood there undecided, at the side of the bed for a full three minutes before cursing and pulling on underwear. Grumbling all the way down the hall, he got to Misty's room and started to knock, then changed his mind. The doorknob turned easily and the door swung open on silent hinges. He could barely see Misty curled on top of the mattress, her room nothing but shifting moon shadows as the trees swayed outside with the wind. But he could hear her soft, even breathing. She was likely exhausted and he promised himself he wouldn't keep her awake, but he wanted to hold her and there was no longer any reason to deny himself.

When he stood next to her bed she shifted and yawned, then opened her eyes to look at him. Immediately she sat up, shoving her silky hair out of her face. "Morgan? What's wrong? Did you just get in?"

Her normally deep voice was even rougher with sleep, and sexy as hell. "Yeah." He bent and scooped her out of the bed, lifted her up against his bare chest, and started out of the room. She had on a thin knee-length cotton gown, and her warm, sweet scent clung to her skin, making him regret his resolve to let her rest.

She tucked her face under his chin. "Where are we going?"

"To my room. I want to hold you while I sleep."

She made a soft, humming sound of pleasure and curled closer. As he toed her door closed from the hallway, he heard another door open. He turned, Misty held tight in his arms, to see Casey leaving the bathroom.

Casey blinked, then quickly averted his gaze. "I didn't see a thing."

"Make sure you don't repeat a thing, either."

Casey waved him off, too sleepy to care. Misty groaned. "How do you always embarrass me like this?"

"Why would you be embarrassed?" He went down the hall to his room and once inside he nudged the door closed. He didn't immediately put her in the bed; he liked the feel of her in his arms, the trusting way she accepted him.

"What will Casey think?"

"That I've got too much sense to sleep alone with you nearby." When she didn't comment on that he turned her slightly to see her face. Her eyes were closed, her expression relaxed. Not really wanting to, he gently lowered her to the mattress and climbed in beside her. "Sleep, sweetheart. We'll talk in the morning."

Before he could pull her against him, she had her arm around his waist, her head on his shoulder and one thigh covering his. And damn, it felt right. He wanted to sleep this way every night for the rest of his life.

Misty kissed his chest. "I'm awake now, you know."

Her voice was even huskier, and he eyed her in the darkness. "Shh. Don't tempt me. It's late and we both need some sleep." And he fully intended to explain a few things to her before he made love to her again.

Her soft little hand slipped down his stomach, making him suck in a deep breath. "Malone," he growled in warning. "Behave yourself."

She sat up, and he expected her to start arguing. He grinned, wondering what she would say, if she'd come right out and admit that she wanted him enough to force the issue.

Instead, she shifted around, and when she curled up against him again, she was naked. She shimmied onto his chest, cupped his face in both hands and said teasingly, "Don't make me get rough with you, Morgan."

He stroked the long, silky line of her back to her lush bottom and gave up. "All right, but be gentle with me. I've had a trying night." She laughed at that, her first kiss kind of ticklish and silly. But he had both hands on her bottom now and the second his fingers started to explore she groaned, and for the next hour neither one of them thought of sleep.

MORNING SUNLIGHT nearly blinded him when he heard Misty's soft, pain-filled moan. He immediately sat up to look at her. She had both hands holding her middle, her mouth pinched shut and her eyes closed. She looked pale. He said very quietly, "Morning sickness?"

She gave a brief nod. "It hasn't been this bad lately. But I don't usually wake up with a hairy thigh over my belly, either."

"Oh. Sorry." Morgan shifted away from her, trying not to shake the bed overly, then said, "Don't move. I'll be right back." When she didn't answer, he said, "Malone?"

"All right."

He pulled on jeans and darted into the kitchen. Honey was there, and Casey and Gabe. They all smiled at him and treated him to a round of inanities. He grumbled his own greetings, then stuck bread in the toaster and water on to boil. He glanced at Casey, who pursed his mouth, silently assuring Morgan he hadn't said a word about Misty.

Not that it mattered now, anyway. The world would soon know how he felt about that woman.

"What exactly are you doing?" Gabe asked as Morgan dug out a tea bag. Everyone in the family knew for a fact he wasn't a tea drinker.

"Misty has morning sickness. Mom said nibbling on dry toast and sipping sweet hot tea before she got out of bed would help."

"Ah."

Honey started to rise from her chair. "If Misty's sick—"

Gabe caught her arm, earning Morgan's gratitude. "It's nothing Morgan can't handle. Isn't that right, Morgan?"

"It's under control." He set the toast and tea on a tray and left the room. He heard Gabe chuckling, then some whispering, but he didn't care. He was going to ask Misty to marry him, so they could gossip all they wanted.

Misty was still flat on her back in the bed when he reached her side. "I have a remedy here. First, nibble a few bites of toast...that's it. No, don't argue. I promise, it'll help."

Crumbs landed on her chest, and he brushed them away. He imagined he'd have to change his sheets more often if this ritual continued, though his mother had claimed the morning sickness usually didn't last that long. Generally not past the first trimester, and Misty should be about through that.

"Now some hot tea."

"I hate tea."

"Tough. It'll help. And I made this real sweet."

She sipped carefully while he held her head, then sighed. "Not bad."

After several minutes of repeating the procedure, she cautiously sat up and smiled. "You're a miracle worker. I won't even need to sneak off to the lake."

Morgan smoothed her hair, thinking she was about the most precious-looking woman first thing in the morning, with her eyes puffy, a crease on her cheek from the pillow. He frowned at himself. "If you ever do want to go to the lake, let me know and I'll keep you company, okay?"

Instead of answering him, she asked, "You've taken care of a lot of pregnant ladies, huh?"

"No, you're my first. Why?"

"How'd you know the toast and tea would help?"

She was naked under the sheet, which barely kept her nipples concealed. Now that she no longer felt sick, talking required major concentration on his part. "I asked my mother."

She jumped so hard she spilled her tea. Yep, his sheets were in for a lot of washing.

He eyed the spill on the top sheet and started to pull it away from her before she got soaked, but she gripped it tightly to her chin and glared at him. "You did what?"

She sounded like a frog. "I asked my mother. I figured she had four kids so she had to have had morning sickness, right? She told me what worked for her. And by the way, she sends her love."

Misty pulled her knees up and dropped her head. "I don't believe this," was her muffled complaint.

Morgan smoothed her hair again. He loved her hair, shiny black and silky. Between the two of them, they'd likely have dark-haired children. He wondered if their eyes would be dark blue like his, or vivid blue like Misty's. It didn't matter to him one whit. "Will you marry me, Misty?"

She jerked upright and thwacked her skull on the headboard. With a wince, she rubbed her head, then eyed Morgan. "What did you say?"

Damn. Morgan took in her expression of stark disbelief and faltered. Her eyes were narrowed, her pupils dilated. Her soft mouth was pinched tight.

And he was hard again.

"I said," he muttered through his teeth, "will you marry me?"

"Why?"

Morgan stiffened, and he knew his damn face was heating. He hadn't blushed since sixth grade! "What the hell do you mean, *why?*"

She didn't blink, didn't look away from him. As if talking to a nitwit, she asked slowly, "Why do *you* want to marry *me?*"

A knock on the door saved him from trying to give a stammering reply. He sure as hell hadn't expected her to answer his proposal with an interrogation. He gave her a glare, waited until she'd pulled the sheet higher, then called out, "Come in."

Gabe stuck his head in the door. He kept his gaze resolutely on Morgan, and not on Misty. "You have a phone call."

"Take a message."

"Uh, Morgan, it's from out of town. I think you'll want to take it."

He could tell by Gabe's tone who the caller was. Hating the interruption, even while he was relieved by it, he stood. "I'll be right back."

Misty nodded, her face almost blank.

He put his hands on his hips. "We'll finish this conversation when I get off the phone."

"All right."

She sounded far from enthusiastic, and he wanted to demand to know how she felt, but knew he'd do better to bide his time. Patience, more often than not, wasn't his virtue.

He didn't look at her again as he left the room.

Twenty minutes later he was lounging against the wall outside the hall bathroom when Misty finally emerged, fresh from her shower. She put on her brakes when she saw him and stared at him warily without saying a word.

Morgan noticed her wet hair, her pink cheeks, her bare feet. She had on a T-shirt and loose cotton drawstring pants. "You going somewhere?"

"I have to be at the diner in about an hour."

He wanted to curse, to insist she skip work today, but he knew without even asking that he'd be wasting his breath. The woman was bound and determined to make all the money she could. Well, that'd be over with soon enough.

"All right. Then I guess we ought to get right to it."

"You're going to tell me why you want to marry me?"

There was no one else in the hallway, but he'd definitely prefer more guaranteed privacy. He took her arm and led her to his room. When he closed the door, he leaned against it and watched her. "Do you remember a woman named Victoria Markum?"

Misty backed up until her knees hit his mattress, then dropped onto it. "Yes. She was Mr. Collins's girlfriend."

He nodded. "Well, I hired some people to talk to her."

She frowned in confusion. "You hired people?" At his nod, she asked, "But why?"

"To prove your innocence. And don't give me that look, Malone. I didn't tell you because I didn't want you to start squawking about me spending my money. This is something I wanted to do, all right?"

"I'll pay you back—"

"The hell you will." Morgan went to her and sat beside

her, then took her hands. "Can't you just accept that I care and I want to help?"

She searched his face for a long time before she grudgingly said, "Thank you. I don't know what to say."

"You could ask me what I found out."

"All right." She bit her lip, her face filled with anxiety. "I hope, judging by the way you're acting, it's good news?"

"As a matter of fact, it is. You see, Malone, I believed you when you said you hadn't taken the money. That meant someone else did, of course. I wondered if perhaps Ms. Markum might have done it."

Misty squeezed his fingers; her hands were ice cold. "I never even considered that. I kept wondering if someone had managed to slip into the store and open the register while I was in the rest room, or if maybe the money had just been miscounted, but... Victoria didn't seem like a thief to me. She was...I don't know. Too ditzy. And I think they were planning on getting married, so she'd have been sort of stealing from herself, right?"

Morgan held both her hands between his own to warm them. "Actually, they were planning on marrying, or at least, Ms. Markum was. But we found out that Ms. Markum and your boss had a falling out. He, it seems, took the money she'd been holding for him in her own savings account, and ran with it, so she was more than willing to talk to us. It didn't even take much prodding, from what the investigator told me. You see, she didn't steal the money...but he did."

"What?"

"Collins had been skimming from himself. Ms. Markum may be a ditz, but she has facts and dates and exact amounts that should corroborate her testimony. All we need to do now is contact your lawyer, who can file for a motion for the first trial to be declared a mistrial, based on the new evidence. The second trial should be scheduled quickly, probably within a month, because they won't want you serving more of a sentence than you've already had to."

She shook her head. "It can't be that easy."

"Actually it is." He smiled, trying to reassure her. "Well, you'll have to see the judge again, of course, but this time I'll be with you."

She stared at him in amazement, her bottom lip starting to quiver.

"Now, Malone," he said uneasily, "don't cry. I can't stand it."

Big tears welled in her eyes anyway. "I can't believe you did this for me."

He pulled her close and kissed the tip of her nose, which was starting to turn red. "I want you to be happy."

She launched herself against him, knocking him back on the bed. She kissed his face, his throat, his ear. Morgan laughed even as he felt himself harden. There was no way Misty Malone could crawl all over him without turning him on. He caught her mouth and held her still for the deep thrust of his tongue, but pulled back slowly before he completely lost control.

He held her head to his shoulder and smiled. "That's one problem taken care of."

She squeezed him tight. "You are the most amazing man."

Laughing, Morgan growled, "So you keep telling me. Now answer my other question. Will you marry me?"

She went still. Very slowly she raised her face. "You still haven't told me why you want to marry me."

Because he'd had a few minutes to come up with a reply, he said easily, "You're sexy and beautiful."

Her smile was radiant. "You're sexy and beautiful, too, but that's not a good reason to tie yourself to someone for life."

He snorted at her compliment. "We have great sex together. Hell, I still feel singed."

Her smile melted away and her eyes darkened. "Me, too. It was the most incredible thing. I'd never imagined sex could be like that." She brushed a kiss over his jaw, then added,

"But we don't have to get married to have great sex. For as long as I'm here, I'm willing, Morgan."

His stomach started to cramp. She wasn't saying yes, and in fact, she was making a lot of excuses to cancel out every reason he gave her. But there was one reason she couldn't refute. "You're pregnant."

"The baby isn't your responsibility."

"It is if I want to make it my responsibility."

"Oh, Morgan. You're not thinking straight. You can't really want to be a fill-in for another man's child."

"The baby will be mine if you marry me."

She touched gentle fingers to his mouth and her expression was one of wonderment. "You say that now because you're feeling protective of me, just like you feel about everyone. But I don't need you to take care of me, Morgan. I can take care of myself, and the baby."

Morgan moved swiftly, rolling her beneath him before she could draw a deep breath. "Let me tell you something, Misty Malone. What you know about men doesn't add up to jack. And for your information, I don't care that the baby isn't mine. It's yours, and that's all that matters to me."

She shook her head, making him curse. He caught her hands and raised them over her head. "I'm going to tell you a little story."

"I have to be at work soon."

"Tough. Don't rush me." She wisely didn't push him on that score. Morgan drew a deep breath, then admitted, "Sawyer isn't Casey's natural father."

Misty's eyes widened and her mouth opened twice before she sputtered, "That's ridiculous!"

"No, it's true. If you want all the details, you can ask Honey. I'm sure Sawyer told her the whole story."

"But..." She searched his face, then looked away. "She's never said a word."

"Likely because it doesn't matter. Not to Sawyer, and sure as hell not to the rest of us. No one could love that boy more than we do. Sawyer knew all along that Casey wasn't his.

But he'd been married to Casey's mother, and she didn't want him. So he brought Case home, a squalling little red-faced rodent, and we all went head over heels. Hell, a baby is a baby. It doesn't matter who planted the seed. All that matters is who loves him and cares for him and shelters him. I want to do that with you, Misty." He swallowed hard, his hands gripping her shoulders. "Marry me."

He could feel her shaking beneath him, saw the tears gathering in her eyes. She bit her lip and sniffed.

"Malone?"

"I...I can't."

Never in his life, Morgan thought, had anything hurt so much. He'd been in brawls, he'd been injured by cars and animals. He'd had broken limbs and a broken nose and more bruises than he could count. But nothing had ever hurt like this.

He stared at Misty, not wanting to believe that she'd refused him. She'd told him all along that she didn't want commitment, that she was through with involvement. But he hadn't believed her, not really. He hadn't *wanted* to believe her.

His head throbbed and his blood boiled. He wanted to rage, he wanted to shout. But he'd made a big enough fool of himself already.

He rolled to the side of the bed and stared at the ceiling. He started to ask her why, but wasn't at all sure he wanted to know the answer. Misty scampered off the bed, and her bare feet made no sound on the carpet. His door closed very quietly.

By the time he followed her, she'd already left for work.

Gabe gave him a questioning look, but Morgan didn't even bother to acknowledge him. He left for work and didn't come home until late that night. He didn't see Misty at all.

MISTY WAS SITTING by the lake when Honey found her. She glanced at her sister, shielding her eyes from the sun. "Hey. What's up?"

"That was my question." Honey lowered herself onto the edge of the dock beside Misty. She pulled off her sandals and dangled her feet in the water. "Morgan has looked like a thundercloud all day, growling at everyone, ready to spit nails. We're all avoiding him. The only one not afraid is the puppy."

Misty looked at the dark lake water and promised herself she wouldn't cry. "The dog has really taken to him, then?"

"Amazing, isn't it? Do you know what he named that little wad of fur? Godzilla. And the dog seems to like it."

Misty summoned up a smile, when in truth, it was all she could do not to bawl like a baby.

Honey made an exasperated sound. "So Morgan is more feral than ever and you're so morose the sun won't even shine on you. What's going on?"

Misty turned her face away, resting it on her bent knees. Hoping Honey couldn't hear the strain in her voice, she said, "Nothing. I just wanted some peace and quiet."

"Funny. That's just what Morgan said."

"Oh?"

"Yeah. He sent Gabe and Jordan running, and Sawyer was ready to hit him in the head, but I insisted he talk to me. He won't growl at me, you know. I think he's afraid it'll break me or something."

Funny. Morgan had never hesitated to shower her with his bad moods, not that she'd minded. He hadn't scared her at all, because she'd seen through him.

Honey cleared her throat. "He told me he just wants to finish up the house so he can get moved out. He's been spending every spare minute up there." Honey hesitated, then said with a dramatic flair, "Tomorrow he's moving in."

Her stomach cramped, because she knew she'd chased him away, but what else could she do? Marry a man who didn't love her?

"I hate to see him go," Honey admitted softly. "The house won't seem the same without him."

Misty didn't reply to that. What could she say? She'd

barely seen Morgan in two days. Even today, at the station, he'd not taken much notice of her. When he had looked at her, his expression had been flat. There'd been no teasing, no lust, no tenderness, none of the things she was used to and that she had begun to expect. Oh, he'd still been courteous, telling her to go to lunch, to take her time, to make sure she ate right. It was as if what had been between them was no longer there.

Misty couldn't bear to think about that, so she decided to do something she should have done already. "I have a confession."

Honey's arm slipped around her shoulders. "I'm still a good listener, you know."

"You're going to be angry," Misty warned her.

"I doubt it."

But when Misty explained all about the theft, how she'd been found guilty, Honey was absolutely livid. Not at Misty, so much, but that her boss had dared to accuse her and that the judge hadn't believed her.

It took some fast talking on Misty's part to make Honey understand that all was well now, or at least on the way to being well, thanks to Morgan, and to explain why she hadn't told her sooner.

"So Morgan is the one that got it all straightened out?"

Misty nodded, once again confounded by his generosity. "He's pretty wonderful, isn't he?"

"*I've* certainly always thought so."

She'd always thought so, too, but what she felt wasn't enough to make a marriage work. Misty heaved a sigh. "I have to leave tomorrow morning. I might be gone overnight. I'm not sure."

Honey stiffened. "Leave where?"

"My lawyer needs to see me. There're some things that have to be done to set up the new trial. Everything should go well, so I'm not worried about that. I already told Ceily, and I told Nate. I know I should have told Morgan that I wouldn't be in, but I just couldn't. Things aren't great between us right now."

Very gently, Honey asked, "Why not?"

Misty squeezed her hands into fists. "He asked me to marry him."

There was a moment of stunned silence, then Honey gasped theatrically. "Well, that bastard! How dare he?"

Shaking her head at her sister's mocking outrage, Misty said, "You don't understand."

"I understand that you love him, sis. Isn't that what's most important?"

"No." Misty dropped her feet into the water with a splash, then watched the ripples fan out until they disappeared. "What's important is that two people love each other. But Morgan doesn't love me. He likes to take care of people, and he thinks I need a husband because I'm pregnant. You've said yourself how old-fashioned he is. But that's not good enough anymore. I've learned a lot through all this, most importantly that you can't cut corners. If there isn't love, then there's nothing."

"And you think Morgan doesn't love you?"

Misty lifted one shoulder, not sure what to say. "I asked him why he wanted to marry me. He gave me a lot of good reasons, but not once did he say he loved me."

"So ask him outright."

Misty stared at her, appalled. "I can't do that!"

"Why not?" Honey kicked her feet, too, splashing them both. "Morgan is a hard-headed man. Actually, he's just hard, period. All over."

"I know, I know." Misty hadn't been able to sleep at night, remembering how wonderfully hard Morgan was. She loved everything about him, but she was crazy nuts about his big, solid body. And after only making love with him twice, she was addicted. She didn't think she could have ever gotten enough of him.

"Hard men are usually sensitive men."

Misty snorted over that bit of nonsense. "Morgan is about

as blunt as they come. He always tells me what he's thinking or feeling, even if it embarrasses me to death.''

Honey looked at the sky and pondered that. ''Well, then, don't you think you owe him the same courtesy?''

She shuddered at just the thought. ''I'm a horrible coward. Morgan's made it clear from the first that he's attracted to me. But that's all.''

''How can you say that?'' Honey frowned at her. ''Morgan's done everything he could to keep you close by. He even made up that ridiculous story about the two of you having an agreement.''

''You knew that wasn't real?''

Honey smiled. ''It was plain on your face.''

Bemused for a moment, Misty wondered if all his brothers had known he was just making up their involvement. Then she shook her head. ''It doesn't matter. He kept me here because he was trying to take care of me—whether I wanted him to or not. He does that for everyone, Honey.'' She turned to face her sister, wanting her to understand. ''Morgan is about the most giving, caring man I've ever met. That's why being a sheriff is so perfect for him. He loves taking care of other people's problems. He's a natural caregiver—though he'd choke if he heard me say that, and probably frown something fierce. He tries to hide his gentleness behind a big tough exterior.''

Honey waved that away. ''I know. But still—''

''No. If he loved me, surely he would have said so.''

''Will you at least think about it? Maybe he's not quite as tough or as confident as you think he is.''

The idea of Morgan being insecure would take some getting used to, but to appease her sister, she agreed to think it over. What would Morgan say if she blurted out that she loved him? Would he be embarrassed? Would he lie and say he loved her, too, just to keep her from embarrassment? She closed her eyes, not sure at all what his reaction would be.

''I was looking for you for another reason, too.''

Honey's serious tone pulled Misty out of her contemplation. "What's wrong?"

After a deep breath, Honey said, "Father wants to visit us. He called a few minutes ago."

That was the very last thing Misty had expected to hear. Incredulous, she stared at her sister. "You must be kidding."

"Unfortunately...no."

Misty narrowed her eyes. "He wants to come here? To Kentucky?"

"Yes. That's what he said. I'm supposed to call him back and tell him when it'd be convenient."

A summons from her father wouldn't have thrown her so badly. But a visit? It didn't make any sense. Unless... "What are we being accused of now? Is he mad about something?" Then a horrid thought intruded. "Oh, God. He found out I'd been arrested, didn't he?"

"I don't think so. Actually, he told me he wants to meet my husband. Sawyer is afraid he's going to bring up his will again, and you can just imagine how that'd go over."

Misty nodded. All her life, her father had claimed to want a son to carry on the family name. Since their mother had died without giving him one, he'd decided that Honey, as the oldest child, would have to supply a husband to fill the role of masculine heir.

Sawyer had flatly refused to accept anything from him. And their father had been peeved ever since. He hadn't even attended the wedding.

"Father said he was intrigued by the notion of men who would blindly turn down money and power. When I mentioned to him that he should have come to the wedding, he actually said he regretted missing it. Can you believe that?"

"Uh...no."

Honey softened her tone. "He also said he was worried about you."

"Since when?" Misty couldn't help but feel bitter over her last conversation with her father. He'd been very disappointed that she'd gotten pregnant, and he hadn't bothered to try to hide that disappointment.

"Here's what I think." Honey pulled her feet from the water and stood, then looked at Misty. "I think I'm so happy that I don't mind hearing him out, seeing what he has to say. Sawyer told me that not everyone is as capable of expressing love as we are. He asked me about Father's upbringing, our grandparents, and you know, I think he might be onto something there. Father was always a cold, detached man, just as his parents were and as they expected him to be. After Mom died, he was all alone. That couldn't have been easy for him, Misty. I'm not saying we have to be all loving and hugging." She shuddered, then laughed. "That would be too weird after all this time. But I'd at least like to make my peace with him. And you're going to be giving him a grandchild. Maybe he'll look at things differently, but either way, I want to know that I gave our relationship every chance."

Honey walked away, leaving Misty to think things over. True, her father had never been the type to hug or even give a quick compliment. But he'd made certain they were always well dressed and well fed, and they'd never wanted for anything material. Just the fact that he wanted to meet Sawyer and the brothers showed a bending on his part, a sort of olive branch. She supposed it wouldn't hurt to listen to him.

As she walked up to the house, dodging stones on the ground and the occasional bee feasting on clover, she smiled. She couldn't begin to imagine her father's reaction to the brothers. They were overwhelming and dominating and they spoke their minds without hesitation.

Her father would be in for a surprise.

EARLY the next morning, Morgan stared at his bedroom ceiling, a habit that had replaced sleeping in the past few days. No matter how hard he worked, no matter how he exhausted himself, he couldn't sleep. He was so damn tired he could barely see straight, but when he closed his eyes, all he could think of was Misty.

Hell, even with his eyes open, she was all he could think of. He alternated between fantasies of making love to her until she begged him to marry her and throttling her for turning down his proposal in the first place. Not that he would ever really hurt her, he thought with disgust. Hell, no.

There was one bright side to all his recent labors; his house was done. He could now move in and live in comfort—and solitude. But he didn't want to. He'd come to think of the house with Misty in it. Without her, it didn't seem complete no matter what he did to it.

Sawyer was right, he was a miserable bastard. He never should have given in to his needs. He should have avoided her instead of finding out for a fact how sweet she was, how right it felt to be inside her, holding her, talking with her, loving her. Now she was still here, a damn relative, and he had to look at her and know she was close, but she didn't want him.

He closed his eyes and groaned.

Two seconds later his bedroom door flew open and bounced off the wall. Morgan leaped out of bed, automatically reaching for his gun. The overhead light came on, nearly blinding him in the gray morning shadows, but showing his brother's angry face clear as day. Sawyer stalked in, grabbed Morgan's discarded jeans and flung them at him.

"Get dressed."

Morgan began pulling on his pants without hesitation. It wasn't often Sawyer issued commands that way. "What's wrong?"

"You blew it, that's what."

He stumbled, his jeans only to his knees. "What the hell does that mean?"

"It means Misty is gone."

Forget the elephant, it felt like his heart was smashed flat. Wheezing, a little light-headed, he asked, "Gone where?"

Sawyer jutted his chin toward Morgan and growled, "She *left,* Morgan. What did you expect her to do with you moping around, ignoring her, acting like she didn't exist? I thought you loved her!''

Morgan dropped onto the edge of the bed. ''I asked her to marry me,'' he said, feeling numb. ''She turned me down.''

''You must have misunderstood.''

Sawyer and Morgan both turned to see Jordan standing in the doorway. Morgan shook his head. ''No, I asked and she flatly refused.''

Jordan crossed his arms over his chest and frowned. ''I can tell she cares about you.''

Gabe walked in. ''She's crazy about him, if you ask me.''

''Oh, for the love of—'' Morgan stood and finished pulling on his pants. ''If that's true, why wouldn't she marry me?''

Honey pushed Gabe out of her way and glared at all of them. ''Because she said you didn't love her.''

''What?''

''She said you were just trying to take care of her, but without love, it wasn't worth it.''

Morgan cursed so viciously that Gabe backed up and Jordan rolled his eyes. Sawyer pulled Honey protectively to his side. ''Get a grip, Morgan. Are you going to go after her or not?''

His head shot up. ''Go after her? When did she leave?''

Honey tapped her foot. ''About two minutes ago.''

Before she had finished, Morgan had snapped his jeans, shoved his gun in his pocket and started out of the room. But his brothers had all congregated inside, blocking his path at the end of the bed, so he bounded over it instead, bouncing on the mattress as he dodged past them. He ran out the doorway, not bothering with a shirt or shoes. Gabe trotted after him, waving a shirt. ''Wait! Don't you want to finish dressing?''

Morgan ignored him, but he couldn't ignore the loud guffaws from his other brothers. He snatched his keys from the peg by the back door and ran into the yard.

''Damn irritants,'' he muttered, then winced as his bare feet came into contact with every sharp stone on the dew-wet grass. He slipped twice, but within thirty seconds he had the Bronco out, lights flashing and sirens blasting. When he caught up to her...

Morgan filled the time it took to get to town by plotting all the ways he'd set her straight.

She was in front of the sheriff's office when he spotted her. She slowed when she noticed his flashing lights, and after a few seconds she pulled over.

Unfortunately, Ceily was just coming to the diner to start preparing the food, and she paused on the front stoop to watch as Morgan climbed out of the Bronco and slammed the door. Nate was at the station already, and he and Howard and Jesse also walked out to see what was happening. It wasn't often that Morgan pulled anyone over with so much fanfare.

By the time he'd circled the front of the Bronco, Misty had already left her car. She gaped at him, then demanded, "What in the world is wrong with you? Has something happened?" She gazed at him from his shaggy hair, his bare chest, to his naked feet.

Morgan stomped up to her, ignoring the sting to his feet and the way the sidewalk was quickly beginning to crowd with curious onlookers. He hooked his hand around the back of her neck and drew her up to her tiptoes. "Where in hell do you think you're going?"

She blinked at him. "I have to meet with my lawyer today."

Morgan prepared to blast her with his wrath—and then her words sank in. "You're not leaving?"

"Leaving, as in for good?"

He nodded.

"Why would you think that?"

He seriously considered going home and choking Sawyer. But first, he had a few things to straighten out. "You should have told me you were leaving."

"You," she said, beginning to show her own pique, "haven't shown the slightest interest in talking to me lately!"

"Because I asked you to marry me and you had the nerve to say no."

A loud gasp rose from their audience.

Morgan pretended he hadn't heard them. "Do you know how many other women I've asked to be wife? Do you? *None!*"

"Well, I'm honored," Misty sneered, then poked him in the chest and her own voice rose to a shout. "But I'm not marrying a man who doesn't love me."

He sputtered in renewed outrage. *"Who the hell says I don't love you?"*

Misty caught her breath, panting, then said with deep feeling, her gaze intent, *"Who says you do?"*

Morgan growled, ran a hand roughly through his hair, then he picked her up. He held her at eye level and said, "Damn woman, I asked you to marry me! Why would I do that if I didn't love you?"

Someone on the sidewalk—it sounded like Ceily—called out in a laughing voice, "Yeah, why would Morgan do that?"

Morgan jerked his head around to face them all. "Can't you people find something to do?"

"No!" was the unanimous retort.

Morgan growled again. "Nate, arrest anyone who doesn't scatter."

Nate promptly looked dumbfounded. "Uh..."

Misty regained his attention by saying softly, "You just want to help me, like you helped that woman with the flat tire, and the dog, and the school kids and the elderly."

Morgan walked to her car and plunked her down gently on the hood. He braced his hands on either side of her hips, then leaned in so close his nose touched hers. "Listen up, Malone. I didn't ask the damn dog to marry me. I didn't ask Howard or Jesse to marry me."

Jesse shouted, "He's speakin' the truth there."

Misty opened her mouth twice before she got words to

come out. She spoke so softly, Morgan could barely hear her. "You said...you said you were looking for a wife."

He gave a sharp nod. "You."

"But..." Her voice faded to a shy whisper. "You said you wanted three children."

"Three total." His hand covered her belly, and he smiled. Breathing the words so no one else would hear, he explained, "This one and two more. I was trying to hint to you that I'd be a good father."

"Oh, Morgan." She cupped his face, and tears filled her eyes. "I already know you'd be an excellent father."

He straightened and put his hands on his hips. "I swear, if you start crying again, Malone, I won't like it." He drew a breath and added, "Hell, it just about kills me to see you unhappy."

She sniffed loudly. "I'm very happy."

"So you won't cry?"

"I won't cry."

A fat tear rolled down her cheek, making him sigh in exasperation. The woman was forever turning him in circles. But since she seemed in an agreeable mood for a change... "Tell me you'll marry me."

She nodded. "I'll marry you."

She started to put her arms around his neck, but he held her off. "Not so quick, Malone. I told you I love you. Don't you have something to say to me?"

With everyone on the sidewalk cheering her on, she grinned around her tears and said, "Morgan Hudson, I love you so much it hurts."

He scooped her into his arms for a fierce hug, then turned to the crowd, laughing out loud. "You heard her. Consider me an engaged man." Then to Misty, "Damn. Do you think we have time for me to go home and get dressed before we go see your lawyer? I'd probably make a better impression that way."

EPILOGUE

MORGAN HAULED MISTY into his lap after her father had left. She protested, saying, "No, Morgan, I'm too fat now!"

Three months had passed. She was rounded with the child growing inside her, but still so sexy he could barely keep his hands off her. Every day he loved her more.

He kissed her cheek and smiled. "I promise to bear up under the weight."

Honey, a little subdued and cuddled up against Sawyer's side, said, "Misty, you look wonderful. Not at all fat."

Gabe laughed. "When I start looking like you two did, you'll have to give me some pointers so I can find my own beauty."

Sawyer blinked. "I wasn't looking. That's why Honey sort of...blindsided me." Honey playfully punched him for that remark, making Sawyer laugh.

Shrugging, Morgan added, "I wasn't looking, either."

The feminine weight in his lap gasped over his statement. "What an outrageous clanker! You even told me you wanted a wife."

Morgan shook his head. "That was just lip service. Sawyer seemed so tamed, I thought I should give it a try, too. But I wasn't putting much effort into it, not until I saw you."

Gabe nodded. "As I said, they're both gorgeous."

"Looks don't matter, Gabe." He tilted Misty's chin up and kissed her lips. "It was Misty's mouthy bluster that reeled me in."

Gabe made a face. "You can say that *now.*"

Jordan shook his head. "Your day will come, Gabe."

"Ha! But not before yours, old man. If we're going in order, you're doomed."

Jordan made a face at him. "If you keep using words like 'doomed,' Misty or Honey are going to flatten you."

Casey flopped down on the sofa. "So, Dad, what do you think about me visiting Mr. Malone?"

Morgan hid a smile. Mr. Malone had surprised them all. True, the man was so rigid he bordered on brittle. But he had made the effort to unbend a little more on each visit. His first had been horribly strained, but with all the ribald teasing going on, he could hardly stay puckered up indefinitely. This time, he'd actually kissed each daughter's cheek.

And rather than trying to offer his money to Sawyer again, he'd asked—actually *asked*—if he could put a good portion of it in a trust for the baby. Morgan and Misty had discussed it, then agreed, as long as equal money was put in for each child either of the sisters had.

That had settled one problem, but then the man had fixated on Casey. All along, he'd seemed very impressed by Casey's manners, his maturity, and within a few hours of this visit, he'd damn near adopted him as a pseudo heir. None of them were overly pleased by it, especially not Honey, but when the man had invited Casey to visit, to look over his enterprises, Casey had shown some interest.

Sawyer pursed his mouth, then hugged Honey closer so she wouldn't protest. Morgan knew Honey hated to let Casey out of her sight. She had a hard time thinking of him as a young man, despite the fact he was exactly that. "I suppose we could all make a trip up there. If after that you want to hang around for a short visit, it'd probably be all right."

"Great." Casey didn't seem overly enthusiastic either way, and when he said he had a date, Morgan understood why. The male brain had a hard time focusing when females were being considered.

They all watched Casey leave with indulgent smiles. Seconds later, Honey and Sawyer left to begin dinner. Jordan had a few calls to make, and when Morgan started kissing his wife, Gabe left the room whistling.

"You about ready to head home?" Morgan asked.

"I thought we were staying for dinner."

"We'll come back," Morgan promised, then gave her a lecherous grin. He picked her up in his arms and suffered through her complaints.

"I'm too heavy now for you to keep doing this!"

Morgan just grinned at her. "Do you know, you're the only one who's ever doubted my strength."

"That's not true." She kissed his chin. "I just like to match it."

Blaze

The Trueblood, Texas tradition continues in...

HARLEQUIN® Blaze™

TRULY, MADLY, DEEPLY
by Vicki Lewis Thompson
August 2002

Ten years ago Dustin Ramsey and Erica Mann shared their first sexual experience. It was a disaster. Now Dustin's determined to find—and seduce—Erica again, determined to prove to her, and himself, that he can do better. Much, *much* better. Only, little does he guess that Erica's got the same agenda....

Don't miss Blaze's next two sizzling Trueblood tales, written by fan favorites Tori Carrington and Debbi Rawlins. Available at your nearest bookstore in September and October 2002.

The Buckhorn Brothers are coming back,
and here's your chance to save $1.00 off the purchase of

Forever and Always

by *USA Today* bestselling author

Lori Foster

Back by popular demand are the scintillating stories of
Gabe and Jordan Buckhorn.
They're gorgeous, sexy and single...at least for now!

Save $1.00 off

the purchase of *Forever and Always*

Available September 2002 wherever paperback books are sold.

RETAILER: Harlequin Enterprises Ltd. will pay the face value of this coupon plus 10.25¢ if submitted by customer for this product only. Any other use constitutes fraud. Coupon is nonassignable. Void if taxed, prohibited or restricted by law. Consumer must pay any government taxes. Nielson Clearing House customers submit coupons and proof of sales to: Harlequin Enterprises Ltd., 661 Millidge Avenue, P.O. Box 639, Saint John, N.B. E2L 4A5. Non NCH retailer—for reimbursement submit coupons and proof of sales to: Harlequin Enterprises Ltd., Retail Marketing Department, 225 Duncan Mill Rd., Don Mills, Ontario M3B 3K9, Canada. Valid in Canada only.

Coupon valid until November 30, 2002.
Redeemable at participating retail outlets in Canada only.
Limit one coupon per purchase.

Visit us at www.eHarlequin.com
PHCOUPONCAN-F&A

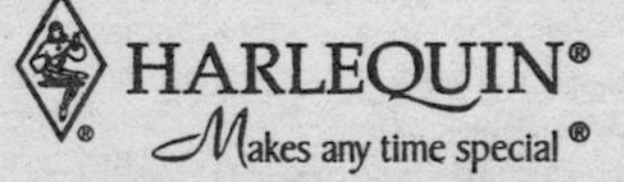